A I *e*

The Family Business 4:

A Family Business Novel

Carl Weber

with

La Jill Hunt

www.urbanbooks.net

Urban Books, LLC
300 Farmingdale Road, NY-Route 109
Farmingdale, NY 11735

The Family Business 4: A Family Business Novel
Copyright © 2018 Carl Weber
Copyright © 2018 La Jill Hunt

The Family Business 2012 Trademark Urban Books, LLC

ISBN 13: 978-1-60162-088-0
ISBN 10: 1-60162-088-8

Frist Trade Paperback Printing February 2019
First Hardcover Printing February 2018
Printed in the United States of America

10 9 8 7 6 5 4 3 2 1

This is a work of fiction. Any references or similarities to actual events, real people, living or dead, or to real locales are intended to give the novel a sense of reality. Any similarity in other names, characters, places, and incidents is entirely coincidental.

Distributed by Kensington Publishing Corp.
Submit orders to:
Customer Service
400 Hahn Road
Westminster, MD 21157-4627
Phone: 1-800-733-3000
Fax: 1-800-659-2436

Prologue

The glass doors of the quaint storefront situated in the Atlantic Terminal of the Long Island Rail Road read: NATE'S SHOE SHINE AND REPAIR. When the door opened, the brass bell clanged loudly and three men of different ages stepped inside. The older of the three, who was more salt than pepper, took a seat in the center of the three shoeshine chairs and made himself comfortable, while his two companions browsed around the store looking nervous.

"Can I help you?" a gentleman situated at the far end of the counter with his back turned to the men called out. He was working on a pair of cowboy boots that had to be worth a thousand dollars or more.

"Yeah, I'm looking for old man Nate?" the older of the three men asked. Unlike the younger men, he was wearing a suit. He had military dog tags hanging around his neck that looked like they'd been dipped in gold.

"You must not be from around here, 'cause my uncle Nate passed away almost ten years ago," the man replied, continuing to work without turning around.

"Sorry to hear that. Nate was a good brother," the man said sincerely. "So, what's your name?"

The man never looked up from his work. "My name's Joe, but folks around here call me Shoeshine. What can I do for you?"

"Get the fuck outta here! You're Shoeshine Joe. Man, you still the best shoeshine boy in town?" He laughed like they were old friends, lifting his shoe. "Man, how about a shine?"

"First of all, I ain't nobody's boy," Joe snapped angrily, still without moving his head. "Secondly, I'm the owner, so I don't shine nobody's shoes no more. We got a kid that comes in at four for the rush hour crowd that can help you with that." Joe stood up and finally turned around with a slight frown on his face.

Then he recognized the man sitting before him. He took a step back. "Shit, I thought you were dead."

"That's what I wanted people to think," the man in the chair answered, gesturing to his shoes. "Now, how about a shine for old time's sake?"

"Sure, sure, no problem." Joe hurried from around the counter and pulled out a shine box. The man eased back in his chair. "What's it been—five, ten years?"

The man ran his hand through his graying hair. "Closer to fifteen."

"Damn, has it been that long?" Joe shook his head. Observing the two younger men, he asked, "These your boys? They look just like you."

"Yes, sir, these two are the best parts of me, Ken and Curt." He pointed at his two sons. "Boys, Joe here is the best shoeshine man on the East Coast. Back in the day, every time I'd come to Brooklyn I had to bring three pairs of shoes just for him to shine. He's that damn good."

"Thanks, but that was a long time ago. It's been a while since I did this for anyone other than myself."

"Man, shining shoes is like riding a bicycle: you just got to get back on it," the man said, and Joe nodded his agreement as he began to apply polish.

"So, Joe, it looks like the neighborhood is changing a lot. How's business?"

"Changing is an understatement, but believe it or not, that's not such a bad thing, because business is good. These yuppies that are moving in don't wear two hundred–dollar sneakers like the old neighborhood folks. They wear expensive designer shoes and boots that need repair. Nobody wants to throw away a seven hundred–dollar pair of shoes, so for now business is better than ever."

The man glanced over at the two younger versions of himself, who were now posted at either side of the door; then he looked down at Joe.

"That's great. I'm happy for you," he said sarcastically. "But I wasn't talking about the shoe business. I was talking about the information business."

Joe froze, peering over his glasses. It had been years since anyone had even mentioned the figure he was now kneeling before. The man was a killer, no if, ands, or buts about it. Word on the street was that he'd been locked up and died in his jail cell, but that couldn't have been true, because he was sitting right there in the flesh, asking for information. Joe just hoped the information he wanted wasn't the kind that might get him killed.

"I don't really know much about nothing other than shoes." Joe shrugged as he tentatively continued to shine the man's shoes. "My uncle Nate was the one who knew everything about everyone. Not me."

"Is that so?" It was obvious from the look he gave his sons that the man thought Joe was lying through his teeth; however, he remained calm. He nodded to Curt, the older of his sons. Reaching into his pocket, Curt pulled out a stack of cash and placed it next to Joe's shoeshine box. It was more money than Joe had seen in a while.

"I'm sure you can be just as helpful as your uncle, don't you think?" Curt spoke for the first time.

Joe stared at the money, thinking of the pile of bills stacked on his kitchen table at home, along with the constant calls from the finance company about the past due note on his wife's car. It was tempting, but still, he didn't move.

"I'm sorry. I'm not big on information." He went back to shining the man's shoes.

"Okay, maybe *information* is the wrong word. The truth is, I'm looking to buy something. Maybe you can help me with that." The man reached into his pocket and pulled out another stack of cash, placing it alongside the money Curt had put down.

"Wha—what you trying to buy?" Joe asked nervously. He swallowed hard as he gathered up the bills and placed the money in his apron pockets. Glancing up at the two other men, he saw that they were amused by his sudden change of heart. Not that it mattered to him. He knew there had to be at least twenty or thirty thousand dollars in front of him, and it was a sum he just couldn't pass up.

"If I wanted to purchase a large amount of dope, where would I go to find it?"

"You're joking, right?" It was Joe's turn to be amused. "If anybody knows where to find dope, it would be you, wouldn't it? You know the key player better than all of u—" He stopped abruptly when the man bopped him on the head just hard enough to get his full attention.

"Motherfucker, don't worry about what I know. Does Verizon go to Sprint when they need new towers? Does Ford go to GM to help them build cars? Of course not! So why the fuck would I go to LC and ask for help? I'm trying to put his ass outta business."

Joe raised his hands defensively, hoping to give himself a moment to collect his faculties. That was not the response he'd been expecting. He thought for a second and said, "Well, you can't go to the Mexicans or the Colombians now that Alejandro's dead."

"Why not?" Curtis asked.

"Rumor has is it LC's son Vegas is fucking—or used to fuck—Alejandro's widow, and she's supplying them with everything they need. But there is always Lee and his people. He's been hurting ever since him and LC fell out over that Sal Dash fiasco."

"I never liked that Asian bastard, but it's worth a try. The enemy of my enemy is supposed to be my friend, at least until you kill the bastard." The man laughed. "All right, so who else you got?"

"Well, there is a guy who's been looking to move some product. He usually moves marijuana, but he's sitting on a shit load of dope, and I heard he wants to unload it cheap." Joe finished one shoe and moved on to the other.

"Why is he sitting on it?"

"Nobody will buy it from him. Guy's got a price on his head, and everyone is afraid of pissing off the Duncans. He's got a lot of dope, but his supply isn't infinite. Where do you go once he dries up? Not to the Duncans, that's for sure."

The older man sat back. He looked intrigued. "Sounds like me and him need to have a talk. What's his name?"

"Vinnie. Vinnie Dash."

He lifted his head. "This Vinnie any relation to Sal?"

"Yeah, he's Sal's son. He's the only Dash left after the war a few years ago. Which LC won, I might add."

"Is that right? So, where do I find this Vinnie Dash?" the man asked.

"You don't. Dude's running his business out of Jamaica. You gotta get in touch with his man Jamaica John in Co-op City if you want him. He runs a vape shop," Joe said matter-of-factly, getting over his initial discomfort now that the information was flowing.

"Okay. Thanks, Joe. For someone who doesn't know much information, you've been extremely helpful. Hasn't he, boys?"

The two younger men smiled and nodded.

"Glad I could be of service. Good doin' business with you."

"Pleasure was ours," the man replied as Joe finished off his shine. "I'm sorry we won't be able to do business in the future."

"Huh?" Joe was confused until he looked up and saw the gun pointed right at his head. Before be could react, a silenced shot entered his forehead and he fell to the floor.

"Damn, why'd you shoot him?" the younger of his two sons shouted. The older son didn't look happy, but he kept quiet as he picked up the money that had spilled out of Joe's apron.

"I wasn't taking a chance of someone paying his ass double what we gave him to tell them what we wanted. Now, help your brother pick up the money and let's go. We got business to handle."

1

Grateful. That was the only word that came to mind as I looked over the balcony of my bedroom into the sprawling backyard of our family compound. The sun was bright in the sky, but a slight breeze dissipated most of the morning heat. It was going to be a scorcher, that was for sure—not that the heat bothered me. I was just glad to be alive. It was a little less than six months since I'd been shot and left for dead, so no one appreciated a beautiful day and a little excess heat more than I did.

For a few minutes, I watched my grandson Nevada practicing his martial arts stances with his instructor, Minister Farah. At one point, he stumbled just a bit, but to his credit, he never lost his composure. I could see he was serious about perfecting the art. He would not quit until he got it right, like a true Duncan.

"Breakfast is ready."

I turned to see my wife Chippy easing up beside me. She was wearing a multicolored caftan and a pair of simple gold sandals. I had been so caught up in watching Nevada that I hadn't even heard her sneak up behind me.

"What's got you out here grinning like that?" She slipped her arm around my waist.

"Thinking about you." I reached over, pulled her close, and kissed her softly.

"Liar." She laughed and shook her head.

"And Nevada," I added, sliding my hands down to caress her butt.

"Mm-hmmm." She flirted, squeezing me back. "What were you thinking pertaining to me?"

I gave her a seductive look and said, "About last night."

"Yeah." She grinned. "Last night was pretty darn amazing and definitely worth smiling about."

"You're so right." I kissed her neck. Even through the flowing material she wore, I could make out the soft curves of Chippy's body, and I became aroused. Even at our age, she still had that effect on me. "We can always go inside and have an amazing morning too."

"LC, you better stop it. Breakfast is ready," she said, trying to get away from me. Her hand rested on my chest. "Besides, the kids will hear us."

I frowned. "You know, I'm getting sick of these kids. They been cock-blocking me for almost forty years."

"I know," she said sympathetically. "Look, it's not just the kids. I'm worried about you. I don't wanna push our luck. You are still recovering."

I looked into her eyes then back down to her hand. Her finger covered the exact spot where the bullet had entered my body and nearly took my life a few months ago. Chippy had always been brave, but I knew the thought of losing me had scared her. I wanted her to feel secure and know that everything was going to be okay. She was my wife, and I always wanted her to feel protected.

"I'm fine, Chippy. We're fine," I assured her.

"I know you are fine, LC, but let's just take today to rest up."

"I wore you out, huh?" I winked.

"Boy, you already know I did that to you. The way you were snoring last night, I'm surprised you even made it out of bed this morning," she said with a satisfied smirk.

We both laughed and again, I was grateful. I turned my attention back to Nevada.

"You see him? He's a natural."

"I wouldn't say all that. He's been training with his mother since he was small. But he is good," Chippy said.

"I want him to be even better. He needs to learn the finer things in life, and you're going to have to show him," I told her.

"Is that so?" I didn't look at her, but I was sure she was giving me the side-eye.

"Yes. He's our future, honey. One day, all of this will be his, and he has to learn not only how to run it, but to appreciate it as well." I walked over and placed my hands on the railing as I watched my grandson take down his instructor. The surprise on his teacher's face was mixed with embarrassment.

Chippy walked up beside me. "Wow, you've certainly had a change of heart." There was a hint of contempt in her voice.

"What is that supposed to mean?" I turned to her with a frown.

"A month ago you weren't even sure he was Vegas's son. You went on and on about how he might not be a Duncan. Now you're ready to turn the reins of the entire business over to him."

"A month ago I didn't know what I know now," I said confidently.

"And what is that?"

"He's definitely a Duncan," I replied, hoping that would put an end to it. Of course, with Chippy, that was never the case.

"How do you know for certain?" she pressed. "Because when I told you he was our grandson, you didn't want to hear it. What's changed your mind all of a sudden?"

"I just know," I said defiantly. This was not a discussion I wanted to continue, because it could go totally wrong.

"Lavernious Duncan, don't play games with me. I know you, remember? It's bad enough you won't tell me who the hell shot you, but you are going to tell me why you changed your mind, or else what happened last night is not going to happen again for a long time."

I raised my hands defensively to stop her tirade. "Okay, okay." Chippy was right. She did know me well. I shrugged and admitted, "I had Orlando swab him and do a DNA test a week ago. He told me the results last night. He's a Duncan, Charlotte."

She looked at me and shook her head. "I should have known. I hope Orlando was discreet, because you know if Vegas finds out, he's going to lose his mind."

"He was," I replied.

"Well, I'm glad we have that settled. I knew he was my grandson the moment I laid eyes on him." She took my hand, squeezing it as we watched Nevada take down his instructor again. "We finally have all of our children and grandchildren under one roof."

I looked over at her. "All except one. And his mother hates us."

Junior

2

It was the perfect ending to the perfect honeymoon. For almost ten days, my new bride and I had enjoyed the palm trees, white sand, and crystal-clear water of Negril. Now we were spending our last morning walking along the shoreline of Seven Mile Beach. In less than ten hours, we'd be home, leaving paradise behind to begin our new routine as man and wife.

"Last chance. Are you going to jump?" she asked.

"Jump where?"

"Jump off the cliff. We still have time to go back to Rick's Café," she said playfully.

"Now, you know better than that. The only jumping I plan on doing is jumping your bones when we get back to the room." I grabbed a handful of her plump ass in my hands, causing her to squeal.

"Don't you think you've done enough of that these past few days? We've got a plane to catch."

"Naw, not nearly enough." I grabbed her ass again and kissed her neck.

"Stop it. People are looking." She slapped me playfully.

"They can't help it, and neither can I," I said, laughing.

Sonya was beautiful every day, but today, she was breathtaking in a white sundress and sandals. With her thick, curly hair hanging loose and free, she looked like a Nubian queen. *My* Nubian queen. She was glowing, and I didn't know whether it was from the relaxing vacation or the baby she was carrying inside her belly. I had thought her marrying me would make me the happiest man on earth, but that feeling was surpassed when I found out she was pregnant.

"You better stop." She tried to swat my hand away as I reached for her again.

"Nope," I said, pulling her closer to me.

"Well, you're gonna have to."

"Oh, yeah? Why is that?"

"Because your baby is sitting on my bladder, and I have to find a restroom, that's why. Wait right here. I'll be back." She gave me a quick peck, and I released her.

She headed toward a nearby restaurant, while I stepped over to a cart where an old woman was selling shaved ice. I loved those flavored ice cones, especially the mango and pineapple.

I guess my enthusiasm was a little too much, because when I took my first big bite, I got major brain freeze. I was glad Sonya wasn't around, because I know I looked like a fool, shaking my head around like a monkey. I squeezed my eyes shut against the pain in my forehead.

When I opened my eyes, I saw a small shadow zip by, and then a small boy skidded to a stop in front of the cart. I couldn't help but smile. The kid was cute, and he looked like he couldn't contain his energy as he fidgeted in his spot, trying to decide what to order.

"Mango? No, orange. No, lemon," he said, until finally he seemed to have made up his mind, and stated proudly, "I'll take cherry."

The cart owner laughed and said, "You sure, mon?"

"Yup!" the kid answered, and the old woman leaned down to scoop the ice.

She handed him the treat and said, "Two dollar."

The little boy reached into his pocket and pulled out a single, crumpled dollar bill. "This?" he said as he tried to hand it to the woman.

"No, you need more." She shook her head. The smile fell from his face, and his little shoulders drooped.

I felt sorry for the little guy. Maybe I was inspired by my own impending fatherhood, but I didn't even think twice before I reached into my pocket and handed the woman another dollar. "I got it. Here you go."

"Thank you." The boy flashed me a quick smile then took the white paper cone from the vendor.

"No problem, little man." I said, "What's your name?"

"Vincent. What's your name?"

"They call me Junior."

"Hi, Junior. I'm a junior too, but they call me Vincent."

"Vincent! You wait right there!" an out-of-breath voice called from a distance.

"That your mom?" I asked, and he nodded his head. "I think you're in trouble."

"I think so too," Vincent replied, but he didn't look upset. He just started eating his ice faster, cracking me up.

I looked toward his mother, who was still a good distance away, but as she came closer, her face became clearer. I looked down at Vincent, and a knot developed in my stomach.

"Boy, didn't I tell you to wait?" The woman marched up to her son, grabbing his free arm.

"Ruby?"

At first, she smiled at me, until her brain registered who had spoken her name.

"Oh my God. How did you find me?" The look on her face was one of sheer terror. She tugged on Vinnie's arm. "Come on, boy. Come on. We have to go."

"Please, don't go, Ruby," I said.

"No. Come on, Vincent. Let's go." She pulled his arm so hard that he dropped his cone.

"Oh, nooooooo!" Vincent cried. "You made me drop it."

"Don't worry. I'll buy you another," I said, turning back to the cart to get him another cone.

"No, you won't!" In one swift motion, Ruby scooped the small boy up into her arms and took off. I went to follow behind her, but she slipped into a crowd, and I lost sight of them.

"Junior!" I heard Sonya yelling behind me, and I stopped in my tracks. "Babe, what happened? Where did you go? And what are you doing?" she asked when she got to my side.

"We've got a problem." I sighed, feeling defeated.

"Why? What's wrong?" Her forehead creased with concern.

"I just saw my brother Orlando's son."

London

3

"Can I have pancakes, Mommy?" Mariah shouted.

"I want waffles!" her sister Maria chimed in.

"I want Cap'n Crunch!" Jordan said.

"I'm working on it, guys," I whined in reply. I was trying to get my two daughters, along with my nephew, settled for breakfast. My husband, Harris, was also sitting at the table, but he was too engrossed in whatever he was looking at on his iPad to offer any kind of assistance. Luckily, our family chef, along with my mom, had prepared enough of a selection that the kids would be somewhat satisfied, even if it wasn't exactly what they'd requested. I put a pancake, a small serving of eggs, a side of fruit, and some bacon on each plate and placed them in front of the kids.

"Apple juice!" Jordan demanded.

"Me too!" the girls shouted in unison.

Just as I was about to head to the fridge, Harris looked up at me.

"Umm, you forget someone?" He looked down at the empty placemat in front of him. "Can I get some breakfast?"

"You're kidding, right?" I cut my eyes at him. I was starting to understand that this being a good mother and wife thing was overrated. I don't know what I was thinking when I decided to have another baby. And then, to add someone else's child to the mix was even more taxing. Don't get me wrong; I love my nephew, but I was getting tired of my sister Paris's absentee parenting.

"Harris, can't you see I'm trying to get these kids ready for daycare and school? The least you can do is fix your own plate."

"Fix my own plate?" You would have thought I had just cursed at him the way he snapped at me. "This is ridiculous. Where's your mother? Isn't she supposed to help you with the kids?" He looked around the kitchen like he was lost.

"My mother is upstairs getting my father. I could use your help," I said with plenty of attitude.

"Sorry, no can do. I'm trying to finalize some paperwork before I leave for the office." He looked up at me, trying to fake a sincere smile. "So, can you *please* make me a plate?"

"Fine." I sighed, totally regretting that blow job I'd given him earlier that morning. The fool should have been making me a plate, yet here he was expecting more service from me.

"What? No syrup?" Harris asked when I gave him his plate. I picked up the syrup, and the thought came to mind that I should just throw it at his head, but I kept my composure and placed it down in front of him.

I heard the front door open, and then I heard laughter. I recognized it as coming from my pain-in-the-ass sister.

"If it was that little, why'd you tell him you'd call him later? I know you, P. You're never gonna give that little-dick brother any again." This time it was my cousin Sasha's voice. The two of them were giggling like lunatics.

"Look, I was trying to be polite, and little dick or not, he is fine as hell! Besides, he promised to take me shopping for a Rolex and to the Jay-Z concert this weekend," Paris announced for the whole house to hear. "Mmmmm, you smell that? I smell bacon!"

"I told you we should have come home instead of going to that diner," Sasha replied.

Their stilettos started clicking on the marble floors of the foyer, and a few moments later, they both walked into the kitchen. Sasha was dressed in tight-fitting black jeans and a shirt that barely covered her breasts. Paris wore a short, sequined mini skirt and a black halter that was even smaller than the shirt Sasha wore. I'd deny it if asked, but they both looked cute, despite being dressed like tramps.

"Mommy!" Jordan jumped up from the table and ran over to greet his mother.

"Hey, baby, how's my little man?" Paris knelt to hug him, causing the back of the skirt to rise even higher.

I glanced over at Harris, who quickly turned his head. Smart man. We'd already had enough arguments about him gawking at my sister.

"You know what? I think I'll eat my breakfast in the study and finish up these files. It's quieter in there anyway." He gathered up his plate and his iPad and scurried out of the kitchen.

"Jordan, sit back down and eat. You don't want your food to get cold," I said.

"Don't tell my son what to do when I'm here," she sniped at me. "He has a mother."

Oh, no, she isn't going there, is she?

"You coulda fooled me," I said, rolling my eyes at her. "But if you wanna call yourself a mother, how about you bring your narrow ass home in time to get your son ready for daycare?"

"Whatever, London. He's dressed and ready, isn't he?" She picked Jordan up and kissed him.

"Yeah, thanks to me and Mommy. But don't make any plans for this weekend, 'cause Mommy and Daddy are going to Sag Harbor, and me, Harris, and the kids are going to Sesame Place."

"Damn, Paris, aren't you supposed to go out with dude this weekend?" Sasha asked.

Paris raised a hand, waving it at her to shut up, then looked at me like the cat that got caught with a canary in her mouth.

"Need something?" I asked.

"Can't y'all take Jordan with you?" Paris was damn near pleading.

"We could, but he's got a mother. Remember, she can take care of him?"

Her mouth opened, but nothing came out. She helped Jordan back into his seat so he could continue eating. I couldn't help but smirk.

"All righty-then, so where is everyone?" Sasha asked, trying to neutralize the situation. She had a tendency to try to play peacemaker between me and Paris, in spite of the fact it barely ever worked.

I gave her a quick rundown of everyone in the house. "Mom just went to get Daddy for breakfast. They should be down any minute. Rio is still asleep, and Nevada is outside training in the backyard. Orlando's in Daddy's office working. Oh, and Vegas is down in the gym with Daryl."

"Umph, umph, umph. Daryl is here? That's one fine man," Sasha said, her voice humming with sexual energy. "I would love to work him out."

"Back off, bitch. How many times I gotta tell you? Daryl's sexy ass belongs to me," Paris warned in the most serious of tones.

I'd seen my sister flirt with Daryl, but I never thought for a minute she was serious, until now. I told her, "You ain't got a snowball's chance in hell of landing that man. He wouldn't touch your ass if you tried to serve it up on a platter. Talk about out of your league." I laughed loudly, knowing I was pissing her off even more, especially considering my history with Daryl.

"You're crazy. I'm in every man's league," Paris responded, snatching an empty plate from the counter.

"Well, cousin, he does brush you off quite a bit, and you've been throwing that ass at him for quite a while now," Sasha teased.

"That's because Vegas is blocking." She began putting food on her plate, and I went to sit with the kids.

"No, that's because Daryl knows who's been playing in your playground, and he's afraid he might catch something," I stated. Sasha and I laughed, but Paris was ready to take it to the next level.

"Bitch—" She was about to launch into a tirade when I looked over her shoulder and noticed my parents coming into the kitchen.

"Morning, Daddy," I said, cutting her off before she could really get going. Daddy didn't need the stress of hearing us fight.

"Morning, everyone." He walked in with a big smile on his face, holding my mother's hand.

"Mommy. Daddy." Paris put her plate down and ran over to greet my parents like she was the same age as one of the kids sitting in front of me. I watched as my father's face lit up and he kissed her cheek. Wasn't no secret who his favorite was. My mother, on the other hand, sat at the table without a word. I could see that she did not approve of my sister's attire.

Soon, we were joined by Rio, Nevada, and Orlando, and the kitchen became filled with chatter. Paris, of course, continued to give me the stink eye. She was a damn expert at that.

"Hey, y'all! Look who I found lurking on the premises!" My brother Vegas's voice boomed, causing all of us to turn around. At first the only person I saw was Daryl, and he wasn't bad to look at, but when he stepped aside, I saw one of my favorite people in the world.

"Oh my God, Aunt NeeNee!" Orlando and I both jumped up and gave her the biggest hug. Rio and Paris didn't know Aunt NeeNee like us older kids did, but she was one of the sweetest women you could ever meet, and she could cook like nobody I'd ever met, including my mom. "How are you?"

"I'm good, girl. How are those babies I been hearing so much about?" she asked, and I pointed at my two girls.

My mother and father eased their way beside me. I stepped aside so Aunt NeeNee could hug Mommy. When they finished their moment, Aunt NeeNee stood face to face with my father. I could see that even though my aunt was forcing a smile, something was wrong. I could tell from Daddy's body language and the way he hugged her, he could see it too.

"What's going on, Nee?" he asked, releasing her from his arms. He was staring at her like he used to do to us as kids when he was trying to get the truth out of us.

"Yeah, it's not like you not to call before making such a long trip," my mother added.

"I never could hide nothing from you two, could I?" Aunt NeeNee replied, a worried look on her face now. "I couldn't take a chance on using a phone. I had to speak to you in person, so I drove straight through."

"What's wrong, NeeNee?" Daddy asked, easing my aunt over to a chair so she could sit down.

Aunt NeeNee looked over at my father with tears in her eyes and said, "LC, we've known each other a long time, ever since we were teenagers. So, I'm asking you." She placed her hands together. "No, I'm pleading with you. Please, please, don't kill my children."

Ruby

4

"Do you tink you can slow down a little?" I glanced over at Vinnie from the corner of my eye. Even without looking at the speedometer of the SUV, I knew he was driving dangerously over the speed limit. "You're gon' kill us."

"Hell, why do you care?" Vinnie snapped.

"What?"

"You're the one trying to get us killed."

"Oh my God, Vinnie. You know dat isn't true." I folded my arms across my chest. Vinnie's maniacal driving was just one more example of the frantic behavior I had been witnessing ever since I told him I saw Junior Duncan. As soon as the words came out of my mouth, he had gone into full-blown panic mode: making calls, grabbing money from the safe, and within the hour, we were fleeing.

"I still don't understand why you didn't call and tell me the moment you saw him. Why did you wait until you got home?" he asked for what seemed like the hundredth time. "You know they want us dead. What's wrong with you?"

"Vinnie, de house was less than a mile away. I got scared and I panicked. I was trying to get as far away from him as possible." Tears were starting to well up in my eyes. "I don't understand why you're mad at me."

Vinnie's eyes left the road, and he stared straight at me. "Ruby, he could have followed you. I can't help you if I'm dead. We've gone over this time and time again. If they know where we are, we have no chance."

"So, I should have just let him take me and Vincent?"

"No, of course not. I apologize for getting so upset with you. You and Vincent are all I care about, and keeping you both safe

Chippy

5

"Please, please, don't kill my children."

I saw the tears running down NeeNee's face and heard the seriousness in her tone, but for the life of me, I couldn't fathom why she thought my husband would do something so horrible. The scowl on LC's face told me he was surprised and probably a little hurt by her words—so much so that he hadn't even opened his mouth to respond.

"NeeNee, what the hell is all this about? You know LC. He would never hurt your children! Hell, your children are our family." LC might have been stunned silent, but I sure as hell wasn't. If he wasn't going to rebuke her comments, then I would, and I'd make sure she understood how irritated I was.

NeeNee swayed her head back and forth, looking very seriously at LC and me. "You say that now, Chippy, but once you've heard what's going on, I'm not so sure you'll be of the same state of mind. Then we'll see how much you consider my children your family."

I still didn't know what she was talking about, but the conviction in her voice had me worried. I glanced over at LC, who shared my look of apprehension. We'd known NeeNee almost forty years, so there was no doubt in my mind that she thought she had a good reason to come all the way from Waycross, Georgia. I just prayed it was a lot less than the drama she'd been building.

LC slid his hand over his hair then took a sip of his coffee to clear his throat. "Well then, sister-in-law, why don't you tell us this earth-shattering news and just why you're here? 'Cause we're all on the edge of our seats."

"Yeah, why don't I do that?" She pointed at LC's coffee cup.

"And in the meantime, can you have one of the kids pour me a cup of coffee and get the little ones out of here? This is gonna be a grown folks' conversation."

"I got it, Aunt Chippy," Sasha replied, heading for the pot of coffee.

I turned to London and Paris. "You two take your children outside while we sort this out."

London did exactly as I told her to, but Paris didn't budge. "I wanna hear what Aunt NeeNee has to say," Paris stated.

I did not have the patience for her, so I turned to LC and said, "Speak to your daughter."

It didn't take but a look from him before she scooped up Jordan, following behind London with a scowl on her face. I tried my best to ignore her, making a mental note to address her disrespect once things with NeeNee calmed down. I turned my attention back to NeeNee, who was now sipping her coffee.

"What's going on, Nee?" LC asked. He was now flanked on his other side by Vegas, who stood there with his arms folded.

As she sipped her coffee again, NeeNee scanned the room, making eye contact with everyone present. She made sure she had our undivided attention before she spoke. "I don't even know how to tell you this, LC, but Larry's back."

There was a silent scream in the room, and I have to admit my knees buckled to the point Orlando had to help me into a chair. There was some combination of shock and dread on everyone's faces.

Larry Duncan was LC's older brother and a homicidal maniac. He was, without question, the closest thing to Charles Manson that I'd ever met. However, what really scared me about him was that he was also the only man who could put fear in my husband's heart.

"What do you mean, he's back?" Vegas snapped angrily. Like most of my kids, Vegas was well aware of what his uncle Larry was capable of, and unfortunately, a witness to his instability.

"He just showed up at the house a few months ago," NeeNee said, sounding either weary or sorrowful; but at that moment, it didn't matter to me which it was, because I was coming to an uneasy realization.

"Nee, he's been back for months and you never said a word?" I stared at her in disbelief. We talked almost every week, sometimes two or three times a week. "How come you never told me?"

"'Cause I love him, Chippy. He's my husband, the only man I've ever loved. If I had told you, you would have told LC. Then he and your boys would have come down to Waycross and got him, or worse, killed him."

"Aunt NeeNee, we understand you love Uncle Larry, but he's a very sick man. He needs to be under a doctor's care," Vegas reasoned, kneeling down and taking her hand.

"She doesn't understand what he's capable of, Vegas," I said.

"I know exactly what he's capable of, Chippy. He's my husband. I know his dark side better than any of you. I'm not stupid, despite what you think!" She raised her voice for the first time. "I would never release an ill Larry on the world." Tears were beginning to well up in her eyes again. "When Larry knocked on my door six months ago, he wasn't sick. He was himself. I swear, he was my Larry again."

"How can you be so sure of that, Nee? You're not a doctor," I said skeptically.

"No, I'm not, but Larry was seeing a doctor, and I went to CVS and filled the prescription myself. He was doing good, too, spending time with the boys, taking them huntin' and fishin'. We were a family again, Chippy, just like yours."

"So, what happened? What changed things?" LC finally spoke up.

NeeNee looked up in LC's face, and tears began to roll down her cheeks. "About three weeks ago on her birthday, he started to visit your mother, and last week he started taking the boys with him."

The kids shook their heads and exchanged glances, while LC started mumbling to himself.

"Hey, y'all, this is some serious shit. Let's try and stay focused," Vegas commanded. "So, where is Uncle Larry now, Aunt NeeNee?"

"Two days ago, I woke up to an empty house and a note that said the four of them were going to reclaim what was rightfully theirs by any means necessary. They took every gun and round of ammunition in the house," NeeNee replied warily, lowering her head. "I assumed they were headed here."

"Uh-oh, that can't be good for us." My son Rio said what everyone else was thinking.

"No, it's not, and neither is this." NeeNee held up a medicine bottle, which Orlando took from her and began examining. "I found it in the bathroom trash. He's off his meds."

Orlando sighed heavily. "I've got news for you, Aunt NeeNee. If these are what he's been taking the past few months, he was never on antipsychotic medication. These pills are generic Crestor used to control high cholesterol, not mental illness. I think he duped you."

"Shit!" Vegas cursed. "Orlando, call the psych hospital and find out when and why he was released."

"There's no need for that, Orlando. He's been out about six months," LC said calmly.

"Six months?" I repeated. All eyes were now on my husband. "How do you know that?" I asked, totally unprepared for his answer.

"Because it was about six months ago that Larry shot me."

Larry

6

"Pass me those potatoes and one of those biscuits," I said, piling two pieces of fried chicken on my plate. My oldest son, Curtis, or Curt as I called him, was so busy stuffing his face that he didn't move. His younger brother, Kenny, was the one who put his fork down and passed me the container of mashed potatoes and then one of the brown biscuits out of the box. "This Popeye's chicken ain't half bad."

"It's all right, but it ain't as good as Ma's," Curtis replied.

"Ain't nobody's chicken as good as my Nee's chicken, but it's damn sure better than that rubber shit they served me in that hellhole of a hospital your uncle had me locked up in."

"Well, you're not there anymore, son, and that's all that counts." My mother, Bettie, placed a reassuring hand on my shoulder then sat down next to me. She nudged me, glancing across the table at my youngest son, who hadn't touched his food and had been a little more quiet than normal.

I put down the chicken breast I was eating and asked, "What's your problem?"

Kenny looked over at Curtis, who kept on eating, and then realized he was the one I was talking to. "Uh, no—nothing."

"Don't lie to me, boy. You've barely said two words since we got back this evening."

"I don't have no problem," he said, picking at the food on his plate.

"You sure?" I pressed.

"Yeah, I'm sure. But I do have a couple of questions."

"Oh, Lord. Here we go with that fifty thousand questions shit again," Momma said with a sigh as she fell back in her chair dramatically. "I bet you LC's kids don't ask him fifty thousand questions. I bet they do what they're told and shut the fuck up."

It was then that Curtis finally stopped chewing. We looked at one another, then turned our attention to Kenny.

"What is it?" I sat back and waited for him to say whatever was on his mind.

He hesitated and then asked me, "Did you have to kill that guy? Was that really necessary?"

"Are you fucking kidding me? That guy had to die." He was starting to aggravate me.

"Why? We just paid him fifty fucking grand. He wasn't gonna say nothing," Kenny replied in an elevated voice.

"Boy, don't you raise your voice at me."

"Kenny, the guy was an informant," Curtis cut in, trying to defuse the situation. "He'll give anyone information for money. Last thing we need is for LC and his folks to know what we're planning. Dad's right. He had to be eliminated."

"I disagree. Whatever happened to the honor amongst thieves you always preached to me, Curtis? Mommy told me that half the reason LC is where he's at is because he's got loyal folks behind him."

"That's bullshit! The reason LC has what he has is because I killed everyone standing in his fucking way, and what did I get for it?" I stood straight up, but Momma pulled me back in my chair. "I'll tell you. I got fourteen years in the nut house."

"Dad, we can't keep killing everyone we encounter. I'm not going to do it!" He folded his arms defiantly like it was the last word.

A slow smile spread across my face, and then I began to laugh. It was a deep, hearty laugh that came from my belly and shook my body so hard that I banged on the table. Momma and Curtis started laughing just as hard. Kenny just stared at us like we were crazy. For some reason, that made me laugh even harder. Then I just stopped laughing abruptly, leaned over the table, and smacked the shit out of him.

"You do what the fuck I tell you to do." I sat back down, and my mother gave me a reassuring pat on the back. "So what, he's dead? There's going to be a lot more people dead when this is all said and done. You wanna be a pacifist, go find LC and join his merry bunch of faggots."

"I told you his ass was soft as cotton. He's been sitting home sucking NeeNee's tit the whole time you been gone. I don't know why we brought his ass with us in the first place," Momma said. I cut my eyes at her then turned my attention back to the table.

"Well, Kenny, is it true? Should I have left you home with your momma?" I smiled at Kenny, who looked at me strangely, then at his brother. Curtis looked down at the table like he was avoiding eye contact.

"No, I belong here just as much as Curtis. I was just wondering, that's all," Kenny said, shaking his head.

"You said you had a couple of questions. What else you need to know?"

"Nothing. Never mind."

I backed off a little. "Look, I'm sorry for slapping you, but we might as well get everything out in the open and on the table now."

"I just want to know what the end game is. Ever since you got back, you've been preaching that family is everything. Well, Uncle LC is your brother. Ain't he family?" Kenny asked.

"Yeah, but he's the worst kind of family."

"Why is that?"

"Okay, let me see if I can explain." I glanced over at my mother, and she nodded her approval. "Who is the one person you love more than anyone in the world?"

"Ma," he said without hesitation.

"As you should. There's nothing like a mother's love. I feel the same way about your grandmother." I glanced over at her, and she smiled. "And then who?"

He frowned then mumbled, "Probably Curtis, and then you."

"Okay, that makes sense. Your immediate family comes first, and hopefully one day you'll find a woman to marry and love her too." Kenny was paying attention, but he still looked confused. "And hopefully the two of you will have kids that you will love like your mother and I love you boys."

I stared at my son, looking just like his momma. He not only had his mother's dimpled smile and nurturing spirit, but he also had her intellect. He liked to think things through. It was something that I appreciated, and I knew it would come in handy with my plans. What I didn't appreciate was him questioning my motives or my actions. I had a method to my madness, at least I wanted to think so, and I needed him to trust me. It was okay for the world to think I was crazy, but not my kids.

"Now, imagine if Curtis, the brother you love and work with every day, took that all away from you. In the blink of an eye, he snatched your mother, your wife, and your children, all to fill his pockets with money." I was sure my voice was starting to sound a little intense, but this was a topic that filled me with rage every time I remembered what LC had done to me. "Imagine him locking you away in a damn psychiatric hospital and telling them to throw away the fucking key."

Curtis stepped in to explain, probably because he could see how worked up I was getting. "Kenny, listen. Uncle LC was the one who had Dad locked up in that dungeon all those years. Shit, he destroyed our family. Momma had to fend for herself and take care of us. Who does that to his own brother and his nephews?" Curtis asked. "What if I did that to you? What would you do to me?"

"Don't get me wrong, Kenny," I said when I'd calmed down enough to speak again. "I'm not perfect. Matter of fact, I'm far from it. Vietnam fucked me up, but I didn't deserve this, and neither did my family. Hell, ask your mother. I didn't even wanna move to New York, but LC, Lou, and I had built a dynasty, and my family has been cheated out of it."

Kenny remained silent. I got up from the table without finishing my meal and sat on the small sofa. I picked up my gun and began cleaning it as I thought about my brothers. At one point, all three of us were so close. If it wasn't for me and Lou, who had bought LC his first service station back in Waycross, he would probably be sitting behind a desk in a bank somewhere, working for someone else. Duncan Motors was a product of a whole lot of blood, sweat, and tears, and not just his, either. After everything I had done to aid him in his success, LC had me locked up like some wild animal. And that wasn't the only thing he had done. Now, it was time for him to be dealt with.

"Boys, I'm not forcing either of you to take this journey with me. If you can't understand that our family honor is at stake by now, then I'm never going to convince you. This is not about the Duncans as a whole. This is about LC and his family, and me and mine. I'm not gonna lie; my intentions are to hurt LC as bad as he hurt me. I tried to kill him, but the son of a bitch won't die. So, I'm going to do something far worse. I'm going to take away the thing that means the most to him."

Suddenly, Kenny walked over and picked up his gun. I frowned, wondering what the hell he was about to do. To my surprise, he sat down next to me and began cleaning it. "Don't worry, Dad. We are going to handle LC and his family. Nobody fucks with our family honor."

"Well, I'll be damned." My mother smiled from her seat at the table. "I guess we gonna make this boy a Duncan man after all."

"Yes, indeed," I said, nodding my head. I had never been more proud of my son than I was at that moment.

LC

7

"Why the hell didn't you tell me Larry shot you?"

I stared at my wife, who'd just entered my home office, followed by Vegas. Neither of them looked happy. This was the first time she'd said a word to me in hours. When I first made the admission, she'd stormed out of the room. She was pissed like I hadn't seen her in a long time.

"I thought I could handle it." I sighed deeply.

"Have you lost your damn mind, LC? What do you mean you thought you could handle it?"

"Like I said, I thought I could handle it," I repeated.

"How the hell were you going to handle Uncle Larry of all people, Pop? You've said yourself on plenty of occasions that even you and Uncle Lou couldn't handle him." Vegas exchanged a look with his mother, who continued their tag-team effort to berate me.

"LC, everyone knows he's crazy. Shit, his nickname for years has been Crazy Larry, and he's always lived up to it. I can't believe you didn't tell me."

"Honey, I know I should have told you, but at first, I really didn't remember. I couldn't recall anything except waking up in the house and you being there beside me. I didn't even know I had been shot at first," I explained. They both looked confused.

"So, when did you remember?" Vegas asked.

"I don't know, maybe about a month or two ago." I turned to Chippy. "You remember when I was having those bad dreams?"

She nodded. "Yeah, you kept waking up in a cold sweat."

"Well, those dreams were about me getting shot. I couldn't see who it was the first few nights, but eventually, more and more details started coming back to me, until I realized it was Larry." The memory of those nightmares still haunted me.

Chippy's face softened. "Okay, so why didn't you tell me?"

"I don't know. Truth is, I wanted to, but in hindsight, I thought it was the best thing for all of us to keep quiet. I figured Larry shot me and maybe he'd just go away. I mean, we hadn't heard from him since."

Chippy shook her head. "You really thought that you were doing the family a favor by not mentioning that your brother shot and almost killed you?"

"I wouldn't exactly put it that way, Chippy, but . . ." I glanced over at Vegas, who looked disgusted. He seemed to have no sympathy for me or my story. "See, I know our boys and Paris. They could say whatever they want, but if they knew Larry had shot me, they would have hunted him down and killed him—or he would have killed them." Vegas lowered his head, most likely because he knew I was telling the truth. "So, let's be honest. What good would that have done our family?"

Vegas exhaled loudly, but I think I was finally getting through to him. "So, how the hell did he get out, Pop?"

"It was your cousin Curtis," I explained. "Two years ago, he had himself placed as Larry's next of kin and administrator of his affairs with the hospital, instead of me. I knew about it, but I never thought it was a big deal. He's Larry's son, after all, and he'd seen firsthand what his father was capable of. Never in a million years did I think he'd orchestrate his father's release."

Again, Chippy stared at me and shook her head. "So, you gave the approval for your brother, a homicidal maniac who's been locked up in a mental institution for years, to have his son, who worships the ground he walks on, be his administrator?"

I cringed with embarrassment as I admitted how badly I'd miscalculated the situation. "It doesn't sound too bright now, but yes, that's exactly what I did. But in my defense, Larry had been getting treatment for years. He's a damn near sixty-five-year-old man. I didn't think there would be any harm in his son taking over his care. It had been a while since he'd had an episode or an incident."

"Well, it almost got you killed," Chippy said angrily. "This is what happens when you go rogue and we don't act together as a team, LC."

"I know that, Charlotte, but he's my brother. All I wanted was for him to live out his days happily." I was damn near crying, but somehow, I straightened my spine and found my resolve again. "I'll take care of this. If I have to put him down myself, I'll take care of it. I promise." And I meant what I said.

"LC." Chippy walked over and put her arms around my shoulders. "Sending Larry away was the best thing you could have done for him. I know you love your brother. Hell, I love him too, but he is a danger to our family. You can't handle him by yourself. This is something we have to do together."

"Ma's right. We have to handle Uncle Larry the same way we handle everything else: as a family," Vegas said with finality.

I nodded my head in agreement. "Okay, from here on out, we do it as a family."

Vegas

8

"What do you mean, I can't go?" Orlando yelled, jumping out of his seat on the sofa. I'd called a family meeting after Mom and Pop had made it clear they wanted me to head up the effort to neutralize Uncle Larry and keep our family safe. Unfortunately, on top of the Uncle Larry situation, Junior had just come home with news that he'd seen Ruby and Orlando's son, Vincent, in Negril. O was losing it, because I had just told him I was putting together a team to find his son, but he couldn't be on it.

"I'm sorry, bro, but there's no way in hell you're sending a team to look for my son without me," Orlando continued. "Key words here being *my son*." He was now in my face looking like he wanted to punch me.

"Which is exactly why you're not going, O. You're too involved in this, and we can't afford for you to be flying off the handle, getting all caught up in your feelings." Orlando was a smart guy, and he could handle himself, but like the rest of us Duncans, he could be hotheaded and stubborn at times.

"This is bullshit and you know it, Vegas! If this was about Nevada, nobody could stop you from killing everyone on that damn island."

"If this were Nevada, I'd want the right people for the job. This situation must be handled like a surgeon, not the Unabomber. You're going to have to trust me on this one, O. Besides, I've got other things for you and Paris to do."

He turned to my father. "Pop, will you please tell Vegas that I'm going?"

My father shook his head. "I can't do that, son, because he's right. Just like I'm too emotionally involved with Larry, you're too emotionally involved with Ruby and your son. Vegas has got a plan. Let him play it out."

"Yeah, but his plan doesn't include me." Once again, he was in my face. If he was anyone else, I would have taken him down, but I let him have his moment. "Don't do this to me, man. My son is the most important thing in the world to me. Ruby and Vinnie have been keeping him from me. I just want to see my boy."

"And you will, but this ain't just about Ruby and Vinnie Dash. We also gotta worry about a whole posse of Jamaicans who work for them. If we don't do this right, people could get killed. People like your son."

"Sit down, Orlando, and let him finish," my father said.

Orlando did what he was told, but he wasn't happy about it.

"What I wanna know is why are you sending Rio to Jamaica instead of me? How much sense does that make? I'm the one who's trained to handle situations like this, not him. The only thing Rio can do in Jamaica is sit on the beach and get a tan," Paris said, pouting.

"Don't do that." Rio rolled his eyes at Paris, wagging a finger. "Don't throw me under the bus because you're mad. You trained your way, and I trained mine. I'm a Duncan. I know how to handle myself."

In some ways, my sister did have a point, but so did Rio. My younger brother was a party animal and didn't have the formal training that most of us had, but he had proven himself to be valuable in the past, and I felt confident in sending him along with Sasha.

"I'm ready. When do we leave?" Sasha finally spoke up.

"Tomorrow night," I told her.

"Great. That gives me time to run to the mall right quick and grab a few last-minute items." Rio smiled deviously. "Sasha, would you like to join me?"

"Sorry, Ree, I've got an appointment with Jenny," Sasha replied.

Orlando glared at me as I continued explaining what was going to happen. "Sasha, Rio, and Daryl will leave tomorrow night for Negril. Harris, I need you to arrange for a discreet Airbnb where they can hole up, along with a few of our best people."

"Daryl's going?" Paris's voice became two octaves higher.

"Yeah, I've already spoken with him, and he's making arrangements as we speak. He knows that island and the people like the back of his hand. He lived there for a few years, remember?"

"What does that have to do with me?" Orlando snapped.

"Orlando, I promise, I'm going to get your son back. You've gotta trust me. That's my nephew too. It's family."

Orlando stood up and announced, "I don't care what you say. I'm going, whether you like it or not. I'll charter my own damn plane if I have to."

"Me too. I'm with you, Orlando. That's my nephew." Paris stood beside him.

"Keep talking like that and I'll lock both of your asses up in the basement," I said to her.

"You got your son. Now I'm going to get mine!" Orlando shouted at me.

I looked over at Nevada, who was taking it all in, not saying a word. My son was quiet a lot of the time, but that didn't mean he wasn't paying attention. He studied everything that went on in this family, and I was sure that one day his observation skills would serve us all well.

"Orlando and Paris, both of you sit your asses down!" my mother yelled, and the room became quiet. They stopped complaining and took their seats, and everyone turned their attention to Ma. "Orlando, your brother is right. You would be spotted as soon as you stepped off the plane. Vinnie Dash would do everything in his power to hurt you, or worse, do something to your son. Let Vegas handle it. He has a plan in place, and that's how it's gonna be."

"Well, if they're gonna do that, what do you have me doing?" Paris asked, still sounding pissed off.

"You and O are going to Waycross, Georgia," I said.

"Waycross? What the fuck is in Waycross? Sasha and Rio are going to Jamaica with Daryl, and you're sending my ass to Waycross! How unfair is that?" She stood up and stormed off in true Paris fashion. This was exactly the reason she wasn't on the Jamaican team. The last thing I needed was her emotional ass wreaking havoc.

The rest of the family members began filing out of the dining room and into the kitchen, leaving only Nevada and me.

"Poppa?" He got up from his chair and walked over to where I stood.

"Yeah, son," I answered.

"I want to help. I want to be on a team."

He was only a teenager, but he was nearly my height. Looking at him was like looking in a mirror. I placed my hands on his shoulders and stared at him.

"You are part of the team. You handle computers and communications."

"No, I mean part of the assault team, going on family missions. I used to do stuff for my mom."

"I know you did, son, but for right now, I need you to stay home and coordinate the computers and communications. Your time will come sooner than you think."

He looked disappointed, but he didn't argue. "Okay."

"Hey, I promise you this: one day, you will be ready. One day, you're going to be the head of the team."

My son looked at me and smiled. I grabbed him and pulled him close to me, knowing that my words weren't just for him, but they were for me. I would make sure that before that time came, he would be well prepared.

Larry

9

"Good afternoon. I'm here to see Lee," I told the tiny hostess as I walked into Ming's Garden, followed by my two boys and Momma. Ming's was a quaint restaurant, located in the heart of Chinatown, right off Canal Street. The smell of garlic noodles, friend wontons, and shrimp filled my nostrils, and my stomach grumbled, even though I wasn't hungry. "Tell him Larry Duncan is here to see him."

The hostess, dressed in a red kimono, shook her head at me. "No Lee here."

I glanced around the sparsely filled dining room and gave the woman a half smile. "Yeah, he's here. I know that he's here. He's always here at one p.m. That's what time his family conducts business over fish and rice."

"No, no Lee." The woman's voice got slightly louder, and she took a few steps near the bar, where an Asian man was watching us closely. She was starting to get on my nerves with this "he's not here" bullshit.

"Look, I don't have time for this shit. Now, tell Lee that Larry Duncan is here to see him." I raised my voice to get her attention, but the bitch kept staring at me.

Okay, you wanna play games, then we can play games.

I was just about to reach into my waistband and take out my pistol when the bartender lifted a phone and spoke some Asian gibberish into it. He motioned to another man, who was seated at the bar, whispering something in his ear. The man's eyes went from him then back to us, and then they spoke some more of that gibberish. The man stood up and went to the back of the restaurant and returned a few moments later.

He said something to the hostess, who nodded and headed directly to us. "My apologies for the confusion. Lee will see you shortly. Please follow me."

We followed her past the bar, through the small kitchen, and into a small, dimly lit room. There was an empty table with several chairs around it. The hostess gestured for us to take a seat on one side of the table, and then she left. I sat in the middle, and Kenny sat in the chair to my left. Curtis went to sit in the seat to my right; but before he could sit down, I snatched him up by the collar, slapping him hard upside the head.

"Since when do you sit to my right when your grandmother's around? You know better than that, Curt. Don't you fucking embarrass me in here," I snapped angrily. "Now, apologize to your grandmother."

Curtis glanced at me then my mother, pulling out her chair so that she could sit down. "Sorry, Grandma Bettie."

"It's all right, baby. You know your granny loves you." She sat down, glaring at me. "I don't know why you always so hard on Curtis. Between the two of them, you know he's the only one you can rely on." My mother loved all her grandkids, but she had a special fondness for Curtis because he was her first.

Curtis took a seat beside Kenny, who was staring at me with his eyebrows all knotted up. He was probably upset that I'd let his grandmother talk shit about him.

Another woman entered the room and smiled politely. "Good afternoon, Mr. Duncan. Can I get you anything to eat or drink? Compliments of Mr. Lee Cheng." She seemed to be a bit friendlier than the hostess.

"Bourbon," I replied. "And two Hennessy on the rocks for the boys."

"Get me a beer," Momma said.

"And a beer," I added.

"Make sure it ain't that sake bullshit either," Momma whispered. "Real beer, you understand?"

"Yes," the waitress said and scurried out the door.

"Listen, Ma, you know how these Asian cats are about their culture. They don't believe in doing business with women, so I'ma do all the talking. Understood?" I looked over at my momma, who didn't seem pleased with the idea, but thankfully she didn't fuss like I thought she would.

"Uh, yeah, Dad." Curtis nodded.

"Fine with me." Kenny shrugged.

A few minutes later, the woman returned with our drinks and some fried dumplings.

"Larry Duncan, how very nice to see you. It's been a long time since we've seen each other," Lee Cheng said when he walked into the room shortly after the waitress left. There were two other men with him, including the one who had been at the bar. Lee took a seat directly across from me, and they sat on each side of him.

"Lee, I was starting to think you were about to pull some shit on me, especially when ol' girl started saying you weren't here."

He offered his hand across the table, and I took it.

"No, no, we have to be wary in times like this. I would never pull anything on a man like yourself." Lee still had that bullshit smirk that just made you wanna shoot his ass. "So, to what do I owe the pleasure of this visit?"

"I would like to do business with you," I told him. "You know, start out small, maybe fifteen, twenty kis to start."

"You know I am always interested in doing business with the Duncans. Of course, I would like a larger order, but we can start with twenty kilos, to rebuild business." Old Lee looked happier than a pig in shit.

"Good. So how much we talking per ki?"

"I can wholesale them to you for thirty thousand dollars a kilo. That should give you plenty of margin for profit."

"That's what I'm talking about, Lee. Always good doing business with you." I felt Momma's hand on my back, and the boys were nodding their approval.

"You as well, my friend. So, your brother will send payment in the usual way?" He stood up.

"No, my brother won't do shit, but my sons will bring by your cash in three days." I stood up to offer Lee my hand, but he was too busy glancing back and forth between himself and the two guys on either side of him. "Is there a problem?" I asked.

"Yes, a slight problem, but nothing a phone call with your brother won't clear up," Lee replied, his forehead wrinkled up like he was really concerned about something.

"What do you mean? Why do you need to talk to my brother?"

"We no longer do business in cash. We need to have it wired and confirmed. Your brother knows that," he said.

"Well, you're not dealing with my brother. You're dealing with me," I snapped, leaning over the table. "And since when is cash no fucking good?"

"Since 9/11, the world is very dangerous for men in our profession, but your brother knows this. He is the one who set up the system of offshore payment." Lee looked confused. "This can all be straightened out with a phone call to him."

"I knew this shit was going to happen. You shoulda let me talk to these motherfuckers," Momma said and rolled her eyes at me.

"This deal doesn't have shit to do with LC. It's me that you're doing business with. Me!" I jabbed a finger into my chest for emphasis.

"Yes, I understand that now, Larry. However, this isn't the way we usually do business. Because of the war between Sal Dash and LC, we lost much business and don't want any trouble. I just have to make sure that I am not involving myself in something that will be detrimental to my business. A simple call to your brother will resolve that, and we will be able to conduct business," Lee explained.

Momma leaned over and whispered to me, "Fuck him. Let's go. I can already see whose side he's on."

"I'm sorry, but that's unacceptable, Lee," I replied. Momma and I stood, and the boys followed suit. "It's too bad, too, because we could have made a lot of money together."

"I do not understand your objection to a simple phone call to your brother."

"Well, maybe you'll understand this." I smirked, buttoning my suit jacket as I ordered, "Curtis, Kenny, kill these motherfuckers!"

Lee's eyes grew large as Curtis pulled out his silenced Glock without hesitation and pulled the trigger. It was Kenny that I was concerned about, but he didn't hesitate either, discharging his firearm until all three men were slumped over.

"Good shooting," I told the boys.

Momma nodded her approval as she headed for the door. I followed behind her until she stopped, glancing back at the boys.

"Those two just gonna stand there?" Momma asked.

Neither one of my boys had moved. They just stared at the three dead bodies sprawled across the room, with blood seeping from their heads. At first I thought they were feeling some kinda way about taking a life for the first time, but then I realized they weren't just staring; they were smirking. You might even call it gawking. Curtis stuck out his fist, and Kenny bumped it with his fist, and they both laughed. Damn, talk about a chip off the old block.

"Hey! They're not gonna get any deader. Let's go!" I ordered. "I'm getting hungry for some real food. Come on, I'll buy you boys a steak."

We all walked out of the restaurant the same way we'd walked in, ignoring the hostess, who ran past us toward the small kitchen entrance near the bar.

Sasha

10

"This color you like?" Jenny, my favorite technician, asked as she held up the bottle of nail polish.

"Yes, that's perfect," I told her then took a sip of my champagne, which happened to be the same color as the polish.

Jenny began prepping the water in the porcelain bowl in front of me. When it was ready, I eased my feet inside and began to relax. I don't know what felt better: the butter soft leather chair I was sitting in, the feel of Jenny's hands massaging my calves, or the satisfying anticipation of my upcoming trip to the islands.

Normally, I worked as a team with Paris, using our beauty and charm, along with our skills as assassins to our advantage. Over the years, I had proven my worth to Uncle LC and the Duncan family, and I understood Vegas's reasoning behind sending me solo instead. Not trying to take anything away from her, because my cousin was good at what she did, but she had a lack of self-control that had put the family in jeopardy on more than one occasion. Being chosen to go to Jamaica without her was my opportunity to show the family that I wasn't just Paris's little sidekick, but I was just as much, if not more, of an asset to the family business.

"Is that Rihanna?" I heard someone whisper.

"I think it's her."

"No, I just looked at her Instagram. She just looks like her."

The Nail Bar was the place for not only the elite and famous to come and be pampered, but anyone else who could secure a coveted appointment and afford the costs. I was a regular customer who indulged weekly. My Diamond Rose manicures and pedicures were essential to my well-being, and the price tag was small change to me.

I was just about to close my eyes and take a quick nap when my cell phone began ringing.

"Hello."

"What's up, heifer? Where the hell y'all at?" Rio asked.

"Rio, you so damn crazy. I'm getting my nails and feet done."

"Let me speak to Paris right quick. I tried calling and she didn't answer, and she didn't respond to my text either."

"She's not here, and I haven't talked to her either." I sighed. I had tried calling Paris to see if she wanted to come with me to the salon, but she sent me straight to voicemail.

"Oh, that little bitch is really in her feelings about this Jamaica trip, huh?" Rio laughed. "Well, she'll get over it. Wanna meet me at the mall when you finish? I got some last-minute stuff to pick up."

"I don't know. If Paris finds out we're hanging out without her, she's gonna really be pissed," I told him.

"So what? She's a big girl. Besides, how's she gonna know?"

"Rio, you know damn well you can't go nowhere these days without putting it on social media. You need to chill with that shit. You know it ain't safe. Or have you forgotten the danger your ass was in a few weeks ago?" I warned him as I pulled up my IG account and went to Rio's page. Sure enough, there was a picture of him posing in his car with the caption *#retailtherapy.*

"I'm hardly ever on there anymore."

I laughed. "Rio, stop lying. I'm looking at the picture you posted ten minutes ago."

"Shopping don't count!"

"You stupid. I'll call you when I leave here," I said and ended the call. Again, I leaned back and closed my eyes.

"Is that the new Chanel Boy Bag Kim K was rocking?" I heard the inquisitor from earlier ask.

"Looks like it, but it can't be real, though. I heard they only made a hundred."

"I think that one is real. Look at her. She's designer from head to toe. That's one bad bitch."

I looked over to see who they were speaking of, and my eyes fell on a well-dressed woman entering the spa. She was the epitome of class and elegance in her YSL suit, Louboutin heels, and Chanel purse, which was undoubtedly real.

"Hello." She walked over and sat in the chair right next to mine, and all I could do was shake my head and frown. "Is this seat taken?"

"No, but there are plenty other empty seats in here. You might be more comfortable in one of them," I replied, gulping down the rest of my drink. Jenny motioned for one of the attendants to bring me a refill.

"No, this will do just fine." She removed her Louis Vuitton sunglasses and placed them in her lap. "How are you? It's been a while since you stopped by the house."

"Let's not do this, okay, Mom?"

Deidra, another technician, walked over and handed her a glass of champagne then proceeded to remove the designer heels from her feet.

"So nice to see you again, Ms. Donna," she said with a smile. "The usual today?"

"I'll have whatever my beautiful daughter is having."

At the sound of the word *daughter,* my head snapped in her direction.

"What do you want?" I hissed. She was totally ruining my mood.

"How about a meaningful relationship with my only daughter?"

I almost threw up in my mouth because she said that shit with conviction.

"How about we don't and say we did?" I refused to look at her.

"Why are you being like this, Sasha?"

Out of the corner of my eye, I could see Jenny and Deidra eyeing each other with concern.

"I'm not being like anything." I shook my head at her.

"I made sure that you've had the best of everything your entire life. Your father—"

"Don't." I interrupted her.

"Don't what?"

"Don't talk about my father. You have no right. That man raised me, and he and his family gave me everything a girl could ever want." I could feel the anger building in my chest, and I tried calming down. I was grateful when the attendant finally showed up with my glass of champagne. Again, I gulped it down, praying that the alcohol would calm my nerves. "So, don't talk about my father. You're beneath him."

"Sasha, despite what you may think, I loved your father, and I always will." She tried to reach over and touch my hand, but I snatched it away.

"If you loved him so much, why did you leave him with a five-year-old to be with another man?"

She stared at me like I had two heads, just like she always did when I asked that question.

"I don't think this is the time or place for this conversation. Why don't you come over to the house? We can have dinner. I'll make your favorites, and we can talk," she suggested.

"Sorry. I've got an early flight tomorrow for work."

"Flight to where? Anywhere good?"

I didn't answer her question. I was not about to make bullshit small talk with her when our issues were so deep.

"Oh, you're ignoring me now?" she said.

"I got nothing to say to you until you answer my question. You said you wanna talk, then talk—here and now," I challenged her.

I knew my mother was all about appearances, especially public ones. Airing out dirty laundry in front of others was making her uncomfortable. She looked at the two women working on our feet, who were diligently trying to act as if they were not eavesdropping. I could see the strain on her face, and it was somewhat gratifying to me. She didn't want to address our real problems, and I didn't want to pretend we were cool with each other, so we both stayed silent for a minute.

Finally, she let out a huge sigh and said, "Fine. The relationship between your father and me had always been a complicated one. Our breakup had nothing to do with me not loving him."

"Obviously, because every time you were broke, I'd wake up to you in his bed. But that never lasted long, did it? You'd milk him for forty, fifty grand then disappear again." I looked over at her. She was still beautiful to me, despite how much I despised her and what she had done to our family. We stared at one another. "I needed you, but you were never there for me. So, if it wasn't Daddy, I guess it was me."

She scrunched up her face like she was in pain. Good. I hoped I'd hurt her feelings, given how badly her abandonment had hurt me.

"Sweetheart, no, it definitely had nothing to do with you," she finally said. "It had everything to do with him being a Duncan."

"What the hell does that even mean?" I asked. "You knew he was a Duncan when you married him."

"I did. Things just became more complicated over the years."

"Yeah, I bet they did when he cut you off and stopped letting you spend all his money." I shook my head. "Jenny, I think it's time we do my nails."

"That's not what happened. Those Duncans are brainwashing you against me."

I chuckled. "Uncle LC talks bad about a lot of people, but you're not one of them. So, brainwashing is out." I lifted my feet, and Jenny began to dry them.

I glanced around the salon and noticed that the women who'd commented on my mother's bag when she came in were over there now, trying to look nonchalant as they ear hustled our whole conversation. My mother must have noticed them, too, because she tried to end it real quick.

"Sasha, this isn't the time or the place for this," she said again. "We'll finish this conversation another time. Why don't you come over to my house on Friday?"

"Sorry, I can't," I told her. "I told you I have a flight to Jamaica tomorrow."

"Really, Sasha, can't you just postpone your vacation?"

"This isn't a pleasure trip. It's work," I said.

"What kind of work?"

"Duncan business. And you said it yourself, you can't handle being a Duncan, so stay out of it," I said with finality.

Ruby

11

Kingston was the last place in the world I wanted to be. Not only did it hold too many painful childhood memories, but being there also was a constant reminder that my older brother Randy was dead. The neighborhood that we were staying in was only a few blocks away from where Randy and I grew up, and although it was a little nicer and the house we were staying in was better, it was still in the middle of Tivoli Gardens, a dilapidated area filled with crime and violence. According to Vinnie, being in the middle of the shanty town was the safest place for us, because we were protected by the gangs and thugs he did business with. I didn't feel safe, though. Most of the time I felt like a prisoner, despite being told I could come and go as I pleased. What good is leaving the house if you don't have anywhere to go but a slum? So, I never left the house, which was manned by several so-called security members that Vinnie made sure were present at all times. Having them in our home only added to my frustration. They were loud, annoying, and made themselves a little more than comfortable. Sometimes I didn't know if they were there to protect us or just to smoke all the weed Vinnie kept around. Luckily, my son made a few friends with some children from next door, and I could watch and listen to them playing in the front yard from our bedroom window.

"Throw me the ball," I heard Vincent say.

"Come closer. You can't make it from way over dere," one of the boys yelled as he stood in front of a plastic goal, holding a soccer ball.

"I bet I can!" Vincent yelled back and ran a little farther across the yard.

"Can not!" another boy said.

"Throw it," Vincent said.

The boy threw the ball at Vincent, and he caught it then placed it on the ground. He eyed the goal, and then took a step back and kicked the ball. They all watched as the ball went up in the air and soared across the yard, stopping short of where it was supposed to go. A look of disappointment came across Vincent's face, and the other boys began laughing at him.

"Shut up," Vincent told them.

"I told you. I knew you couldn't make it," they teased.

"I don't care. My daddy is gonna help me when he gets home anyway," Vincent said. "I'm going to kick it even farther."

"Where is your daddy now? Where does he live?" the boy asked him.

"He lives here with us. He's da boss," Vincent bragged.

"That's not your daddy," one of the boys told him, and I felt my stomach drop.

"He is too my daddy," Vincent insisted.

"He's a white man. You're not white. You're black," another boy said.

Unable to listen to the conversation any longer, I yelled out the window, "Vincent! Come inside. It's time to eat."

I took off running down the stairs and out the back door. When I made it to the yard, the boys had all scattered, and my son was standing alone, soccer ball in hand.

"Come on. It's time to eat," I said, putting my arm around his shoulder and pulling him toward me.

He looked up at me and asked, "Mommy, where is my daddy?"

"He's out working. He will be home in a little while," I told him, hoping that would be enough to satisfy him. Of course, it wasn't. Those boys had planted the seed in his mind, and now he would want answers.

"Marko said that he's not my daddy because he's a white man and I'm not white." Vincent had a confused look.

I inhaled deeply. I knew that this conversation would happen eventually; however, I had hoped it would take place much later.

"Vincent, he is your daddy. You are his son, and he loves you very much. You know dat, right?"

Vincent nodded at me, and then he said, "But he is not black like me. So, how?"

I tried to answer in terms his young mind would understand. "There is a difference between a father and a daddy. A father is a man who helps create a baby in a mother's stomach. A daddy is a man who loves you and protects you and takes care of you. He is your daddy, Vincent."

He asked the next logical question. "So, who is my father?"

If I didn't answer, he would keep pestering me until I did, so again, I answered him, trying to keep it short and simple. "Your father lives in New York. He's a powerful man who is also very dangerous."

His eyes widened. "Like the Duncans?" I had tried to shield him over the years, but he had overheard many conversations and arguments between me and Vinnie about Orlando's family. As far as my son was concerned, the Duncans were the definition of "bad guys."

"Yes, but you don't have to be afraid, because your daddy is gon' to make sure dat you are safe." I leaned down and kissed him on the cheek. "Now, go inside and wash up fo' dinner."

Vincent opened the back door and went inside. I could hear his small feet running up the steps as I walked into the kitchen. I stopped, suddenly overwhelmed by the smell, which was so strong it almost made me nauseous. I followed it into the garage, where three men were smoking and tossing dice.

"What de hell is dat smell? What de hell are y'all doing in my house? Have ya lost ya damn minds?" I screamed so loud that one of the men dropped the brown cigarillo he had just placed to his lips. "My son is right upstairs. What de hell is de matter wit' you?"

"We not in ya house! We out here away from you and de boy. Why you out here clownin'?"

"Clownin'? If you don't get de hell away from here, I swear I will—"

"What's wrong? What's going on out here?" Vinnie's voice came from behind me. "I could hear you yelling as soon as I walked in the door."

"Vinnie, dey out here smoking ganja in my house with our son inside. Dey got to go." I brushed past him and walked back inside.

"Ruby, wait. Come here," he called after me. A few seconds later, I felt his hand on my arm. "Ruby, you can't be yelling at the men like that."

"Help? Who de hell are dey helping, Vinnie? Dey don't do nothin' but sit around, eating all de food, watching TV, running dey mouths all day long and smokin'. I don't need help. Dey got to go. Now!" I snatched away from him.

"They can't go. They're here to protect you and Vincent while we're here."

"I don't even wan' be here, Vinnie. I hate dis place. You say you want us safe, but you bring us here in de middle of a fuckin' war zone. My brother and I left dis place to get away from dis shit, and now I'm right back where I started. You wan' me and your son safe, den you shoulda found us a place in Discovery Bay. We've got money to afford it," I spat at him.

"Ruby, calm down. I told you we're only here temporarily, until I make some moves and get everything situated. I got some shit lined up, trust me. Think about it. If we woulda went to Discovery Bay, those white folks would be all in our business and talking up a storm if anyone came around asking questions. The Duncans would be sure to find us there, and shit, anyone else looking. Is that what you want?" Vinnie asked.

I thought about what he said, but I didn't respond.

"I'm going to get us out of here. But, for now, this is where we have to be."

"And dem?" I motioned toward the door leading to the garage.

"I'll talk to them. But they gotta be here too. There's no way I'm leaving my wife and son alone. I love you too much, and I have to know you're protected, Ruby." Vinnie pulled me close and kissed me. I knew he meant well, and had we still been in Negril, I might have felt the same passion that he kissed me with; but, although I kissed him back, the only thing I felt in my heart was worry.

12

After a quick stop at the security gate, we pulled into a gated neighborhood in Manhasset, Long Island, in three black SUVs like we were a presidential motorcade. Being a man of discretion, of course you know I hated this, but I had no choice. Despite my vehement objection, Chippy had Vegas place a security detail of six men on me any time I left the compound. I did understand that they were doing it for my own good, and I had to set an example from the top that I was taking this situation seriously, but that didn't change the fact that I hated it.

The SUVs pulled to a stop in front of an impressive Tudor-style house, the passenger's side rear door was opened, and I stepped out. All six men of my detail were posted on either side of me, looking like they'd just auditioned for *Men in Black*.

"Mr. Duncan, it's Vegas," said Willie, my new driver, as he handed me a cell phone.

I took the phone from him and placed it to my ear. "Yes, son?"

"Pop, I just got confirmation that Uncle Larry is definitely in New York." Vegas's voice was filled with anxiety.

"Confirmed how?" I asked as the front door of the house opened.

"He killed Lee Cheng, his brother, and his uncle this afternoon," he replied.

"What the fuck! We don't even do business with Lee anymore," I said as a female figure appeared in the open door. Her long hair was neatly pulled back into a tight chignon, she was wearing high heels and a gauzy negligée, and on her face she wore a pair of large designer sunglasses. For a woman her age, she was sexy as hell. Once she was sure she had everyone's attention, she began to pose.

"Apparently, he was trying to do business with them, and it didn't go so well from what I was told," Vegas replied.

"Does his family understand that we had nothing to do with it?" I asked.

"I tried to explain the best I could to his son, Pop, and for now he's cool. But that doesn't mean he won't change his mind once it all sinks in. I mean, look at it from his side. The guy's father and uncles are dead at the hands of the Duncans. Doesn't matter if Uncle Larry's with us or not. He's still a Duncan, and everyone knows he's your brother."

"Yeah, I know." I bit my lip as I continued to watch the woman in the doorway. She had always been naturally flirtatious, so I couldn't tell if she was posing for me or for my men.

"Put the word out on the street that Larry's the one who shot me. Put a hundred grand on his head, dead, and a million on his head for anyone who brings him and the boys to us alive."

"That will work. Good thinking, Pop."

"Yeah, I come up with a good idea occasionally," I said, and we both chuckled. "Hopefully it'll keep these trigger-happy motherfuckers from killing my brother and his sons until we can get his ass back in a hospital."

"I guess. We'll see." Vegas didn't sound optimistic.

"Yeah, I guess we will. Look, son, I gotta go. Keep me posted."

"Sure, Pop."

I headed up the walkway, followed by my men, half of whom had one eye on me and one eye on the woman in the doorway.

When I reached her, she leaned over and gave me a light kiss on the cheek, which I didn't reciprocate, mostly because of the heavy smell of alcohol on her breath. She stepped aside in an obvious gesture for me to enter, but I stayed where I was.

"Good morning. You're looking well for a man who was shot six months ago. How are you feeling, LC?"

I took a deep breath. *Better to be cordial than nasty, LC.*

"I'm fine, and I wanted to thank you for the support you gave my family while I was incapacitated, Donna. Chippy told me you stopped by every day. You didn't have to do that considering our past, and I appreciate it."

"I appreciate you saying that. However, we are family, and family sticks together when times are tough. Isn't that what you always say?"

"Yes, I do say that," I replied halfheartedly.

There were times that I still couldn't believe that Donna, my ex-fiancée whom I'd left standing at the altar to marry Chippy, had somehow ended up married to my older brother Lou. At first, I had questioned their relationship, and so had everyone else, but after a while, nobody even blinked when he announced they were getting hitched and she was becoming my sister-in-law. Of course, that didn't change the fact that I didn't particularly like spending time around her, and Chippy surely didn't like it. Unfortunately, our complicated family arrangements made it necessary to do so from time to time, even now that Lou was deceased.

She looked past me at my men, eyeing them like fresh meat. Donna fancied herself some type of cougar. "So," she said, "you must have a lot going on when you show up with six men to come see me. What's going on?"

I ignored her question. "Listen, Donna, you called and said you needed to talk to me and it was urgent, so I'm here. Now, what do you want? And why are you dressed like that?"

"Because I'm at home, and I like to be comfortable when I'm home. Your men don't seem to mind." She was back to posing again.

I turned back and looked at my bodyguards. They tried to look away, but some let their eyes fall back on her. "Well, I mind. Put some damn clothes on. You're embarrassing yourself."

Even with her sunglasses on, I could see the slight sneer as she cut her eyes at me. "I didn't ask you here to argue or be ridiculed, LC. Why don't you and your men come on in and have some coffee? I've made some mimosas for those who don't mind a little alcohol in the morning."

"My men are fine right where they are, and so am I, so let's get on with this, shall we?" I checked my watch. "I don't have a lot of time. What do you want?"

She stiffened her demeanor. "Well, I was hoping this was going to be a friendly meeting, but I can see that I was wrong." She took the shades off and looked in my eyes. "What I want is for you to stop putting my child in harm's way. That's what I want."

"*Your* child?" I frowned. "Lay off the mimosas, Donna. They're starting to make you say things you really don't mean."

"No, they make me say exactly what I mean!" She stood up straight, trying to show confidence. "So listen to me, and listen good. I want you to stop using my daughter for your fucking underhanded illegal business. I already lost Lou to your bullshit; I'm not going to lose Sasha to it too."

I have to admit I was a little relieved. For a second there, I had thought she was talking about something entirely different; but now I had to figure out where the fuck this was coming from. She had never complained about Sasha participating in the family business, so this sudden change took me by surprise.

"Sasha is a grown-ass woman. She can make her own decisions. And don't you dare act like you even care about my brother's death. You went out of your way to make him miserable when he was alive."

She shook her head adamantly. "That's a damn lie and you know it. Lou made himself miserable chasing behind you and Larry. It didn't have shit to do with me. If he'd listened to me, he'd be alive today."

"I'm not gonna stand out here and argue with you, Donna," I warned.

Lou and Donna had hung in there for quite a few years. I'd never seen him happier than when she gave birth to Sasha and gave him a child. I'd also never seen him more upset than when he caught her cheating with a man half his age. Donna's betrayal damn near destroyed him, and from that point on, her relationship with the family varied from cordial to strained.

"We both know the truth. You broke Lou's fucking heart."

I could see the shame in her eyes, but typical Donna, she wouldn't back down or admit fault. "I'm not arguing, LC. I'm just stating facts. I loved Lou Duncan, but he loved you, Larry, and Levi more, and I just stopped trying to compete. I was his wife. I shouldn't have had to come after anyone. He should have put me before you or your stupid-ass family business."

"Don't, okay? Just don't! He put you first. Why do you think he worked so hard? You never had to work or ask for nothing, Donna, because Lou provided everything for you. But none of that mattered once you met that pretty-boy Mark."

Mentioning her infidelity to my brother was always a sure way to get her to shut up, and it worked this time too. She tried to end the conversation in a hurry.

"Just leave my child out of your family's bullshit before she gets shot like you, or killed like her father." Donna looked me straight in the eye and said, "'Cause I'm warning you, if anything happens to her, it's gonna be hell to pay."

Her threats meant nothing to me. I'd known Donna for years, and she had no power to make me do anything.

"Like I said, Sasha is a grown-ass woman who can handle her own affairs. You need to take this up with her. But let's make something clear: if she didn't work for me, she'd be working for one of these cartels or mercenary outfits. Her life would be much more dangerous. She knows what it means to be a Duncan. Lou made sure to teach her that. There's nothing you can do about it. You should have been a mother when you had the chance."

"Fuck you! I'm a good mother. My children have always had the best of everything. I made sure of that."

"Really?" I chuckled, determined not to be undermined by the authoritative tone of her voice. I knew when she called requesting to speak with me alone that it was going to be some bullshit, and she hadn't disappointed. "Going to Toys R Us on Christmas and birthdays doesn't constitute being a good mother."

She glared at me, her eyes full of resentment. "You're traveling down a slippery road, LC, a road these bodyguards won't be able to protect you from."

I could feel my blood pressure rising, and the words of my doctor echoed in my head, telling me to avoid stress. That was a sure sign that it was time for me to leave. "Good-bye, Donna."

"We're not done yet."

"Yes, we are. You said what you had to say, I listened, and now I'm leaving. As far as I'm concerned, this conversation is over."

"LC, one thing I learned from you and your brother is that family is everything. And you get to a point where you stop at nothing to protect them, at all costs, sometimes hurting others in the process. So, in an effort to protect my family, here's what's going to happen: you're going to back the hell away from Sasha. Encourage her to maybe spend a little time with her mother."

I laughed out loud. "You have lost your damn mind. Sasha is my family too. I'm not telling her shit."

"Oh, you're telling her."

"And if I don't?" I asked, curious as to what her end game was.

"If you don't, then 'Aunt Donna' will have a long talk with her favorite nephew, Junior, and tell him some things I think he should know about his lineage." She made sure to use air quotes and emphasize the words.

"You know I don't take kindly to threats." I stepped back. I couldn't believe what she was threatening to do. The only reason Chippy and I continued to keep in touch with her at all was that she was one of the few people left who could expose a family secret that we'd kept from our children for almost forty years. If she revealed it, my family would be ripped apart, and my wife would most likely kill her. Chippy and Donna played nice, but the truth was they could not stand one another. I hadn't told Chippy I was going to see Donna that day because I didn't want the drama, but now that I was here, I was starting to regret not bringing her with me. If anyone could handle Donna and put her in her place, it was Chippy.

"And I don't make threats unless I plan on using them, so I guess we're at an impasse," she said with her arms crossed defiantly over her chest.

I didn't dignify her with an answer, and Donna didn't wait for one. She put her designer sunglasses back on her face, stepped back, and closed the door. My men and I were left standing in front of her house like a bunch of Jehovah's Witnesses handing out copies of the *Watchtower*.

Larry

13

After I brushed my teeth, I finished drying off and pulled on a pair of sweatpants and a T-shirt, hung up my towel, and walked into my bedroom. The small apartment was quiet except for the TV in the living room, where Momma was watching some old cowboy movie. I'd let the boys go out hoeing to celebrate the job they'd done at Lee's. I was proud of them, especially Kenny. I knew Curtis wouldn't disappoint me, but I was surprised by how into it Kenny had been. I didn't think he had it in him. I figured he was too much like his mother, but I can admit when I'm wrong, and I had been really wrong about him. He was a true chip off the old block. There was a lot of Larry Duncan in his DNA.

Lying across the bed, I opened my wallet and pulled out a picture of NeeNee. The picture was about twenty years old, and I'd been carrying it around since the day she gave it to me. It was from the last real vacation we took together down in Virginia Beach, and she was wearing a sexy-ass red bathing suit. My goodness, she was one beautiful woman, and even now, with grey hair, a few extra pounds, and some wrinkles, she still did it for me. Damn, I missed my wife.

I reached into a duffle bag and pulled out one of the prepaid cell phones we'd bought at Walmart. Powering it up, I dialed her cell phone number.

"Hello?"

I froze, savoring the sound of her voice.

"Hello. Hello. Kenny, is that you, baby?" It was logical that she'd think Kenny would be the one to call her, because they'd always been so close. She'd be surprised by how much he'd changed in a week's time.

I finally exhaled the breath I'd been holding, and she said, "Larry, I know that's you. I'd know that sigh anywhere." She paused, probably waiting for me to speak, but I stayed quiet. "Larry, honey, are the boys all right?"

"They're fine, Nee," I finally said to comfort her. "They're at some bar chasing after girls."

"That sounds like them, especially that Kenny." Listening to her voice, I could almost hear her smile. "And you? How you doing, Larry?" she asked warmly.

"You know me. If Nam and the nuthouse didn't break me, nothing will."

"Larry, what are you doing? I thought we agreed that you'd just stay in Waycross and forget about LC and them."

"I know, Nee, but that was when I thought he was dead. Once I found out he was still alive, it just started eating away at me. I have to reclaim what belongs to me. What belongs to us—you, me, and my boys. LC is going to return what's rightfully mine, and I'm going to crush him in the process."

"You are going to get my boys killed; that's what you're going to do, Larry," NeeNee shouted, surprising me. She wasn't one to raise her voice to me unless she was really upset.

"They're soldiers. They know what they've signed up for." I thought that might pacify her, but it didn't.

"They are not soldiers. They are our sons—my babies—and I don't want anything happening to them. I swear to God, if either of them gets hurt, I'll never forgive you." Her tone was resolute. There was no doubt she meant every word of what she'd said.

"Nee, they're not going to get hurt."

"Can you promise me that, Larry? Can you? Can you?" she badgered. "LC's boys have been trained their entire lives for this type of thing."

"And so has Curt," I snapped. "And Kenny ain't no slouch, either. I'll take my two boys against LC's three and a half any day."

"You still didn't answer my question. Can you promise me that my boys won't get hurt?" she asked again impatiently. Damn, it didn't look like there was going to be any happy ending to this conversation.

I lowered my head as I spoke into the phone. "No, I can't. When the shit hits the fan, there's a possibility any of us could go down."

"Then let me offer a suggestion that could keep our family alive," she said, her tone softening just a little.

"Sure, what's that?" I asked optimistically.

"Talk to your brother, Larry. Tell LC what you want; tell him what you think you deserve. He just might give it to you. He doesn't want a war, and he doesn't want to kill you and the boys. So, talk to him. Please."

I hesitated for a second, thinking about what she was asking me. The first thing that ran through my mind was doubt that LC would even consider returning to me what was rightfully mine. And if he did agree to it, could I trust him?

"It would be nice to be a family again, wouldn't it?" I said. The thought of having the whole family together was appealing to me.

"Yes, it would," she said happily.

I sat up in the bed. "So, you think we can just talk this through and he'll give me everything back?"

"Yes, Larry, I do."

"You don't think he'll try and put me back in that hospital, do you?" I mean, that was a legitimate question.

"Not if you take your meds, he won't."

"Well, Nee," I said, raising my voice, "all I can say is, if you believe that, then you're a damn fool, because if LC and them don't put a bullet in me, they're going to cart me right back to that hospital, and our boys are going to be right there with me." I said with finality, "I know my brother. He can't be trusted."

"God dammit, Larry, then bring my sons home to me," she shouted. "Do you understand? I want you to bring my sons home to me."

"I'm sorry, but I can't do that. Not right now at least." I hung up the phone, took out the battery, and snapped it in half. Suddenly, I could feel the weight of the world on my shoulders.

"What the hell's going on in here?"

Startled, I reached under my pillow for the gun I had tucked away. Within seconds, I was turned around, aiming at Momma, who was standing in the doorway of my room.

"Dammit, Momma! You scared the shit outta me. You're lucky I didn't blow your dag-gone head off by accident." I lowered the gun and placed it back under my pillow. "I thought you was watching TV."

"I was until I heard you screaming at somebody. The boys acting up again?" she asked.

"No, the boys are fine. They're at the strip club down the block."

Momma chuckled. "Shit, I should have gone with them."

"Me too," I said, joining her laughter.

She sat down on the bed next to me. "What's going on? What's got your face all in a twist? You wanna talk about it?"

"Nothing to talk about," I mumbled.

"You're lying. Who you been talking to?" She pointed at the broken phone in my hand.

I looked down at the dusty floor and paused a few seconds before admitting, "NeeNee."

Momma didn't chuckle this time; she let out a loud, raucous laugh. "You mean to tell me that you talked to NeeNee for five minutes and she got your head turned around that quick?"

"My head's not turned around, Momma. I'm just wondering if what we 'bout to do is the right thing, that's all."

"What the fuck? Why wouldn't it be? Larry, LC had you locked away in a damn nuthouse for fourteen years, away from your wife and children, and then he stuck me in some nursing home to wither away and die because I had the nerve to say something to him about what he was doing to you. I done missed out on great grand after great grand being born, so he gets no pass from me."

"Me neither, but I was thinking, maybe if we talk to him—"

SLAP!

The palm coming across my face stunned me. My first instinct was to make a fist to retaliate, and then I quickly came to my senses when I remembered that the blow came from the woman who had given me life.

"Stop thinking. Ain't nothing to think about," she yelled. "LC's not going to give you back those years he stole from you. He's my son, Larry, so you know this is hard for me to say, but he's violated everything this family stands for. Your brother has singlehandedly destroyed what your father built. So, right now, all you need to do is stick to the plan. Do you understand, son? Stick to the goddamn plan."

I listened to everything Momma was saying. My being gone had taken its toll on my family, and the last thing I wanted was to have the legacy of my father destroyed. My father had always emphasized the importance of family sticking together. He was one of the main reasons my brothers and I had worked so hard to build a family business, a legacy for all of us. And then LC had turned on me, like the Duncan name didn't mean shit to him.

I looked at my mother and nodded. "Yeah, Momma."

"Good. Now, put LC and his nonsense out your mind. We got a lot to do tomorrow, and dealing with them Jamaicans is not going to be an easy task, so we're going to need our leader at his best." She kissed my forehead and eased her way toward my bedroom door. "I love you, son.

"Love you too, Ma."

She shut the door, and I closed my eyes. I loved my wife, but I can't lie; there is nothing like a mother's love and comfort. My momma could talk me into damn near anything.

Sasha

14

I finished putting the final items in my Louis Vuitton suitcase, zipped it shut, then did one last look around my room to make sure I hadn't forgotten anything. It looked like I had everything, so I tucked my Ray Bans into my purse and headed downstairs. I decided to have one of Junior's guys grab my bag, because Vegas had sent me a text saying he and Uncle LC needed to speak with me. Most likely they wanted to give me some last-minute instructions about our trip, and undoubtedly lecture me about mine and Rio's behavior while we were working. My excitement about the trip was slightly minimized, because Paris was upset she wasn't going with us. I'd tried calling her, but she was still in her feelings.

"You wanted to see me?" I said when I walked into Uncle LC's office. He was sitting behind his desk, while Vegas stood in the middle of the room on his phone.

"Have a seat, Sasha." Uncle LC pointed to one of the empty chairs in front of him. He was being formal, which let me know that this was going to be one of his longer lectures. I sat down and waited for his instructions.

He leaned forward and announced, "There's been a slight change of plans."

"What kind of change? We're not flying out today?" Uncle LC was a very hard man to read, so I glanced over at Vegas, who had ended his call and took the seat next to me.

"Actually, you're not flying out at all," he replied.

"Excuse me?" I sat up in the chair. "What do you mean, not at all? I can't very well drive to Jamaica."

"We're gonna need you to stay here. There's some other business you can help us with," Uncle LC said.

"I don't understand. Why can't I go?" This time, I turned and addressed the question to Vegas. "Surveillance and intel are my specialties."

He shrugged and said, "I know that, but this is not my call."

I turned back to my uncle. "What did I do? You know I can handle this, Uncle LC. This is a piece of cake."

"I'm not questioning your ability, Sasha. I just think this job is better suited for someone else."

Fuck, this can not be happening. He is not replacing me with . . .

"Paris! You're taking Paris?" I huffed, glancing back and forth between them. "You mean to tell me she bitched and whined enough to get her way again? I should've known this was gonna happen. Paris always gets what she—"

Uncle LC interrupted me. "Paris isn't going either."

Now I was even more confused. I knew Vegas needed a female operative to help, if only to act as a companion to Daryl so he wouldn't stick out like a sore thumb, and sending Rio in that role would be pushing it. If I wasn't going and neither was Paris, that didn't make sense.

"Then who? Who's going?" I asked.

Vegas hesitated before he said, "London."

Clearly, I had misunderstood him, so I asked again, "Who?"

"We're sending London." Uncle LC answered this time.

"London? What's she supposed to do if things get sticky? She hasn't picked up a gun since I've been here."

"I wouldn't say that. She and Ma are down in the range two or three times a week before you and Paris even get up," Vegas said.

Okay, that was surprising, but that didn't change the fact that she was far less qualified than me or Paris. "She wouldn't know what to do—"

"She's trained. Who do you think killed Tony Dash?" Uncle LC said, interrupting me again.

Again, I looked at Vegas, who nodded and said, "I trained her myself. She can handle it, but this is Pop's call."

"Uncle LC," I said, pleading, "why can't we both go?"

"Because I said so. Now, we have business for you to handle here, Sasha. It's already been decided. All right?"

"Yes, sir," I replied, but as the words escaped my mouth and I tried to wrap my head around my uncle's sudden decision to keep me from leaving, it dawned on me where this was stemming from.

"One last question."

"Sure," Vegas replied.

"This is about my mother, isn't it? She's the one who's pulling the strings to keep me in New York, isn't she?"

Vegas seemed completely miffed by my comment, but one look at Uncle LC's face and I knew that I was right.

"Sasha, your mother's just a little worried about you," Uncle LC said.

"My mother is full of shit! And if she's going to dictate our relationship, then maybe it's time I go back to work for the Syndicate!" I stood up and told them, "Donna Washington-Duncan-Wilson-Ferguson may pull your strings, but she damn sure doesn't pull mine. I ain't one of her puppets." I stormed out of Uncle LC's office and headed out to call the woman who found it necessary to keep interrupting my life.

Larry

15

"Stay alert, boys," I told Kenny and Curt as we moved across the Co-op City parking lot toward the stores. From the second we'd stepped out of the car, I could feel hostile eyes on us. I glanced up at the twenty-story buildings, which were a sniper's wet dream. If someone wanted to take us out, we'd be dead, and there was nothing we could do about it. "We are definitely in unfriendly territory."

"Copy that," Curt replied. "I count five potential unfriendlies between eleven and one."

"And another five at my three o'clock," Kenny added. We were now about five feet from the sidewalk. "How you want to handle it, Pop?"

"Don't do a damn thing unless I do. Far as they're concerned, we're here to purchase some vaping equipment," I said, pointing at the storefront with a huge Jamaican flag painted on its window.

By the time we reached the door, the two groups of unfriendlies had gathered in front. None of them said or did anything other than stare, so we continued past the crowd and entered the shop.

A pungent herbal smell greeted us as we stepped into the hazy atmosphere. The gathering of thugs on the inside was not as big as the one on the outside. A few glanced up when we walked in, but most of them were too focused on the stuff they were smoking to even be concerned. Various photos and paintings of famous Jamaicans from Marcus Garvey to Bob Marley covered the red, black, and green walls.

"This ain't like no vape shop I've ever been in. It smells like weed in here," Kenny whispered to me. "Think we can get some samples?"

"Will you shut the fuck up?" Curt hissed.

"Can I help you, mon?" the slim, dread-headed man behind the counter yelled over the reggae music blaring from the speakers. "We got all types of smoke. Whatcha need today?"

We walked over, and I said, "What I need is to speak to a man by the name of Jamaica John. You wouldn't know where I might find him, would you?" I slipped a hundred-dollar bill across the counter.

He looked at me for a moment and then said, "Sure ting. Be right back." He disappeared through a doorway covered with long, dangling beads.

A few moments later, the beads were parted by a jovial, brown-skinned man who had to be every bit of four hundred pounds. He squeezed his way through the doorway wearing a colorful T-shirt. He smiled and spoke to a few of the customers, who laughed at the fun-loving man. I watched and waited.

"You looking for Jamaica John?" he finally asked warmly, with no hint of threat in his tone.

"Yes, I am," I told him.

"Why you lookin' fo' me?" He gave me a half-smile then sucked hard on a large rectangular vaping device.

"I need to talk to you."

The slim guy had returned and was now standing beside him, staring at us.

"You wanna talk, brotha, then talk," John said, taking another long hit from his device.

I looked around at the shop full of vaping fiends. "Nah, I prefer to conduct my business in private if you don't mind."

"What kind of business you talkin'? You lookin' for smoke?"

"No, I don't want no smoke," I said, beginning to feel agitated.

He lifted an eyebrow. "Then what?"

"I'm looking for a different kind of product, so to speak, but I ain't gonna discuss it out here around your customers. I only discuss business in private."

"Fine, let's go to de back where we can talk." That fat motherfucker was still smiling. "But only you. Dese two have to stay here." He glanced at the skinny guy, who lifted a makeshift countertop for me to pass through, then closed it in front of Kenny and Curt.

"You sure about this?" Curt asked, sounding concerned.

"Doesn't seem like I have a choice," I replied.

"He'll be a'ight, mon," John said, gesturing for me to follow him as he squeezed through the beaded doorway.

I followed him down a dark hallway into a large makeshift office, where two men sat at a card table, smoking weed and playing dominoes. There was a large desk, a full-size refrigerator, a microwave, and in the corner was a large safe.

One of the men jumped up and asked, "Who da fuck is dis?"

"Calm down, mon. This man is here to talk business. Have a seat," John said, maneuvering behind a large desk. I sat down in one of the card table chairs.

"Now, what is dis business dat is so important we must discuss in private?" Jamaica John asked, reaching into his desk drawer and pulling out one of the biggest blunts I had ever seen. He laughed as he lit it.

"I am looking to buy a large quantity of your product," I told him.

"What product is dat?" he asked, taking a drag of the brown cigar and then offering it to me. "You said you don't wan' weed."

"I don't," I said, shaking my head. "What I'm looking for is a large quantity of heroin."

Jamaica John's jovial smile disappeared, and I could hear the dominoes game behind me stop as if E. F. Hutton had just spoken.

"John, ya know ya can't trust a man who won't smoke witcha. He's probably po-lice," the same dominoes-playing man said.

"He's got a point. You a cop?"

"Nah. I hate cops." I pointed at his blunt. "Almost as much as I hate smoking that shit."

"Den who are you?"

"My name's Larry. Larry Duncan."

Jamaica John's eyes widened. "Duncan?"

"Yes, Larry Duncan," I said, maintaining my calm demeanor so they wouldn't feel like they had the upper hand, in spite of the fact that I heard the distinctive sound of bullets being chambered behind me. I was actually glad that we'd left my momma behind, because her smart-ass mouth would not be helpful in this situation.

"We no do business wit' LC Duncan and his bunch of bloodclots! John—" It was the same man yelling behind me. His job with the crew seemed to be to protest every fucking thing.

I looked directly at him and said calmly, "I ain't come here asking you for shit. I ain't even talking to you, so you need to sit your ass down and shut the fuck up." I turned back to John and said, "I ain't LC Duncan. I'm Larry, and I don't fuck with my brother and his bloodclots either. That is why I'm here."

"Liar!" the guy behind me shouted. Finally, John had heard of enough of him too.

"Dexter, let dis man talk." Jamaica John put the blunt back into his mouth and pulled on it again. "I apologize for my friend's behavior. You would tink de ganja would make him a bit calmer." He shot a look at the man, who understood it as an order and sat his ass back down.

"Now, Mr. Duncan," John said, "what did you—"

"John, de Duncans are not to be trusted!" It was Dexter again, and this time he had raised his gun to my head.

"My man, if you gonna use that gun, then use it. Otherwise, sit yo' ass down. Can't you see we are trying to conduct business?" My hand eased under my jacket. I wasn't sure if I could take all three of them, but it would be fun trying.

"Dexter!" John barked, and that was enough to defuse the situation. Dexter lowered the gun but remained standing.

"How much product are you looking to buy?" John asked.

"All that you have."

He looked surprised by my answer. "Dat is a lot of product."

"Okay, then how about we start with twenty kilos?"

John shook his head. "I don't have dat kind of weight."

"But you know someone who does," I said.

"And who might dat be?" John peered at me suspiciously.

"Vinnie Dash."

"John, dis man is lying. Why are you even tinking—" Dexter argued.

"Didn't you and I both tell this motherfucker to shut the fuck up?" I looked at John before I pulled the pistol out and aimed it right at Dexter. The look of terror on his face was priceless. I pulled the trigger, and a bullet hit him right in the neck. His body hit the floor with a loud thump, and I put the gun back in my pocket then turned around to face John as if nothing had happened.

"Oh shit, mon!" John stared at me for a second, and then to my surprise, he laughed loudly. "I guess he will shut de fuck up now, won't he?"

"My apologies," I told him. "But at least we have one thing out the way. I'm definitely not a cop."

"No worries, mon. I didn't like dat motherfucker anyway." The other men at the table were smart enough to keep their eyes on the dominoes and remain silent.

"So, back to what we were talking about," I said. "Set the meeting up."

"How do I know dat you are not in fact working wit' your brother?" John challenged me. "Vinnie Dash is a powerful man, and I am not trying to become an ally wit' his enemies. He would kill me just as fast as you ended de life of my friend lying on de ground." He pointed to Dexter's lifeless body.

"I'm not asking you to become my ally. I tell you what—" I reached into my pocket. John's fat body stiffened until he realized I was only pulling out a small piece of paper. I held it out to him. "Call Vinnie and just ask him about Larry Duncan. I'm sure he can confirm that my brother and I are not friends. Once you've done so, give me a call."

Jamaica John took the slip of paper from my hand and said, "I will do that."

"I look forward to your call." I stood up and stepped over Dexter's body as I left the office.

London

16

"This is some bull!" Sasha mumbled, almost knocking me and my mother down as she exited my father's home office while we were entering.

"Sasha, what's wrong, baby?" my mother asked.

She paused briefly and looked at me, then turned to my mother and said, "Nothing, Aunt Chippy. I'm just having a bad couple of days." She stormed off without waiting for a reply.

"What's that all about?" I asked.

"I don't know." My mother shrugged. "But I hope it doesn't have anything to do with why your father wants to see you."

"Me too," I said, pushing the door open. We entered the office and sat down in the chairs next to Vegas.

"LC, what's wrong with Sasha?" my mother asked. Both my father and Vegas looked up at me.

"She's not happy with a decision we made, that's all." Daddy sighed.

"What decision?" Mom looked a little puzzled, if not annoyed. According to her rules, if any decisions about the family were to be made, she should be there when they were making them.

"Sorry, Pop. I didn't mean to throw you under the bus, but this was your decision." Vegas raised his hands defensively. "I didn't have anything to do with it."

All eyes turned to my father as my mother spoke. "LC, what's going on?"

Before Daddy could answer, the door to his office flew open, and my husband came rushing in, looking agitated. "LC, what the hell are you thinking? Sasha just told me what you're doing.

There's no way in hell you're sending my wife on this wild goose chase halfway around the world after some mobster. I won't allow it." Harris was visibly upset and stood with his hands clenched by his sides.

"What are you talking about, Harris?" I looked at my husband like he was crazy then turned my attention back to my father. "Daddy?"

"We're sending you to Jamaica, London," Daddy said.

My heart began pounding. From the tone of his voice and the way he looked at me, I knew that the decision for me to go had been one he thought about long and hard. My father had never put me in danger before, so without question, I knew it was because it needed to be done.

"She's not going anywhere. Have you forgotten that she has a husband and children to care for?" Harris asked. I hadn't heard him this passionate about anything other than sex in years.

"And when were you going to tell me all this?" my mother snapped at Daddy with attitude. "You're making a lot of decisions without talking to me, LC, and I don't like it."

Before Daddy could respond, Harris was at it again. "Why would you even ask her to do something like this? My wife doesn't handle that kind of thing. She's not capable or trained the way your other children are."

Vegas tried to reason with Harris. "Oh, she's quite capable. I trained her myself back in the day. You don't give your wife enough credit. I heard about the way she handled the situation when Mariah was kidnapped. That should show you that she knows what she's doing."

I didn't say anything, but I was flattered by my brother's vote of confidence. It wasn't often that I got credit for anything in this family.

"I'm sorry, but I forbid it. End of discussion," Harris said, then turned to Daddy and asked, "Why not send Sasha, or better yet, Paris? She's dying to go. Send one of them."

"You forbid it?" Vegas laughed. "Obviously I've been away too long."

"Listen, we have two fires to put out, Harris: one here, and one over there. We need Paris and Sasha to help handle Larry. I know you're concerned about London, but I have all the faith in the world in my daughter," Daddy said in an effort to reassure him.

"Bullshit. She's not going." Harris stood his ground.

"Harris—" I started, but before I could speak another word, Vegas cut me off.

"No, London, maybe Harris is right. There is a better candidate." Vegas stepped up and faced my husband. "We can always send Harris instead of London. I mean, after all, he did kill Vinnie's dad. Why not send him to handle the son? What d'you think, Pop?"

A look of fear came over Harris's face. I'd always known my husband wasn't the bravest guy, but he backed down so fast I was almost embarrassed for him. He glanced over at me and then quickly looked away.

"No, that was a one-time thing," he said. "I . . . I'm the family's lawyer. I should be in the country if anything legal comes up. So, maybe you're right; London's probably the right person for the job. When do you want her to leave?"

"That's what I thought." Vegas rolled his eyes.

I couldn't believe Harris. Talk about throwing someone under the bus! He'd just thrown me under a tractor trailer. I knew as well as everyone else in the room that there was no way Daddy would send Harris anywhere other than to handle paperwork. The fact that he wasn't built for the dark side of my family wasn't a secret, but to watch him visibly cower and, rather than stand up like a man, offer me up instead, was heartbreaking in a sense. I looked over at Vegas, who seemed amused by his reaction.

"Daryl and Rio are going with you," Daddy said.

At the sound of my former lover's name, I felt a shockwave through my body. For the longest time, I'd been fighting thoughts about Daryl and purposely avoided putting myself in any situation where the two of us would be alone. It had been months since I'd dared go into our home gym, because I knew that was where he would sometimes work out when he was visiting. Now, it seemed as if we would be spending more time together than I ever imagined, and in Jamaica of all places.

"London? London?" I heard my name being called.

"Huh?" I asked, realizing that I had zoned out and missed part of the conversation that had taken place.

"Did you have any questions?" Daddy asked me.

I looked over at Harris, standing with his arms folded and a scowl on his face. He was the polar opposite of Daryl, who was bold and fearless. I turned to Daddy and smiled. "When do I leave?"

Orlando

17

I took a deep breath and squeezed the trigger of my 9 mm Glock, sending bullets into the head and chest of the paper target. Satisfied, I put the gun down and removed the large headphones I was wearing. I'd been down in the basement shooting range of our house for almost two hours, shooting round after round, hoping to release some of the tension I'd been feeling over my son. Unfortunately, it hadn't worked.

"Nice shooting, O." I turned to see Junior standing behind me, staring at the target, now full of gaping holes.

"Thanks. You know what they say about visualizing your target," I responded.

"Damn, who you visualizing, Vinnie Dash or Uncle Larry?" he asked.

"Vegas," I replied, ripping off my safety glasses.

"Funny." Junior smiled.

"That wasn't a joke."

"It was still funny." He shrugged and leaned on the edge of the wooden counter.

"I'm glad you're finding humor in this fucked-up situation. I mean, why should you or Vegas even be bothered? Both of you know where your kids are. His is in the house, and yours is in Sonya's belly. Vegas won't even let me go and find mine. Fuck it. What I should do is get on a plane my damn self and go."

"Come on, O. You need to stop talking that rogue shit. You know that would be a mistake."

"Would it?" I glared at him.

"It would, so stop acting stupid. You know Vegas is just as anxious to get your son back as you are, and so is everybody else. We're your family."

"Yeah, but that's my son."

"And that's our nephew," Junior snapped, sounding a little agitated himself. "You know, for someone so smart, you can be real stupid sometimes. Why does everyone have to tell you the same damn thing repeatedly, huh? You'd be spotted the minute you step foot in Jamaica. We gotta play this smart, O, or somebody is gonna get hurt, and we don't want it to be your son."

"I get it, but what the fuck am I supposed to do?" I asked in frustration. Everything Junior was saying made sense, but it still didn't help ease my frustration. I hated the feeling of being powerless. "I can't just sit around here and do nothing."

"You're not doing nothing. You and Paris are headed down south to Waycross in two hours. Vegas and Pop want you to see if you can find any clues to Kenny and Curt's whereabouts. Hopefully it will lead us to Uncle Larry."

"Why aren't they sending you with us? You and Curtis grew up together, didn't you?"

"Yeah, we were pretty much best friends when we lived down in Georgia and first came to New York. Heck, we was still close until Uncle Larry went batshit crazy." Junior's expression revealed his sadness at the loss of his one-time best friend. "After that, Curt was so pissed about Pop putting his old man in a mental hospital he stopped taking my calls."

"All I remember was I always used to try and avoid him because he would beat me and London up when you and Vegas weren't around."

"Yeah, that sounds like Curt. He was a real bully." Junior chuckled to himself. "He used to do that stuff to us too, until me and Vegas locked his ass in a closet one night. He came out the next morning humble as shit."

"So, what do you think his take on this is? Anything I should know about him?"

"Crazy or not, he'll do anything for Uncle Larry. The two of them have this crazy obsession with each other. Uncle Larry could do no wrong in Curt's eyes."

"Do you think he can be reasoned with?" I asked.

Junior got a troubled look on his face. "Curtis is more like Uncle Larry than anyone realizes. He used to light animals on fire and shit like that when we were kids."

I couldn't believe what I was hearing. "Get the fuck outta here. That's some making-of-a-serial-killer type shit."

"Exactly. Like father like son, so whatever you do, don't sleep on him."

"I won't," I replied sincerely. "What about Kenny? What do you know about him?"

"Nothing really. He was in elementary school when Uncle Larry went away, so you might wanna check with Paris or Rio on that. They know him better than me. He seemed cool last time he came to the family reunion with Aunt NeeNee a few years back, though."

"Yeah, he did." We stood silently for a few seconds, and then I asked, "Junior, what does my son look like?"

"He's your complexion and has the same big-ass, oblong head you had as a kid. He's a cute little fella, with his mom's dimples."

I tried to imagine a younger me with a smile as beautiful as Ruby's. "She does have a pretty smile, doesn't she?"

"She looked good. I'm not gonna lie. She looked real good," Junior told me.

"Junior, I don't mean to sound negative, but do you truthfully think I'll ever see my son?" I asked. I had butterflies in my stomach, anticipating my brother's answer.

"Yeah, London, Rio, and Daryl will figure something out, or they'll call us to come help. So, I wouldn't worry about that. You'll see your boy," Junior replied, but his voice and expression were troubled.

"What?" I asked, but all he did was bite his lip. "Don't hold anything back, Junior. What's on your mind?"

"Let's say we get him. What're we going to do, have London and Daryl bring him back here? Rip him from his mother's arms? I mean, O, you may be his father, but he don't even know you."

I could hear Junior's words, but my brain would not allow me to comprehend them.

"And even if we get Ruby to see the light," he continued, "that kid's been poisoned about you and our family since birth. Bringing him back here might not be in his best interest."

"What are you trying to say, Junior?"

"I'm not *trying* to say anything; I said it. You're his father. You have to decide what's best for your kid, and in the end, that might not be what's best for you."

I let out a long, aggravated breath, because he was right. "Dammit! This is all his fault. Vinnie Dash orchestrated this shit." I put the headphones back on, picked up a gun, and fired it several times, ripping more holes in the target. I took the headphones off again, not feeling any less frustrated.

Junior looked at me and sighed. "I'm not trying to cause you drama. I just need you to be prepared. This is not going to be easy."

"I know. And you know what the real fucked up part of this is?"

"What?"

"As much as I love my son, I still love his mother too—and I'm probably going to have to make a decision on whether she lives or dies." I put the gun down and walked off.

Curtis

18

"Place looks closed to me, Dad," I said, driving through the opened gate to the front of the building. It was well after eight o'clock, and as I expected, the large warehouse building looked closed.

"Don't worry about what it looks like. Pull up over there." I began to pull into a parking space, and he yelled, "God dammit, Curt! Not here, you fool. Pull around back. Don't you see that big-ass security camera that's pointed at us?"

"Sorry." I shrugged and drove around to the back of the building.

The open garage doors once again proved that Dad was right and the place was still open. I parked the car in the shadows between two trucks and waited for his instructions, because I had no clue what the plan might be. We'd just driven almost fifteen and a half hours from New York City to Atlanta, Georgia, and Pop had barely said a word, other than to give directions. I'd never seen him this quiet, except for the day he had me drop him off at Duncan Motors and he shot Uncle LC.

"Curt, you're on my right. Kenny, you're on my left," Dad said, uncovering two semi-automatic rifles and passing one to each of us. He took his own pistol out, sliding a bullet into the chamber. As we got out of the car, Kenny and I hid our weapons under our jackets, and we all headed toward the building.

We walked into the first bay, where a man was leaned up against one of the tractor trailers, smoking a cigarette. I could see the anguish on my Dad's face as he read the words *Duncan Transports* on the side of the truck

"Can I help you?" the guy asked, tossing the cigarette onto the ground and stepping on it.

"I'm looking for Frankie B. Is he anywhere around?" Dad said.

At that moment, I knew the plan, and I was sure Kenny did too. We were going to kill everyone in the building. You see, when we'd finally gone back to talk to Jamaica John that afternoon, he said he'd spoken to Vinnie Dash, and Vinnie refused to deal with any Duncans.

"Did you tell him I don't fuck with LC and that I'm going to put my brother out of business?" Dad had yelled at Jamaica John.

"Yeah, mon. I told him all about dat you're tryin to make a deal. De problem isn't de deal; de problem is he doesn't trust ya," Jamaica John tried to explain. I almost felt sorry for the guy, because in a few minutes, he was probably going to be dead.

"Well, how the fuck can I get him to trust me when he won't even sit down and talk?" my dad asked. I could see his hand twitching, which meant he was about to reach for his gun. I made eye contact with Kenny to make sure he was going to be ready. Jamaica John had about six guys with him, and they all looked high as hell, which placed the odds heavily on our side.

"Dat depends on whether or not you're sincere." Jamaica John was sweating bullets.

"What does that mean?" Pops looked at him strangely.

"Maybe you can do someting to help him, as a sign of good faith? Show him you can be trusted." Jamaica John grinned, and I wondered if he knew he had just saved his own life.

"Show him how?"

"Dere is a man by de name of Frank Bosworth. Maybe you have heard of him?"

My dad frowned then spit out, "Frankie B? Hell yeah, I know him. He's LC's driver."

John shook his head. "Maybe he used to be de driver fo' ya brudda, but that must have been some time ago, because he is LC's transporter. Handles everyting shipped, domestic and international, legal and illegal. De boss of transport and logistics."

"Get the fuck outta here," my dad said. "Fucking Frankie B got my old job."

"And he is a pain in Vinnie's ass. Vinnie can't get shit to where it needs to be because Frankie and LC blackballed him. Now, if Frankie somehow was no longer to be a pain in Vinnie's ass, den maybe—"

"Consider it done," Dad had said before John could even finish. "And tell Vinnie there is no maybe. I want to meet with him day after tomorrow, or he'll suffer the same fate as Frankie." Dad turned and walked off.

John had looked at me and Kenny as if he expected us to explain, but we didn't. We followed Dad out the door, and now, here we were.

"He's in the office." The man pointed toward the back. "But it's kind of late, and he hates to be disturbed. Who can I tell him is looking for him?"

"You don't have to tell him shit. I'll tell him myself," Dad told him, pulling out a dagger and throwing it into the man's chest. He fell to the ground.

We moved through the building, and two guys wearing coveralls came out of nowhere to confront us. They were both unarmed, so Kenny and I took them out with our own knives within seconds. Somewhere in the building, someone had to have cameras, because soon after, two other guys came running toward us with guns. Dad blasted them before they even realized what was happening.

"Kenny, go get the C4 and caps out the car. Spread them around. I don't want one of these motherfucking trucks standing once we leave this place," Dad ordered.

Kenny nodded and headed for the car. Dad walked over to where the first guy had indicated the office was, and we entered, killing three more armed men in the process. Guns at the ready, we could hear someone yelling as we walked down the hallway.

"Larry just shot this whole fucking building up! And he's heading in here now. I can see him on the fucking monitor! Shit, he's here!"

"Hey, Frankie B. Long time, no see!" Dad shouted. Our guns were pointed directly at him through the glass partition. He was empty-handed, but there was a 9 mm on his desk that I was sure he was thinking about grabbing as we entered the office.

"I wouldn't touch that gun if I were you, Frankie. You see, this here is my oldest son, Curt, and he's real sensitive about people pointing guns at his pops. Now, why don't you put down the phone?"

Frankie eyed me as I stood next to Dad with my gun raised.

"Sure, sure." He hung up the phone, placing it on the desk. "So, how've you been, Larry?" he asked, his voice shaking uncontrollably.

Dad sat in one of the chairs in front of Frankie's desk. "I'm good, Frankie. Glad to be outta that nuthouse my brother had me in."

The color drained out of Frankie's face. I could tell that he was scared shitless as he stuttered, "I–I–I'm sorry about that, Larry."

"Sit down, Frankie. Let's have a chat. I know you got some good-ass bourbon around here. You was always a bourbon man. Pour me a drink, why don'tcha?"

"Just don't get stupid while you're doing it," I said.

Frankie opened the desk drawer and took out a silver flask and a glass. His hands were shaking so bad that some of the liquor spilled as he poured it. He slid it across the smooth mahogany surface and finally sat down.

"Good stuff," Dad said after drinking it all in one gulp.

"L–l–look, Larry, you . . . you and I go way back. I–I've always respected you, and you know that," Frankie said.

"Damn, Frankie, you stuttering so bad that you're sounding like my brother Levi." Dad laughed. "Say what the fuck you gotta say."

Frankie took a deep breath, cleared his throat, and said, "La–Larry, whatever this shit you and LC got going on, it don't have nothing to do with me."

"Bullshit, Frankie. That's a lie and you know it. All this shit belongs to me. I started Duncan Transports. It was me that created this and built it up with my blood, sweat, and tears. You were there watching me put in all the work over the years. Then you and LC stole my fucking company!" Dad pounded his fist on the desk, and everyone jumped.

Frankie frowned and said, "Larry, that's not true. You sold your share of the company to me years ago. I didn't steal anything. I got the paperwork to prove it."

He reached into the drawer again, pulled out a tattered folder, and slid it across the desk. My dad opened it, looked through it for a moment, then shut it.

"Curtis," Dad said.

"Yeah?" I answered, fully expecting him to tell me to shoot this poor bastard.

"Go check on your brother. Make sure he's rigging that C4 properly. I'll be down in a minute. Me and Frankie have to discuss this paperwork in private." He drummed his fingers across the folder.

"Okay, it was nice meeting you, Frankie," I said, knowing it would be the first and last time I saw the dude. By the time I found Kenny, Frankie's screams could be heard from every corner of the building. Ten minutes later, we were all in the car, driving away, when a huge explosion erupted. It was so strong we could actually feel its heat as it shook the car.

I pulled over, and we all looked back at the building in amazement. The flames had to be a hundred feet in the air. The satisfied look on Dad's face was priceless. It was the first time he had looked genuinely happy since he'd come home.

"Okay, show's over. Let's go." Dad tapped my shoulder, and I pulled back on the road. "Now, I want you boys to drop me at the Amtrak, then head back home and have a real good time, because you deserve it. I'm real proud of both of you."

Both Kenny and I beamed with pride.

"What about you? Where you going to be?" Kenny asked.

"Me and Grandma Bettie are going on a trip to visit an old friend's son," Dad answered. It wasn't too hard to figure out he was going to see Vinnie Dash.

London

19

I was trying to be as inconspicuous as possible as I stood in front of the house we'd rented in Negril. When Rio and I had arrived, I called Vegas to let him know we were there, and was surprised to hear that Daryl would be picking me up in fifteen minutes. That felt like an hour ago. My stomach was a bundle of nerves, partly from the anticipation of seeing him, but mostly from the fact that I had been sent here along with my brothers to help take care of family business. That was something I hadn't done in a long time. A very long time.

Life for me was unusual because I grew up as a Duncan. My parents made sure we lived in the finest of homes, wore designer clothes, and traveled the world. We were not only educated in the classroom, but we learned other unique skills. At the age of six, my mother enrolled me in ballet class, and my father taught me how to use a knife and handle a gun. By the time I was ten, I was fluent in Spanish, French, and Russian. My mother instructed me on proper etiquette, and yet, she made sure I received formal martial arts training, and I was awarded a black belt in Brazilian Jiu-Jitsu and karate. Although I wasn't shipped off to finishing school like Paris, I was still capable of killing a man if necessary. Unlike my younger sister, I never had until Vinnie Dash's brother kidnapped my child. I think my family just assumed that I preferred being in the more traditional role of wife and mother. I was the "safe" one of the family. I was also the bored one, which was why, when Daddy and Vegas decided I would be sent to Jamaica to help find Orlando's son, I was secretly ecstatic.

"This makes absolutely no sense at all," Harris had grumbled when we were alone after he found out I was leaving. "Why the hell would you be the one to go? What about Paris or Sasha?"

"Look, I'm just as surprised as you are," I told him.

"Who's going to take care of your kids while you're off in Jamaica looking for Orlando's?" he asked. "Or hasn't anyone thought about them?"

I stared at him. "*My* kids? Is that what you just said?"

"You know what I meant, London."

"I know what you said. And in case you didn't realize, my kids have a damn daddy who is more than capable of taking care of them while I'm gone—although sometimes he does forget. Also, my kids have a nanny who will be here, along with their grandmother," I said matter-of-factly.

"You know how I feel about having other people raise my children, London."

"I can't tell sometimes." I rolled my eyes at him, but then decided to take a different approach. "Listen, Harris, I get it. You don't want me to go? Fine. You march yourself back downstairs and tell Daddy and Vegas I can't go. And this time don't back down."

Harris continued to grumble and complain, but he never said anything else to my brother or my father. I left a list of instructions with him about the kids that I knew he probably wouldn't even look at, since my children would be the sole responsibility of the nanny and my mother anyway. By the time I entered the car to the airport, we were barely speaking.

"You called for a taxi?"

I turned to see Daryl yelling from a jeep he was driving. I smiled and walked over, then waited for him to get out and open the door for me.

"Well, I definitely wasn't expecting this," I said, motioning toward the all-terrain vehicle.

Daryl's body brushed against mine as he opened the car door. He was close enough for me to smell the sweet scented oil he wore as I tried to maneuver around him. Somehow, he managed to brush his hand across my chest as he helped me with my seat belt, sending a shockwave down my body. I hated that he still had the ability to do that to me. I did my best not to stare, but as usual, he was looking sexy dressed in a casual pair of jeans that made his ass look even more spectacular than normal.

"What's wrong with this?" Daryl asked, climbing back into the jeep and putting on a pair of aviator shades before taking off.

"I just figured you would be in something a little more upscale, I guess," I told him, making sure my eyes stayed forward.

"Come on, you know I ain't the flashy type. Besides, we should remain low key while we're here. The last thing we need is to be seen in some kind of luxury ride that people will remember. My goal is to blend in as much as possible," he said. "When in Rome, do as the Romans do, ya know?"

"That makes sense." I pulled down the bottom of the sundress I wore, which had risen slightly over the top of my knees. From the corner of my eye, I could see Daryl peeping at me and smiling.

"You don't have to do that," he said.

"Do what?"

"Pull your dress down. It ain't nothing I haven't seen before." He laughed, and I peered over my glasses. Although he was smiling, it wasn't laughter in his eyes; it was lust. I looked away before he could see the same thing in mine.

Stay focused, London. You're not here to break your vows. This is business. The last thing you need is to get distracted by Daryl. Just keep it cordial.

"Not since I've been married, you haven't." I pulled my dress down a little farther to make sure he got my point.

"Touché," he replied.

What most people didn't know was that Daryl and I had secretly dated off and on for years before my engagement to Harris. In fact, Daryl was the first man I'd ever slept with, and you know what they say about your first.

"I don't know what I was thinking. I apologize if I was outta line," he said.

My eyes looked up and met his. I didn't want to be so cold, but he was starting to get a little too comfortable, and I'd just arrived.

"No problem. I just want to make sure we have clear boundaries." I turned my legs slightly away from him.

"So, what's going on back at home? What's the deal with this uncle that everyone is worried about?"

"Uncle Larry," I said.

"Yeah, your uncle Larry. I remember him. He was a pretty bad-ass dude, but from what Vegas is telling me, he turned psychotic."

"He did." I nodded. "My uncle served in the Vietnam war, and they say when he came home, he was still Larry, but he just wasn't the same. Being in the middle of all that combat and seeing all of that death messed with his mind, I guess," I explained.

"That shit messed with a lot of guys' minds. They don't say war is hell for nothing. A lot of men came back from Vietnam with PTSD."

"Naw, this wasn't just PTSD. Uncle Larry is way beyond that. He was always a little out of control, but Aunt NeeNee and my dad and Uncle Lou could kind of reel him back in when he needed it. But then he got worse. Even his meds didn't help. He became a lunatic."

"For real?"

"Yeah, Uncle Larry got to the point where he would shoot somebody for getting his order wrong at the drive-through."

"Damn, now that's what you call anger issues." Daryl, who had no doubt seen plenty of crazy shit in his lifetime, seemed genuinely surprised by this.

"Tell me about it. It broke his heart to have to do it, but Daddy had to put him away. It had to be done. Uncle Larry was instutionalized for years, until he showed up and shot my dad."

Daryl took his eyes off the road and stared at me. "You mean LC was shot by his own brother?"

"Watch out!" I warned, seeing the car in front of us stop in the middle of the road.

Daryl slammed on the brakes just in time.

"You trying to kill us?" I asked, my heart pounding.

He looked at me calmly and said, "I couldn't think of a better person to die with."

I shook my head. Despite my previous protest, he was still flirting. "Well, I'm not trying to die anytime soon, so keep your eyes on the road."

"I'm trying, but it's hard not to look at other things," he said and glanced down at my cleavage. I reached out and turned his head forward.

We drove a little while longer, until we came to a small food store. He parked the car on the side and told me, "Wait here. I'll be right back."

"What? Hell, no. I'm coming with you." I reached for the door handle, but he reached over and grabbed my hand.

"Look, I'm not gonna be in there that long. I just gotta go see this cat I know that's a butcher here and see what I can find out. I'll be back in a few minutes."

"What if something happens to you while you're in there?" I asked.

"Nothing's gonna happen. I know this dude. Just relax. These folks don't like outsiders."

"Fine," I said, sitting back and folding my arms.

"London, I mean it. Stay your ass in the car."

"I said fine."

Daryl gave me a final warning look then went inside. While I waited, I took my phone out and tried calling Harris. He didn't answer, so I just sent a quick text telling him I was checking on him and the kids. Then I called Momma, who assured me everything was fine. By the time I finished talking with her, Daryl was opening the car door.

"That was fast," I said. "Did you find out anything?"

"Yeah, I think I know where they're staying. It's not so hard to find a rich white guy, married to a black woman with a son, who is hanging with a bunch of thugs."

"Great. This is gonna be easier than we thought," I said.

Daryl shook his head. "I wouldn't go counting your chickens before they're hatched. The place they're staying at is built like a fortress."

Paris

20

"Welcome to Waycross, Georgia," Orlando announced as I stretched myself awake.

I glanced at the scattered houses with makeshift storefronts in between as we drove into what appeared to be the black portion of town. I hadn't been here in like fifteen years, and I couldn't believe this was where my parents grew up, especially my mother. Who would've thought the self-proclaimed queen of all things couture had survived this rural area? I had only seen one grocery store, let alone anything remotely resembling a mall. It looked pretty scary, like an abandoned ghost town, but I knew that had a lot to do with the fact that it was almost nine o'clock at night and the streets were dark.

"Talk about small beginnings," I murmured. Both Orlando and I had been quiet most of the trip. We'd slept on the plane and barely talked on the two-hour drive from Jacksonville into Waycross. Although I was still pissed about not being sent to Jamaica, I knew he was even more upset. Daddy had tasked us with heading to his hometown in search of information regarding the whereabouts of Uncle Larry, Kenny, and Curtis. Neither Orlando nor I was enthused about the assignment, but we did what we knew we had to do.

"Yeah, this is where it all started." He sighed as we passed a Piggly Wiggly.

"I can see why they got the hell away from here. This place is a dump."

"Yeah, but believe it or not, they were doing pretty good for themselves while they lived here. Dad had the gas station, and Uncle Lou and Uncle Larry had their side hustles, of course."

"Of course!" I laughed, knowing he was referring to the gambling, numbers running, loan sharking, and in Uncle Lou's case, pimping.

"Gotta love the Duncans," he said with a chuckle.

"So, how do we even know where to start looking?" I asked, feeling irritated. It had been a long day, and I was tired. The last place I wanted to be was on a wild goose chase in the middle of nowhere. "How far is the nearest hotel? It's too late to do anything else tonight. I mean, we are in Waycross."

"Nah, it's early for where we're headed."

"What? Where is that?"

"We're going to another Duncan family establishment here in Waycross." He was smiling, but I groaned.

"Ugh. Are we going to the gas station?"

"Nope, something way better than a gas station."

I was not in the mood to play Twenty Questions with him, so I just shut up, leaned my head back, and closed my eyes. We continued traveling in silence until finally, we arrived at the infamous Oak Street, where Orlando parked in front of a large house with a wraparound porch. There was a neon sign above the porch that read: BIG SHIRLEY'S.

"Oh, shit! Big Shirley's still exists?" I laughed, remembering the stories about the brothel named after my aunt. It was the place where my parents had met. "Is it still a whorehouse?"

"It's more like a strip club now," Orlando said.

"Get the fuck outta here. You know I love strip clubs."

"So do I, little sister. So do I."

Suddenly I was feeling more energetic. We walked up to the front door, where we were searched by a burly guy who looked more like an oversized door holder than a security guard. He was so overweight that he was winded just from waving the security wand over our bodies.

"You got any ID?" he asked breathily as he stared at my breasts instead of my face.

"You ain't ask him for ID," I said, pointing at Orlando, who had just gone through the door with no problem.

"I wasn't interested in his name, sexy." He grinned at me, and I was immediately repulsed. Reaching into my pocket, I pulled out one of the many fake IDs I kept for work purposes.

He looked at the ID I handed him. "Sky. That name suits you."

"Can I go in now?" I asked.

"By all means." He held the door open, and I walked inside.

I didn't know how it compared to other strip clubs in the deep South, but it definitely wasn't like any of the clubs I'd ever been to. First, there wasn't a stage, just some strobe lights and a random pole with a chick swinging on it in the corner of the room. There were a few tables with ladies dancing on top, and of course, a couple of other naked women walking around. Trap music blared from some speakers, but I didn't even see a DJ at first, because he was blocked by the crowd of folks near the pole. Although I wasn't impressed by the place, clearly the crowd of male patrons was, including my brother, who was staring at some redbone with the biggest nipples I had ever seen.

"Damn," he muttered, practically drooling on himself.

"Stay focused, Orlando." I nudged him.

"I'm trying, but she got my full attention right now," he said.

I tugged his arm and pulled him over to the bar. "Lemme get a pomegranate martini," I told the bartender, who stared at me blankly for a few seconds.

Finally he said, "We're fresh outta those."

Orlando leaned over and whispered, "Paris, I know we're in a bar, but we're in Waycross."

I rolled my eyes and said, "Fine, lemme get a vodka and cranberry. Can you handle that?"

"Now, that I can handle." He commenced to making my drink, along with the shot of Hennessy Orlando ordered.

"Well, hello. I haven't seen you before." The nippled woman who'd caught Orlando's eye walked over and greeted him.

"Yeah, it's my first time here," he said.

"Well, welcome to Big Shirley's. What brings you in here?" She eased her body so close to him that her breasts were now pressed against his chest.

"Actually, I'm here for two reasons," he told her. I could see him trying not to stare.

"And what's that?" She gave him a seductive look.

"Well, one, to buy me a drink and enjoy the atmosphere."

"I can see you're already doing that. Is there anything else you might be interested in buying?" she asked, moving her torso slightly so she was basically caressing him with her breasts.

"Not right now," I told her. She shot me a dirty look but quickly turned her attention back to her mark. No doubt she saw dollar signs, judging by the way she was sizing up Orlando's gold watch.

"And I'm looking for someone," Orlando told her.

"You've already found her. I'm Lydia." She introduced herself by touching his leg, and I could see Orlando struggling even more. I had to give it to her: this chick was good, real good.

"Well, we're actually looking for Curtis and Kenny," I said, deciding to take control of the conversation since my brother was so distracted.

"Who?" the bartender asked as he placed the drinks on the bar.

"Curtis and Kenny Duncan, the owners of this place," I told him.

"Oh, naw, we haven't seen them in a minute," he answered.

Lydia looked over at the bartender with a frown. "What are you talking about? They were just here this afternoon."

"Shut the fuck up," he growled at her. Orlando and I exchanged glances.

"Why don't we go somewhere that we can chat in private?" Orlando said, picking up his drink and taking Lydia by the hand. "Y'all give private dances?"

"We give way more than that," she answered happily. "Right this way."

I watched as Lydia led him through the crowd. I guess this place still was a whorehouse after all. Knowing that they would probably be gone for a while, I decided to sit on one of the worn barstools rather than stand. A couple of men tried to catch my eye, but I made sure to avoid eye contact, and instead, turned my attention back to the man behind the bar.

"Can I get another?" I said, pushing my empty glass toward him and making sure I gave him a smile as seductive as the one Lydia had given Orlando.

He gave me a double take then shrugged. "No problem."

When he came back a few minutes later, I made sure my cleavage was a little more apparent by pulling my shirt down farther and leaning against the bar.

"Thanks. I'm Sky," I told him.

"Nice to meet you," he said, glancing at my chest then back up at me. "I'm Barry."

"Well, Barry, listen. I really need to find Curtis and Kenny. It's really important."

Barry shook his head. "Look, I don't want no trouble. I can't help you with that."

"It's not like that. We're not causing any trouble. Really, we're not. The truth is, they're my cousins."

Barry folded his arms. "Yeah, right."

"No, seriously, they are. I can prove it. Big Shirley was my aunt too."

"Anybody would know Shirley and the boys were family," he said.

"Would anybody have this?" I whipped out my real ID and flashed it to him.

Barry looked at it and then at me. "Well, I'll be damned," he said.

"I told you. They really are my cousins, and I need to find them. It's a family emergency."

The way he looked around to make sure no one was listening, I thought he was about to give me some valuable information, but then he spoke, and all he said was, "Sorry, miss. Kenny and Curt aren't here."

"When are they coming back?" I asked him, pressing for more.

"I honestly don't know. They haven't been around much ever since their dad came back around a little while ago. They only pop in to pick up the cash and that's it." He shrugged.

"Do you know where I might be able to find them?"

"Can't really say. They live out on their family farm. I'm sure you know exactly where that is, if you're really a Duncan as you claim."

"Yeah, I do," I replied. Or at least Orlando knew. "Thanks."

My phone rang, so I stepped away from the bar to answer it.

"What's up, Vegas?"

"Where are you guys?"

"We're in Waycross. I just got a line on Kenny and Curtis. If they're here, Uncle Larry can't be too far behind."

"Good. Find those motherfuckers before they cause any more trouble," he said.

"More trouble? What the fuck happened?"

I could hear Vegas take a breath and pause, which was never a good sign. "Those motherfuckers blew up our Atlanta hub and killed Frankie B."

"They killed Uncle Frankie? Shit, O's not gonna like that. We might be bringing these dudes home in body bags."

"That's for Pop to worry about. Personally, I don't care how you bring their asses back. Just don't take any chances. Family or not, these are some dangerous people. Understand?"

Larry

21

"Well, mon, this is it!" Jamaica John waved his arm dramatically, as if he were revealing the grand prize on a game show instead of a tiny-ass cargo plane that was only slightly larger than his oversized body. I stood back and stared for a second, hesitating for several reasons, the first being that I hated to fly. Always had. Something about being suspended up in the air, knowing we could fall at any moment, made me fearful. I enjoyed being on the ground, where I was in control. The second reason for my hesitation was that not only was the plane little as hell, but it didn't look safe at all. It was pretty banged up and rusted. When Jamaica John told me he had a friend who could get us to our destination without passports, I knew it wasn't gonna be a damn Learjet, but I damn sure wasn't expecting a piece of shit like the one we were standing in front of.

I glanced over at the pilot, who looked barely old enough to possess a driver's license, let alone a pilot's. "You sure this thing is gonna make it to Kingston?" I asked.

"Of course, mon," Jamaica John said. "It made it from Kingston wit' no problem. Gus here flies back and forth all de time. Right, Gus?"

The lanky guy, dressed in cutoff jeans and a colorful tank top, shrugged. His lackadaisical attitude definitely wasn't helping me gain any confidence in his ability to fly or in the damn plane itself.

"Neva had no problem at all. Don't see havin' none now. But it's gettin' late, and I need to be takin' off. You say you need to get to Jamaica; I'm goin'. You pay, you go. Your choice, mon." He sauntered off, opened the door of the winged vehicle, and began placing a couple of boxes and bags inside.

"Hey, you say you need to speak wit' Vinnie. Dis is de only way to get you dere wit' no passport or red tape," Jamaica John said.

I turned and looked at Momma, who was waiting for me to make a decision.

"What's the fucking problem?" Momma hissed. "Pay the man and let's get on the fucking plane. We got shit to handle."

"One thousand apiece, right?" I asked Jamaica John.

He nodded. "Dat's right. A bargain, I'd say."

I slid my hand in my pocket, counted out two thousand dollars, and handed it to him.

He counted the stack, counted it again, then glanced up at me with a weird look on his face.

"Is there a problem?" I asked him.

He stared at me for another second, like he was trying to read something on my face, then he smirked and said, "No. No problem at all, mon."

"Good, then let's get the hell outta here and get this shit over with. The faster we take off, the faster we can land," I said.

I walked over to the opened door where Gus stood, smoking what I hoped was a cigarette. I paused to let my mother go inside first; then I followed behind her. The inside of the plane was even smaller than I expected, with a pilot's seat, two small seats, and an open space for whatever other cargo Gus happened to be delivering. I strapped myself into the seat next to Momma, and a few minutes later, Gus climbed inside.

As he began fidgeting with the dials and controls, I prayed that this wasn't truly the death trap I felt it was. The engine started up with a stutter, and I half expected it to cut off. Jesus Christ, what had I gotten myself into? Gus fiddled with a few more knobs, and then, thankfully, it began purring like a loud kitten. He then reached down to the floor beside him and turned on what I assumed was a radio, because reggae music began playing.

Gus gave a thumbs up. The plane jolted a bit, and then we reversed. I peered out the window and saw Jamaica John waving at us. When the plane changed direction and we began moving forward at a faster pace, I braced myself for takeoff. The plane rocked and rattled, causing all of us to shift back and forth. I closed my eyes and held on to the side of the raggedy seat. And then, the plane stopped shaking so much, and I knew we were in the air. I released my grip on the seat, but my heart still raced, and I didn't open my eyes.

"I can't believe we're going to Jamaica," I heard Momma say. "I ain't never been over there. I'ma get me a drink with an umbrella and lay out on the beach. Hell, who knows? I might meet me a man over there. A nice Jamaican man with muscles who can help me get my groove back. Shit, Larry, who knows? You might end up with a Jamaican stepdaddy!" She laughed.

"Momma, please," I mumbled, my eyes still closed. I was trying my best to hold it together, but her nonstop chatter wasn't helping me any, especially with the constant thumping of the music Gus was playing. It was all too much. Being in the small compartment of the plane, which was bumping up and down in the air, was causing me to feel more and more constricted. I could hardly breathe.

"What the hell is wrong with you?" she hissed. "Why are you acting like a scared rabbit? It's just a plane, Larry. You act like your ass ain't fly when you were in the war."

The plane jumped a little, and I gripped the chair even tighter.

"Momma," I pleaded, "can you just stop talking for a little while? Please."

"Boy, you look white as a ghost," she said, laughing at me.

"Momma, please! Will you just sit back and shut up till we get where we're going?" I said, reaching in my suit jacket for my silver flask. I unscrewed the cap, taking a long swig without even knowing what was inside. The smooth liquor burned as it went down my throat, but it made me feel a hell of a lot better.

Gus, who must've heard what was going on, suddenly changed the music to something a little more soothing. I sat back and started to enjoy the soft ballad that was now playing. I took another, longer swig from the flask.

"Feel better?" Momma asked.

"Yeah," I said.

"Good. Now gimme some of that so I can feel better too," she said, and I passed her the flask. I closed my eyes again, and this time, I drifted into a deep slumber, knowing that when I woke up, we would be on the ground.

Curtis

22

"Hold the damn light closer this way!" I yelled at my brother.

"I am! Damn," Kenny said, shining the light from his cell phone in the direction I was pointing. "Are you sure there's even anything down there? This could be another one of his fantasies, Curt."

I ignored him and kept digging in the dirt. I was on my hands and knees behind the barn of our family home, in the exact spot my father had instructed us to go. Although I had wondered the same thing a few seconds before Kenny asked the question, there was no way I was gonna stop looking. People called my dad Crazy Larry all the time, and although he was a little quirky, I always felt that he got a bad rap most of the time. So, when he called with specific instructions to get a "package" that he had buried behind the barn on the Duncan farm, even I was a little skeptical, but I was going to keep shoveling in that dirt until I found it or China.

"Hey, you hear something?" Kenny whispered and moved the light again.

"Dammit, Kenny," I said, my frustration increasing, "of course I hear something. We're on a fucking farm with noisy-ass hogs, chickens, and cows. Now, hold that damn light over here."

"I don't care what you say. I'm telling you I heard something," he whispered.

"Shit, I think I found something." I squinted and leaned closer to the ground. "Give me that damn phone."

Kenny passed me the phone, and I held it into the shallow hole that I had dug. Sure enough, I saw something that looked like fabric.

"Well, I'll be damned," I said.

I handed him the phone and used the hand shovel to dig around the area a little more, then I reached my hand in and tried to pull out whatever it was. It didn't budge. A part of me was afraid that it might be a fucking corpse.

"What is it?"

"If you hold the fucking light still I'll be able to see and tell you," I shot back. He finally held the light still long enough for me to see that it was a duffle bag. I continued digging and pulling until it was finally free.

"What's in it?" Kenny asked.

"Money," I said when I unzipped the bag and saw rolls of bills, held with rubber bands and stacked together in clear plastic bags. The duffle was full of money. "Must be over a million dollars in here."

"Damn, you think this was here the entire time he was away?" Kenny asked.

I shrugged, zipping the bag and standing up. "Knowing the old man, there ain't no telling. He might have bags of money all over the country. But this is the only one he sent us to get, and it's the only one I'm digging for. Come on. Help me put the dirt back in this hole so we can get the hell outta here."

Kenny hesitated then froze up like a scared doe caught in headlights. "I'm telling you, Curt, I hear something," he said.

"Man, if you don't bring your paranoid ass on and help me fill this fucking hole so we can get the fuck outta here, I swear—" I stopped mid-sentence when I heard a branch snap.

"You heard it too this time, didn't you?" Kenny asked.

"Cut that fucking light off," I said, dropping the shovel and pulling the gun from my waistband.

Kenny turned the light off and wasted no time taking out his own weapon.

"Yo, I don't know who the fuck you are, but this is private property, and you're trespassing, so prepare to die," I said, aiming my gun in the direction of the sound.

"I could say the same thing to you, Curtis," someone replied.

He stepped into the moonlight, and I could make out the silhouette of a gun. I was about to shoot when I realized that I knew the person.

"Orlando?" Kenny recognized him too.

"You were expecting maybe Wonder Woman?" he joked. Orlando had always been a little corny like that, brainiac that he was, but just because he was super smart didn't mean he was any less dangerous than the rest of my cousins. After all, they were raised by my snake of an uncle.

"What are you doing here?" Kenny asked, but he sounded a little shaky.

"I should be asking you that." He glanced at the hole and the duffle bag.

"We live here. And what we do is none of your damn business." I raised my gun, pointing it at him. Kenny did the same. "Now, what are you doing here?"

"I'm here to talk, cousin," Orlando said. "Where's Uncle Larry?"

Kenny glanced over at me, and I shook my head. "Again, that's none of your business."

"First of all, lower your gun," he said forcefully. "Secondly, that's where you're wrong. You and Uncle Larry made this my business when you blew up our transport hub and killed my god-father."

"Godfather?" Kenny repeated.

"That's right. Frankie B was my godfather and one of the nicest men I've ever met in my life." He stared at us arrogantly, as if he had no doubt he was in control. "Now, put down your guns. We're gonna have a little talk about your father."

"I ain't putting shit down. You put your fucking gun down!" Kenny shouted erratically.

I'd always known LC had raised his kids to think they were better than us, but Orlando was a little too sure of himself for a man who had two guns on him. I tried my best to look around without taking my eyes off him, but I didn't see anyone or anything. "Who else is here? I know LC didn't just send you after us alone."

"He didn't. He sent me along with him," a female voice said from behind me.

I glanced to my right, and there was my baby cousin Paris, holding guns to the back of Kenny's and my head. Bitch had to be some kind of ninja, 'cause I had no idea how she had sneaked up on us like that.

"Now, I'm not playing with you, Curtis. You either, Kenny. Put the fucking guns down."

"Ain't nobody playing with you either," Kenny told her.

Paris glared over at my brother, who still had his gun aimed. I was surprised by her confidence and cockiness.

"Orlando, we ain't got time for this shit. Larry's crazy ass could show up at any minute," she said.

"I know, Paris, but they're our family. I don't wanna kill them if we don't have to." Orlando sounded as if he was more concerned about her pulling the trigger than us. "Now, fellas, just put the guns down and tell us where to find Uncle Larry."

"Not gonna happen, Orlando," I spat at him. I wasn't about to fall for their good cop/bad cop routine.

The four of us stood, guns drawn in the darkness, with only the moon lighting our faces. The tension was so thick that you could hear the beating of all four hearts simultaneously. We were all ready to kill as we watched and waited with anticipation to see who would pull the trigger first.

"All of you put the damn guns down!"

Our bodies remained still, but we all glanced over to see my mother running toward us, carrying a big-ass shotgun.

"Did you hear me? I said put the guns down!" Momma kept yelling, but none of us listened. Our Mexican standoff continued until she stepped in between Kenny and me, looking directly in my eyes.

"Momma, what the hell?" Every time I moved my gun, she'd move with it.

"Put the gun down, Curtis! Put it down now," she demanded.

"Momma, this ain't got nothing to do with you," I told her.

"And this mess between Larry and LC ain't got nothing to do with y'all," she said.

"He put my daddy in a mental hospital, Momma!" I said, beginning to get choked up.

"I know, and he might do it again, but that's between the two of them. Not you kids."

No one moved, and no one lowered a gun, and Momma started crying.

"Curtis, you and Kenny are my sons." She looked at me and my brother, then turned to Paris and Orlando. "And you are my niece and nephew. You can't do this to one another. I won't allow it." My heart ached as she sobbed, but I refused to lower my gun. "Y'all are family," my mother cried.

Orlando took a step closer, lowering his gun. "Look, Curtis and Kenny, we are not here to hurt anybody. We're here to help."

"How the fuck are you gonna help us?" I asked, feeling a little pissed off that he'd been the one to react to my mother's tears and lower his weapon. The bastard had made me look like a bad son.

"We're here to help with your father. Your dad needs help, Curtis. He has some serious mental issues."

"Says who? You? Your old man? You're a piece of fucking work, Orlando. You think you can come down here to our home and talk shit about our father being ill when neither you or your old man came to visit him in that hellhole once?" I shouted. "Fuck you! We don't need that kind of help!"

"He's not going to listen to you, Orlando. Curtis is just as crazy as Uncle Larry," Paris interjected.

"My brother's not crazy," Kenny snapped.

"And neither is our dad," I added.

"Curtis, Kenny, Orlando, Paris, please," my mother pleaded.

"Momma, go inside," Kenny told her.

I looked over at my brother, who had always been a momma's boy.

"Aunt NeeNee, for once can you listen to your dumb-ass son and do what he says? You really don't wanna be here when your sons die," Paris sneered.

I don't know what those words did to my mother, but suddenly she charged at Paris like a wild animal, pointing the shotgun directly at her chest. Paris instinctively pointed her guns at Momma.

"You wanna kill someone, then kill me!" Momma shouted.

"Paris, no!" Orlando yelled.

"Then tell her to stop pointing that thing at me! You know how I am, Orlando!" Paris responded.

"No, you put yours down. This is getting outta hand." Orlando walked over and guided his sister's hand to her side. "She's our aunt. She's not going to hurt you."

But to his surprise and mine, Momma cocked both hammers of the shotgun and said, "I'm sorry, Orlando, but I can't let you hurt my boys. Y'all drop those guns."

"Aunt NeeNee." Orlando sounded so disappointed, but he dropped his gun in the dirt. Paris took a little more coaxing, so Kenny and I raised our guns too.

"I'm sorry, baby, but I'm not doing anything that your mother wouldn't do," Momma said to Orlando. Then she spoke to me. "Curtis, you and Kenny get in that car and don't you come back, you hear?"

"Yes, ma'am," we said in unison. Kenny went over and kissed her on the cheek, and then I did the same. Orlando and Paris looked sick to their stomachs as I picked up the duffle bag and slowly backed away, heading to the car.

Ruby

23

The house was quiet. Vincent had eaten, bathed and gone to bed hours ago, but I tossed and turned in bed, flipping channels on the television as I waited for Vinnie to come upstairs. When I got tired of waiting, I got up and pulled on a robe and slipped into a pair of slippers before I quietly eased down the stairs. The house we were staying in was so much smaller than our house in Negril. That house was open and spacious, with natural lighting that brightened every corner when the sun was shining. Here, it was old and cramped, and it didn't matter if it was day or night; it always seemed dark and depressing. I walked downstairs through the small living area into the bedroom that Vinnie used as an office. The door was slightly opened. I peered inside and saw that he was alone, staring at the computer.

"Whatcha doing?" I asked as I entered the room.

Vinnie, startled by my voice, jumped in his seat. "What's wrong with you, sneaking in here like that, Ruby?"

"I wasn't sneakin'. Why you so jumpy? You in here looking at porn or something?" I folded my arms and walked closer so I could see what was on the screen.

"Why would I need porn when I have you?" he said seductively.

"What is dat, Vinnie?" I said, looking closer at the image on the computer. It looked like a live video of some sort. "Is dat de house in Negril?"

"Yes." Vinnie turned back around in his chair. "That's our house."

"Why you lookin' at it?"

"I'm waiting on something, and it's frustrating as hell."

"Waiting for what?" I was confused.

"Waiting on the Duncans to show up."

"De Duncans are at our house in Negril? Where?" I leaned in, watching the video closer. The screen flickered, and another view of our house appeared, this time of the back door. I didn't see anyone or anything resembling a Duncan, though.

"They're not there yet, but they're coming. I know they're coming, and when they get there, there is gonna be a big surprise."

"What kind of surprise? Ya sounding like a crazy man, Vinnie. What is going on?" I turned his chair so he was facing me.

"The entire house is wired to blow the fuck up. All I gotta do is push a button and the whole place goes up like the fourth of July." He gave me a sinister grin.

"Vinnie, I don't understand. Why would you blow up our house? I love dat—"

His phone rang, and he hit the speaker button. "John, what's the good word?"

"He's on de way, boss."

"So, he went through with it? Frankie B is dead?"

"Not only is he dead; de man blew up de entire Duncan transportation hub and half de damn block. He crazy!"

"Get the fuck outta here." Vinnie suddenly had a huge smile on his face. "You couldn't have paid me to think that he would go through with it. My God, this is fantastic. John, I owe you, man! This won't be forgotten."

"Thank you, boss."

Vinnie hung up the phone and reached for me. He pulled me into his lap and kissed me.

"What was dat?" I stared at him.

"That was the best damn news I've gotten all week, baby. You're not gonna believe this."

"What?"

"Well, it seems that the Duncans may not be a problem for us after all. And that dope I've been sitting on the past six months may have a buyer."

"What? How?"

"The Duncans have a bigger, more important enemy to deal with than Mr. Vinnie Dash—someone who is itching to come directly after them."

"I don't understand what you're talking 'bout." I had an uneasy feeling in the pit of my stomach, and I didn't like it one bit.

"Someone blew up their entire transportation warehouse to smithereens." He laughed. "It's one of the most important pieces of their business. Without it, they can't move product. The motherfuckers are crippled."

I gasped. "Someone like who? Did you do dis? Because dey will come after us for it."

"Well, not exactly, but kinda." He couldn't stop laughing. "Anyone who would do something like that directly would have a really big problem with the Duncans, and they would stop at nothing to exact revenge."

"Vinnie, you're confusing de hell outta me. I just heard you thank John for doing it."

"That's the beauty of this entire thing, honey. It's entirely confusing. Yeah, sure, I put the wheels in motion, but I didn't push the button. It was one of their own. LC's brother Larry did it for us. We're teaming up to put the Duncans out of business, and they don't even know I'm involved. He's on his way here now."

"Whatcha mean he's on his way here? Have you lost your mind dealing with dis man? You don't even know him." I couldn't recall Orlando ever mentioning Uncle Larry when we were together. "How do you know dis not some type of trick, Vinnie?"

"Trust me, it's not. They wouldn't destroy their entire transport operation just to set me up."

He had a point, but there was something not right about this. "So, why would dis man do dis to his own family?"

Vinnie began to twirl his finger next to his ear. "Because he's crazy, honey, like for real. He's certifiable, straitjacket crazy. So crazy the Duncans have a bounty on his head."

"And you wan' deal with dis man?" I was getting a really bad feeling about this guy Larry.

"This is our one shot at taking out the Duncans once and for all, including Orlando. And isn't that what you've wanted, to finally be rid of the man who killed your brother?"

"Yes," I said, although I felt my heart beat a little faster at the thought of Orlando actually being killed. Still, if that was what had to happen for me to get my life back, then so be it. "And dat would mean you don't have to blow up our house and we can finally return to Negril, right?"

"Maybe." Vinnie turned around and stared at the computer. "Or maybe we'll go back to New York."

London

24

"I'm gonna ask you this one more time. Where the fuck is Ruby?" Daryl yelled at the top of his lungs. The guy he directed the question to had been captured by Daryl's guys, who had been keeping an eye on the house Vinnie and Ruby were allegedly staying at. I say *allegedly* because other than him, there had been no activity at the house in the past 48 hours. Rio and I had returned to the rental house to find this dude tied up in a chair in the middle of one of the empty bedrooms. Daryl and his guys took turns beating him in between questions.

"I don't know who you talking 'bout," the guy said, blood seeping from the corner of his mouth.

"You don't, huh?" Daryl gestured at one of his guys, who hit the dude so hard that a tooth came flying out of his mouth and skittered across the floor.

"Damn," Rio said, sounding disgusted.

"Keep lying to me and you're gonna be gumming your next fucking meal—if you live long enough to have one," Daryl threatened. "Now, tell me where Ruby and the boy are."

Daryl got no response, so I decided to take matters into my own hands. I walked over and took the gun out of Daryl's hand, then stood in front of the man. He looked at me, his eyes full of confusion and fear.

"Look, I'm tired, and I'm not gonna play games with you all night like these guys. As far as I'm concerned, my nephew's life is at stake here. So, I'm gonna need for you to tell me where the fuck Ruby is." My voice was calm, unlike everyone else who had dealt with him, which made him let down his guard a little. That was exactly what I wanted him to do.

He looked me right in the eye and said, "Fuck you, bitch!"

I looked around at Daryl and his people. Everyone was staring at me, waiting to see what I would do. "Fuck me, you say?"

"Yeah, fuck you!"

I lowered the gun slightly, and my eyes never left his as I pulled the trigger. I don't know what scared him more—the sound of the gunshot, or the bullet that entered his foot. He screamed so loud I was worried someone in one of the neighboring beach houses would hear him.

"Damn," Rio said for the second time. "That shit hurt *me*. I know that shit had to hurt, didn't it?"

"Now, tell me where Ruby and her son are." I aimed the gun at his other foot. "You think I'm playing?"

The guy looked at me, panic-stricken, shaking his head. "Okay, okay, dey in de house."

"What house?" Daryl's voice boomed over my shoulder.

"Vinnie's house on de beach," he said. "Dey are upstairs. Her and de boy. He makes dem stay low so nobody can see 'em."

"Let's go!" Daryl motioned for the two guys we had been working with, and they headed out the door.

"Wait!" I snapped. "Where are you going?"

Daryl looked back at me. "We're going to check it out. We've got his keys to get in, and I wanna do it before they realize he's gone."

"You better pray we find them in that damn house. You've already lost a tooth and a foot. I'd hate to have you lose your life," Daryl warned the man.

"Be careful," I said to Daryl and his men as they left.

The guy was groaning in pain. I looked down at his foot and stared at the blood as it oozed out of what used to be an Air Jordan sneaker. I didn't know why, but I had an uneasy feeling about Daryl and our men busting up in Vinnie's house on the word of some idiot. It just didn't sit well with me. Daryl's logic was sound, but somehow it didn't feel right.

"London, something ain't right. This dude is lying about something." I guess Rio was having the same thoughts as me.

I looked over at the guy, who shifted his eyes away in a hurry, like he was afraid to make eye contact. Yeah, something wasn't right.

"Remember the last time when Sasha went into a house where we thought Vinnie was hiding?" Rio continued. "He blew the bitch up and killed Ruby's brother and almost killed Sasha."

"Shit, you're right. I completely forgot about that." I glanced over at dude, and I swear I saw what looked like a grin come across his bloody face. There was no doubt in my mind now that something wasn't right. I aimed the gun at the guy's other foot. "What the fuck did you do? You think this is a fucking joke?"

"Fuck you," he said then spit at me. I clocked him upside the head with the gun. It didn't do much damage, but it felt good and got his attention.

"Say good-bye to your other foot." I pointed the gun at his good foot, prepared to pull the trigger, but the bastard had the nerve to sit up like he was gonna take it. I guess he figured we were going to kill him anyway, so why the fuck should he talk?

"You know what, Rio? Fuck shooting his foot. I'm gonna shoot his dick off."

You should have seen the guy stiffen up then. And that damn smirk was gone too.

"Oh, that sounds painful." Rio laughed, grabbing his groin. "And by the way, who are you, and what did you do with my sister London?"

"I locked her away until we go back home, but remember: what happens in Jamaica stays in Jamaica."

"No problem. I love this side of you."

"Me too." I moved the gun to dude's crotch, and his eyes went huge. "You might wanna turn your head. This is going to be messy."

"No! No! Please don't!" The guy was trembling and shifting in the chair.

"Then stop playing and tell us the truth!" Rio chastised, getting in the guy's face.

"Fuck it, Rio. He ain't gonna talk. Vinnie's been sucking his dick too long."

"But not anymore," Rio added in a sarcastic whine.

"De house. De house is wired. Vinnie is watching it from the surveillance cameras. He can see everything on de property," the dude spit out in a hurry.

I was out the door and behind the wheel of the rental car before I heard him say anything else. The tires screeched as I pulled out of the driveway and took off down the street. I had only been a passenger in the car when Daryl and I went over to stake out the house a few days ago, so I had to rely on my vague memory to find my way back there. I navigated through the dark, unfamiliar streets, breaking all types of speed limits and driving laws. I could feel perspiration forming on my brow and between my breasts as I prayed out loud.

"God, please let me get to him. Please let me get to him."

Finally, I arrived on the right street and saw the neon sign of the jerk chicken restaurant directly across from the house. As I got closer, I could see Daryl and the guys standing at the edge of the beachfront property. I laid on the horn, but he didn't look up as he stepped onto the walkway, headed for the back entrance.

I screamed, but they didn't hear me. If they got too much closer and the house blew up, they could be killed by flying debris. *Fuck it.* I slammed my foot on the accelerator and headed directly for the house, through the shrubs and onto the lawn.

"Daryl, no! No!" I slammed my foot on the brakes two feet from the house and jumped out. I'd gotten his attention now, that was for sure.

"London, what the fuck?" I heard him yell.

"Don't go in there!" I screamed, running toward him.

Daryl grabbed me, and I pulled him back toward the street, screaming, "The house is booby trapped!"

"Get away from the house!" he ordered his men.

When we were far enough away from the property, we stood under the neon lights of the restaurant sign, Daryl holding me tight. I was totally out of breath when our eyes met. "I didn't think I was going to get here in time."

"Well, you did, and I'm grateful for it," he said, rubbing my back. "So, are you okay?"

"Am I okay?" I laughed, despite how my heart was racing. Tears filled my eyes, and I became overwhelmed with emotion. "I can't believe I almost lost you."

"You'll never lose me." Daryl cupped my face in his hands, then slowly, he kissed me.

25

My heart sank as we came around the bend of the road and what was left of Duncan Transports' Atlanta hub came into view. The entire complex looked like a roped-off war zone, with chunks of concrete, stone, and twisted metal scattered all over the place. Thirty-six hours after it was bombed, there were still firemen putting out pockets of smoldering debris. And if that wasn't reminder enough of all that we had lost, there was still one wall and some trucks that remained to mock the fact that everything else was completely gone.

"Pull over there," I instructed the driver, who did what he was told. He placed the car in park, and before he could get out, I had opened my own door and was halfway over to where Vegas was standing, surveying the damage.

"What are you thinking?" I asked Vegas.

"It's pretty much all gone." Vegas and I stared across the road at the dozen firemen and half dozen cops going through the rubble. "The building is totally demolished, along with twenty or so trucks. They've already pulled out twelve bodies, including Frankie B. I've got Harris over there dealing with the cops now."

"Twelve dead?" I repeated, slamming my fist into my palm. "You know Frankie B was one of my best friends. Since you came back, he was planning on going down to Florida to retire."

"Yeah, I know. He was a good man, that Frankie. He taught me a lot. He's gonna be missed."

"Dammit, I should've seen this coming."

"Pop, no one could've predicted this. We all thought Uncle Larry was in New York. Why would he even come here?" Vegas gritted his teeth in disbelief.

"Because this is where it all started." I knew my brother was on a path of destruction, but this told me he was only beginning. "He's trying to send me a message."

"And what's that?" Vegas asked.

It took a moment for me to choke down the emotions that were welling up inside me. "That he's going to destroy everything he, Lou, and I built, and he doesn't care who gets hurt in the process."

"Yeah, but Pop, we don't even use this hub for that kind of stuff anymore. Frankie B was running a legitimate business."

"I know that, son, but Larry doesn't—or at least he doesn't care," I said. Just then, a car rolled up behind my SUV. "You expecting someone?" I asked Vegas.

Before he could reply, Paris jumped out of the car and ran over to us. She hugged me tight. "Hey, Daddy. I missed you."

"Missed you too." I swear, despite her reckless foolishness, that girl always brought a smile to my face.

"Did Uncle Larry and them do this?"

"Everything seems to point to it," I replied sadly.

"Shit, what the hell did he use, an atom bomb?" Orlando asked as he walked up.

"You find any clues to Curt and Kenny's whereabouts?" Vegas asked his brother.

"We ain't find no clues. We actually found Curt and Kenny," Paris exclaimed.

"Get the fuck outta here," Vegas said, a satisfied grin creeping up on his face. "Where do you have them stashed? I wanna talk to those two."

"We kind of had to let them go." You could hear the disappointment in Orlando's voice as Vegas's expression soured.

"I told you we shoulda just snuck up on their asses and blasted them," Paris snapped. She began pacing back and forth as she deflected all blame on her brother. "But no, O wanted to try and talk shit out." She threw her hands in the air. "Yeah, well, he talked shit out so well Aunt NeeNee pulled a shotgun on us and let them go!"

"So, you found them at the farm?" I asked Orlando, knowing that Paris was too riled up to give me any useful information.

"Yeah, but they didn't have any plans on staying there. They were digging for something," Orlando said.

"It was probably a body," Vegas said.

"Nah. Larry would never bury a body on the farm. It was most likely money," I answered.

"Money?" Vegas and Orlando asked at the same time.

"Yes, it's an old school thing. Guys like Larry never kept their money in banks. They'd hide it where they could get to it whenever they needed it. Larry's probably got money and gold stashed all over the place." I sighed. "Did they find what they were looking for?"

"They left with a big army duffle bag. Looked pretty full too," Orlando answered.

"What do you think they're gonna do with all that money, Pop?" Vegas asked me.

"I don't know. But whatever it is, it's probably not gonna be good for us," I told them.

"Vegas, make that hundred-grand bounty on Larry's head a half million."

"But what about Curt and Kenny?" Vegas asked.

"Put a hundred grand on each of them too," I said coldly. "Dead or alive."

"Damn, Pop. You sure? I mean, those are our cousins." Vegas seemed uncharacteristically hesitant.

"Yeah, and Larry's my brother, but I refuse to allow him to go on a rampage across the country killing innocent people like he did last time. We've already got twelve dead, and that's not including Lee and his people." I turned and looked back at the crumbled transport center, becoming even more angry. "The body count is getting too high. Those boys made their bed; now they're gonna have to sleep in it."

Larry

26

Once we arrived in Kingston, I got Momma settled into the hotel, then called Vinnie Dash to arrange a meeting. Surprisingly, he was more than happy to meet with me. He even sounded excited about it. He offered to send a car over to get me and promised to buy me the biggest steak in Jamaica—although from the looks of the skinny-ass cows around here, I might order jerk chicken instead. I guess now that I'd taken care of our mutual pain-in-the-ass problem Frankie B, Vinnie's business would no doubt expand, and I was going to be his new best friend. Hell, I didn't have a problem with that. Me and him being friends would just piss LC and his brats off even more. The mutual hatred between the Duncans and the Dashes went way back, and from what I'd heard, it had only become more intense after LC orchestrated Vinnie's father Sal being killed.

"You sure you don't want me to come with you?" Momma asked as I was heading out the door. She hugged me like she had the day I went off to the Vietnam War. With Lou dead and LC's betrayal, it felt good to know someone cared for me that way.

"I'm sure, Momma. You stay here and relax. Why don't you go down to the pool and see if you can get one of these Caribbean gigolos? I got this. I wasn't scared of Sal, so you know I'm not scared of his son." I was just joking about the gigolo thing, but I really did want Momma to relax.

"You've never been scared of anybody, but that don't change the fact that I got a bad feeling about this, son."

"Momma, you were the one who pushed me to set this meeting up. Now you're changing your mind?" I frowned.

"I ain't say shit about changing my mind or the deal," she snapped. "I just got a bad feeling about this, so much so I wish those hard-headed grandsons of mine were here." She let me loose, wiping her glistening eyes. "So, I'm just telling you to be careful with these people by yourself."

"Okay, Momma. I'll be careful." I kissed her cheek, picked up the package I'd brought with me from the States, and walked out the door.

By the time I got downstairs and exited the Courtyard Kingston, the car Vinnie had sent was waiting for me. The driver, a slim, older Jamaican, didn't say much while we were in the car, which was a good thing, because I wasn't the type for small talk anyway. Soon, he pulled up to a small cafe. I waited for him to open the door for me, and then I followed him inside. The smell of marijuana was so strong, I halfway expected to have a contact high by the time I was ready to leave.

"Holy shit. There he is, Larry fucking Duncan," I heard someone say from across the room. I squinted in the dusty, dimly lit space and saw an olive-skinned man I assumed to be Vinnie Dash sitting at one of the tables nearby.

"Man, I can't fucking believe this. You're a fucking legend," he said as I approached.

"Yeah, but only in my mind," I said.

Vinnie stood up and stretched his hand out. We shook hands, then he motioned for me to sit in the chair beside him.

"You look just like your daddy," I commented.

Vinnie nodded. "That's what everyone says. Thanks."

"That wasn't a damn compliment," I told him with a laugh.

"Damn, Crazy Larry Duncan. I'm in awe right now." Vinnie took a long drag of the joint that had been lying in the ashtray in front of him. When he passed it to me, I declined. I didn't want to cloud my thinking.

"You really are a fucking legend. You know that? I mean, old man used to always say 'LC is the smart one, Lou is the big-dick one with all the women, but Crazy Larry, that's the one you want on your team. That guy is going to get the job done, no matter what.' You did a lot of work for him back in the day, didn't you?"

"I completed a contract or two for him," I said nonchalantly.

"Yeah, that's what I heard. And now look at this. I'm sitting here doing business with you. My dad would be proud, don't you think?" Vinnie asked.

"He would be if the deal is right," I told him. "Sal Dash was a true businessman, very professional."

"That he was. And I'm sure you'll find me to be just as professional. But I need to be assured of one thing. Are you sure Frankie B is dead?" Vinnie's face had no expression as he stared directly in my eyes, making me laugh.

A dark look passed over his face for a second. "What's so fucking funny? All I'm asking is if the guy's dead. I didn't ask for his head on a silver platter or anything."

That comment made me laugh even harder as I reached down to pick up the wrapped box I'd brought with me. "Hey forget about that shit for a moment. I brought you a present." I set it down in front of him.

"Really? What the hell did you bring me?"

Vinnie seemed a little confused by me, and I liked it that way. It's good to keep people guessing; let them know they can never predict your next move. It gives you the upper hand.

Vinnie opened the package, making sure not to rip the gold wrapping paper. He looked inside then snapped his head back, trying unsuccessfully to hide the look of disgust on his face. "What the fuck is this?"

"That's Frankie's head," I said. "I'm sorry, but I couldn't find a platter on such short notice. I had a flight to catch."

Vinnie managed to recover from his initial shock, and he laughed along with me.

"This motherfucker really is crazy," he shouted, raising the box for all to see. "He's got a fucking head in the box. You are one crazy son of a bitch!"

The smile fell from my face. "Not crazy. Eccentric. I hate the word crazy."

"Okay, you're eccentric, motherfucker. Now that Frankie's gone and the Duncans are having some transportation issues they gotta deal with, I have a little present for you." Vinnie motioned toward one of his men and instructed him, "Get one of those packages from the bar."

The guy walked behind the bar and returned with a package wrapped in brown paper.

"You're looking for dope, so try this on for size." Vinnie tossed it over to me.

I caught it, then took out a small knife from the pocket of my suit jacket, cut into the package, and licked the blade.

"That's good stuff," I told him.

"Wow, now that's some old-school shit. Most of the people I've ever dealt with have like a mini chemistry set, and if it don't turn blue, your shit ain't pure."

"Well, I'm old school all the way. How much of this shit you got?"

"I got five hundred kis." Vinnie beamed with pride.

"You got five hundred kilos? Of this?"

"Yep. I can sell it to you for thirty grand per ki."

I grinned. "No, you're gonna let me get it for twenty grand a ki. Okay?"

"What? Why the fuck would I sell it to you for that?" Vinnie snapped. "Nobody else is going to sell it to you for thirty. Wholesale is thirty-five, and that's on a good day. I'm giving you a deal."

I shook my head. "Come on, Vinnie. We both know no one wants to buy from you at any price; otherwise, this shit would be gone. Now, let's stop playing games and make a deal."

He hesitated for a minute, but he couldn't deny the truth of what I was saying. Finally, he gave in a little. "I can't sell it to you for twenty, but I'll split the difference with you and make it twenty-five. What d'you say?"

"You got a deal, but I buy it in four shipments, a hundred twenty-five kis at a time." I reached my hand across to him, and he took it, sealing one hell of a good deal for me. Shit, if he had stuck to thirty, I still would have bought the shit.

Vinnie picked up the blunt and took another long drag, then put it down and looked at me. "Well, I guess there's only one thing missing then."

"What's that?"

"The money."

"My boys will be here tomorrow. I'll have your money then," I told him as I stood up, offering my hand, which he took.

"Larry, this is definitely the start of a beautiful friendship. LC is not going to know what hit him," Vinnie said with a chuckle.

If things worked out the way I planned, this was just one of the many ways I'd be hitting my treacherous brother LC.

Sasha

27

I was lying across the bed, watching some new Beyoncé video on my phone when Paris stuck her head in the room.

"Get dressed. I'm bored, and I can't take it anymore. We're going out. We're leaving in thirty minutes."

She didn't have to tell me twice. Of course I was bored, considering my damn meddling mother had basically made Uncle LC put me on lockdown instead of sending me out on jobs. I jumped off the bed and walked over to my 10 x 10 walk-in closet. "Where we going? 'Cause you know I ain't got shit to wear."

"I know, right?" Paris agreed. "Same here, but find something. We ain't got time to go shopping."

"A'ight, but are you gonna tell me where we're going or what? I need to know what style to wear."

"Wear something expensive. We are going to a charity event," she said, sounding very proper and high society.

"A charity event?" I whined. I hated charity events. They were more boring than sitting around the house looking at everyone's long faces about the warehouse being blown up in Atlanta and Uncle Larry's recent killing spree. "What kind of charity event? You know I hate these things, Paris."

"Sasha, stop it with all the damn bitching and moaning. Trust me on this. You're gonna have fun," she said with a confident smile. "Now, get dressed. I'm serious about leaving in a half hour."

An hour later, we pulled into Jake's 58 Hotel and Casino out in Long Island. At first I thought Paris must have been lying about it being a charity event, but sure enough, the sign in the front lobby read: LADIES NIGHT OUT BENEFIT AUCTION. We were directed to one of the casino hotel banquet halls, which was set up for a fashion show, complete with a runway and a small stage. The audience was an eclectic group of women, all ages, dressed in everything from Sunday's best to high fashion couture. Now, I love fashion, but the vibe in this place was way too low key for me. I needed more excitement than these bougie ladies could ever offer.

"Paris, the last place I wanna be is a boring-ass fashion show. I could have stayed home and watched *Project Runway* reruns for this."

"Trust me, it's going to be fun." Paris shrugged and handed me a glass of champagne from the bar before we made our way to the seats she had reserved in the VIP section.

"How much fun can a charity auction be, Paris?" I asked as we settled in to our seats.

Before she could answer, the lights dimmed, and the intro to R. Kelly's *12 Play* came blasting out of nowhere. Women began screaming, which totally confused me. This was like no fashion show I'd ever been to. Then I looked toward the stage, and everything made sense. One by one, some of the finest men I had ever laid eyes on began strolling out, each one wearing jeans, Timberland boots, and nothing else. Their muscular chests and shoulders glistened as they gyrated to the beat of the music. The group of men was just as varied as the women in the audience, all races and ages. But there was one thing they all had in common: they were all fine as fuck. My eyes widened, and I drank my champagne in one gulp.

"Yesssssssss!" Paris jumped up and screamed along with the rest of the women, and I couldn't help laughing. One of the men dove onto the floor in front of us and proceeded to demonstrate his stroke game. My mouth gaped open. He had the body of a Nubian king and the face of a model. Watching him dance in front of me, I could only imagine what he would do to me in bed.

As the song ended, he slowly stood up, and our eyes met. He smiled at me, and I almost forgot where I was. In one leap, he was back on the runway stage, and then he disappeared behind the curtain along with the other guys.

"Ladies, ladies, ladies! What's going on?" a woman yelled into the microphone. As she walked onstage, I recognized her as a reality star turned rapper whose song had been number one on the charts. The audience went wild.

"Is that—"

"Yep, I told you it was gonna be fun." Paris nudged me playfully.

"Welcome to Ladies Night Out Benefit Auction. I can already see that the show's opening got y'all excited as hell, right? Y'all like those fellas, huh?" The host held her microphone toward the audience, and we all screamed. "So, that means that y'all are ready to show them some love and bid on them, because tonight, each and every one of their fine asses are up for auction! Get those wallets ready, ladies!"

"Oh, shit." I turned and looked at Paris. "That's what the hell they're auctioning off?"

"Yep." Paris smirked. "And I got my eyes set on one or two. What about you?"

A smile spread across my face, because I knew exactly who I would be bidding on.

"All right, ladies," the announcer said, "first up for grabs we have Victor, who also happens to be a volunteer firefighter right up the road in Huntington."

A sexy white guy wearing a fire hat and suspenders walked out and stood in front of the microphone. "Hey, ladies. I'm Victor, and I'm ready to come put out the fire of the hottest bidder tonight."

"Four hundred dollars!" the woman sitting beside Paris yelled out.

"Four fifty!" another one yelled.

The bidding for Victor continued until it reached two thousand dollars, and the winner ran onstage and gave him a big hug. Victor didn't seem to mind that she looked more like a lukewarm grandma instead of the hottie he talked about, because he picked her up into his arms and carried her offstage. The crowd went wild, clamoring for the next specimen to be brought on stage.

We all laughed and screamed as each guy came out and explained why we should bid on him. Some, like Victor, went for two thousand dollars. A few went for slightly higher, but most of them stayed at around twelve hundred.

"Are you gonna bid?" I leaned over and asked Paris, who was staring intensely at the gorgeous, deep chocolate guy who had just walked onstage wearing a chef's hat and carrying a spatula.

"Hey, ladies, I'm Bilal, and I'm a private chef who would love to whip something up for you to taste," he said.

"Nah, not this one," Paris said, although she continued staring and smiling at him.

"Why not? You're damn near drooling at his ass," I told her.

"Because I've already fucked him for free." She looked over at me and laughed. I couldn't help it; I laughed right along with her.

"You know I gotta ask," I said.

"And I have no problem telling you—yes, he can cook his ass off," she said, trying to keep a straight face.

I shook my head. "Your silly ass. You know that's not what I wanna know. I wanna know if he can fuck."

"Oh, I would definitely fuck him again," she replied happily. "He's a three-tool player, and proficient at them all."

"Fingers, tongue, and dick," we chanted in unison then high-fived each other.

Paris finally caught his eye, placing her hand to her ear and mouthing the words, "Call me." He nodded his head then went back to working the rest of the crowd.

I was waiting in anticipation for the sexy guy I had mentally staked my claim on during the show's opening. Finally, he walked out wearing a stethoscope.

What's up, ladies? I'm Dennis. I'm a doctor from Dix Hills, and I have no problem examining you from head to toe and coming up with the proper diagnosis to cure whatever ails you. So, bid your highest and best for me, because after your visit, I promise you'll feel much better," he said and smiled right at me. As they had been doing all night, the crowd went wild.

I sat up and got ready for the bidding war that I knew was about to take place.

The same woman seated beside Paris who had lost the bid for Victor screamed out, "Six hundred!"

"Six fifty," I yelled.

Paris looked at me. "Yes, bitch. Get his fine ass."

"Seven fifty," another woman yelled from the other side.

"One thousand dollars," I countered.

"Ten fifty!" The lady beside Paris winked at me.

I winked back at her and said, "Two thousand." Then I looked at Dennis, who seemed impressed.

"Three thousand!" a woman yelled from behind us.

"Ohhhhhhhhhhh!" The crowd reacted in unison.

The woman behind Paris sat back in her seat, letting us know that the doctor was out of her budget. Hell, three grand for some dick was out of my budget, too, I thought.

Paris looked at me and gave me a nod. "Get your man, cuz. You can afford him."

I figured that was her way of letting me know that if I was a few dollars short, she would have my back, so I said, "Thirty-five hundred!"

"Damn, Dennis. They really want that checkup. I have thirty-five hundred. Do I hear four? Anyone? Anyone? Going once, going twice . . ."

No one said anything, so I stood up and got ready to head toward the stage to claim my prize.

"Five thousand dollars!"

I froze for a second, then I slowly turned to see who was bidding. The woman was in the shadows in the back, but she finally stepped into the light for all to see. I stared at the bidder. She smiled at me and waved.

"Oh, shit. Is that—" Paris mumbled.

"Yes, it is," I snapped. "That's my mother."

"Five thousand dollars!" the hostess repeated. "Five thousand going once, going twice." It felt like all eyes were on me as I sat down in anger and defeat. "Sold, to the lady in the back for five thousand dollars!"

The sound of applause that erupted was deafening, and I refused to stay and watch in humiliation as she claimed the prize that was supposed to be mine. I grabbed my purse and headed toward the exit.

"Sasha, wait." Paris tried to grab my arm, but I snatched away from her and kept going.

I wanted to leave, but Paris was driving, which meant I had to wait for her ass. I paced angrily in the lobby while Paris took her sweet time.

"Sasha."

"What the hell do you want?" I turned around and yelled at my mother. "Aren't you supposed to be onstage?"

"Don't act like this, Sasha." Donna walked toward me, and I took a step back.

"Leave me the fuck alone!" I yelled, causing the other folks in the lobby to stare.

"You're causing a scene, and I know you were raised better than this," she said.

"How the fuck would you know? You didn't care enough to stick around to see how I was raised," I spat.

Our eyes locked, and I could see that my words had hurt her, causing me to feel slightly vindicated. She walked away without saying anything else.

"Sasha, you okay?" Paris asked as she came walking up.

"Yeah, I'm fine. I can't believe she did that. I hate her," I said.

"Why are you so mad? It's a charity auction. If you want his ass that bad, all you gotta do is ask for his number. He was checking your ass out just as hard as you were checking him," Paris said. "Look at it this way: you and your cougar-ass mother have the same taste in men."

"Fuck you, Paris. It's not about him. How would you feel if Aunt Chippy was in here bidding on Bilal's Chef Boyardee ass?"

Paris blinked for a second and then said, "I'd kick her fucking ass, that's what I'd do. My mom's in her sixties."

"Exactly, and so is mine, so you should understand why I wanna kick her ass right now," I replied.

We walked toward the exit, and as we passed a doorway leading into the hall, I saw my mother and Dennis laughing and talking. I realized that my feelings were deeper than what I'd just admitted to Paris. I wanted to kick my mother's ass each and every time I saw her.

Ruby

28

Although it was Sunday, the church was fairly empty when I entered. I knew it would be, because I'd picked a time late in the evening when all the so-called saints would be home enjoying dinner after a long day of praising and singing. It was a small church, the same one my mother had dragged my brother Randy and me to each and every Sunday. As I walked into the sanctuary, I felt as if I had walked into a time warp. Everything was the same, including the sense of peace I felt when I looked at the large, gold cross hanging on the wall behind the pulpit. I smiled at the sight of the wooden pews we would squirm in as we endured the long, drawn-out services each week. The back of the pews held the same red hymnals and tattered Bibles.

I sat at the end of the front pew. Praying had become unfamiliar and uncomfortable to me, which was why I had decided that if I went back to the place where I first learned to pray, maybe it would help. I had been up for three nights, tossing and turning, unable to sleep because of the dreams I was having. I needed help before I went crazy, and I knew the only one who could help me was God. I closed my eyes and tried to focus.

"Please help me, Lord," I whispered, then began, "Our Father, who—"

"Ruby?" I opened my eyes, startled by the sound of a woman. My heart pounded, and I quickly stood up. "Ruby, is that you, gal?" The large woman dressed in all white smiled at me, and I instantly recognized her.

"Mother DuBoise," I said.

"You lookin' good; still beautiful. How's ya brudda Randy?" she asked, sitting on the pew and pulling me down beside her. "He was such a good boy to ya mudda, God rest her."

I looked down sadly as I thought about Randy. "He's dead, Mother Duboise. Randy died three years ago."

"My God." Mother Duboise made the sign of the cross over her body and clutched the crucifix she wore around her neck. "Did a white man kill him? I had a dream about him bein' killed by a white man."

I shook my head. "No, he wasn't killed by a white man."

"Okay, not all me dreams is true." Mother DuBoise left the uncomfortable subject and turned her attention back to me. "So, what brings ya here in de chapel dis late in de day? I can see dat you're troubled in ya heart, Ruby."

"Peace." I sat back and looked down at the floor. "I just needed to come here and see if I could find some peace of mind."

"Dis is de place fo' dat. You've come to de right place, all right. But why is your spirit so vexed? Ya pretty, but ya look tired." She took hold of my hand.

"I am. I'm very tired. I don't sleep as of late."

"Dat's not good. What keep ya up, child?"

"It's funny you talked about dreams. I keep dreaming about my son's father. Very intimate dreams."

"Why is dat a bad ting?" She smiled, looking down at my hand as she said, "I see dat ring on ya finger, so ya must be married."

"I am, but dat's de problem. The man I'm married to is not my son's father." I lowered my head.

"Oh, I can see how dat can be troubling." Mother DuBoise nodded, and her kind voice lacked any hint of judgment against me. "You still have feelings fo' de fada of your son."

I hesitated then frowned. "No, I love my husband."

"I did not say you did not love ya husband. I said you have feelings fo' de fada. Dat is why you cannot stop him from coming to you in ya sleep. Tell me, is someone bringing harm to him in dese dreams?"

I tried to recall exactly what had been happening in the dreams I had. In most of them, it was Orlando and I being intimate, then, a white bird would come down and attack us, causing us to separate and run away. I would call for my son Vincent, but he would run after Orlando, and I couldn't catch either one of them; and finally, the bird would catch me in its talons. I would wake up in a cold sweat and run into my son's room, making sure he was safe. Then, I would climb into bed with him, holding him until it was time to wake up.

"My son chases after his father, and I chase after both o' dem, but I can't catch 'em," I said, leaving out the part about the bird.

"Maybe you are chasing after de love you both have fo' dis man?" Mother DuBoise suggested.

"No, my son has never met his father," I said.

"Neva? Why not?" She looked appalled.

"Because his father is de man who killed my brother. Which is why I can never love him."

"Ruby," she said, her eyes wide with surprise, "you are still tinking about him after all of dat? Dat means you still love dis man."

I sat and listened to Mother DuBoise as she told me something that, deep down, I already knew.

London

29

The small charter plane we were riding in landed with a bump. It had taken less than thirty minutes for us to arrive. There was no conversation between us during that ride, and I told myself it was because of everything that had taken place over the past twenty-four hours, and not because of the kiss that neither Daryl nor I had yet mentioned. As soon as we had returned to the house after the explosion, Daryl had gone crazy on our captive, who finally told us that Vinnie and Ruby were in Kingston, which was where we'd just landed.

I had spent most of the night wrestling with the idea that Daryl was going to knock on my door, and what I would or wouldn't do when he did. Only he didn't. I honestly didn't know how I felt about that, and with Rio all up in our faces, we really hadn't had a moment alone to discuss it.

As we taxied on the runway toward the small terminal, I glanced over at Daryl, and he smiled. I smiled back, remembering the feel of his lips on mine and the warmth of his arms as he held me in front of that house. We needed to talk, but I knew this wasn't the time. Would there ever be a right time? Should I even be thinking about finding a right time to talk, especially since my husband had already called demanding that I come home? I probably should have been more concerned with that, but I wasn't.

My mind was all over the place, not only with thoughts of Daryl. There was also the fact that our men were at least three hours' drive away, and we had no idea how we were going to find Vinnie, Ruby, or my nephew.

When the plane finally stopped, I unfastened my seat belt and stood up. There was another jolt when the door opened, and I instinctively grabbed Daryl's arm to steady myself. Again, our eyes met, until he looked away.

"I'll go find a cab," he said as soon as we stepped off the plane.

"We'll meet you out front," Rio told him and then turned to me. "What the hell is going on? Why is he acting so strange all of a sudden? Did you fuck him?"

I did my best impression of being offended by his assumption. "No, I didn't fuck him. I'm married, or did you forget that?" I held up the marquise diamond on my left hand.

"Don't act like I'm stupid. What happens in Jamaica stays in Jamaica, remember? Your words."

"I do remember, and I'm gonna need to hold you to that, okay?" I gave him a don't-play-with-me look. "And just so you know, we did have a moment, but that was it. Just a moment, nothing else. So, anything you think, or think you're thinking, stays right here on this island, you hear? I don't want anything misconstrued when we get home."

"I got you, but whatever is going on, y'all need to get it together, 'cause both of y'all are acting weird as fuck, and I don't like it. It could get one of us killed." He picked up one of the suitcases as if there was no more to say. "Oh, fuck." Rio gasped.

"Please don't start with that again," I warned, thinking he was about to start ranting about the weight of my luggage. Then I turned to see him staring at something, and I asked, "What is it, Rio?"

"Look." He leaned over to me and whispered, "Over there, getting into that car."

"Look at what? Where?"

"There," Rio pointed emphatically. "There, over there, London."

"Oh, fuck." I repeated his words because I couldn't find any of my own. I literally couldn't believe my eyes. "Am I seeing things?"

"Not if you're seeing Curtis and Kenny," Rio snapped back.

I grabbed him by the wrist and headed for the door. "Come on. We gotta find Daryl."

We stepped outside, and I looked around for Daryl. He was a little farther down the walkway on the phone. Rio whistled loudly and waved wildly until Daryl noticed him. Meanwhile, I approached a van that had been sitting in front of the airport and spoke to the driver.

"I got a hundred U.S. dollars if you can give us a ride and follow that car," I told him.

"Yes! Yes! Get in," the man said without hesitation. "My brother can wait."

Rio and I quickly threw our bags into the van and climbed in the back seat.

"What the heck is going on?" Daryl asked, climbing into the front seat.

"My cousins Curtis and Kenny are in that car." I pointed to the black Mercedes that was half a block ahead of us.

"Whatever you do, do not let that car out of your sight," Daryl said to the driver.

"No worries, mon. I'm a good driver." The man smiled as he sped behind the Benz.

True to his word, the driver continued following the car through the streets of Kingston until it pulled in front of a downtown apartment building.

"Stay right here," Daryl told the driver. "Don't turn. Just pull over."

The driver obliged and eased over. We watched as the doors to the Benz opened, and Curtis and Kenny got out carrying a large army duffle bag. As confusing as this whole scenario was, the coup de grace was when the sliding glass doors to the building opened and Uncle Larry walked out.

Curtis

30

The car pulled in front of a high-rise apartment building, and I was happy to get out and stretch my legs. I was tired as hell, and from the looks of him, so was Kenny. It felt like we'd been sitting forever between driving to Maryland from Georgia last night and the flight over here. There was one good thing about it, though. It was good to see my old man. It had only been a few days, but I missed his eccentric ass.

"Hey, Dad," I said happily when he walked out through the sliding glass doors.

"What the hell took so long?" He hugged Kenny then me. "You guys left six hours ago."

"We weren't exactly in a Learjet," I joked. "Where'd you find that bush pilot anyway? He was high the entire ride over here."

"He's one of Jamaica John's people."

"Well, that answers the question," Kenny said.

"It does, doesn't it? But at least you're here in one piece. Come on in. We got shit to do. You got the bag?" Dad asked.

I held up the duffle bag full of money that I had been holding onto for dear life ever since I dug it up. "Yes, sir. Right here."

"Good. The sooner I pay Vinnie and get home the better," he said.

"Home? We just got here." Kenny said with a frown. Like me, he was hoping for a few days of fun in the sun.

"This ain't no fucking vacation, boy. We gotta get back and get shit done. From what I'm hearing from Vinnie, LC has a price on our heads. We have to hit them before they hit us."

"Speaking of hitting us, I think there's something you should know," Kenny told him.

"What?" My dad looked past me to my brother, who was standing on the other side of me.

I frowned, hoping he wasn't about to say what I thought he was. We'd talked about it during the ride to Maryland.

"Come on, Kenny. Spit it out!" Dad yelled at him.

Kenny sighed. "While we were digging the bag up, Paris and Orlando showed up at the farm."

"What? How the fuck did y'all let that happen? I told you to go at night so no one would see you," Dad snapped.

I closed my eyes and shook my head. I had warned my brother that telling Dad wasn't a good idea, but he thought he knew better than me.

"We did go at night," Kenny replied.

"How the fuck did they even know y'all were in Waycross? Who the fuck did you tell? Or fuck?" Dad turned around and directed the questions at me.

"We didn't tell anyone, Dad. I swear." I raised my hands as if I was surrendering. I cut my eyes at Kenny, who now looked at me as if this was somehow my fault. "We did everything the way you told us to."

"Well, you're here and they ain't, so I guess we got two less of LC's brats to worry about. You did kill them, didn't you?"

Kenny's shoulders slumped as he admitted, "No, Dad. We didn't kill them."

The old man's head snapped back so fast I thought he might have given himself whiplash.

"What do you mean they're not dead?" He grabbed Kenny by the throat, not caring who saw or heard him. "I told you if you saw any of those little fuckers to kill them. Why the fuck aren't they dead?"

I had to give my brother props for his bravery. He didn't even try to resist. By now, I was standing next to Dad, trying to pry his fingers from around Kenny's neck.

"We were about to kill them, Dad, and—"

"And what?" He tightened his grip.

"We didn't have to. Momma dealt with them. She pulled a shotgun on them and everything," I told him, hoping it would be enough to bring him to his senses before he killed my little brother.

"Your momma?" Dad's voice softened slightly, and his eyes widened. Finally, he let go of Kenny's throat.

"Yeah," Kenny sputtered, rubbing his neck. "She pulled a shotgun on them."

"She always did love shotguns. It's been her preferred weapon since we were kids." To my surprise, his body relaxed and he smiled. "That damn NeeNee. I swear, I love that woman."

"We know, Dad," I told him.

"What the fuck y'all looking at?" Dad shouted when he realized we were being watched by everyone outside the building. Most of them went about their business once he yelled at them. "Come on, boys. I've got someone I'd like to introduce you to," he said like he hadn't just almost choked the life out of Kenny.

"We'll be back in a little while. Go wait in the parking lot," Dad told the driver, who responded wordlessly with a nod.

We walked past the reception area and rode the elevator to the top floor. When the doors opened, there was an armed man waiting in front of a door.

"I'm here to see Vinnie. He's expecting me," Dad told the guy.

"What ya name?" he asked and went to frisk my father.

"Don't put your hands on me." Dad pushed him away, and the man reached for his piece. Before he could unholster it, all three of us had our guns aimed at him.

"Whoa, what the fuck is going on here?" The door was opened by a white guy.

"I told this motherfucker you were expecting us, and he tried to manhandle me, Vinnie," Dad said, his gun still pointed.

"Come on now, Leviticus, man. Is that any way to treat our guests? You know better. Come on back, Larry." Vinnie Dash opened the door wide and welcomed us inside. His apartment was a fully furnished man cave with a pool table, fully stocked bar area, and even a Jacuzzi in one corner. Rap music played through the surround-sound speakers, and there were a couple of guys playing Madden on one plasma TV, while porn played on another. We followed him to another open living area with a black leather sofa, oversized chair, and a coffee table, which had the biggest pile of marijuana I had ever seen sitting in the center.

"Nice place, Vinnie," Dad said.

"Thanks. This is my corporate office." Vinnie laughed. "Isn't that what it's called in the business world?"

"I ain't never seen no corporate office like this," I mumbled, taking it all in.

"The only thing missing is some naked strippers up in here," Kenny said, laughing as he looked around.

"It's a little early for them, but stick around for another hour or two and they'll be here," Vinnie assured us.

Dad introduced us. "Vinnie, these are my boys, Curt and Kenny. Boys, this is our new business associate, Vinnie Dash."

"Nice to meet you, fellas. Sit down, sit down. Y'all want a drink? Some smoke?" Vinnie asked, sitting on the oversized chair. Dad sat on the sofa, and we remained standing. We knew not to sit down unless instructed by our father.

"No, we're good." Dad declined his offer, although I could have used a good hit. "Let's get down to the business at hand. You got the dope?" Dad asked Vinnie.

Vinnie nodded. "It's waiting to be transported to the plane when you leave. You got my money?"

Dad looked over at me and said, "Pay the man."

I placed the bag on the floor and took out three-fourths of the cash, placing it on the table next to the weed. Vinnie picked up one of the bundles and flipped through it, then called for one of the men playing the video games to come and get it.

"When are you heading back?" Vinnie asked.

"Today," Dad told him.

"Why so soon? I thought you'd hang around to celebrate. There's going to be plenty of ass, and these Jamaicans love some American dick."

"Or at least the dick they think can get them to America," Kenny joked, and Vinnie laughed along with him.

I looked over at Kenny. I knew he was hoping that Vinnie would somehow convince our dad to stay so we could enjoy this shit. It's the same thing I was hoping.

"Come on, Larry. Have a little fun," Vinnie prodded.

"Sorry. I'm flying back with the product. The sooner I get back, the sooner I can get shit done. You want me to be a return customer, don't you, Vinnie?"

"Indeed, I do. And I gotta tell you, Larry, doing business with you has certainly been a pleasure for me, and I appreciate it. Anything you need, you got it. Jamaica John and his people are at your disposal, and you may utilize him wherever he can be helpful," Vinnie told him.

"I appreciate that," Dad said.

"No problem. But I gotta ask you a question, though."

"What's that?"

"How exactly are you gonna use that dope to put your brother out of business?"

I listened closely, because I'd been wondering the same thing.

Dad stood up with a big smile on his face. "I'm gonna give it away."

Vinnie looked at him like he was crazy. "Did you say *give it away*?"

"Well, something like that."

Vinnie walked us back through the fun-filled office space and out the same door we'd entered. When we got into the hallway, the same guy was there.

"Leviticus, apologize to my friend and his sons for giving them a hard time," Vinnie commanded him.

"But I was just doing my job, boss. You told me—"

The shot seemed to come from nowhere, and it hit Leviticus right in the forehead, leaving a small hole. My heart began racing, and I reached for my weapon, prepared to retaliate—until I heard laughter. I turned around and saw it was Vinnie who was laughing.

"Somebody clean this mess up," he shouted.

"What the fuck?" Dad hissed.

"Oh yeah, Larry. I'm a little crazy myself." Vinnie smiled wickedly. "Come on. I'll walk you guys out. I could use some fresh air."

We didn't waste any time getting on the elevator to exit the building.

Vegas

31

"What's going on?" Pop asked as he entered the den, followed by Harris and Nevada. I'd sent my son to find his grandfather because things had just gone from bad to worse.

"Take a look for yourself." I motioned toward the big screen hanging on the wall then pressed a button on my phone. The video I had received began to play, and I could see from the hardened look of disbelief on my father's face that we were in trouble. "Shit just got complicated."

"That's an understatement," he said.

"That right there is the work of the devil himself," Orlando added angrily. He and Junior were sitting on the sofa and had already seen the clip of Uncle Larry, Kenny, and Curtis in front of some tall building, all hugged up and laughing like they were best friends with Vinnie Dash.

"Play that video again," Pop said, easing into a chair. "Do we know what the hell they were doing together?"

"Nope, but if I had to guess, it looks like they've formed some kind of alliance."

"The enemy of my enemy is my friend," Pop muttered, leaning forward to see the video closer. "That was one of Larry's favorite sayings."

"I remember that," Junior replied. "Uncle Larry used to always say stuff like that to Curtis."

"Words to live by, Larry used to call them." Pop exhaled, running his hand through his hair. His frustration was written all over his face. "Despite his mental issues, that brother of mine is one who practices what he preaches."

"So, what do we do now, Pop?" Junior asked.

"Why don't we just take them all out now? Give our guys the kill order," Orlando said. "I wouldn't lose any sleep over Vinnie's death; I can assure you that."

"No can do on that, little brother. Our people ran up on them purely by accident and without support. If they had made a move, it would have been akin to a suicide mission," I replied, playing the video again.

"We sure as hell don't want that. Where are they now?" Pop asked.

"They split up pretty fast after their love fest. Our people are following them. We should be getting reports in the next ten, fifteen minutes."

"So, who took this video? That was some pretty quick thinking," Pop commented.

"Yeah, it was," I replied, studying the images. "Rio really came through on this one."

"Rio!" Harris spoke for the first time, stepping in front of the television and blocking our view. "Rio is in Jamaica with London."

"We are well aware of that, Harris," I said.

"Obviously you're not, because my wife is still there, and now you're telling me these fucking psychos are there too. If they spot her, she's dead. That son of a bitch Larry is insane! Now, what's the plan to get her the fuck out?" Harris stepped up boldly, getting in my face. His reaction was exactly why I had tried to stay away from mentioning the names of our team with him in the room. He was already pissed that London was in proximity to danger; I didn't need him to be reminded that she was there with Daryl Graham. Harris was the most jealous dude I'd ever seen.

"Calm down, Harris. London's gonna be fine." I tried in vain to reassure him.

He pointed an accusatory finger in my face. "Easy for you to say. It's not your wife out there stalking a stone-cold killer." He looked over at Orlando in an attempt to drag him into this bullshit, then looked back at me. "Or your son we're trying to rescue."

My brother-in-law had a way of pushing people's buttons. I don't think it was intentional; it was simply that he was an asshole. There was no denying that. Why London had married him was one of the biggest mysteries of the Duncan family. But, as much of an asshole as Harris was, he was also smart, meticulous, and a damn good lawyer, all qualities that the family had benefitted from many times. I glanced over at Pop, hoping for a sign that he'd be okay with me knocking Harris's ass out, but he, in turn, glanced toward Nevada, reminding me that my son was in the room. So, I decided not to punch Harris in the face—for the time being.

"No, it's my sister, my brother, and my nephew, you prick. Now, get that finger out my face before I break it." I shoved him backward.

"Vegas, your phone," Junior said.

I ignored Harris for a second and answered the Face Time call. Rio appeared on the screen.

"What up, Ree? We got you on the big screen. Pop, Orlando, Junior, and Harris are here." I held up my phone so he could see everybody.

"Can you hear me?" Rio asked.

"Barely," I said. "There's a lot of wind noise in the background."

"Yeah, I'm at the airport. Uncle Larry, Curtis, and Kenny just left."

"Left? Where the hell did they go?" Pop shouted, standing up.

"The flight manifesto for the charter plane says they're headed to Farmingdale," Rio yelled over the background noise. "I'm getting ready to hop on a plane there now."

"Farmingdale! Out on Long Island?" I asked.

"Yeah," Rio replied. "Look, I gotta go. Have y'all heard from London?"

"No, not yet, but they should be checking in soon."

"Well, tell her I'm okay. I'm getting on this Learjet, and I guarantee we'll land before that piece of crap Uncle Larry and the boys just got on. I'll see you in a few hours."

As soon as Rio hung up, Harris started flipping out. "What the fuck did he mean, have you heard from London? Why isn't she with him?"

"Not now, Harris. Just calm the fuck down," Junior yelled then looked at our father. "So, what's our next move, Pop?" he asked.

Pop looked stressed. "Well, boys, I guess we better break out the welcoming committee. Looks like we're about to have a family reunion."

London

32

One hour earlier . . .

Uncle Larry and his boys had only been in the building about fifteen minutes before they walked out, followed by Vinnie Dash of all people. I was so surprised by Vinnie's appearance I could barely talk, let alone move. Thank God Rio had the foresight to pull out his phone and start recording, because I was there, and I still couldn't believe what I was seeing, so I knew the folks back home would have a hard time believing it.

"Rio, send that video to Vegas right now," Daryl ordered intensely. He kept looking at Rio and me, and then at my uncle and Vinnie. Finally, he shook his head and exhaled, mumbling to himself, "Nah, it's not worth the risk."

To tell the truth, I was a little offended. "If we were Vegas and Junior, or Paris and Sasha, you'd try to take them, wouldn't you?" I snapped.

"Maybe, but you're not, so there's no sense in thinking about it. Just because there's opportunity doesn't mean you should take it."

"I can fight, Daryl, and so can Rio," I told him.

"This is not about fighting, London. This is about the odds being stacked against us."

"Six on three is not great," I agreed, "but we have the element of surprise on our side."

He pointed to the top of the building, where I hadn't noticed two men standing, then at two cars, parked but still occupied, that I had also missed. "There's almost a dozen men outside of the six you're looking at in the parking lot. How many are hostile?"

"I don't know," I replied, feeling stupid all of a sudden.

"Neither do I, so why take a chance?" He began texting somebody on his phone. "Rio, there's a cab right up the street. Go get in it."

"What? Why me?" Rio protested.

"Because your uncle and cousins are headed to the parking lot, and Vinnie and his entourage are heading back inside." He put down his phone and stared at Rio. "And because even Miss Chippy wouldn't recognize you with that purple hair."

"True." Rio smirked as he reached for the door.

"Rio," Daryl said, stopping him before he got out of the van. "Whatever you do, stay out of sight and don't take any risks."

"Okay. Gotta go." He kissed me on the cheek then hopped out of the van and crossed the street. Rio got into the cab just as the Mercedes that had delivered Uncle Larry and the boys to this spot eased out of the parking lot. I held my breath, hoping my brother would be able to catch up to them. We'd been lucky to find a fast driver from the airport, but would that be the case a second time? I was finally able to breathe when I saw the cab pass by with only one car between them and the Benz. Rio waved at us from the back seat.

"So, now what do we do?" I asked.

"We wait," Daryl told me.

"How long is dat gon' be?" Our impromptu van driver looked worried. Things had been so intense that I'd almost forgotten he was there.

Daryl reached into his pocket and handed him another hundred-dollar bill. "As long as it takes. You'll get one of these every hour."

The driver took the money and wiped the frown off his face. "No problem."

About an hour and a half later, Vinnie and five other men came out of the building and got into three different vehicles.

"Follow that car." Daryl pointed to the yellow Lamborghini that Vinnie and another man were in, which was being followed by the other two cars. The driver immediately got behind them and tried to keep up, but it wasn't easy because Vinnie was flying. Soon, I realized that our surroundings had begun to change.

We were no longer in the vibrant, busy downtown of Kingston; instead, we were approaching a dilapidated urban area. When we got to a busy intersection, the driver pulled over.

"What are you doing?" I asked in a panic as I watched the Lamborghini and other cars continue down the street. "You're letting him get away."

The driver turned to Daryl and said, "Dis is as far as I can take you. I can't go no further. Tivoli Gardens is de most dangerous part of West Kingston, and I value my life. I don't know who dat white man is, but if he traveling somewhere in dere, den he is a very bad mon. White men are not welcome in dat area, especially ones with fancy cars. You are not familiar in dese parts, and someone will see you, and you will not make it back out."

"What if I give you a thousand dollars U.S.?" Daryl asked.

He shook his head. "Can't spend it if I'm dead."

Daryl nodded as if he understood what the man was saying. "Is there a hotel near that building we came from?"

"Dere is one not far from there, but it is not a fancy hotel. It is more like a motel," the driver told him.

"Take us there."

"I'm not staying in some beat-up motel," I objected.

"London, don't start." The look Daryl gave me made me feel ashamed. "Now is not the time for us to be checking into the Four Seasons. You're starting to sound like your sister Paris."

"Fine," I relented. "This is my nephew we're talking about."

"Take us to the place," Daryl told the driver; then he dialed Vegas's phone to tell him what was going on.

when they pulled their guns out on us down in Waycross," Paris interjected with her usual take-no-prisoners attitude.

"Paris makes a good point. If they give you any resistance or a reason, take them out," Pop said without hesitation.

"A'ight, Pop, don't worry. If the feds don't get them, one of our people will." I clamped a firm hand on my dad's shoulder. Although he was cool and calm, I knew this was hard for him, and I wanted him to know we had his back.

The sound of aircraft caused me to grab my binoculars and aim them at the sky. Sure enough, a small plane was approaching the tiny runway. It landed with a bounce, and before it even came to a complete stop, at least a dozen vans and unmarked cars rushed toward it, blocking its path. Officers armed with guns, wearing helmets and bulletproof vests, jumped out of the vehicles.

We all watched as the door to the plane opened and a tall, skinny guy climbed out with his hands up. Within seconds, they had him on the ground. We waited for my uncle and cousins to follow suit, but they didn't.

"You! In the plane! Come out with your hands up," a voice yelled through a loudspeaker.

"Where the fuck are they?" Paris hissed.

"They're not going down without a fight. I know my brother. He's not giving up that easy, if at all," Pop told her.

After a twenty-minute standoff, the cops took position around the plane, throwing tear gas into the opening the pilot had exited. They waited a few more minutes, but still no one exited, so they stormed the plane.

"No shots," I said, pressing the binoculars against my eyes. "Why the fuck don't I hear any shots?"

"Silencers, maybe?" Junior asked.

"No, maybe Larry and the boys, but I didn't see any of those cops with silencers." The next thing we saw were bales of marijuana being tossed out the back of the plane, one by one.

"Damn, that's a lot of weed for such a little-ass plane," Paris commented as the five officers who had stormed the plane exited—with still no sign of Uncle Larry, Curtis, or Kenny.

"What the fuck is going on? Where the hell are they?" I asked.

"Should know in a second. That's Captain Wilcox calling me now." Junior put the call on speaker so we could all listen. "Hello."

"This is Captain Wilcox, I—"

Junior didn't let the man finish his sentence. "I don't have time for pleasantries, Captain. Did you get them?"

"We got almost thirty bales of marijuana and the pilot, but your uncle and his sons weren't on the plane."

"Captain, this is LC Duncan. What do mean they weren't on the plane?" Pop cut in, moving closer to the phone. "They were on the damn thing when it took off."

"The pilot said he stopped in Maryland to refuel, and that's where they got out, Mr. Duncan," the captain replied. "I'll give your son a chance to interrogate him if you'd like, but that's about all I can do."

Pop let out a frustrated sigh. "Thank you, Captain. I think we'll take you up on that. My sons will be in touch," he said, and then Junior ended the call.

"What do we do now?" Paris asked.

"We wait until my brother makes his next move. And if I know him, it won't take very long." Pop sat back in his seat. "Vegas, you and Junior go see this pilot. I wanna know everything he knows about Larry, Vinnie, or anybody else involved with them. My brother may have given us the slip this time, but as your grandmother used to say, I've always been the smartest one of her boys."

Larry

35

"This makes no sense whatsoever. We could be in New York by now, instead of on the Jersey Turnpike," Kenny complained from the back seat. "I don't understand why we got off the plane."

"First of all, I done told you about questioning what I do. Secondly, who said I didn't have business in Jersey?" I replied, handing my cell phone to Curtis so he could read a text message I'd just received. "I been in this business a long time, Kenny, and I learned to trust my gut. My gut told me to get off that damn plane. Now, stop complaining. You're starting to aggravate me."

"No offense, Pop, but there's a first time for everything," Kenny said, pouting like a little bitch. "Maybe that feeling in your gut was a stomachache."

"Oh, really?" I replied. "Curtis, show your brother that text message."

Curtis shook his head, handing my phone to his brother. Kenny read it and became unusually silent. The message was from Jamaica John, telling us that the pilot had been arrested and the plane was confiscated by the DEA.

"Humph! Cat got his tongue now, huh?" Momma shouted to me. "He need to start listening to his father. You ain't a stupid man, and he should know that. Or else you should put your foot in his ass."

"I think you owe Dad an apology, Kenny," Curtis snapped.

Kenny hesitated for a minute then grudgingly said, "Sorry, Dad."

"I don't know why we gotta keep bumping heads, Kenny. You're my son and I love you, but you have to stop second-guessing me."

"I know, but . . ."

"But what, Kenny?" Curtis sounded a little agitated himself. "If we listened to you, we'd all be in jail right now, sharing jelly sandwiches with that damn bush pilot!"

"There you go! Tell him about himself, Curtis!" Momma shouted.

"Turn off here at this exit," I instructed Curtis. A few minutes later, we passed a sign that announced we'd just entered Mount Laurel, New Jersey. "Go in there where it says Sage Diner."

Curtis pulled into the parking lot, and we all got out.

"Momma, we'll be right back. Kenny, grab one of those bricks and put it in the bag."

The parking lot was fairly empty. Somehow, we had managed to miss the lunch crowd and beat the dinner one, so the timing was perfect. We walked inside, and sure enough, the only diners were a small group of older men sitting in a corner near the rear of the diner.

"Can I help you?" a heavyset guy in his fifties asked.

"Yeah, I'm looking for Joey the Wop," I told him.

"You mean Joey?" the guy asked again. "I take offense to the name Wop."

I gave a nod. "Yeah, whatever."

I looked past the first guy to see Joey sitting at the end of a table in back. Joey was Italian and well into his late fifties, but he still didn't look a day over thirty-five. His wavy hair was slicked back, and in typical Joey fashion, his white shirt was unbuttoned to show off the gold chains he wore.

"Come on, boys." I walked past the guy and headed for Joey.

"Larry Duncan." Joey smiled when he looked up and saw me approaching the table. "The last time I saw you, we were in a holding cell. I went to prison—"

"And I went to the fucking crazy house." I finished the sentence for him. "I'm gonna make your day, Joey. I got something really special for you."

"Oh yeah? What you got for me?" Joey asked.

"It's a gift." I had to hold back a laugh because most of the time, this was when I would pull out my gun and shoot the poor bastard. Instead, I turned to Kenny and said, "Give him the bag."

Kenny handed him the bag, and Joey looked inside to see the ki of heroin it held. He handed it to one of his men and said, "Take this in the back and test it." The man got up and disappeared through the kitchen door.

"So, Larry, you do know there's a substantial price on your head, right?" Joey asked as we waited.

"So I've been told. You planning on collecting?" He had no idea I had a hand grenade in my pocket and would have no problem pulling the trigger.

"I guess that depends on how good that dope you just gave us is. I'm a long-term thinker. Plus, I hate that bastard LC for killing my uncle Sal and cousin Tony." He sat back in his seat, and no one at the table said much, until his man returned and whispered something in his ear. Joey smiled like a kid on Christmas. "So that brick you gave me. That's a gift?"

"How much is LC selling these to you for?" I asked.

"Forty-five a brick."

I let out a long whistle, looking at him pitifully. "Wow, that's expensive!"

"Really. I thought that was pretty fair, actually. How much you selling yours for?"

"Tell you what I'm gonna do. I'm gonna let you have this one for free, and when you need more, I'm gonna let you get it for thirty."

"What?" Joey's eyes widened in surprise, and everyone at the table started shifting in their seats like they were trying to contain their excitement. I now had their full attention.

Once he had a minute to get himself under control again, Joey must have thought things through a little more, because all of a sudden he looked at me suspiciously. "Hold on. This shit right here is pure. We could step on it three, four times and nobody would know the difference. What's the catch?"

"No catch," I said calmly. "I'm just setting the new price for the market. Tell your friends. I'll be in touch in forty-eight hours." I turned to walk out.

"Larry, wait. I got a question for you. How much of this shit you got?" Joey asked.

I turned back around to face him. "More than you can sell. Spread the word, Joey. Larry Duncan is back in business." I tossed him the hand grenade with the pin still intact. He and his buddies looked like they were about to shit themselves as I walked out of the diner with Curtis and Kenny.

"Why would you sell it to him so cheap? We easily coulda got thirty-five, forty," Kenny said.

"Now, here you go questioning what I'm doing again." This boy and his damn questions. "Listen, what's our objective in this whole thing?"

"To put LC outta business and take back what is ours," Kenny replied.

"Exactly, and the best way to put your competition out of business is to undercut their prices. Just look at what Amazon and Walmart are doing to the Mom and Pop shops. Well, we are about to become the Walmart of dope. You get it?"

"Yeah, actually I think I do," he replied. "So why didn't Vinnie do this?"

"Because Vinnie is an idiot, just like his daddy. A guy like that could never beat LC. You can't beat someone you're afraid of. That's why LC can't beat me," I told them, easing back into my seat. Momma reached out and patted my shoulder, giving me her approval.

"All right, then, enough of the chit-chat. Let's get going. We've got quite a few more stops to make, boys," I announced, and we were on our way again. Everything was falling into place, and I was feeling great about my plans.

London

36

"You've gotta be kidding me," I said, feeling totally exasperated after fidgeting with the raggedy door of the so-called motel we had just checked into and finally getting it to open. I walked into the small room, stopping just beyond the doorway and dropping my bag.

"What's wrong?" Daryl's voice came over my shoulder.

"This place looks like it has bedbugs." I felt like my skin was crawling.

"Well, it's the only room they had available, and we said we wanted it. If you want, you can check into the Sheraton and I'll stay here. No need for you to suffer." He was serious, and I'm sure he was trying to be nice, but I wasn't going nowhere, especially by myself.

"What, and have you talk about how bougie I am to Vegas for the next year?" I retorted, shaking my head. "I don't think so."

"Okay, suit yourself." He pointed at the lumpy bed. "So, what are we going to do about sleeping arrangements? There's only one bed."

"You're gonna have to deal with sleeping on the floor," I answered without hesitation. My cell phone rang, saving me from having to hear him respond.

"Hello."

"London, dammit, you need to get your ass on the next flight and come home. This shit is getting out of control, and nobody seems to care about your safety but me."

"Hello to you too, Harris," I snapped.

Daryl glanced at me briefly then put his bag on the bed and pretended to search for something. I walked over to the small window to have a little more privacy. The last thing I wanted him to hear was my overly emotional husband's tirade through the phone.

"I'm not kidding, London. Rio brought his ass home, and you should've been with him. What the fuck are you thinking?" Harris ranted.

"I know he flew home. He was trailing Uncle Larry, who, by the way, we had no clue was even here until we saw him meeting with Vinnie Dash. We had to split up," I tried to explain.

"So, instead of following your uncle back to the U.S. where you knew you would be safe, you sent your brother and decided to stay in Jamaica to keep tabs on a ruthless drug lord by yourself. What kind of sense does that make?"

"First of all, when we split up, we didn't know where Larry was headed. Rio found out he was flying back to Farmingdale after he took off."

"Well, let me give you a little update, London. He didn't fly back to Farmingdale. We don't know where the fuck he or his kids are right now," Harris stated.

I frowned and turned toward Daryl. "What do you mean he didn't fly back to Farmingdale?"

"Like I said. The plane landed, and his ass wasn't on it. And before you ask, neither were Curtis or Kenny. For all we know, they could very well be back in Jamaica helping Vinnie. Which is why you need to get your ass back home."

Daryl's phone rang, and he answered. I heard him say, "What's up, Vegas?" before he stepped outside the room.

"Hello? London? Do you hear me talking to you?" Harris asked.

"I hear you, Harris, but I'm not coming home. Not yet anyway. I'm sure my father and brothers are handling the situation with Larry. If I was in any danger, they would call and make sure I came home."

"Oh, so your husband calling and telling you to come home doesn't mean shit, huh?"

"I didn't say that."

Daryl stepped back into the room. I searched his face for any signs of alarm but saw none. I grabbed a shawl out of my bag and spread it on the bed before sitting down. "Now, listen. I'm not alone. I'm safe, and I'm gonna stay here until we find my nephew. Orlando and the rest of the family risked their lives to rescue Mariah when the Dashes kidnapped her. How can I do any less?" I told him. "I'll talk to you later."

I ended the call and put Harris's number on DO NOT DISTURB. It was something a wife shouldn't have to do to her husband's number, but I didn't want to deal with hitting IGNORE when he tried calling and texting me multiple times later. For someone who barely paid me any attention when I was actually home, he sure as hell got his panties in a bunch when I wasn't there. Most times I was the dutiful wife and ended up giving in whenever he threw one of his tantrums, but something about being away, being on a mission, had me feeling like I could get used to having more independence once in a while.

"You good?" Daryl asked.

"Yeah, I'm fine. What did Vegas say?" I asked.

"He confirmed what you already know. Your uncle and cousins weren't on the plane when it landed. They got folks looking for him now."

"And what did he say about us?"

"He said nothing's changed. Complete the job that we were here to do and let him know if we need backup since Rio is home. I told him we were good for now."

"Okay, cool." I relaxed a little.

Daryl came over and sat beside me. We both remained quiet for a few moments, until I said, "So, are we gonna talk about the elephant in the room?"

He laughed and looked around. "What elephant?"

"I'm serious." I tried not to smile. "I'm talking about what happened last night in Negril."

He turned toward me, leaning his face so close to mine that I could feel his body heat. "What happened in Negril, London?"

"You know what happened," I said, biting my lip. I was breathing so hard that I could see the rise and fall of my chest with every breath I took. "You kissed me."

"You mean like this?" He reached out and touched the side of my face in an effort to guide my mouth to his, but he didn't need to, because just being this close to him was an aphrodisiac.

My desire to kiss him overwhelmed me, and it was my arms that pulled his head to mine. It was the kiss that I had been wanting for the past twenty-four hours. I savored the taste of his mouth, our tongues dancing as if they were partners in a choreographed routine it took years to master. I wanted more, and I knew that he did too. My hands pulled his shirt over his head, and my perfectly manicured fingers ran down his chiseled chest. I could feel the muscles of the six pack he worked so hard to maintain. His body was nothing like the slim frame of my husband. Daryl's was cut, firm, and thick. It was a welcome change.

His mouth eased its way to my neck, then my ears, giving me succulent kisses. The sound of his lips kissing my flesh was like some crazy sexual stimulant to my brain. I let out a moan, and he continued his kisses down to my chest. I held my breath in anticipation of his lips licking and sucking my extremely sensitive hardened nipples.

"Ahh," I exhaled when I felt the warm wetness of his tongue on one, then the other breast. I leaned back on the bed, pushing away thoughts about bedbugs or any other possible critters that might have been present as Daryl slipped my lace panties down my hips so I could kick them off. I unfastened his jeans and slipped my hand into his boxers, where his aroused manhood was waiting.

He stood up to take his pants off, and I sat up and smiled at him. With my fingers still wrapped around it, I welcomed his hardness into my mouth, taking him by surprise. I hadn't been very big on blow jobs when we were together, but I'd learned to love the power I wielded when I had a man's penis in my mouth.

"Oh, shit," he groaned, turning me on even more. I licked him from the tip of his dick to the base of his balls, and when it was all said and done, I deep-throated him to the point where he could no longer stand and gently pushed my head away.

"Fuck! When did you learn to do that?"

"I've learned a few tricks over the years," I said with a self-confident smirk.

"Oh, yeah? Well, you're not the only one who's learned a few new tricks," he said, guiding me into position. "Now it's my turn. Lay back."

I did exactly as he told me to do. Oral sex is not something you just let anyone do, because when it's bad, it's frustrating as hell. Oh, but then again, when it's good, it's like the Fourth of July, Christmas, New Year's, and your birthday all combined into one. My husband wasn't very good at it, so we tended to stay away from it, but if my recollection of Daryl's abilities was still accurate, I was about to be sent to holiday heaven.

He opened my legs, kissing down my inner thighs until I could feel his warm breath on my lips, which he licked until they were moist and glistening. I let out a loud, long moan when his tongue finally slid against my clit. He began to suck and lick it like he'd done to my nipples.

Fuck! It had been years since I'd felt that type of pleasure, and I arched my back as an invitation for him to give me even more. It didn't take long for the pressure inside me to build up to a boiling point, and before I knew it, an even more intense wave of pleasure had taken over. I would have been happy with one, but quickly one became two, and two became five, and to be honest, I stopped counting after five. *Phew!* At that point he could just send me the bill.

He continued until I begged him to stop, and that's when he flipped me over, mounting me from the back. He slipped his dick into me and grabbed a handful of hair in the process. Who the hell would have thought that would turn me on? But it did. It turned me on like a motherfucker. I clawed the sheets and called out his name as he fucked me harder and harder into a state of ecstasy. I'd always been a pleaser, so at that point, I began to concentrate on his release, but you have no idea how great it was when we both arrived at the height of pleasure and climaxed together.

Exhausted and covered in sweat, he collapsed beside me. I closed my eyes, realizing what we had just done. It had been unexpected, but certainly not unappreciated. It had been just as much of an emotional release as a physical one for me and, I suspected, for him too. I felt his lips press against my shoulder, and he reached out and pulled my body into his. My back was pressed against his chest. The sun had now set, and the room was dark.

"You okay?" he asked.

"Yeah, I'm fine," I replied.

He wrapped his arms around me, and our legs intertwined as we lay in the darkness. My mind was filled with a million thoughts, but no regrets, and I fell asleep to the sounds of his snoring beside me.

Chippy

37

"Are you nervous?" I asked Nevada. He looked a little uncomfortable, and I wasn't sure if it was because of the shirt and tie he wore, or where we were headed. We were traveling in the back of a black SUV being driven by Rodney, who also served as the head of my personal security.

"A little," he said with a shrug and a typical teenager's indifference.

"That's a good thing," I told him.

"It is? Why would being nervous be a good thing, Grandma?" He had such an innocent look to him.

"It's healthy anxiety, and that's normal. People think of nerves as a bad thing, but that's not always the case. Those butterflies we sometimes feel in our stomach don't always mean something bad. It just means you're about to do something unfamiliar, and that feeling will help keep you on your toes. You're more aware."

Nevada sat back and seemed to relax a little bit. "Hmmmm, I never thought of it that way. I remember the day my mom was bringing me to meet my father and my Duncan family. I was so nervous that I almost threw up. I didn't know what was gonna happen."

"You had every right to be nervous. But I hope it was nerves and not fear, Nevada," I said. Since arriving, he had seemed to enjoy our family and fit right in. I had never seen any indication that he was uncomfortable among us.

"No, Grandma. I'm a Duncan. I ain't scared of anything." He shook his head. "It definitely wasn't fear."

I couldn't help but laugh. He might not have been raised by his father in his younger years, but he'd definitely inherited his courage. "That's good."

"As soon as I walked in the house and saw you, I felt like I belonged."

"You do belong, Nevada, and I'm so glad that you're living with us. You're right. You are a Duncan, and that is both powerful and special," I told him. "Which is why you're going to this Beautillion."

"I guess, but, Grandma, I already have manners. You say so all the time."

"This isn't just about manners, Nevada. This is formal etiquette training. Being a part of Jack and Jill is about being a part of tradition. It's about culture and becoming exposed to the finer things in life."

"But being in this beau–beau . . ." he stammered.

"Beautillion."

"Beautillion," he repeated. "Is this really necessary?"

"Yes, Nevada. Trust me, you will enjoy it. This is a rite of passage that will introduce you to society as a man of dignity, strength, and grace."

"Doesn't my being a Duncan tell society all of that?"

"Yes, but participating in the Beautillion Ball and learning how to waltz—"

"Waltz? Wait a minute, Grandma. You ain't say nothing about my having to learn how to waltz." Nevada shook his head.

"What did you think you'd be doing at the ball, Nevada? Crunk dancing?"

Nevada laughed so hard that he snorted. "You mean krump dancing, Grandma?"

"Crunk, krump, whatever you young people are calling it these days. You won't be doing that. You'll be waltzing. And it'll also give you the chance to spend time with some young ladies."

"Oh, really?" A smile crept up on his face. He was definitely his father's son.

"Who do you think you'll be learning to waltz with? You have to have a partner. And I know how much you enjoy the young ladies. I've seen you checking them out at church."

He smiled. "Naw, Grandma, they were checking me out."

I shook my head at him. "Of that I'm sure. You're a very handsome young man. Now, are you ready to get measured for your tuxedo?"

He groaned. "It's not like I have a choice."

"Glad we understand each other," I said, looking out the window as we pulled up to the Miracle Mile shopping center in Manhasset. The trail car pulled up behind us. The driver opened the door, and Nevada climbed out first then waited as I eased out of the SUV.

"I'll be right in after I park, Mrs. Duncan," Rodney told me.

"That's okay. Stay in the car. We won't be in here long. He's just being measured, and then we'll be done. You don't have to come in if you don't want to."

Rodney looked at the front entrance, then back at me with skepticism. "I don't know. Vegas said—"

"It's fine. Louis and Tito have already gotten out of the other car. It'll take all of fifteen minutes," I assured him. "I'll call when we're ready, and you can pick us up right here. Besides, if anything happens, which I'm sure that it won't, Nevada can take care of me."

Nevada beamed with pride as he put his arm around my shoulder. "Yeah, Rodney, I got her."

Nevada and I set off toward the designer men's store where Rio had made us an appointment with his personal tailor. Just as we were about to enter the store, I saw her walking toward us on the sidewalk, where she had stopped to look at one of the window displays. Had it been anyone else, I probably would have admired the couture pantsuit she wore, along with the exquisite diamond brooch, but there was nothing admirable about Donna. I had some choice words for her, and she needed to hear them.

"Wait right here for a moment," I told Nevada then made my way over to her. It was obvious by the way she jumped that I was the last person she expected to see.

"Oh, Chippy. Hello." She acted like we were old friends who had just bumped into one another.

"Don't hello me," I snarled. "I don't know why you keep forgetting this, so consider this a reminder or even a warning: stay the fuck away from my family. I mean it. LC told me about your little meeting."

"The meeting I had with LC was concerning my family, not yours." Her voice remained calm and pleasant, which caused the anger in me to rise even higher.

"The only family you have is whoever the latest pitiful soul who was dumb enough to put a ring on your finger happens to be."

"This isn't about a man, Chippy. This is about my daughter, and unlike you and LC, who have no problem sending your children off on suicide missions all in the name of Duncan family business, I want to make sure my daughter is safe and sound."

"Daughter? You mean the same daughter who was raised by her father and you barely kept in contact with since she was thirteen because you were too busy jetsetting around the world with random men? The same daughter who's lived at our house for the past three years and you never once stopped by to see until your nosy ass heard my husband had been shot?" I snapped. "Or are you talking about the daughter who cried herself to sleep in my arms because her mother showed her up at a charity auction? Is that the daughter you're talking about? Because I'm more her mother than you are."

I could see the anger in her eyes when they met mine. I had struck a nerve, which had been my intention. I was tired of everyone, including LC, acting like Donna had position in our family. She only had what I was willing to let her have and nothing else.

"You are not her mother. You will never be her mother. Do you understand me? That's my fucking daughter. She's all I got. You already stole one of my children, but I'll never let you have both, bitch," she said, seething with a barely suppressed rage now.

"Stole?" I took a step toward her, lowering my voice. "If I recall, you abandoned him, and his father and I saved his life—and yours." I gave her a superior smirk. "Now, if you ever contact my husband and threaten him with your bullshit, I'll—"

She cut me off, matching my expression with a haughty one of her own. Neither one of us was willing to back down; it had always been that way between us. "You'll what? Call my bluff? Keep it up and your little family secret won't be a secret anymore."

Without thinking, I lunged and grabbed her by the collar, slapping her as hard as I could three times. Her eyes widened in surprise, and she gasped. The next thing I knew, her hand was in my hair, and she was yanking it, so I did the same. We both stumbled and fell against the window of the store we were in front of, and people began yelling.

"Grandma! Grandma! Let her go!" Nevada grabbed me from behind and pulled me off her, while the rest of our security team grabbed Donna. "Grandma, calm down!"

Once I was free, I stood up and readjusted my clothes.

"You've lost your mind!" Donna yelled as she struggled to get away from the grip of my security team. "Let me go, you creep!"

"Are you okay, Grandma?" Nevada asked, still holding my arm.

I nodded, out of breath but happy I'd gotten in a few good shots. "I'm fine. Come on. Let's go before we miss your appointment with the tailor."

We started to walk away, but then I stopped and turned back to Donna to get in the last word. "By the way, I will tell Junior myself before I let you destroy my family. How do you think he'll react when he finds out the woman who birthed him abandoned him at birth? Then again, him and Sasha will have a lot to talk about, won't they?"

"It wasn't abandonment and you know it! You are playing with a mother's love, Chippy!" she screamed at me. "You of all people should know that's a dangerous game, so stay away from Sasha and I'll stay away from Junior."

"Call it what you want, Donna, but the bottom line is you were incapable of caring for a child, and *you* know *that*. If LC and I hadn't stepped in, who knows what could have happened to that baby."

My men had let her go but were hovering nearby in case she tried something again, so Donna shot them the middle finger then picked up the bags she had dropped during our tussle and walked away.

"Grandma, what was she talking about? About Uncle Junior?" Nevada asked when she was gone. My poor baby looked so confused.

I put my hands on either side of his face and stared him in the eyes. "Nevada, remember I told you that being a Duncan means there are some things you may see and hear that are not to be talked about?"

"Yes." He nodded.

"Well, what you saw happen, and more importantly, what you heard is something you will take to your grave. This is our little secret. Do you understand?" I felt the tears forming in the corners of my eyes, but not one fell.

"I understand," he said and hugged me tight.

We started walking toward the men's shop, Nevada keeping a protective arm around my shoulder. "You know, Grandma," he said before we entered the store, "I don't know if what just happened really fits in with that dignity and grace stuff you were just telling me about the Beautillion."

I looked at him and saw a sly smile on his face. He sort of had a point, but I wasn't about to tell him that. I playfully swatted his hand away. "Nice try, Nevada, but you are still going to Beautillion whether you like it or not."

He gave me a kiss on the cheek and opened the door for me. "After you, ma'am."

God, I loved that boy.

38

Chippy was in the den, drinking a glass of wine and listening to Al Green when we got home. She barely looked up when I walked in. I took off my jacket and loosened my tie then poured myself a drink. I could hear my children mumbling in the living room, and I was sure they would make their way into the den soon.

"Hey." I sat on the sofa beside my wife and took a long swallow of bourbon.

"Hey."

I could hear the irritation in her voice, and I wondered if one of the kids had called and given her an update about what had happened at the airfield. I waited for a few moments, expecting her to start fussing, but she didn't, which made me realize that something else was wrong.

I moved a little closer and said, "Okay, Chippy. What's wrong? You got the old school music playing, and you ain't saying much."

When she turned to me, I saw a red mark on her cheek and scratches on her neck.

I sat up and leaned in to get a closer look at her injuries. "What the hell happened to you?"

"I'm fine, LC. Calm down. I just ran into someone who never fails to bring out the old me." She sighed loudly and took a sip of wine.

"Let me guess. You ran into Donna."

"I did. And what the hell happened to you? You walked in and went straight for the top-shelf bottle," she said, gesturing to my glass, filled almost to the brim with bourbon.

"Well, while you were slugging it out with Donna, I was out looking for Larry and the boys," I told her.

"I take it you didn't find them."

I swallowed the rest of my drink and was about to explain what happened when Vegas walked in, with the rest of his siblings behind him.

"Hey, Mom," Vegas said.

"Hey, Vegas. Junior, Orlando . . ." Chippy frowned. "Rio, what are you doing here? Why aren't you in Jamaica?"

"I followed Uncle Larry back here."

"Followed him from where?"

Rio looked over at me, and I nodded, letting him know it was okay to give her the details. Sometimes I liked to leave out a few things if I knew they would upset her too much. Anything that put her kids in extreme danger was usually on that list.

"Uncle Larry was in Jamaica," Rio told her.

"What the hell was Larry in Jamaica for?" She put down her wine and stood up.

"He was meeting with Vinnie Dash, and when—"

"This isn't making any sense. Where the hell is London?" Chippy demanded to know.

"She's in Kingston," Vegas said in an attempt to calm his mother down and save Rio from her wrath at the same time. "But Daryl is with her."

"Chippy, London is fine. She and Daryl are keeping an eye out on Vinnie, while Rio was instructed not to let Larry out of his sight," I explained.

"Well, you said you couldn't find Larry, LC. I'm so confused with all of this." Chippy folded her arms.

Vegas's phone rang, and he stepped out to take the call.

I pulled her down to sit beside me and explained what had taken place over the past few hours.

"Well, what are we going to do, LC?" Chippy asked me when I was finished.

"I don't know."

"What do you mean you don't know? We need a plan." The worried look on her face mirrored exactly how I was feeling.

"I mean I don't know. There is no plan at this point," I told her. The room became silent.

"Pop, things just got a little dicey," Vegas said when he came back.

"Now what?" I sighed.

"I just heard from our Dominican friends. They just re-upped with Uncle Larry. He sold them five kilos for thirty thousand a piece," he said.

"How? That's damn near what we pay," Junior said.

"Damn it! He knows what he's doing. He's undercutting our price," I said, starting to get a clearer picture of what Larry was up to.

"Yeah, but at those prices, none of us will make any money," Orlando said.

"I think that's the point, son," I explained. "Larry doesn't care about making money. All he wants to do is hurt us."

"Well, is the product any good?" Orlando asked.

Vegas delivered bad news. "According to my people, it's just as pure as ours, maybe a little purer."

"Where the hell did Uncle Larry get that kinda dope from?" Junior shook his head in amazement.

"He got it from Vinnie Dash," I said matter-of-factly as I stood up. "Vegas."

"Yeah, Pop."

"I wanna know where the fuck Vinnie Dash got his product from and I wanna know how much of it he has."

Vegas nodded, a grimace on his face. "So do I, Pop. So do I."

Ruby

39

Once again, I had woken up from a dream about Orlando that was so real I could still feel his lips and hands on my body. It was bad enough that I saw him every time I looked in Vincent's face, but now he was haunting my dreams on a daily basis. I decided that what I needed was some retail therapy. Shopping was the ultimate stress reliever, and I hadn't been shopping in a while. So, I called Vinnie and told him that Vincent and I were going out for the afternoon.

"Where're you going?" he asked.

"I'm just going to pick up a few tings from downtown, Vinnie. Maybe a dress and some underwear for you and Vincent. I won't be gone long. I promise," I told him.

"You can't go by yourself," Vinnie stated, sounding more like my father than my husband. "Take Henry and Charles with you."

I was glad he couldn't see the disgusted expression on my face. Henry and Charles were two of the men that spent more time smoking weed and harassing the women that walked by the house than protecting Vincent and me, and I couldn't stand them, especially Charles, who was always ogling me. There was no way I was going anywhere with them.

"I don't know where dey are. Besides, I already asked Blake to take us," I told him, hoping that Blake, one of the few men who was still around from when my brother was in charge, was nearby.

"Okay, that's fine. Blake knows what to do. Oh, and boxers not briefs, Ruby."

"I know, Vinnie. I'm not de one who buys briefs. You are."

"That's right, isn't it? Okay then, I'll see you later. Be careful. I love you."

"Love you too," I told him, relieved that he hadn't put up much of a fight.

Half an hour later, we were climbing into the back of Blake's jeep.

"Are we going to buy toys?" Vincent asked me.

"Maybe," I told him as I fastened his seat belt.

"Vincent, my man. How ya been?" Blake greeted my son with a big grin.

"Hey, Blake!" Vincent smiled back. "We're going to buy toys."

"I know." Blake nodded.

"I said maybe," I corrected them. "And only if you're a good boy."

"He's always a good boy," Blake said as the jeep pulled forward.

Blake had been around it seemed like forever. He was one of the last links between my brother's regime and Vinnie's so-called new Jamaican posse. He was a laid back, friendly guy who I always felt comfortable around. Where many of Vinnie's employees gawked and stared at my body, some even going so far as to make lewd comments that they thought I didn't hear, Blake was always respectful and pleasant, and on more than one occasion, I had overheard him putting people in their place. Vincent also liked him a lot. I was glad, when we moved from the States back to Jamaica, that Blake was one of the guys who made the move with us.

"Blake, you can pull over dere," I said. We were at a stop light almost at the edge of town. It was a rough area, and I knew it wasn't the safest part of town, but there was a small boutique on the corner with a beautiful dress hanging in the window.

"Dis is not a good place to shop," he said, giving me a warning look in the rearview mirror.

"I just wan' see how much de dress is, Blake. It's fine," I assured him.

He pulled the jeep over and parked right in front of the store.

"I'll be right back. You wait right here for Mommy," I told Vincent.

"But what about my toy?" Vincent asked. His voice quivered, and I could see he was about to throw a fit, which was exactly what I didn't want to happen.

"Dere ain't no toys in dat store, son. Dere ain't noting in dere but fancy lady tings. Ya don't wanna go in dere, I promise," Blake told him. Vincent didn't look like he believed him.

"If you stay here and be good, we'll go and get you a toy when we leave," I said, which was enough to make him sit back in his seat and calm down a little.

"Okay," he said quietly.

I quickly walked into the store. There were several racks filled with gorgeous items, but I knew I only had so much time before Vincent would be asking for me. I looked around for a salesperson but didn't see anyone.

"Hello?" I called out.

"I'll be right out," a woman yelled from the back, and a few moments later, she appeared. "How are you? How can I help you?" She sounded friendly.

"Hello. I wanted to know about de dress in de window. De green one," I said.

"Oh, yes. Dat's one of my favorite dresses. I can help you in one minute. I have someone in de dressing room, and I'll be right back to get one fo' ya," she said.

"Okay, maybe I should come back. My son is in de car—"

"No, no, I'll be right back," she sang as she rushed off.

I began admiring a few of the dresses on the racks and listened as she assisted another customer.

"Are you sure dis looks okay?" I heard another woman ask.

"It looks beautiful. It's de perfect dress fo' de occasion," the saleswoman told her. "Ya brudda would be proud."

"I can't believe I'm picking out a dress fo' his funeral." The other woman sniffed, and I could hear that she was crying. My heart sank, because I knew exactly how she felt. I recalled having to do the same thing.

"Ya will be fine, child. We are all sad dat Leviticus is gone. He was a good man."

At the sound of the name Leviticus, I felt my stomach tighten. It was the same name as one of Randy's childhood friends. I waited anxiously so that I could confirm if it was the same man. The saleswoman returned, this time with her arm around the customer she had been helping, and it confirmed what I had feared. They were talking about Randy's friend.

"Mary," I said, my eyes filling with tears. She was Leviticus's sister, and like our brothers, we'd gone to school together. "Oh my God. Did I hear right? Leviticus is dead? I'm so sorry."

Mary looked over at me, holding the black dress. Her face went from one filled with sadness to one full of anger. "Yes, he's dead, but me no need no pity from you or your crocodile tears."

"What? What do you mean?" I was confused by her reaction.

"Don't play games. It was ya man dat killed him," she spat at me.

"Oh, Jesus." The saleswoman grabbed the crucifix hanging around her neck, kissed it, and made the sign of the cross.

"Dat's not true. My husband would do no such ting. You are mistaken."

"I know you, and I know your husband de white man. He killed Leviticus de same way he killed ya brudda Randy. Everyone knows dis. Randy was a good man de same as Leviticus. Dey were friends from grade school. Ya marry a white man who kills our people, and now ya wan' say you sorry? You go to hell wit' ya sorry, because we no want it," she yelled, tears streaming down her face. I recognized her pain.

"My brudda was killed by someone else, not my husband. And he didn't kill your brudda either. You don't know what ya talkin' 'bout." I shook my head at her, telling myself that it was grief over her brother's death that was causing her to say these horrible things about Vinnie.

"No, you don't know! Everyone knows. Everyone except you!" She turned to the saleswoman. "You know who killed Big Randy over in the U.S., don't you?"

The saleswoman looked at her, then me, and said, "Dey say it was his partner, a white man, who killed him."

Not wanting to hear anything else, I ran out of the store and snatched the door of the jeep open so hard that it surprised both Vincent and Blake.

"What's wrong, Momma?" Vincent asked.

"Drive," I said. Blake put the jeep in gear, and we drove for about five minutes before I said in a whisper, "Did Vinnie kill Leviticus?"

Blake's eyes widened, and he looked away.

"Answer me, Blake. You're one of de only people in de world dat I truly trust. I need you to tell me, please," I begged him.

Blake nodded his head slowly. "Yes, Vinnie killed him."

My eyes welled up with tears. "And Randy? Did he kill my brother Randy?"

"De truth is I don't know, ma'am," he finally said.

"Well, den I need you to find out, and Blake, dis is between you and me. I don't want anyone knowing 'bout it." I glared over at him until he relented and gave me a slight nod.

Vegas

40

I sat in Pelham Park and watched for almost an hour as one man after another sat at the rusty card table and lost their money playing heads up dominos with the overweight champion. He was lively and loud as he conquered them one by one. As the sun began to set, I stood and made my way over and sat in the empty chair across from him, placing five crisp hundred-dollar bills in the center of the table.

"Shuffle 'em up," I said.

"Five hundred dollars? You sure you wanna lose dis, mon?" He laughed, spreading the black pieces across the table.

"I ain't worried," I told him and began selecting my bones.

"Is your loss. Not mine." He shrugged, placing a stack of bills next to mine.

Once the game began, he barely looked up from the table. Each move I made was strategic and calculated. Studying him in that short amount of time had given me a preview of his skills. I'd had one of the best domino educations in the world—jail. Just as he had during the previous games I'd watched him play, he was talking shit in the beginning; but as the game moved on, he became quiet, and his boastful rants disappeared. A crowd gathered around us to get a closer look. I could sense his frustration, and it made my victory even sweeter when I simply said the word, "Domino."

It was at that moment that he decided to look up to see exactly who had broken his winning streak. I slid back my hood, and he boldly removed my sunglasses. He recognized me immediately, and his eyes widened in terror.

"Jamaica John." I smiled at him.

"Fuckin' Duncan," he hissed.

He tried to slide his chair back and reach into his pocket, but his belly was so big that it got caught on the edge of the table, shaking it and almost causing it to flip over. He stumbled back down into his seat, looking around.

"Looking for your men? My guys took them for a ride. You'll find them over by Yankee Stadium," Orlando said as he reached around him from behind and took out his gun.

"What de fuck you want, Vegas?" He looked scared but tried to hide it.

"I wouldn't take that tone with me, John. I'm really not in the mood. Now, I need some information, and you're going to give it to me."

"I no got no information fo' ya. Sorry," he said.

Orlando kicked the leg of his chair, causing him to fall to the ground. I got up and stood over him. "Get your fat ass up."

Jamaica John struggled, and I looked over at my brother, who was trying not to laugh. I almost felt bad for him as he used the folding chair to lean on as he pushed his large body off the ground.

"Where is—"

"I don't know nothin'," John insisted before I could even get the name out.

"I haven't even told you what I want."

"Whatever it is, I don't know shit."

"Oh, you know." I sighed. "Now, tell me, where the fuck is my uncle?"

A strange look came across his face. "Your uncle?"

"Yeah, you thought I was gonna ask about your fucking boss, Vinnie Dash. I know he's in Tivoli Gardens, so I ain't thinking about his ass right now, John. Right now I'm more concerned with the whereabouts of my uncle Larry."

"Why would I know where he is?" John asked.

"Because I know he's been working with Vinnie, and I know that you're the one who's been helping him."

Once again John's eyes grew wide. "No, I ain't—"

"Listen, before you lie to me again, I need you to know we talked with your nephew, Gus. He's pretty much filled us in on everything."

"Dat is a lie. My nephew is no snitch." John glared at me.

"Really? Well, he told the feds all about how you set up the meeting with Vinnie and Larry and arranged for him to fly Larry and his sons over to Jamaica and back with a whole bunch of dope. Now, we can do this one of two ways: one, I can haul your fat ass over to the feds, or two, I'm sure you know all about the bounty on my uncle's head right now."

John looked even more confused. "What are you saying?"

"Man, I told you to just offer that reward to Gus. We're wasting our time with this dude," Orlando yelled.

I raised my hand and played my part in our good cop/bad cop exchange. "Hold on a minute, O. Let the man at least answer us." Looking at Jamaica John, I asked, "What's it gonna be?"

"Look, Vegas, I don't know where ya uncle is at. Dat's de truth, mon. De numba I had fo' him is not workin' no mo'." John shrugged, but I swear I could see him trembling beneath all that fat.

"But he will call you eventually." I pulled out a chair and sat directly in front of him, looked him in the eye, and said, "Fine. You don't know where my uncle is. But you do know how the hell Vinnie got all that dope he sold him. Let's talk about that."

London

41

We had been staked out at a small outdoor cafe for almost two hours. I was on my third cappuccino, and Daryl was on his fourth cup of tea. The cafe was located directly across the street from the building where Uncle Larry and Vinnie had met up. Daryl had decided that returning to the forbidden neighborhood Vinnie disappeared into would be like looking for a needle in a haystack. The only other lead we had was to return to the downtown building in hopes that we would see him again. Now that our team had made their way from Negril to Kingston, we set up around-the-clock surveillance of the building. As luck would have it, just as our shift started, Daryl and I spotted the same yellow Lamborghini that Vinnie had been driving, parked in the building's lot. Instead of going inside in search of him, we sat at the coffee shop and waited for him to come out.

"I'm not gonna lie. I forgot how good we were together," I said to Daryl. My body was still feeling the effects of round two this morning.

"Yeah, we've always had crazy chemistry. I think we both know that." He reached across the table and covered my hand with his. "Look, I ain't trying to mess this up right now, because we're both enjoying it, but you do know that eventually we have to go home."

I nodded sadly. "I don't wanna think about that."

"Neither do I, but—"

I touched my finger to his lips. "Sssshhhh. You said you didn't want to mess it up."

His emotion-filled eyes met mine. "This is a very dangerous game we're playing."

His words sank in, and that warm, satisfying sense of contentment that I'd felt since waking up in his arms began to fade. My eyes darted from his face back to the building in an effort to avoid his stare.

"Oh, wow, Daryl. Vinnie's walking out the door. We've gotta go." I stood up and placed some money on the table.

We quickly made our way back to the rental car as inconspicuously as possible. Vinnie pulled out of the parking lot, followed by another dark-tinted SUV, and we eased behind them. Daryl continued to maintain a loose tail.

"He's headed back to Tivoli Gardens," Daryl said.

"I don't care if he's headed to the moon. Just don't lose him." We had just crossed over into the neighborhood when a large box truck suddenly reversed from an alley and stopped in the middle of the road, preventing us from going any farther.

"What the fuck is he doing?" I said, unable to see around it. "Blow the horn."

"Get the fuck out of the way!" Daryl yelled as he leaned on the horn.

A loud rapping on the driver's side window startled both of us. Daryl lowered the window slightly so that he could hear the tall, scary-looking guy with shoulder-length dreadlocks hovering next to the car. I couldn't help but notice the long machete bat he was swinging back and forth in his hand.

"Are ya lost, mon?" he asked. That's when I noticed three other machete-wielding men on my side of the car.

"Nah, man, we're not lost. We're tourists, and we just happened to make a wrong turn," Daryl told him. I touched Daryl's arms as a small group of six or seven men came and stood beside the one holding the bat. Now there were a total of ten men surrounding the car.

"Dat mean ya lost. Let me help ya, mon. De way out is dat way, and dat's de only way you should be headin'. Ya understand?" He pointed the machete in the same direction we had come from.

"That way. Got it," Daryl said, putting the car in reverse and turning around.

"We're leaving?" I asked him.

"Yep."

"Are we gonna come back later tonight?"

"Not unless we have a death wish. This is not a place where we wanna get caught after dark."

LC

42

I stepped out of the back of the SUV, along with Orlando, Junior, and Harris. We were then followed into a sleek Canal Street office building by my four bodyguards.

"LC Duncan to see Jun Cheng. He should be expecting me," I told the young woman sitting at the reception desk.

"One moment, Mr. Duncan. You may have a seat over there if you'd like." She pointed to the waiting area.

"I'll stand and wait here."

She picked up the phone and announced us to whomever was on the other end, then said, "You can follow me this way."

I ordered the bodyguards to sit tight as the rest of us followed the woman down a long corridor, and she opened the door to a massive office, where Jun Cheng sat in an oversized chair. Two of Cheng's men were positioned near the door, while two other men stood on both sides of him.

"Jun Cheng." I nodded at him.

His face was emotionless as he stared at me silently, causing me to wonder if he was going to greet us. Finally, after a few seconds, he stood and said, "Mr. Duncan, I was expecting Vegas to be with you."

"These are my sons, Orlando and Junior. I think you know my son-in-law, Harris, who is our attorney."

Without offering his hand, he said, "You gentlemen may have a seat."

I waited until everyone was seated before I spoke. "Jun, your family has known me for a long time, and I wanted to make sure you knew I had nothing to do with your father's and uncle's deaths."

"That is what Vegas tells me, but I must admit, I find it hard to believe that your brother killed them without your knowledge."

"I can understand your point of view, and if I were you, I might come to the same conclusion, which is why I wanted to clear the air and bring you proof of my innocence." I gestured to Harris, who opened his briefcase and handed Jun a folder.

"My brother has been in a mental hospital for almost fifteen years," I explained as he thumbed through the folder. "Nine months ago, they somehow miraculously deemed him competent and released him without my knowledge or consent."

Neither Jun nor his associates seemed impressed, until I ripped open my shirt dramatically, revealing the scars from the bullets that had been removed from my chest. "He then came to my place of business and shot me three times." Harris handed him another folder with my medical records. "I should have been his first victim, not your loved ones."

Jun sat back in his chair, contemplating my words. "I'd heard you were shot. My father even came to visit you; although, like me, I'm sure he did not know it was your brother who shot you." Jun handed the paperwork back to Harris. "I'm glad you came by to explain this. It has helped to stop what could have been an uneasy conflict between us." The men beside him stepped back a fraction of an inch, and the tension in the air came down a notch.

"Well, I'm glad to hear that," I said. "If you didn't know, we've put a sizable bounty on my brother's head."

"We did know. It's the only reason we were willing to meet with you." He leaned forward, finally offering his hand. "Thank you for coming."

I grasped his hand firmly. "I have something else for you to see."

Orlando took out his phone and showed Jun the video.

"My brother and his sons are the men on the right in the video. The man on the left is—"

"Vinnie Dash," he said, finishing my sentence. "Why is your brother with Vinnie Dash?" Jun looked over at me, and I could see his anger growing. "Did Vinnie have something to do with my father's death?"

"We don't know that, but we do know that Vinnie has supplied him with enough heroin to make a deal with the Dominicans and a few of our best customers," Orlando told him. "Well over a hundred kilos."

"Where would Vinnie Dash get that much product?" Jun asked with a frown.

"According to our sources, it's yours," Orlando said.

"How? We haven't provided him with any product." Jun glanced at his associates curiously.

"Are you missing any product?" Orlando asked.

Jun motioned toward the man on his right, and when he leaned down, the two began whispering in their native language.

"We did have a container on a freighter that was lost in the recent hurricane. It was being shipped to Puerto Rico. My father wrote if off as a casualty of business, but perhaps it wasn't," Jun fumed.

Orlando informed him, "From what we've been told, that container you're talking about ain't at the bottom of the ocean. It somehow turned up at a container terminal in Kingston."

Jun again motioned for the man on his right and whispered something. This time, the man left the room. "How do we know that container was ours?"

Orlando reached into his pocket and pulled out two small vials, which he placed on the glass coffee table in front of us. "You probably don't know this, but I am a chemist and a licensed pharmacist. These are samples of heroin: one we got from a Dominican street dealer yesterday, and the other from one of your associates last night. I tested them, and the chemical breakdown of both are exactly the same. There's no mistaking that the dope my uncle got from Vinnie belongs to you."

Jun stared at the two vials sitting on the table, then looked up at me.

"He knows what he's talking about, Jun. It cost me a fortune to put him through pharmacy school, and he graduated at the top of his class." I chuckled, attempting to lighten the mood. It didn't work, because now Jun looked like he was ready to rip someone's head off. Actually, that wasn't a bad thing, because I could help him direct his anger right where we needed it.

"Obviously, you didn't come here unprepared. What do you have in mind?" Jun asked.

"We have a plan that I'm sure you will find beneficial to both of us. Harris and I have another meeting to attend. Orlando will stay here and give you the details," I said as I stood. "Thank you."

When we exited the building and were in the car, Harris turned to me and said, "Are you crazy? You're going to leave Orlando by himself to handle something like this? LC, we have to make sure nothing goes wrong. You should have stayed."

"Calm down, Harris. Orlando can handle this, and Junior's there. Me and you have bigger fish to fry right now."

"We do?" Harris replied, looking confused and a little scared.

Donna

43

"Sasha, dammit! Stop acting like a child and answer the phone!" I shouted into my cell as I pulled into my driveway. I'd been calling and texting my bratty daughter nonstop ever since the charity auction she'd stomped out of, but she wouldn't answer. I was starting to think she'd blocked me, which was no way to treat your mother, no matter how mad you are at her. Hell, for all she knew, this could be the last call I ever made—or worse, I could be dead in the morning. And all this because I'd outbid her on some doctor who could barely keep it up.

After leaving a scolding message, I took out the endless number of shopping bags I had managed to collect after my trip to Roosevelt Field Mall, and headed toward the house. I stepped inside my townhome, the heels of my Oscar de la Renta pumps clicking on the marble floor as I walked the short distance to the alarm system keypad. I didn't hear the beeping noise that normally came from the wall panel, and when I reached it, I saw that the alarm had been deactivated. I could have sworn I turned the alarm on when I left the house that afternoon, but I chalked it up to a senior moment. Then suddenly, I stopped, sensing that there was movement in the house and I wasn't alone.

"Sasha?" I called out. Maybe she'd decided to grace me with her presence, I thought for a second, but as I slowly moved into the den to investigate, my heart seized with fear.

"Who the hell are you? What the hell are you doing in my home?" I gasped, backing away from a man I'd never seen before, only to spot another man standing on the opposite side of the room. I dropped the shopping bags and clutched my expensive purse against my chest with both hands. No way was I giving up my shit. "What do you want?"

Neither of them said a word as they began moving toward me. *Fuck!* Was I about to die? No! I was a survivor. No way was I going to lose my life over shit that could be replaced. I held my handbag out toward them.

"You want money? Here, take my purse. There's probably a thousand dollars in there and fifteen credit cards. The purse itself is worth four thousand dollars."

Instead of taking it from my hands, the two men just crept closer, staring at me. That's when I realized maybe it wasn't money they were after.

"Please, please don't rape me," I begged them. "My keys are in the purse. You can take my car too. It's the Maserati parked right out front."

Then, the sound of laughter came from the doorway leading into the dining room. I looked over to see a face I hadn't seen in years. This time, I dropped the purse in the middle of the floor.

"Oh my God, if you could see your face," he said, still laughing.

"Larry, you fucking bastard, where the hell did you come from?" I stood staring at my ex-brother-in-law as hard as the two strange men had been staring at me. I hadn't seen Larry in almost eighteen years. As a matter of fact, his brother Lou and I were still together, and Sasha was just a toddler at the time. "And how did you get into my house?"

"The front door. You know I've always been resourceful. I picked the lock."

Okay, that answered one question, but how the hell did he manage to get past a state-of-the-art burglar alarm system?

"And you and Lou always used Sasha's birthday as your alarm code," he said, answering the question I hadn't voiced out loud. He smiled as he walked over and tried to give me a hug that I did not reciprocate. "How are you, Donna? Now, you can believe it or not, but I missed you."

"I thought you were . . ."

I didn't want to say it, so he said it for me. "In the nuthouse?"

I shrugged my shoulders. "Well, yeah. That's what I was told. They said you went bonkers."

"From who? LC?"

"No, Lou told me a few years before he died."

"So, what's up, Donna? You don't look happy to see me," Larry said, sounding like this was just a normal social call instead of the bizarre break-in that it was.

"I'm not used to finding uninvited guests in my house, Larry," I said, not hiding my annoyance. Now that I wasn't as scared, my attitude was back in full force. "And who the fuck are these scary-ass guys?" I glanced over at the two men.

"Those are my boys. You may not remember my youngest, Kenny, but you remember Curtis, don't you?"

Now that I took a closer look, there was no mistaking the menacing man I'd spotted first. His face was a perfect combination of Larry and NeeNee. "Yeah, I remember bad-ass Curtis. He gave me the best laugh of my life when he cut off both of London's pigtails." I chuckled at the memory. "I thought Chippy was gonna lose her damn mind the way she was jumping around screaming about those damn pigtails."

"Damn, I forgot all about that." He joined in my laughter. "She wasn't so high and mighty that day, was she?"

"She sure as hell wasn't. And poor London looked a hot mess for a few months." Despite our earlier feuds during our younger years, what most people didn't know was that Larry and I got along. Maybe it was because we were both outcasts, or maybe he just decided I was here to stay. I don't know why, but I could relate to him more than anyone else in the family besides Lou.

"You still drink bourbon? Let me fix you a drink," I offered.

"I sure do, but I actually have a surprise for you." He took me by the arm and led me into the dining room, where I saw the table had been set for four, and dinner was prepared like it was the most normal thing in the world.

"How long have you been in my house, Larry?" I asked.

"Oh, I don't know. Maybe ten, fifteen minutes after you left this afternoon." He sat down at the table then patted the seat beside him for me to sit. "Come sit."

Although I didn't like the fact he'd broken into my house, after all these years, I had sense enough to do what Larry instructed. He had never done anything to harm me, but it was no secret that he had done some unthinkable things to others.

"Here you go." He passed me a glass of wine. "Cabernet Sauvignon from Napa Valley. Your favorite."

I took the glass from him but didn't drink. "Thank you?" I said warily.

"Don't worry, Donna. I didn't put anything in there to hurt you. You can drink it." He laughed and pointed to the silver ice bucket. "Curtis, pass me that bottle. See here? Look. It's Harlan Estate."

I stared at the bottle. Sure enough, it was from my favorite vineyard. In normal circumstances I might have been impressed that he'd remembered my preferences, but all I could think about was what reason he could have to be at my house. I knew he wasn't going to ease up until I drank some wine, so I relented and took the tiniest sip. It didn't taste like he had put anything in it, but to be safe, I held the glass without drinking more.

"What's this all about, Larry?" I frowned. "What do you want?"

"You never were one to beat around the bush, were you?"

"No, that's Chippy's game."

He chuckled. "Okay, I'm here because I have a business proposition for you."

"A business proposition? What are you talking about? Why would I want to go into business with you?"

"Because we share a common enemy—and an enemy of my enemy is my friend." Larry picked up his glass and drank the wine in one gulp. "Me and the boys are going to take LC down, put him straight out of business, and I want you to be my partner."

"Oh, really? Just like that you're going to take down the mighty LC Duncan?" I asked skeptically.

"I've already got him and his brats on the run."

I laughed so hard that I almost spilled my wine. I didn't know what was funnier: the fact that he said he was going to take his brother out of business, or that he seemed as if he actually believed it. "Yeah, you're definitely crazy. How the hell do you think you're going to do that?"

"I'm going to become his biggest competition," Larry said matter-of-factly.

I looked over at Curtis and Kenny to see if they were in on the joke that clearly was being played on me. They stood in the doorway, looking at their father as if what he was saying made sense.

"Larry, you can't be serious."

"I am. And I need your help."

"Help how?" I giggled. He had me so amused at this point I actually took another sip of wine.

"I'm fucking serious. I need an inside person. Someone who can give me the schematics of their house, plant bugs and stuff like that, so I can start planning their demise," he said.

Damn, he wasn't kidding. I put down my glass and shook my head. "No way. I'm not doing that. We come from two totally different worlds. My last name may have been Duncan at one point in time, but I ain't like the rest of y'all. You should know better."

"You've always been a bourgeois bitch, Donna." He sighed. "Everyone knows that."

"And you've always been a crazy motherfucker, Larry." I shrugged. "Everyone knows that too. Besides, I don't be in that damn house like that anyway. They'd be suspicious of me right away."

"Fine." He leaned toward me, kind of hovering in my personal space. "Then there's another way you can help."

"How?"

"I need you to recruit your children to our side. They're both important pieces in this chess game we're playing," he stated. "We both know what Junior is capable of, and Kenny tells me your daughter is a bad-ass bitch."

I blinked. After the way LC and Chippy had been disrespecting me lately, it would feel like sweet revenge to somehow use my kids against them; but at the same time, it made me uncomfortable because I had no idea what Larry was proposing. So, I tried to shoot down his idea. "She is, but she wouldn't do it for me. We're not close like that anymore."

"Well then, work on your relationship. You may be a bourgeois bitch, Donna, but you're far from dumb. All you have to do is tell Junior you're his real momma, and his instincts will do the rest. Worst case scenario, he destroys them from the inside. Give LC a little internal strife."

We stared at one another for a few seconds as I mulled it over in my mind. When I made my decision, I told him, "Hell, no. My leverage with my kids is the only thing keeping LC writing checks. Besides, I don't even want my kids involved in this family business crap."

"Look, I don't have a whole lotta time," he said, obviously getting frustrated. "I need to know: are you with them or me?"

"I'm not trying to waste your time, Larry. I'm just trying to explain."

"My momma said you were gonna act like this. That's why she didn't wanna come. But I didn't believe her!" He stood up, yelling, "So, spit it out, Donna. Are you in or not?"

What the hell was this crazy fool talking about? Why would he be bringing his momma into this right now? I had already given him my answer anyway. "No! I may be a bourgeois bitch, as you call it, but they are still my children, and I love them. I don't want any harm coming to them. If I bring them into this, one, if not both, will end up dead."

"Well, my dear, if you're worried about either of your kids ending up dead, I'll let you know ahead of time: I'm gonna kill them both." A sinister look came across his face as he started pacing the floor. "There is a silver lining to all this, though. You won't have to worry about it, because I'm gonna kill you first."

He swung his arm at me hard, and it was a miracle that all he did was graze my face. I felt the wetness on my thigh and realized I'd dropped the glass of wine. I stared at the red stain soaking into my pants leg and dripping onto the floor. My face was stinging, and when I reached up to my cheek, I realized it was wet too. At first, I thought maybe the wine had splattered to my face, but then, I looked at my fingers and saw a different shade of red. It was blood. My blood.

"You cut me, you psychotic motherfucker! Now I see why LC had your crazy ass locked away." I tried to get up from the table, but it was too late. Before I could move, Curtis and Kenny were on each side of me, pulling me up. "You're fucking crazy! Get the fuck off me! Larry, you crazy bastard."

"The enemy of my enemy is my friend, Donna. But you're not acting like a friend; you're acting like you're his friend," Larry growled insanely at me.

I turned my head and caught a glimpse of the steak knife in his hand as he loomed over me. "You really are fucking crazy!"

"You haven't seen crazy yet," he said with an evil grin.

LC

44

Almost an hour after we'd left Jun Cheng, Harris and I were in Brooklyn, parked on Livingston Street. We weren't there long before Vegas slid into the front passenger's seat to join us. He had a look of pure satisfaction on his face.

"Where the heck did you come from?" Harris asked, startled.

"Taking care of something," Vegas answered, glancing toward me in the back seat. "How did everything go with Jun?"

"Better than we could have hoped for," I replied with a grin. "Orlando and Junior are with him now. Everything in place?"

"Oh, yeah," Vegas said confidently, glancing at his watch. "Things should be going down any moment now."

"Can someone please explain to me what the hell is going on?" Harris whined. He'd been looking annoyed ever since we left Orlando and Junior with Jun Cheng. One thing about Harris: he hated to be out of the loop, and with his attitude about London being over in Jamaica, we'd been leaving him out of the loop quite a bit.

"See that building over there?" Vegas pointed.

"Yeah," Harris answered. "The strip club?"

"Mm-hmm. Keep your eyes on it."

Harris made a face. "Why? What's so important about that nasty-ass joint? The girls in there are so low-class."

My son-in-law had had issues with remaining faithful in the past, so I wouldn't be surprised if he'd spent plenty of nights in a private room in this very club. I glared at him but held my tongue.

"Just shut the fuck up and watch, Harris," Vegas told him, probably thinking the same thing I was.

Within a minute, the sirens and horns of an NYPD emergency response team truck were blaring as they pulled up, followed by six regular units and two undercover. We watched as they entered the club with bulletproof vests, masks, and shields, their guns ready.

"Oh, shit! They're raiding that strip club?" Harris yelled. "I'd hate to be in there right now."

"Yeah, I bet you would," Vegas said, shooting him a dirty look. "Keep watching. It ain't tits and ass they came looking for."

After a few minutes, they began bringing people out of the building. Half-dressed strippers yelled and complained as they were piled into the backs of vans and police cars. An array of men, from well-dressed businessmen to blue-collar uniformed workers were escorted out.

"What are we waiting on? Did our mailman make a pit stop?" Harris quipped.

"Shut the hell up," Vegas said. "I'm getting sick of your sarcasm."

"There he is," I said.

We watched as a Latino man was brought out in handcuffs and put in the back of an unmarked car.

"Who is that?" Harris asked.

"That's your new client," I told him. "His name is Julio Vargas. He was my biggest New York client until a few days ago, when he became Larry's biggest client. He's about to be booked for gun possession and possession with the intent to distribute."

"You orchestrated this, didn't you? You set him up." Harris looked miffed but impressed.

"He recently bought ten kilos from Larry. They now belong to the NYPD. First thing in the morning, you're gonna need to go to his arraignment and eventually bail him out," Vegas said with a smile.

"Oh, and make sure you remind him that his bail and legal fees are compliments of LC Duncan," I added.

London

45

It had taken damn near all night, but I had finally convinced Daryl that the easiest way for us to get into Tivoli Gardens was to take the bus and try to blend in with the rest of the people in the neighborhood.

"For the record, I would just like to say that this is a bad idea," he whispered in my ear as we stepped on the bus. I looked over at him and shook my head. He already looked like he belonged, dressed in a pair of slacks and a long white shirt. It was the same outfit damn near every man on the bus wore. His attire, along with his smooth chocolate skin and his beard, which had grown out since we had been in Jamaica, made him look like he was exactly where he belonged.

"It's going to work. Stop being so negative," I told him and stared out the window at the people on the streets. There was nothing about us that made me think we would stand out; especially in the various groups of people I saw.

The bus came to a stop and we got off, along with most of the people on the bus, and headed into the neighborhood. I made sure to keep my head down and not make eye contact with anyone. I also didn't say anything for fear that they would recognize my American accent. I figured that once we had gotten further down the street, I would ask about Ruby. Asking about Vinnie Dash would send up a red flag immediately.

My confidence started to diminish as we passed one deteriorated building after another. If it weren't for the women and children sitting outside of them, I would think that they were abandoned, because none of them looked livable with their broken windows, cracked walls, and doors hanging off hinges.

I saw Daryl glancing over his shoulder, and then he took my hand rather forcefully and tugged me into a crowded store. I knew not to say anything, because his body language sent a strong enough message that something wasn't right. We walked up and down the aisles, until finally he stopped and picked up a jar of something, pretending to examine it.

"What's wrong?" I mumbled, pointing at the label so it would look like we were discussing the item in his hand.

"We're being followed."

"Are you sure?"

He gave me a quick look that said *What the hell do you think?* and I looked past him down the aisle. The only person I saw was a guy, about thirty years old, on his cell phone; but I knew Daryl well enough to know that if he said we were being followed, then we probably were.

"Come on." He put the jar back on the shelf, and we quickly walked out of the store. I glanced back and saw a little boy and a teenager walking out behind us. I did not like the look on the older one's face. We sped up the pace for another two blocks, then turned onto what looked like a small street but turned out to be an alley. The teenager behind us let out a yelp, and suddenly there were three men coming around the corner at the other end of the alley.

I stopped in my tracks when I saw that the one in the middle was holding a machete, and his partners by his side held large knives. I turned around, and the boys were still behind us standing there like they were prepared to stop us from going back.

"We don't want no trouble," Daryl said. "We're just filmmakers scouting out locations for a documentary we're making."

"Is dat so, mon?" yelled one of the men who were now approaching us from the other end of the alley.

"That's right," Daryl told him, easing his revolver out of his waistband. "You want some, then come and get it." He raised his gun.

My heart raced as I reached in my purse for my own gun and got into position. Daryl's arm went up to protect me. We were at a standstill for a few heated seconds, until they realized their weapons were no match for our bullets. They stopped advancing and lowered their weapons to their sides.

"Get de fuck out!" the man yelled at us.

We moved quickly, our guns still pointed as we backed out, past the boys who had stepped to the side, and then we hauled ass down the street.

"Put your gun away," Daryl told me, and I didn't hesitate to do it.

I looked back, and now, in addition to the men we had faced in the alley, there were another four with them, all walking behind us. They kept their distance but made it clear they wouldn't stop following us until we got the hell out of their neighborhood. We didn't slow down as we hustled down four blocks and crossed the main street that led out of Tivoli Gardens; then we went another two blocks before Daryl finally stopped.

When I finally caught my breath, I asked, "How did you know they didn't have guns?"

"I didn't. I took a chance," he said.

"What the fuck, Daryl? That was pretty risky, wasn't it?"

He shrugged. "Better than being dead, but maybe not as much as you'd think. Believe it or not, you get caught with a gun here in Jamaica, that's some serious shit. A gun charge here ain't no simple six-month sentence like back in the States. They give you a year for each bullet. Now, I'm sure Vinnie's guys have guns, but the average thug's just carrying a machete or a knife down here. And they will use those fucking knives for sure. If they don't kill you, they'll cut off your feet."

I looked down at the black Tory Burch flats on my feet, the simplest shoes I owned. Thank God I hadn't been wearing heels as we ran for our lives. "Wow."

"Exactly." Daryl nodded. "Oh, and London?"

"Yeah?"

"Risky was coming down here in the first place. I told you this shit was a bad idea."

Sasha

46

"About time you got out here. We were supposed to leave an hour ago."

I rolled my eyes at Junior and hopped in the passenger's side of the car. I knew I had been the hold up, but I didn't care. Hell, I didn't even want to go. But Uncle LC and Vegas had tasked the two of us with heading upstate to the mental facility that had housed Uncle Larry for nearly two decades to see what information we could get.

"Let's just hurry up so we can get back. Paris and I got plans for later tonight," I told him.

Junior laughed. "You and Paris always got plans. Don't worry. I wanna get back here just as fast as you do, because me and my wife got plans too."

"What kinda plans you got?" I eyed him. Junior was the least social member of the Duncan family. He pretty much never went out, other than to take Sonya somewhere, and I couldn't remember the last time they went to a club. I always teased him about being the strong, silent type. He was just as handsome as his brothers and Uncle LC, but Junior was bigger, way bigger than them, and he was as strong as an ox. I always felt safe around him, even as a kid. Paris may have been like a sister to me, but there had always been a connection between me and Junior. Maybe it was because he was so close to my father.

"What you mean, what kinda plans do I got? I'm a newly married man with a gorgeous bride at home waiting for me. I plan to make the whole damn house shake!" he joked.

Seeing him so happy and in love with Sonya really made me happy. I knew that he was going to make a great father, but still . . .

"Ewww, TMI." I shook my head. "TMI!"

"I know you ain't talking, with all of the information you and Paris find it necessary to volunteer. That was nothing and you know it."

I took out my cell phone and turned it on. It had been off since the night before because of my mother, who had been calling and texting nonstop. After that stunt she pulled at the auction, I was done with her for real. You couldn't tell me she'd didn't do that shit on purpose. Since then, she'd been trying desperately to reach me, but I was ignoring her. She just wouldn't let up, and it was so damn annoying. Sure enough, when the phone powered on, it alerted me that I had seventeen missed calls and just as many texts, all from the contact with the name BIRTH GIVER.

"Fuck. Leave me alone," I said aloud as I deleted the calls and texts.

"Uh-oh, must be one of your ex-boos trying to come back. Or is it one of your stalkers whose heart you broke?" Junior teased.

"Oh, it's a stalker all right. It's my stalking mother," I said with a sigh.

"Aunt Donna?"

"The one and only. She's been blowing me up for days because she knows I'm pissed. I can't believe her sometimes. Here's a woman who didn't give a shit about me and pretty much abandoned me, yet she still thinks she can tell me what the fuck to do. She's got some nerve."

"Yeah, Aunt Donna is pretty intense. I don't know what it is about her, but Pop always seems to back down when she snaps off. I've seen her and Mom go at it a couple of times over the years, too," Junior said, "and it was not pretty."

"That's 'cause Aunt Chippy is the only one who can see through her bullshit."

"I hear you. Ma does have a bullshit detector on her nose, but I'm not gonna lie. Aunt Donna ain't shown me nothing but love over the years. You should have seen the wedding present she got me and Sonya."

"Take off the rose-colored glasses, Junior. She's a bitch, plain and simple."

He looked over at me and said gently, "That may or may not be true, but maybe you should just talk to her and get it over with. Seems to me the longer you avoid her, the longer you avoid the inevitable."

"What?" I looked at him like he was crazy. "I don't want to talk to her. I just want her to leave me the fuck alone."

"Then tell her to leave you alone."

"I have! And if my words haven't been enough, I've avoided her for the past five years. That should be obvious."

"Look, I get it. But maybe it's time you had a heart to heart with her. Put your cards on the table. When it comes down to it, Sasha, she's your momma, and you only get one of them. Do it the same way you would do a Band-Aid. Just rip it off and get it over with."

I thought about what Junior said, and once I let it sink in a little, it made sense. If I didn't handle this situation, it would go on just like this for years. I picked up my cell phone and said, "Siri, call Birth Giver."

Junior looked at me and shook his head.

"What?" I said. "You didn't think I'd have her in my phone as *Mom*, did you?"

The phone rang over and over, but there was no answer. I hit the redial button and called again. Still, she didn't answer the phone.

"You mind if we make a pit stop?" I asked, irritated because the tables were turned and now it was her ignoring me.

"No problem. We already late as hell anyway."

Fifteen minutes later, we pulled into my mother's driveway and parked next to her Maserati. At least now I knew she was home. Knowing her, she had some man over, and that's why she wasn't answering her phone.

"I'll be right back," I said, opening the car door and hopping out.

I stood at the front door and rang the doorbell several times. When she didn't answer, I started banging. I knew she would be pissed. She might have been a crappy mother, but she was the queen of decorum and proper etiquette. Not only was I at her house unannounced, but I was beating on the door like I had lost my mind. I could just imagine the disgusted look she probably had on her face as she was running down the steps to scold whoever was at her door. I waited, now excited because I was going to get the opportunity to say what I wanted to say to her face and then be done with her once and for all. Junior was right; I needed to handle this woman to woman, and if she had some dick over who would hear it too, then all the better.

I waited a few moments more, ringing and banging, before I remembered the spare key that she kept. As bourgeois as my mother was, she was still old fashioned in some areas of her life. She always left a key under the watering can sitting near the flower bed. I waved at Junior, who seemed to be quite entertained by all of this, and used the key to unlock the door.

"Hello?" I called out when I stepped inside. No one answered. "Mom, it's me. Sasha."

There were a couple of shopping bags laying discarded in the den. That was weird. She was usually pretty careful with her designer purchases, because as far as she was concerned, her wealth and style defined her. I called up the stairs a little louder.

Still no answer. Her and her beau must have decided to take things up to the bedroom. I rushed up the stairs, thinking it might be funny to bust in on them in the middle of the action. But the bedroom door was open, and the room was still as pristine as ever: the bed perfectly made, her dresser lined with jewelry boxes and bottles of expensive makeup and perfume. She was nowhere to be found. I searched all the other rooms upstairs to no avail.

I walked back down the steps into the den and noticed my mother's purse on the floor in the corner. Something was wrong. My mother loved her designer bags more than she loved me. There was no way in hell she would ever allow one to touch the floor.

I grabbed my gun out of my purse and headed over to search the rest of the first floor. I stepped into the dining room, and that's when I let out a scream loud enough for Junior to hear me outside.

At first, I was unable to make my body move. There she was, sprawled out in the middle of the floor, a pool of blood around her head and chest.

"Mom? Mommy?" I squeaked out, even though I already knew the truth: she was dead. Donna Washington-Duncan-Wilson-Ferguson, my mother, was dead. I squeezed my eyes shut and told myself to wake up, because I had to be in the middle of some horrible nightmare; but then I opened them slowly, and she was still lying motionless. She was still dead.

"Noooooooooooo!" I screamed and ran over, collapsing onto my knees and pulling her lifeless body to me. "Please, God, no. Please. I'm so sorry. Please, Mommy." I rocked back and forth, crying so hard that I could barely breathe.

"Sasha! Sasha!" I heard Junior calling, but I couldn't answer. Seconds later, he entered the room.

"Oh my God. No, this can't be happening," I heard him whisper, then I felt his arm around me. I continued to rock her in my arms as the tears poured down my face.

"She's . . . She's . . . " I couldn't bring myself to state the obvious.

"I know." He sat with me for a few moments, and then I heard him dialing his phone.

I thought about all the missed calls and texts that I'd ignored. She had tried over and over to reach me. Did she know something was wrong? Was she calling because she needed my help? Was someone after her?

"Yeah, Vegas, it's me. I'm over here at Aunt Donna's with Sasha. Bro, something horrible has happened." He paused to listen then said, "Yeah, she's dead, and it looks like something Uncle Larry would do."

"Mommy," I whispered through my tears. "I'm so sorry. I'm so sorry, Mommy."

"Yeah, I'm bringing her home right now," Junior said softly. "Sasha, we have to go."

"No, I can't leave her. I can't," I wailed.

"Sasha, please. Come on, sweetheart."

"No! You don't understand. I know she's a bitch, and I know no one likes her, but she's my mom and all I had left. And now. . ."

"Sash," Junior said, reaching for me.

I snatched away, still holding my mother's head against my chest. "Now she's gone. I have no one. I have no one left. My daddy's gone, and now she is too. My family is gone."

"Sasha, you're not alone. You still have family. You still have me. I'm always gonna be there for you. You know that. We all are." Junior's voice cracked a little. "But we have to go."

"I can't leave her by herself. I'm all she's got." I looked up at him and shook my head. "I have to stay with her."

"Sasha, you can't stay. Vegas is on his way with a team. They will make sure she's okay."

"No."

"We've gotta get you home and get you cleaned up. Come on." Junior eased my arms from around my mother's body and pulled me up off the floor to embrace me. He held me tight and let me cry on his shoulder until I had no more tears left. Then he released me and held my hands as he looked in my eyes. "It's gonna be fine. We're gonna find who did this. I promise."

His words sparked the fire of fury in me that I knew would be burning for a long, long time. "Stop pretending, Junior." I turned and kneeled, leaning over to give her one final kiss. "We both know who did this. It was Uncle Larry, and when I find him, he's going to find out that he ain't the only crazy one in this family."

Orlando

47

"Okay, okay, you're right. Going there was a bad idea," I heard London saying as she came around the corner of the motel. She stopped dead in her tracks when she spotted me leaning against my rental car. "Orlando! What are you doing here?" She ran up and hugged me.

"I hear you're having some problems getting into Tivoli Gardens," I told her as she released me from our embrace. From the look she gave Daryl, I guess that comment had struck a nerve. "I'm here to help."

I turned to Daryl, giving him a pound with my fist. "What's up, Dee?"

"Just trying to make it, O. Good to see you," he replied. Daryl was always low key, but for some reason he seemed a little standoffish. "Right now, we could use all the help we can get."

"Don't worry. The cavalry has arrived," I said confidently.

"You do know Daddy and Vegas are going to lose their minds when they find out you're here, right?" London gave me a disapproving look, which prompted Daryl to take a step back, glancing in every direction but ours. Now I knew what the problem was: London thought that I was there to step on her toes. "We've got the situation well under control," she said, full of attitude.

"Pop and Vegas know I'm here, London. They're the ones who sent me." I saw the disappointment on London's face as her confident demeanor deflated. I'm sure she thought my presence was the result of her failure to find Vinnie Dash, but that was far from the truth. "And for the record, we all think you've done a phenomenal job," I added to gas her up a little. London didn't get involved in the business too often, so she deserved some credit for stepping out of her stay-at-home mom role as eagerly as she had this time.

"You do?" She perked up quickly. "I was just doing the same thing any Duncan would do."

"Yeah, Rio told me how much of a bad-ass you were, shooting that guy in the foot and saving Daryl's life." Daryl couldn't help but laugh along with me as I teased, "Who the fuck you think you are, Annie Oakley?"

"No, I like to think of myself as Pam Grier in *Brown Sugar*," London joked, laughing along with us. It seemed all she needed was that little reassurance, because her insecurities were gone, just like that.

"Any word on Uncle Larry and the boys?"

I leaned back against the car and took off my sunglasses. "No, not yet. We got eyes and ears everywhere, though, so I'm sure it won't take long. They sent me down here to help you with Vinnie and your Tivoli Gardens problem." Of course, it went without saying that I didn't hesitate for a second when they told me to get on a flight to Jamaica. It was what I'd wanted all along.

"Orlando, getting in there is damn near impossible," London said. It didn't matter to me. Nothing was going to dampen my spirits now that I was one step closer to getting my son back.

"So I've been told, but as Pop always says, nothing's impossible. It just depends on how much you're willing to give up to get it."

"You sound awfully confident," Daryl said.

"Time to take the fight to them, Dee. Come on. Grab your stuff and let's go," I said.

"Where are we going?" London asked.

"The Sheraton—unless you prefer to stay in this place." I gave the raggedy motel the once over and chuckled. Nobody back home was going to believe that my bourgie-ass sister had even dared to stay in a place like this. I was starting to see there was more to London than any of us had given her credit for.

"Hell, no! Hot showers and decent bedding, here I come," my sister said happily.

***

It was early afternoon by the time I got London and Daryl checked in. I told them to meet me in the presidential suite in half an hour, and they were actually on time.

"Come on in," I said, opening the door then gesturing for them to follow me. We walked past a half-dozen Asian men wearing headphones and working on computers.

"What's going on?" London asked.

"Why don't I let our host explain that?" I waved my hand at Jun Cheng, who took off his headphones and walked over to me. "Jun, this is my sister, London, and one of our main guys, Daryl."

"Him, I already know," Daryl said, stepping up so the two of them could share a brotherly embrace. "Good to see you, Jun. It's been a long time."

"Yes, it has, my friend." Jun politely shook London's hand. "Pleasure to meet you."

"Nice to meet you," she replied. "Now, can someone tell me what's going on here?"

"Jun and his people have agreed to work with us on taking care of the Tivoli Gardens problem we are having," I told London and Daryl.

"How? If we can't get into West Kingston without being detected and we're black, how are his people going to manage to do this?" London asked.

I shot a glance at Jun to see if he had been offended by her comment, but if anything, he seemed amused.

"My people are invisible," Jun said with a smirk.

London rolled her eyes as if Jun had a screw loose. "Excuse me? What did you say?"

I answered for Jun. "You heard him, and he's correct to an extent. His people are invisible, London. Maybe not literally, but figuratively."

"Have you had the chance to enter any grocery stores while you've been here?" Jun asked her.

"One or two." London shrugged. She still wasn't getting the point.

"And did you notice anything about them?" Jun continued.

London looked at him, her face full of confusion. "They all had food in them?"

Jun laughed and said, "Yes, that is true, but they also had Asian workers—which you did not even notice."

"Son of a bitch." Daryl nodded his head. Clearly, he understood what Jun was getting at.

"Can someone tell me what the hell is going on?" London sounded totally frustrated, so Jun patiently explained it to her.

"All the major food stores on the island are owned and run by my people," Jun said matter-of-factly. "Locals don't pay attention to us. We're like furniture to them. We're—"

"You're invisible! Yeah, now I get it," London said, looking almost relieved that she now understood. I guess after being out of the loop with the business for so long, she didn't like to feel stupid or uninformed.

"We can get into every neighborhood in this country, including Tivoli Gardens and anywhere else that yellow Lamborghini you have been searching for goes."

"You know the apartment building downtown that you followed Vinnie from?" I asked.

"Yeah," London replied.

I pointed at a computer screen that was divided into four video images. "Take a look at this monitor."

"Is this in real time?" she asked as she watched over two dozen Asian men walk in the building and then, in another quadrant of the screen, the same men storm the apartment.

"It happened about five minutes ago, right before you arrived," Jun responded.

"Did they capture Vinnie?"

"Vinnie was not there, but his men who were, the ones that are alive, have been taken to our safe house in Saint Mary's. Locating him will not be a problem. I assure you," Jun said.

One of the Asian men brought over a cell phone and held it out for Jun to talk. Jun stepped away and carried on a short conversation in Chinese. When he ended the call, he said to us, "We've located the house in Tivoli Gardens where the yellow Lamborghini has been seen, and it has been confirmed that a white man with an island woman and child live there. My people are heading there now to take care of it. We should know something in the next ten to fifteen minutes."

"Are you sure you want them to do this?" London asked me.

I guess I looked worried, because Jun read my expression and said to reassure me, "I've given them specific instructions that they are not to harm the woman or the child." He paused for a second and then added, "Provided the woman does not become involved, of course. However, should she pose a threat . . ."

"Take her out," I replied before he could finish. "If she gets in the way, take her fucking ass out."

Ruby

48

Blake had been avoiding me ever since I'd asked him to find out if Vinnie was behind my brother's death. I got the feeling that it was more by design than coincidence, and I was starting to get pissed and a little worried. Most times, he was the one who stayed close to the house, keeping an eye on Vincent and me, but I hadn't seen him in days, and that wasn't a good sign for any of Vinnie's men. Thankfully, my heart jumped for joy when I looked out the kitchen window and saw his jeep pulling up.

"It's been four days since me seen ya. Where ya been? Vincent has been asking for ya." I ran and buried my head into his chest the second he walked into the house. I may have used Vincent as an excuse, but I'm sure he knew I was worried about him from the strength of my hug. I was confused, scared, and overwhelmed at the same time. When we separated after a few moments, I took a step back and said, "I don' know why, but me thought you was dead."

"No, girl. I'm alive. I've been lookin' into some tings," he said hesitantly, taking a glass and filling it with water.

"Well, did you find anyting?"

His eyes softened. In that moment, I saw how much he had aged since the first time we met. He was only fifteen years older than I was, but he seemed much older now. His hair was grayer, and there were worry lines on his face. "Blake, did you?"

He took a sip of water then placed the glass down, looking around the corner as if he expected someone to be there. "I tink so, but we can't talk here. Your husband has ears everywhere."

"Why don't we take Vincent for a walk?" I suggested.

"Dat's a good idea," he said.

The front door suddenly opened, startling both of us, as Vinnie and his men came rushing inside. I quickly wiped my face and recomposed myself, not wanting Vinnie to see my tears.

"Ruby!" I heard him call up the stairs. He had run past the kitchen so fast he didn't even see Blake and me. "Ruby!"

"I'm right here, Vinnie," I yelled.

He ran into the kitchen, his face flushed and perspiration pouring from his forehead. "What's wrong? What happened?" I asked.

"They're after us. They came to the office looking for me. They shot the entire fucking place up. Ten of my men are dead." He was panting as he paced around the kitchen.

"Who? The Duncans? I told you not to trust de uncle!" I felt myself beginning to panic. My life was going from bad to worse. I was married to one killer while on the run from another, who also happened to be the father of my child.

"No, not the fucking Duncans. The Chinese!" he snapped.

"Chinese? But why? Why would dey be after us?" I became even more confused and nervous as I waited for his answer. Now, not only were we running from the Duncans, but Asians as well. It was becoming too much for me.

"I don't know." He shook his head and slumped into a chair.

"What did you do?" I asked. The way Blake had been acting before, I was quite sure he was going to deliver some bad news to me about the true facts of my brother's death, so now I couldn't put much faith in anything Vinnie said. Who knew what was the truth anymore?

"What do you mean, what did I do? I didn't do nothin'."

"Lies! Why do you keep telling me lies?" I stared at him angrily until he relented.

"Okay, okay, it probably has something to do with the containers," Vinnie replied.

"What containers?"

"The containers we got the dope from. They belonged to some Chinese dudes. I just don't know how they found out it was us. I thought I covered my tracks pretty well."

"Well, evidently you didn't." I was starting to think that, whether he killed my brother or not, maybe it was time to separate myself from Vinnie.

"Dat explains de groceries. Now it all makes sense," one of Vinnie's men mumbled. I suddenly remembered what he was taking about.

I gasped. "The man making the food delivery."

"What the fuck are y'all talking about? What food delivery? What man?" Vinnie demanded to know.

"Dere was a Chinese man here earlier. I went to de door and he said he was delivering food for de man wit' de yellow car. I took it and brought it to Miss Ruby," Jasper explained.

"And nobody thought to question this man who just gave you free groceries?" Vinnie shouted.

"No, we thought you had dem delivered," I replied.

"Fuck! They know where I live?" He got up and began pacing nervously again.

Blake said, "Perhaps we should leave, boss. Dis place is not safe for your wife and child."

"You're right." Vinnie turned toward me. "Go get Vincent and let's get outta here."

I hated everything about this situation. I hated that we were in danger, I hated that we needed to leave again, and I also hated the idea of going anywhere with Vinnie until I learned the truth about Randy's death. "I need time to pack. I can't keep leaving tings behind on a moment's notice, Vinnie," I stated.

"We can always buy new things, Ruby, but we can't buy a new us," Vinnie told me, speaking softly. I glanced at Blake, and he nodded his agreement.

"Can we go back to Negril?" I suggested.

"No, dat's not possible," Blake insisted. "De Chinese are all over de place. People will talk, especially when dey tryin' to feed dey families."

"What are we gon' to do?" I asked.

"We are going to get the fuck outta here like I said." Vinnie sounded more forceful now. "Now go get Vincent and meet us at the jeep."

I turned and looked at Blake, who gave me a slight nod, and I rushed upstairs to once again grab my son and a few bare essentials.

By the time I went outside, Vinnie was behind the wheel of one car, and Blake was behind him in the jeep. I was torn between which car to get into. Hesitantly, I climbed into the back seat of the vehicle my husband was driving, and we took off.

We had barely made it to the corner when two cars sped past us, filled with Asian men.

"Good thing we left that Lamborghini," Vinnie said as gunshots rang out behind us.

"Mommy!" Vincent cried out. "Where we going?"

"I don't know, baby. Let me ask your father." I pulled him down low in the seat, held him tight, and began praying. I knew that the bullets had been meant for us, and we had barely escaped death.

When I felt that we were safe and out of the range of danger, I sat up. I looked at Vinnie in the rearview mirror and said, "Where are we going?"

"I don't know yet, but we're getting the hell out of Jamaica."

London

49

I don't know what was more shocking: the fact that Aunt Donna was dead, or that it was Uncle Larry who had killed her. Once we received word of her death, we immediately flew home to be with my family for a few days. None of us could argue that Jun's people were better equipped to find Vinnie and Ruby than we were. After all, he did have an invisible army at his disposal.

When Orlando, Daryl, and I arrived at the airport, Vegas was there waiting. We were just about to get into the car when Harris pulled up behind us.

"I see your Prince Charming has arrived," Orlando commented.

I rolled my eyes at him and briefly thought about pretending I didn't see Harris, but I knew there was no way he would allow that to happen. Instead, I grabbed my purse, which was on the back seat beside Daryl, and said, "I'll get the rest of my luggage from the house."

Our eyes met briefly, and he shrugged before looking away. I knew in that instant that we were back to reality, and my heart sank. I didn't want to leave, not without at least talking about our situation, but now wasn't the time or the place, and he didn't seem interested in saying much to me.

"Welcome home," Harris greeted me when I walked over to the Infinity SUV that he had given me last year as a birthday gift. Of course, he drove it more than I did.

"Thanks," I said, giving him a brief hug.

"Where are your bags?"

"In the other car. I'll get them later. We're all going to the same place, aren't we? You know you didn't have to come and get me, Harris. I'm sure you knew Vegas was coming."

"What kind of husband do you think I am?" he said sarcastically, almost daring me to give him an honest answer.

Instead, I asked, "Where are the girls?"

"They're home." He opened the door for me to get in. "They're excited to see their mommy, of course."

"I'm excited to see them too."

"Well, you certainly don't seem too thrilled to see me," he commented as he got in and started the car.

I didn't respond to his comment because I was focused on the back of Daryl's head in the back of the other car as Vegas pulled off in front of us. As the distance between us widened, I couldn't help but wish I was in that car too.

"London? Hello?"

"Huh?" I realized Harris had been talking to me, but I hadn't heard anything he said.

"What's going on with you?" he asked with a frown.

"Nothing. I'm just thinking about Aunt Donna. Have they made any arrangements yet?" I tried to get Daryl out of my head.

"No. Well, Sasha has decided to take care of everything. It's going to be a closed casket funeral. Larry messed up her face pretty bad," Harris said.

"That's horrible. I can't believe that he killed her," I told him. "This is crazy."

"Kind of makes me glad I'm just the son-in-law," Harris replied with the usual selfishness and lack of compassion I'd learned to expect from him.

We spent the remainder of the drive home listening to the radio. As soon as I got to the house and walked in the door, my daughters came running.

"Mommyyyyyyy!" Mariah screamed. Maria toddled behind her as best she could. I knelt and grabbed them, holding them close to me.

"I missed you both so much."

"We missed you too. Even Jordan missed you, Mommy," Mariah announced.

I looked up and saw my nephew standing in the doorway of the kitchen with a big smile on his face, and I beckoned for him to come. He ran over and hugged me just as tightly as my own children had. One thing was for certain: I was glad to be home.

"I'll go get the rest of your things," Harris said.

"No need. I already got them out and took them upstairs. They're waiting by your bedroom door," Daryl said as he walked down the stairs into the foyer.

"Thank you." I glanced over at him, hoping his eyes would meet mine, but he didn't even look at me.

"We appreciate that, Daryl. Oh, and I appreciate you looking out for my wife while you were in Jamaica." Harris placed his arm around my shoulder, and I could see Daryl grimace slightly.

"Just doing my job." Daryl picked up his travel bag and headed for the front door. "Tell Vegas I'll give him a call later."

"You're leaving?" I asked.

"Yeah. There's nothing around here for me," he said and walked out. He might as well have carried my heart in his pocket, because Lord knows I wanted to run behind him.

50

I sat on the back patio of our home with my oldest sons, nursing the snifter of eighty-year-old Scotch and trying to comprehend everything that was happening. The past twenty-four hours had been a whirlwind of emotion, and the shock of Donna's death was taking its toll on me. No doubt, she had been a pain in my ass for most of my adult life, but she had been my first love, my ex-fiancée, and technically was the mother of my first born. I'd never admit it to Chippy, but I did care for her in my own way. Now, she was gone, her life taken by a man who I had watched turn into a monster right before my eyes. He was the same monster who had nearly taken my life and was on a mission to destroy everything I had worked so hard to build. I felt anger, grief, and most of all, I felt helpless.

"So, no word from anyone? No one has seen hide nor hair of Larry or the boys?" I asked Vegas.

"Not a peep. We had one guy say he thought he saw one of the boys in Staten Island, but that was a false alarm." Vegas sipped his drink. "We've got folks looking up and down the East Coast."

"I can't believe I let this happen." I looked down at the ground.

"This isn't your fault, Pop. No one expected Uncle Larry to do something like this to Aunt Donna," Junior told me. "She was a civilian."

"He doesn't know what a civilian is anymore. You're either for or against him," I tried to explain angrily. "His intention wasn't to kill her anyway; his intention was to recruit her against us."

"What makes you say that?" Orlando asked.

"Because not only did he serve her favorite wine, but he cooked duck to go along with it. He was trying to wine and dine her to be on his side, and she didn't give him the answer he was looking for, so he killed her."

"You know, that makes sense," Vegas replied. "The table was set for four, and dinner hadn't even been served."

"Dammit, this is all my fault. If he was locked away, none of this would be happening. Lou told me to let them take his ass to jail and throw away the key, but I couldn't let them do that. He was my brother, and I felt like what he needed was help, not to be caged up like some wild animal." Tears began to form, and I closed my eyes to stop them from falling. The anger inside of me grew, and I held the glass so tight that it broke in my hand.

"Pop!" Junior jumped up and took the broken pieces from me.

I opened my eyes and stared at the brown liquor running down my arm. "Lee, Frankie B, Donna, all those people at the transportation hub: they're all dead because of—"

"You've gotta calm down, Pop. The last thing we need is for you to get your blood pressure up and end up back in the hospital. Listen to me. We're going to find Uncle Larry, I promise you." Vegas looked me straight in the eye.

"When, Vegas? Is it gonna be before he murders someone else? Who's next? You, Paris, Nevada?" I snapped.

"Pop, we're going to stop him. I don't care if I have to go on a one-man mission myself and hunt this son of a bitch down." Orlando put his hand on my shoulder.

I shook my head. "You have a son to find. You, Daryl, and London concentrate on that and find my grandson."

"If he's still on that island, with Jun's help we'll find him, Pop," Orlando reassured me.

"I know you will, but that's no comfort to me until he's found. With Larry and Vinnie now in cahoots and sharing notes, there's no telling how much damage they can do until they're caught."

"You want me to lean on Jamaica John a little more before I leave?" Orlando asked. "He might know where Vinnie is."

"That might not be such a bad idea, but wait until after the funeral. We are all gonna need to be here for Sasha." I stood up. "Once Donna is laid to rest, I want you all to take the kid gloves off. Use every contact and favor we have to find Larry, the boys, and Vinnie. I want this over by the end of the week."

London

51

Although Aunt Donna wasn't what you would call a close family member, her death had affected all of us. The entire household was quiet and somber; even the kids seemed to be toned down, and that wasn't easy with my nephew Jordan around. We tried to make small talk during dinner, but there was no denying the tension. I hadn't seen Sasha yet. If I was so upset by this turn of events, I couldn't begin to imagine how she felt.

As soon as the kids had cleared their plates, I gathered them, and we went upstairs to our living quarters, where I bathed them and put them in bed. After they were settled, I took a long, hot bath myself and changed into a pair of satin pajamas.

I stepped onto the balcony of our bedroom to enjoy the night air. I could hear voices in the distance and walked closer to the rail to see who it was. I peered over and saw Vegas, Orlando, Junior, and my father near the pool area, talking and smoking cigars. I secretly wished Daryl might be with them, but now I knew he really had gone home. I could only hope that there was a chance I would see him in the morning.

I walked back into the bedroom just as Harris walked in, taking off his tie and smiling seductively. *Oh God, no.* He was giving me the "I want sex" smile. I had no desire whatsoever to be near him, but I knew that there was no way I would be able to get out of having sex, especially after being away from home for the past two weeks. It was my first night back, and I knew he was going to expect me to give him some.

"I'm going to take a shower. I'll see you in a few minutes," he said, raising his eyebrows to send me what he thought was a sexy message.

"Okay," I replied, smoothing my hands down the front of my silk pajama top.

He undressed then went into the bathroom, and I climbed into bed, turned on the TV, and started flipping channels. I hadn't even realized I drifted off to sleep until I felt him climb into bed beside me.

"I'm so glad you're home, honey," he whispered as he touched my thighs.

"Yeah, it's good to be home, even for a few days." I sighed.

He froze and leaned up on one arm, staring at me. "What the hell do you mean, for a few days?"

"Harris, we only came home for the funeral. We still have to go back and find my nephew." *Thank you, Lord, this might just be my out*. A good fight was the perfect reason not to have sex. "Vinnie Dash has—"

Harris's voice took on the angry tone I was so accustomed to hearing. "You've lost your damn mind, London. You're not going anywhere. You're staying your ass home where you're safe. You think I'm gonna let you continue this wild goose chase for Vinnie Dash? You don't even know where he is. He's in the wind. When they raided his house, he and Ruby were already gone."

"And they have my nephew, so we're going to find them," I insisted.

He blinked and paused for a second, probably surprised by my defiance. I didn't often buck his authority because usually, it was easier to just give in.

He started, "I refuse to let you—"

"Let? Did you really just say *let*?"

There was a knock at the door, and our argument stopped.

"Mommy?" Mariah's small voice called from the other side of the door.

"Yes, baby? Come in!" I yelled.

The door slowly opened, and she walked in, holding her younger sister's hand.

"What's wrong, Mariah? Why aren't you in bed?" Harris sounded frustrated, which pissed me off. He was always trying to control those kids, just like he wanted to control me.

"I want Mommy," Maria, my youngest, told him.

I sat up and lifted the covers, making sure Harris had on pajama pants. I patted the center of the bed. "Come here, sweetie. Get up here."

"London, no." Harris frowned, but I didn't care. Not only did I want to comfort my daughter, who I hadn't seen in a while, but letting her in the bed had just given me the ultimate excuse not to have sex with Harris.

My two daughters climbed into our bed and snuggled beside me.

"Can we watch Disney channel?" Mariah asked, ignoring her father.

"We can watch whatever you want, baby." I smiled at her.

"Mariah, you and your sister need to go into your own room. You have a TV," Harris said, sulking.

I picked up the remote and turned the TV channels until some cartoon appeared on the screen and the kids started singing along. Harris wore a look of disgust on his face.

"How long are you gonna let them stay in here?" he asked.

"I don't know, Harris. Probably not that long," I lied, then said. "But you may wanna go ahead and go to sleep. It looks like they're gonna be up for a while."

I kissed the top of Mariah's head, then did the same to Maria. I'd never been more grateful for my children than I was at that moment. Motherhood definitely had its privileges.

Sasha

52

I had barely spoken ten words since my mother was killed, and most of them had been to the funeral director. My aunt, uncle, and cousins tried to be as comforting and accommodating as possible, even offering to assist me in planning my mother's funeral, but I declined. Having people, especially people who had openly despised her, make the arrangements would not be the best idea. Like it or not, dead or alive, two facts still remained: the Duncans hated Donna, and as strained as our relationship was, she was still my mother. I handled everything myself.

Her body was cremated, and a service was held at First Jamaica Ministries, the church she attended. It was well attended by the crème de la crème of black New York's high society, those who my mother found worthy of associating herself with. The designer suits, stilettos, and handbags in the building were probably worth enough to fund a small third world country. The attendees were arrogant, decked out in their ridiculously high fashion, all vying for attention. As each one pranced their way to the front of the church, admiring the hand-painted portrait and then walking over to me to pay their respects, I knew my mother was probably looking down and loving the attention. I sat at the end of the front pew, dressed in an all-black Yves St. Laurent suit, heels, and a pair of oversized Gucci sunglasses that she had owned. Beside me was Junior, who had suddenly taken on the role of my protector. He was the only person I felt inclined to talk to when something needed to be said. The remaining family members filled out the rest of the row and the one behind.

I couldn't remember the last time I had even been in a church. I was pretty much raised by my father, and religion wasn't at the top of his list of priorities for me to learn. I felt weird as people

I had never seen before walked up and told stories about Donna. They spoke about committees she sat on and fundraisers that she had chaired, how giving and supportive she had been to local substance abuse programs. One woman even said that my mother helped save her life. I realized that Donna was a stranger to me. I didn't really know her at all. All I knew was that she had abandoned my father and me to marry a rich man—or at least that's what I had been told. This woman that people were now speaking about was a woman I'd never known, and now it was too late. She was dead. It's funny how most of my life I had wished she were dead, thinking I would be happy because she would no longer be a thorn in my side. Now that I was sitting there, looking at the brass urn that held her ashes, it wasn't joy that I felt at all. It was sadness. It was confusion. My mind was all over the place.

I closed my eyes. The deep voice of Bishop TK Wilson, who was now speaking, had a lulling effect on me, and I allowed it to soothe my aching heart.

"And we all know that there is an appointed time for all of us. The Bible says that there is a time to be born, and yes, there is a time to die. We are grateful for the time that we had with this beautiful woman," Bishop said. "And although her death seems untimely to us, God knew what time it was. Amen."

Not long after, soft chords emanated from the organ, and people began filing out. I remained seated, unable to move.

"Sasha, baby, I'm so sorry."

It seemed like the millionth time someone had said that to me. I glanced up. Aunt NeeNee stood in front of me, tears streaming down a face full of sadness. Aunt Chippy stood beside her, comforting her. I stared at her blankly, not saying a word.

"I can't believe this happened to you. If you need anything, you know I'm right here for you, honey. I'm so sorry. This is horrible," NeeNee continued.

Slowly, I stood. I lifted the sunglasses from my face and stared at her. She went to hug me, but I took a slight step back. I could feel the seat of the pew on the back of my legs, then felt Junior's arm steadying me. As we stood face to face, I felt the smoldering heat of pain, which had been in my chest ever since I found my mother's lifeless body, suddenly start to rise.

"Your husband and your sons did this to me," I said, my voice calm and steady. "Trust me, they will pay."

"Sasha, honey," Aunt Chippy said, a look of surprise on her face. "Please. Not here. Not now."

I ignored her and continued, "You'd better pray to God that Uncle LC finds their asses before I do. You might wanna get the number of the funeral director before you leave. Start planning now, because they're all gonna die. Like the pastor just said: it's their time."

Curtis

53

We'd been digging up another one of my dad's stashes, this time out in the woods of Pennsylvania. Kenny had been quiet, which was unusual, because most of the time you couldn't shut him up. In that respect, he was kind of like my old man, who always seemed to be talking. But not today. He was moping around like someone had put down his dog. I asked him over and over what was wrong, and each time he responded with a simple, "Nothing." I knew my brother well enough to know that he was lying. I listened to him sigh over and over again before I decided it was time to find out what the hell was really going on with him.

"Kenny, what's wrong with you?" I asked him, tossing a shovel full of dirt to the side. "And don't sit there and tell me nothing, either."

"I don't wanna talk about it," he mumbled, jamming his own shovel into the ground.

"I ain't ask you what the fuck you wanted to do." I reached for his shovel to stop him from digging so that we could address this.

He turned and scowled at me. "Let go, Curt."

"Nah. Not until you tell me what's wrong."

"Okay, you wanna know? I'm so sick of this shit," he said as he let go of the shovel and started walking away.

"Sick of what? Where the hell are you going?" I demanded to know.

He didn't say anything, and he didn't stop walking. I started shoveling again for a brief second before I realized I couldn't just let this go. Something was seriously wrong with my brother, and I had to fix it before it got in the way of our mission.

I followed behind him. He was leaning against the Explorer that we had been traveling in since getting back from Jamaica.

"I thought you quit," I said, pointing to his cigarette.

He exhaled a cloud of smoke. "I did, but these are the only thing that calms my nerves."

"What's going on, bro? What's got your panties in a bunch?" I asked again, leaning up against a pine tree with my hands in my pockets.

"This. You. Him." He shrugged his shoulders then finished his cigarette. "This whole situation is fucked up."

"What does that mean?" I decided that after we dug up this bag, I was going to take him to get laid. Maybe that would help his sour mood.

"It means I'm not down with this shit anymore. It's not fun, and I'm starting to see what everyone is talking about. Curtis, Pop is—"

Before he could finish his sentence, I was in his face, grabbing him by the collar. "Don't you say it, God dammit! Don't you say it. He's not crazy!"

"Then what was that shit he did to Aunt Donna, huh? If that wasn't crazy, then what was it?"

I stared at my brother, stunned by the things he was saying. "Shut up, Kenny. You're wrong."

"I ain't wrong. That was sick and uncalled for. Donna didn't do shit to him or us. Innocent people are dying at this point, and I don't like it. Dad is saying that all of this is for family; well, she was family too. He lied to us, Curt. He said we were going over there to talk to her about joining forces and being allies, but because she said no to us, he ended up killing her. Whatever is going on with him, it's getting worse. He's out of control, and I don't wanna be a part of this shit anymore."

I let him speak his mind, but I didn't see things the same way. "He's not out of control, Kenny. He's pissed. Don't you see he's doing all of this for us?" I said in defense of my father. "We can't let him down. He's depending on us. He's our dad."

"Curt, we out here killing people and blowing shit up all on the strength that he's our dad."

I thought about what Kenny was saying, and for the first time, I had to admit he had a point. We really didn't have any information other than what my dad had told us. I'd never doubted his story or wondered if there might be another side, especially since his story about LC taking everything from him hadn't changed over the years. Whenever I went to visit him in the hospital, he would talk about how my uncles had put him there because they wanted him out of the way. They wanted a bigger portion of the Duncan empire that Pop said rightfully belonged to him.

He wouldn't lie to us; at least, I didn't think he would. He promised us that Kenny and I were the reason he was doing all of this, so that the legacy that was stolen from him would be passed on to us once it was recovered. That was what he said, and that was what I wanted to believe, but Kenny's faith in our dad had become weak.

"I can't do this anymore. He killed Aunt Donna, man. Shit, how was killing her helping us get his portion of the business back?" Kenny folded his arms and waited for my answer, which I really didn't have.

"It's a respect thing, Kenny. I don't necessarily think killing Donna was the right thing to do, but maybe it had to be done. We got all this dope, the streets are talking about the Duncans, and they ain't talking about LC, or Vegas, or Orlando. They're coming to us now." I straightened my spine and threw back my shoulders proudly. My entire life, I had lived in the shadows of my cousins, and now because of Pop, we were coming into the light. We were taking back our power, and I enjoyed that feeling.

"He's gonna get us killed, Curt, and I ain't trying to die over nothing stupid." Kenny stood just as straight as I was, and we came face to face.

"So, what the fuck are you saying, Kenny? You just gonna leave me?"

"No, but the next time something like this happens, I will, so you better have a talk with him, because you can bet on that."

Ruby

54

"Is Daddy going on the boat ride with us, Mommy?" Vincent excitedly squirmed in the seat beside me.

"Yes, Vincent. Now, sit down and play wit' your Transformer," I told him as Vinnie stepped on deck. We'd just boarded a yacht that Vinnie must have secretly purchased just for this purpose: our escape from Jamaica. "See, there he is now."

"I need you to get that dope over to me and on this damn boat now, CJ!" he yelled into his phone, pacing back and forth. "I told you to have it here before I arrived. I don't care about any of that shit. You saying it's on the way means it's not on the damn boat."

He ended the call and flopped down in the seat across from me. He was sweating so much that his shirt clung to his chest. I shook my head at him in disgust.

"De captain says he's ready when we are," Blake said, stepping onto the deck and sitting beside Vincent.

"Yeah, well, we ain't leaving until my extra luggage gets here. After that, I want to get as far away from this island as possible."

"Dis is getting ridiculous, Vinnie. We keep running away over and over," I told him. "I can't keep doin' dis to my son."

"*Our* son, you mean." He gestured for Vincent to come to him, and he did, jumping in Vinnie's arms. "Vincent is our son. Don't you ever forget that. Right, buddy?"

I glanced over at Blake, who tried to maintain a neutral expression, but I could see by his clenched fists he was not a happy man.

"Vinnie, dis is not de life I want to live."

"And you think it's what I want?" he replied angrily. "What do you want me to do, stay at the house and have them kill us? We're running away so we can stay alive, Ruby."

"I knew dat Larry Duncan was going to bring trouble. You never listen to me," I snapped.

"Listen to you about what? Larry's not the problem here, and neither am I. We're not the ones who just happened to run into Junior Duncan in Negril. It was you; so don't blame this shit on me."

"Me can't believe dis. You blaming all this on me?" He wouldn't look at me, so I continued ranting. "I don't sell drugs. I didn't steal a container of drugs. All I did was follow you."

"Shut up, Ruby. I can't deal with this right now." Vinnie stood up and walked back into the cabin of the boat. Vincent followed behind him without even glancing back at me. Sometimes it made me sad that my son admired Vinnie so much.

When they were gone, Blake leaned over and said quietly, "Listen to me, Ruby. Now nuh de time to anger him. Truss what me saying to ya."

"You not saying anyting to me, Blake. You still haven't told me if Vinnie killed my brother."

"Dat's because I don't know yet. I'm waitin' to hear back from a man."

"What man?"

"A man in de States by de name Flynn. He's de only one other than your husband and de Duncans who know de truth." The look on Blake's face was sincere. "So keep quiet 'til me and him have a chance to speak. You may be barking up de wrong tree."

"From de look on your face, you don't tink so," I replied.

Blake looked left then right, placing a finger to his lips.

"What you want me to do? Just sit here and shut my mouth?" I glared at him.

Blake nodded seriously. "Fo' right now, yes. He unda enough pressure. Man like that could snap and kill you and de boy."

I decided to take Blake's advice. I folded my arms and inhaled in an effort to relax my nerves, which were all over the place. I couldn't keep living like this. Not only was my life in danger, but so was the life of my son. Here we were, fleeing our second home in two weeks, and not only were we running from the Duncans, but now the Asians too. The number of enemies we had was increasing by the minute, and I was tired of running.

Vinnie came back, and he seemed a bit calmer.

"All right, the dope is here. Soon as they load the boat, we can get the hell outta here," he told us.

"I'll go make sure dem handle it properly." Blake stood up and left.

"Where are we going now, Vinnie?" I asked. My hope was that he would say Montego Bay or somewhere close, but from what I had gathered, staying in Jamaica was definitely out of the question. I hoped wherever we were headed would at least be nice and tropical, where my son and I could still enjoy the beach.

"I hear Florida's nice this time of year," he said.

"What's in Florida?" My eyes widened and my voice cracked.

He looked into my eyes and said, "Hopefully Larry Duncan and the rest of my money."

Larry

55

"Do you know what to do? You want me to send Curtis with you?" I asked Kenny. We'd just pulled up to the Kings County Courthouse in Brooklyn, and I was sending Kenny on an assignment, but I was concerned because he hadn't said a word since we left the safe house in Long Island.

"I got it," Kenny mumbled as he got out of the car, carrying a small knapsack. "Go in, pay the bail money, and bring him out. It's not rocket science, Dad. Nobody needs to get killed in the process." He headed down the sidewalk and up the steps into the building

"What the hell is that all about?" I turned and asked Curtis. I was hoping he wasn't still in his feelings about Donna being killed. It had been a pretty tough night of arguing and name calling when Kenny and Curtis returned from digging up one of my stashes. *The things you do for your kids.* I had actually ended up promising him I wouldn't kill anyone without talking it over with him or his brother first.

"I thought we cleared the air last night," I said.

"We did." Curtis shrugged. "I think he was fucking with you."

"He better straighten his damn attitude up before I straighten it up for him. I saw him talking to his grandmother this morning." The thing that pissed me off the most was that despite her feelings about Donna, Momma actually agreed with Kenny and started chastising me for my temper and anger issues. All of a sudden, she was Kenny's biggest advocate, spewing off about how they'd proven themselves and I needed to start listening to them, or I was going to be a lonely old man with only my guns as friends. She was so upset she'd decided not to even take the ride into Brooklyn with us.

Curtis didn't confirm or deny that Kenny had gotten his grandmother on his side. Neither one of my boys liked talking about her very much for some reason.

"Give him a break, Dad," he said. "If not for him, then for me. I need him. I can't do this without Kenny."

"Okay, son. I'll do it for you." I patted his shoulder from the seat behind him. "But your brother needs to remember I'm still his damn daddy."

Curtis didn't respond, and we sat in silence until the front door opened five minutes later and Kenny came out of the building. The problem was, he was alone.

"Damn, that was fast," Curtis said when Kenny got in the car.

"Where the hell is he?" I asked.

"He's already been released. Somebody posted his bond about an hour before I got there." Kenny shrugged nonchalantly.

"What the fuck you mean? His people called us bitching and moaning they ain't got no money!" I yelled.

"Don't ask me. The lady said he was released about five, ten minutes ago. He might have walked right past us," Kenny said, still sounding unconcerned. I don't know what was making me angrier: the fact that my best dealer was now in the wind or the fact that my son was acting like he really didn't give a damn.

"Wait. Ain't that him right there?" Curtis said. "Coming down the steps."

"Where?" I turned my attention back to the courthouse, squinting as I tried to find him.

"Yeah, that's him." Kenny pointed, and I followed his finger until I spotted Julio, an up-and-coming Dominican drug broker who'd been working for me. He had somehow been pinched in a raid at a strip club he owned and landed his ass in jail.

We'd been introduced to Julio by Joey the Wop down in Jersey. The only reason I agreed to spring his ass was that he'd distributed almost twenty kilos in a less than a weeks' time and had proven himself somewhat beneficial to my plan to put LC out of business. I was hoping to use me bailing him out as an example of why people should use my services over LC's.

"He's walking with that guy in the suit," Kenny said.

"He must have gotten a bail bondsman, 'cause his people swore they didn't have enough money to get him out," I added.

"Wait. I think I know that man from somewhere." Kenny sat up in his seat. "Curt, isn't that Harris?"

"Damn, I ain't seen him since the wedding, but that is Harris," Curtis said. "I'd recognize that corny-ass dude anywhere."

"Who the hell is Harris?" I asked.

"He's London's husband," Kenny answered.

"What the fuck is London's husband doing with Julio?"

"Well, he is a lawyer. Actually, he's the family lawyer. He handles everything. Mom even uses him," Kenny said. "He's probably the one who bailed him out."

"Come on." I hopped out of the car.

"What are you doing?" I heard Kenny yell from the car.

I stuck my head back through the open door. "Do you know what kind of hostage that guy will make? We might be able to end this whole thing with one phone call."

Kenny and Curtis looked at each other then nodded at the same time, reaching for the car doors.

"We are just snatching him. We're not going to kill him," Kenny stated emphatically.

Ignoring him, I called out, "Julio!"

"Oh, shit. Uh, hey, Larry," Julio said as we approached the two men at the bottom of the courthouse steps. "I was, uh, getting ready to call you. I just got my phone back when they let me out."

"Don't worry about all that. I'm just happy you're among the free." I stared at Harris, who looked nervous. I could see that he recognized exactly who I was. I reached inside my suit jacket, making sure they could see I was pointing a gun at them through the material.

"Uh, hey, what's this all about?" Harris asked.

"You know exactly what this is about, Harris."

At the mention of his name, he looked like he was about to shit himself.

"Yes, Counselor, I know who you are, and I know who the fuck you work for. And it ain't Julio."

Harris's eyes widened. He glanced over at Kenny, who now stood on the opposite side of him with his hands in his hoodie's pockets as well.

Julio looked back at me. "Larry, listen. I swear, I didn't know he was com—"

"Shut up, Julio. We're all going for a little ride." I gestured toward the car just as a black SUV screeched to a halt in front of us. Curtis put an end to the life of the man in the passenger's seat before he could exit the vehicle. The driver must have decided that Harris wasn't worth it, because he pulled off, letting the passenger's body drop to the curb. Curtis's gun was silenced, so she didn't hear the shot, but when she saw the body, a woman nearby screamed and ran up the courthouse steps. Now we had to hurry up and get the hell out of there, but I wasn't leaving without my hostage. I pulled out my gun and pointed it at Harris.

"Larry, please don't do this. I don't know what's going on with you and LC, but I don't have anything to do with it," he said.

"Fuck you, nephew," I growled. "You probably helped them do this to me."

"I didn't. I swear. I wasn't even married to London then." As soon as he finished his sentence, Harris bolted across the street. He was ducking and dodging cars like he was in that old video game Frogger that the kids used to play back in the day.

I lifted my gun to take his ass out, but Kenny shouted, "No, Dad! He's got two kids. Let his ass go."

I reluctantly lowered my hand, but it didn't matter, because within seconds, Harris had been struck by a truck and flew twenty feet in the air, landing on a parked car.

"Ouch, that had to hurt," I said, grimacing.

"We've gotta get the hell outta here," Curtis said. "Come on. Get in the car."

Curtis jumped behind the wheel of the car, where the engine was still running. I turned to get in and looked back. I had no idea where Julio had gone to, but Kenny was still standing there, staring at Harris's limp body, lying on top of a car. I could hear sirens in the distance. As they came closer, Kenny still didn't move. It was as if he were in a trance.

"Kenny! Let's go! He's dead. Ain't nothing we can do for him!" I yelled at him. Finally, he turned, and after taking one look back, he walked toward us, passing right by a group of cops running down the steps. Fortunately, everyone was so focused on the car accident that they didn't even notice us. Kenny climbed in the car, and Curtis pulled off before his brother could even close his door.

London

56

My father put his arm around me as we sat on the uncomfortable plastic sofa. The entire family, with the exception of Vegas, sat in the private family waiting room of the hospital. We'd been there ever since we got the call that Harris had been hit by a truck.

Until we got that call, we were unsure about what was going on, but Daddy knew that Harris was in danger. His driver had called Daddy and told him about the shooting in front of the courthouse. My brothers would deal with him later, because there was no excuse for a bodyguard leaving the scene the way he had, but in the meantime, they were all scrambling to figure out what had happened to Harris and where he was. The driver had left too quickly to get a good description of the shooter, but it was a group of three men, one older, so there was a good chance it was Larry and his boys. Daddy sent another crew racing down there, but it was too late. By the time they got there, Harris was being loaded into the ambulance, and Larry was nowhere to be found.

Harris was still in surgery, where he had been for the past three hours, and no one had come to update us on his condition.

"Everything's going to be okay, baby," my father said.

"I know, Daddy." I inhaled deeply and stared at the neutral-colored carpet, wondering if all hospitals got their ugly décor from the same supplier. Although the initial shock of what had happened was wearing off, I still felt numb for some reason. My husband was fighting for his life, yet I wasn't emotionally overwhelmed or falling apart like I'm sure most wives would be. I didn't even feel the need to cry. I felt nothing.

"This is fucking crazy," Paris snapped. "Don't you think we should be out there with Vegas, looking for Uncle Larry instead of sitting in here doing nothing?"

My mother, who sat on the other side of my father, glared at her. "Paris, being here to support your sister while your brother-in-law is in surgery is far from nothing."

"She can leave if she wants. I'll be fine. And she's right. There's no point in everyone sitting here." I shrugged. If there was one thing my sister was good at, it was making a situation all about her and what she wanted to do. Her wanting to leave was actually a good thing. "There's really no point. I can just call and update everyone if there's any news."

"Great." Paris stood up.

"Don't be ridiculous. No one is going anywhere." My father gave her a disapproving look. Just as she was about to sit down, the door opened, and a doctor walked in.

"Mrs. Grant," he said, and I eased from under my father's arm.

Standing, I tried to read the doctor's face for any signs that would indicate whether the news he was about to deliver was good or bad, but he was emotionless. "How is he?" I asked.

The tension in the room grew as we all waited for his answer.

"Well, it was touch and go in there for a while. Right now he's stable, but not out of the woods yet. We were able to secure things, but his back has been broken in three places. There is a strong chance of paralysis, but we won't know the severity until he regains consciousness," he explained, again devoid of any human feelings. I guess doctors get so used to delivering shitty news that they have to be like robots.

"And when will that be?" I asked.

"I can't really say. Of course, right now he's intubated and sedated. We will probably keep him sedated for a while because we don't want him to move until the swelling in his spine decreases. I don't expect that will be for a few days." He looked around the crowded room.

"Doctor, you said there is a strong chance of paralysis. What did you mean by that?" My mother came and stood by my side.

"Like I said, it's too soon to say, but I will be honest. He most likely will have limited to no mobility in his legs."

"My God, are you saying that my son-in-law is going to be in a wheelchair?" my father asked.

"I think it's best that that's what you all prepare for. He's receiving the best care, and of course, when the time comes, we will set him up with physical therapy and any other type of support he may need. But right now, our main concern is his getting through the next forty-eight to seventy-two hours."

"Thank you, Doctor." I nodded, not knowing what else to say. My mind felt empty.

"One of the nurses will let you know when you can see him." He shook my hand and gave me what he probably thought was a reassuring look.

"Is there anything else that can be done right now?" Junior asked just as the doctor was about to walk out the door.

"Besides pray, nothing," he told us.

I don't know if anyone was actually praying, but after the doctor left, everyone was silent for a few minutes. Personally, I couldn't even form a complete thought, so there was no way I could say a prayer. I just went back to staring at the ugly floor, wondering why I wasn't crying. After a while, I convinced my family that it was time for them to leave.

"Really, everyone, I appreciate your support, but you heard the doctor. There's nothing we can do but wait right now. Y'all might as well go back to handling the rest of our issues. I promise I'll let you know if anything changes," I said.

Everyone else left, and my parents stuck around a few more minutes before they would agree that it was okay for them to go too.

"Oh, London, I'm so sorry, honey." My mother hugged me tight against her body. "We're going to get through this together as a family."

"I know, Momma." I sighed.

"Do you need me to bring you anything?" She dabbed at the tears in the corners of her eyes. It was strange to see that she seemed more upset about my husband's prognosis than I was.

"No, I'm fine."

My father said, "London, I don't want to leave you here alone. Larry is out there . . ."

"Daddy, Vegas and Junior have people all around this hospital. You've made sure of that. Nothing is going to happen to me."

"Well, I'm gonna send a couple more guys to wait up here with you, just in case." He hugged me and walked out the door, leaving my mother and me alone.

"You know whatever you need to make sure Harris is taken care of, we'll get it. You're not going to have to take care of him by yourself."

I shook my head. "Momma, I'm not taking care of Harris."

"I'm talking about when he comes home, London." She smiled weakly.

"So am I," I told her.

Her face was a mixture of shock and something close to disgust. I'm sure she would never dream of saying something like that about Daddy. But her marriage wasn't like my marriage, that was for sure.

"London, what do you mean? He's you husband. Of course you'll take care of him." She reached out and touched my hair.

"Momma, this isn't some Tyler Perry movie, and I'm not an angry black woman writing in a diary. You know what I've realized these past few weeks?" I didn't wait for her to answer. "I've slowly become someone I don't like, in order to please someone that I don't like."

"You're sounding crazy. You can't just abandon him because times have gotten tough. You took a vow for better or for worse." She stared at me like she didn't know who I was.

"I'm not abandoning him, Momma. He's the father of my children. But I don't have the energy or the desire to keep on pretending." As the words came out of my mouth, I realized that I was finally saying what I'd wanted to say for years, and I decided to keep talking. "I'm tired of being the responsible wife and mother and safe member of the family that everyone expects to be reserved and make all the right decisions. Everyone acts like I'm supposed to be perfect, and God forbid I make a mistake; then I'm the worst person in the world. Paris can sleep with whomever, whenever, wherever, and have a baby by God knows who, and it's no big deal. But I'll never forget how you reacted when you found out I had an affair. I'm tired. So, yeah, Harris will have the best care in the world, Momma, but it won't be from me."

"London, this is about you and Daryl isn't—"

Thank God, there was a knock on the door at that moment, so we didn't have to get into that conversation.

A nurse entered the room. "Mrs. Grant?"

"Yes?"

"You can come and see your husband now."

I followed her out into the hallway, leaving my mother standing alone in the waiting room.

Sasha

57

It was after ten o'clock and way past visiting hours when I went back to the hospital. I was headed toward the entrance when I noticed a woman near the edge of the parking lot, smoking a cigarette. I paused for a second, then eased a little closer to get a good look, making sure she was who I thought she was.

"London?"

"Shit, Sasha! You scared me." She jumped, tossing the lit butt out of her hand like a tween who had been caught by a parent.

"My bad. Oh my God, you smoke?" I laughed.

"Actually, I don't. Not anymore. But I used to in college. I needed something to calm my nerves, so I bummed one from one of the security detail. I figured I'd give it a try," she said with a sigh.

"I feel you, but you probably need something a little stronger than tobacco. You shoulda asked Rio for some of that ganja he brought back from Jamaica. It's been working wonders for me the past few days."

"Rio brought weed back from Jamaica?" She shook her head. "Why am I not surprised?"

"You know your brother." I shrugged. "How's Harris?"

"Still asleep. No news."

"Damn. I can't believe this," I told her.

"What's going on, Sasha? I know you didn't come all the way back over here to ask about Harris. You don't even like him like that." Her tone surprised me. She certainly didn't sound like a concerned wife with a really sick husband.

I looked up and saw her waiting for my answer. Our eyes met, and after a few seconds, I said, "I came back to talk to you."

We noticed the security guard watching us from the front of the hospital, and another one to the left side, in the parking lot where we were standing. I didn't want to say what I had to say while anyone was in earshot.

"Let's go back to the waiting room," she suggested.

We entered the hospital and went back to the same waiting room that the family had been in earlier.

"So, talk," she said after she closed the door.

While driving back to the hospital, I had played the conversation I wanted to have with London in my head. In my version, the conversation took place in the confines of the hospital, but finding her smoking in the parking lot had been surprising and almost distracted me. To get myself refocused, I reflected on everything that had taken place over the past few weeks and what I had endured over the past few days. Then, I looked at London and thought about Harris and why we were at the hospital. My thoughts became clear, and I was renewed with my intention.

"London, Uncle LC and Vegas have everyone looking everywhere for his brother, but I think they're going about it the wrong way. They're looking for a needle in a haystack," I told her.

"So, what do you want them to do?" she asked.

"It's not about what they do anymore, London. That crazy motherfucker killed my mother. It's about what I do at this point. I'm going to find him." My voice was calm and even.

"Sasha, how do you—"

"Larry's undercutting Uncle LC's distribution business. He's giving away fucking dope like he's Oprah and it's one of her favorite things. You get a brick! You get a brick!" I pointed my finger at invisible people in an imaginary audience, and London laughed. "When it runs out, he's gotta go back for more. We find his supplier, then I guarantee we will find his ass.

"Sasha, you know what you're saying, right?" London folded her arms and waited for my answer.

"I'm gonna find Vinnie Dash. You know finding him will eventually lead us to Larry." I raised an eyebrow at her and watched her reaction as she processed everything I'd said.

She was quiet for a while and finally said, "Sounds like you're just trying to build a new mouse trap, but what do you need from me?"

"I need you to tell me everything you found out in Jamaica. I wanna know everything you know about Vinnie Dash." I could feel my excitement rising, but I contained it because she hadn't said yes, and I really didn't know if she would. London was older and way more reserved than Paris. Had I gone to Paris with my plans, there would have been no hesitation. She stayed on ready. London was the total opposite.

"But I don't want Uncle LC to know. I don't want him, or Vegas, or Junior, or anyone else's help but yours."

"I can help, but on one condition," she answered.

I frowned, wondering what she could possibly want in return. "What is it?"

"I go with you to find him."

My mouth fell open. I truly hadn't expected that to be her response, and I couldn't understand why.

"I don't know London," I said skeptically.

"That bastard put Harris in here, and he has put me in a fucked-up situation, not to mention that he tried to kill my daddy. I want his ass just as much as you do. I'm down," she responded in a truly un-London-like way.

"Okay, London. You can go. Let's go get these motherfuckers." Then a moment later, after reality settled in, I added, "I know I said I didn't want anyone else involved, but do you think we should get Paris?"

London shook her head vigorously. "Have you lost your mind? That's the last person in the world we need. That bitch is a loose cannon, and her only way of getting shit done is riding dick and killing dudes. I know Daddy and Vegas find those skills of hers useful, but we don't need them in this situation."

"I get what you're saying, but I will ride as many dicks and slit as many throats as I need to if it's gonna help me find those bastards. So, you best be prepared to do whatever it takes or keep your ass home, because I don't need you or anyone else getting in my way."

Larry

58

"Are you sure about this?" Curtis asked.

"Not many things I'm sure of in this life, son, but black women and their hair? That, my boy, is something you can count on. She'll be here," I told him.

Sure enough, at precisely 4:55, a sleek black Town Car pulled up to the front door of Diana's Salon and Spa in the strip mall across the street from us, followed by a black Escalade. Two men got out of the SUV and stood watch, while the Town Car driver got out and opened the back door to help my sister-in-law, Chippy, out of the back.

I watched her walk into the salon, surrounded by her security team. It had been almost fifteen years since I'd seen her. From what I could see, she was maybe a few pounds heavier, but she still looked pretty much the same. Chippy had always been a good-looking woman, and considering she'd kept this standing appointment at the same salon for all these years, she'd worked hard to maintain her looks. Someone else might consider LC a lucky man to have a wife like Chippy, but I knew the truth about her. She was a conniving back-stabber just like him.

Once she was safely inside, the driver got back into the Town Car and drove off, while the two men positioned themselves at the front door. The SUV turned into the parking lot of the salon and drove around back.

We waited another twenty minutes before I finally told Curtis, "Okay, drive around back. Slowly." He did as I instructed, and when he turned into the parking lot, I could see two men posted at the back door. We were still several yards away, so I told him, "Park here and wait for my signal."

I took out my 9 mm and twisted the silencer on the barrel before I stepped out of the van. Casually, I walked along the back side of the building, making sure there were no security cameras in the vicinity. The two guys were so busy talking to one another that they didn't even see me approaching, and the bullets struck them before they realized what was happening. I reached into their pockets and disarmed them, then waved for Curtis, who had parked at the edge of the building. He drove down to where I was, and I tossed the guns I had taken from the now dead men into the van.

"Keep an eye on the parking lot, and move those bodies over to the side," I told my boys.

I trusted them to follow orders, so I didn't wait around to watch them work. I turned the knob on the back door of the salon and slipped inside.

I heard the familiar beauty-salon sound of women gossiping. "I can't believe her husband had the nerve to tell her that chick was his cousin. He knew he was lying, and so did everyone else, with his trifling ass!" one woman was saying.

I stepped into what looked like the storage area of the salon. There were shelves holding all types of shampoos and hair dyes, along with towels and boxes.

"You know she's gonna stay married to him anyway," I heard another woman respond.

I walked past the shelves and arrived in the back of the salon, where a row of hooded dryers lined the wall. I searched for Chippy, but I didn't see her.

"Can I help you?" a startled woman asked, looking me up and down.

"Uh, I'm looking for Mrs. Duncan. I'm a member of her security team," I said when I saw her eying the gun that was sticking from the waistband of my pants.

"Oh, she's in the shampoo room." She pointed. "Can you let her know Katrina will be right there?"

"Yes, ma'am." I nodded and went into the room she had directed me to. Sure enough, there was Chippy, all alone, a towel wrapped around her neck and her eyes closed as she laid her head back in one of the porcelain sinks. I eased over beside her and turned on the water, and she jumped a little, but her eyes remained closed.

"Katrina, that water's a little cold. Make it a little warmer for me, sweetie."

I turned the knob on the other side, and the water instantly warmed up. I picked up the rubber spray hose and held it over her head, running my fingers through her soft hair as the water flowed over it.

"Mmmmmm, that feels so nice. With everything going on in my life, I needed this," Chippy said with a smile.

I looked up at the shelf above the sink and spotted a bottle of shampoo. I poured some into my hand and rubbed it into her hair, then began massaging her scalp.

"You're being a little rough today, huh?" She opened her eyes, and the look on her face went from surprise to horror as she realized whose hands were on her head.

"My, my, my, you've come a long way since the good ol' days when you worked at Big Sam's," I taunted.

I could see her back stiffen, and she slowly sat up. Water dripped from her hair onto her ears and to her towel-covered shoulders.

"Larry?" she questioned nervously.

"You don't look happy to see me, Chippy," I said. "Why is it nobody seems happy to see me these days?"

"I—How? Where did you come from?"

"Oh, I been around, Chippy." From the corner of my eye, I noticed her hand easing into the large purse on her lap, then she moved to stand up. I touched her arm and motioned toward the gun in my waistband. "Now, Chippy, you don't wanna be responsible for me killing all of the lovely ladies in this salon, do you? That's a lot of blood on your hands."

"Miss Chippy, is everything okay?" The shampoo girl walked in and gave Chippy a worried look.

"Yes, Katrina. This is my brother-in-law. It's fine," she answered, her voice sounding tight. "Can you give us a minute?"

"We're just catching up on old times, which ain't got shit to do with you." I gave her a threatening look, and she quickly walked away.

"What do you want, Larry?" Chippy asked.

"Well, I figured talking to you would be easier than talking to my brother. The last time I tried that, it didn't end well for him, as I'm sure you already know," I said. "So, we're gonna go and have a little talk. Come on. I've got a car waiting out back."

"We can talk right here," she said as if she had a choice.

"Get your ass up and let's go, Charlotte. Or would you rather I put a bullet in your head right now?" I said through clenched teeth.

Chippy stood up, and I grabbed her by the arm and guided her out the back door.

Sasha

59

One hour earlier

London and I watched as Jamaica John and two guys pulled into a Chinese buffet restaurant that was close enough to his vape shop that they could have walked across the parking lot. We timed getting out of the car perfectly so that we were about twenty feet in front of them as they headed into the restaurant. I never realized it before, maybe because she was always wearing that conservative shit, but London had what the guys call a *badunkadunk*: her ass was so phat in those jeans I was starting to understand why Paris was jealous. It didn't take long before they were mumbling to themselves behind us.

Once inside the restaurant, we didn't stop at the hostess station. We went straight to the restroom.

"I think we got their attention. What do you think?" London asked, touching up her makeup.

"I think the big guy took one look at that ass of yours and fell in love."

"Let me ask you a question. How the hell did you know he was coming here tonight?"

"The boy genius told me."

"Nevada?" She looked confused, but she shouldn't have been. Nevada had a genius IQ of over 170 and was being trained in something by everyone in the family.

"Yeah, think about it. He has access to Vegas, Uncle LC, and Orlando's files. He even hacked into Harris's computer when

Vegas and Uncle LC couldn't get into it last night," I explained. "All I had to do was play some Tour of Duty with him and bring up Jamaica John, and he started telling me the guy's life story. He eats here every Tuesday and Thursday when they serve crab legs."

She started to laugh.

"What's so funny?"

"Nothing big. This just reminds me of Jun Cheng and his people in Jamaica. Nevada's like a piece of furniture. He can go anywhere he wants in the Duncan household and gather information because he's invisible."

"True, but listen. We better get back out there. You deal with him, and I'll distract his friends." I closed my lipstick, placed it in my purse, and reached for the door. "Oh, by the way. I wanna know where you got all that ass and why it skipped my side of the family."

We were laughing as we exited the restroom. Jamaica John and his posse were already at the buffet station, piling food on their plates. London made her way toward them as I headed to the hostess station so we could be seated.

"Oops, I'm so sorry," I heard her say. I eased a bit closer and saw that she was standing in front of Jamaica John, smiling up at him.

"Nuh problem, pretty lady." John grinned back at her.

"Oooooh, those look so good. I love crabs." She peered at one of the plates he held, piled high with steamed crab legs.

"Me too," John said.

"There's just something about cracking that hardness, then sucking all that juicy meat in your mouth." She bit her bottom lip and raised an eyebrow at him, and John damn near dropped his plate.

"Da–dat's mi favorite part," he stuttered. "Dis place has de best ones, I promise."

"Well, I hope they taste as good as they look. I'll have to try them and see." London winked at him then turned around to look for me. John barely moved, staring at London like a lovesick high schooler, until one of his men snapped him out of it, and he headed for his table.

I couldn't help but laugh and relax a little as I watched from my table near John's. I knew it was his because the jacket hanging on the back of the chair was so big it could only belong to the super-sized Jamaican. The hostess had tried to lead me to the opposite side of the restaurant, but I steered her this way. London slipped into the chair across from me. I made sure she would be seated where John could look directly at her.

The hostess brought two glasses of water to the table and then told us we could serve ourselves, so we went up to the buffet. I really didn't care for Chinese, especially at an all-you-can-eat restaurant. To be honest, I really wasn't even hungry, but I put a dab of rice and vegetables, along with an egg roll, on my plate. London made sure to put crab legs on hers, and she made eye contact with John as we returned to our seats.

London picked up one of the legs and cracked it open, seductively placing it in her mouth and sucking it gently. Her eyes were on John the entire time.

"Damn, bitch, your ass is turning me on with that shit," I teased.

"Let's hope this shit works." She laughed as she licked her fingers.

I looked over my shoulder and saw that not only was John enjoying the way London was devouring her crab legs, but so were his boys. They were staring just as hard, mumbling and nudging him.

"Oh, it's working," I told her.

A few moments later, John wobbled over to our table and asked, "Ya like dem?"

"Mmmmm, yeah," London said. "I could suck on these things all night."

"Me told ya." He smiled.

"You were right. Thank you," she said.

"My name is John."

"Nice to meet you, John. I'm Devin," London told him.

"Devin. Nice to meet ya. I wan' take ya out tonight. Dey havin' reggae night at my man's club. I can get ya in VIP," he said. "We headed over dere after we eat."

"I don't know. My girl and I have plans." London gestured toward me. John looked like he was only now noticing that I was sitting at the table with her.

"Oh, bring ya girl. She can come wit' us." He asked me, "You wan' come wit' us? It's fine. We can have some drinks, smoke some weed, dance on de dance floor."

"Sounds like fun." I nodded, realizing that our night was going to be longer than we had anticipated. No worries, though, because it would all be worth it in the end. We agreed to meet John at his friend's reggae spot, and he walked away.

London looked down at her phone and cursed. "Shit. I hope the damn hospital hasn't called, or anyone else for that matter. I turned my ringer off. By now I'm sure the guys at the hospital have realized I gave them the slip."

"Any missed calls?" I asked as she checked the screen.

"Nope. Just a text from Momma checking on Harris. I better call her," London said.

"That would probably be a good idea. I'll keep an eye on these three."

"Hey, Mom. . . . Yeah, I'm okay. . . . Nothing's changed since you left this morning. They say he's stable, but they don't know how long before he regains consciousness. . . . Yes, I'm going to spend the night here. . . ." She glanced over at me with a smirk as she lied her way through a conversation with Aunt Chippy. "No, that's okay, Mom. If you can just keep an eye on the girls once you get your hair done, that would be great. You don't need to come to the hospital. I'll call you in the morning. . . . Yes, I'm sure. . . . I love you too. Bye."

London ended the call and put away her phone.

"Damn, you're good. I haven't been giving you enough credit, cousin," I said with a laugh.

One thing that London and I had agreed on was that we had to be strategic, which basically meant we couldn't let anyone know what we were doing. Ironically, Harris being in a coma worked to our advantage. The family never questioned London's whereabouts; they always assumed she was at the hospital with him, and they had no idea that most of the time, she was with me, working on our quest to find Vinnie Dash.

Steering clear of the family had also been easy for me, especially since I hadn't really been saying much since my mother's death. They assumed I was still in mourning. No one suspected what we were doing. The most difficult thing to deal with was ducking the numerous members of security that Uncle LC and Vegas had on us 24/7. We had already been gone for a few hours unnoticed, and I hoped that it would continue. One thing was for certain: there was no turning back now.

Chippy

60

I'd been in more than my fair share of life-threatening situations over the years, but the sense of fear I felt as Larry led me out the back of the hair salon was nothing that I'd ever felt. All I could think about was the number of lives he'd already taken, including Donna's, and the fact that he'd also tried to kill LC and Harris, who was still fighting for his life. My fear grew stronger as he pulled me past the dead bodies of my two security men and opened the back door to an old van that was waiting for us.

"Get in," Larry commanded.

I hesitated, trying to reason with him. "Larry, don't do this."

"Get in the fucking car, Chippy," he said even louder.

"Aunt Chippy, it's okay. Please just get in the van."

I looked up and saw my nephew sitting in the back seat. Kenny was such a handsome boy, and I'd always had a soft spot in my heart for him, even despite everything that was going on. I glanced at the driver and saw that it was his brother Curtis. I loved him too, because he was family, but Curtis definitely had more of an edge to him than his younger brother.

Larry pushed me hard, and I almost stumbled. Kenny reached his hand out to help me, and I grabbed it to steady myself as I climbed into the back seat beside him.

"Let's go!" Larry snapped as soon as he got in the front passenger's seat. He slammed the door shut, and Curtis drove off. I wondered how long it was going to take someone to realize that I was gone from the salon, but it didn't matter. I knew that by that time, we would be long gone—and most likely I'd be dead.

"Kenny, you keep an eye on her. Don't make me have to come back there," Larry said with his voice full of evil intentions.

"Don't worry, Aunt Chippy. He's not gonna hurt you," Kenny said, trying to reassure me. "He just wants to talk."

"I know your father's way of talking, Kenny." I was trembling both from fear and the cold water that dripped from my hair, soaking through the towel and down my back. "I'm sure he had talks with Frankie, Donna, and Harris, so excuse my skepticism."

"Seriously, Aunt Chippy, we are not going to hurt you," Kenny said.

"You look so much like your mother, Kenny." I purposely brought up NeeNee to see what type of reaction I would get. Curtis didn't flinch, but I could see a flicker in Kenny's eyes. "She misses you boys."

"And we miss her," Kenny said, smiling happily, until Larry glared into the back seat.

"Are you trying to talk my boys into being against me, Chippy?" Larry grumbled.

"If their mother couldn't talk them into anything, then why would I think I could, Larry?"

"Because you think you're better than everyone else."

"Whatever, Larry. You know that's not true," I said, hoping to at least sound brave. "What do you want? Nobody wants to fight with you, and nobody wants a war."

Larry hesitated, and his brow wrinkled up as if he was confused. "I want my portion of the business back."

"Larry, you sold your portion of the business, remem—"

"Bullshit! That motherfucker stole it from me, and you know it! He knows it, and everyone knows it!" he screamed, spit flying everywhere.

I jumped in my seat, praying I hadn't pushed him too far. "Okay, Larry," I said quietly. "I'll talk to LC, get him to give you your portion back. Just calm down, please."

That was enough to bring his stress level down a notch, I guess, because he sounded calmer when he said, "I don't want things to be like this, Chippy, but what kind of father would I be to let everything I worked for be stolen right from under me? Don't you think I wanna leave a legacy for my boys? Hell, Chippy, you're Curtis's godmother and NeeNee's best friend. I tried to talk to your husband. I told him he needs to give me back what's rightfully mine. And you know what he did?" Larry asked.

"No." I shook my head.

"He called me a liar. Now, I may be a lot of things—hell, I may be crazy—but, Chippy, you know I ain't a liar, don't you?"

"I know that, Larry. At least I used to," I said. In my head, I was thinking, *You might not be a liar, but you tried to kill my husband, you psychotic piece of shit.* I was scared, but my blood was still boiling as I thought of how close LC had come to dying after Larry shot him.

"What's that supposed to mean? You think I'm a liar?"

"It doesn't matter what I think, Larry. You're still going to kill me. You're going to use me to trap LC, and then you're going to kill me. You know it, and I know it. You used to be a standup guy, Larry. Now, not so much." I was trying to appeal to a sense of decency or honor in him, if there was any of that left. I had no idea if it would work, but I had to try something. Obviously, I miscalculated, because my words just pissed him off.

"Fuck you, Chippy, with your high and mighty bullshit!" he raged.

"Then tell me in front of your sons that you're not going to kill me."

He took a breath and held it. The car became so quiet I could hear my heart pounding.

"Tell her, Dad," Kenny urged. He sounded like he was pleading, like he wanted to believe his father was a good person. I sensed that I had found a weak spot, so I pressed on it.

"He can't, Kenny, because he knew the minute he walked in that salon that he was going to kill me."

"God dammit, you want the truth?" Larry yelled from the front.

"Yes, Larry, I would like the truth." I glanced at Kenny, who was hanging on his father's words.

"Yeah, I'm gonna kill you, Chippy. More importantly, I'm going to make that piece-of-shit brother of mine watch as I cut you one piece at a time." He held up a switchblade, clicking a button so the knife sprang to life. "LC took my world from me. Now I'm going to take his world from him, and I'm going to start with you."

I looked into his eyes and knew that his face would be the last one I saw before dying. *Dear God*, I silently prayed. *Help me.*

"These boys and NeeNee are your world, Larry," I said, refusing to give up just yet. "Do you want them to have to fight with my boys for the rest of their lives, like the Hatfields and the McCoys? Because if you kill LC or me, my boys will never give up."

"Neither will mine," Larry replied pridefully.

"Pop, what are you saying?" Kenny yelled out, sounding distressed. "You said you weren't gonna hurt her. You promised."

"Shut the fuck up, boy," Larry growled, the knife still pointed at me. "She's just as evil and conniving as LC is."

"I'm not so sure they're the ones who are evil." Suddenly, Kenny reached over the seat and pushed Larry's hand up, gripping it as he yelled at me, "Get out, Aunt Chippy! Open the door and get out now!"

The van swerved as Curtis was distracted by the commotion. The car behind us blew its horn. I was confused for a brief moment; then I grabbed the handle and opened the door. I can't say for certain, but I think Kenny pushed me out onto the street. Thank God we had been on a narrow city street and he wasn't traveling too fast, or I might have died from the fall. My body tumbled against the pavement, and I cried out in both panic and pain. I lifted my head in time to see the van stop and Larry's door open, but then he must have realized there were witnesses around, because the door closed again, and the van sped off down the street.

"Oh my God! Are you okay?" I heard a woman screaming behind me just before I passed out.

Sasha

61

"Are ya havin' fun?" John yelled over the loud music. It wasn't a very large club, but the crowd was decent, and the DJ was popping. I spent most of the night in VIP, declining invitations from various men offering everything from drinks to straight-up dick. London hadn't left John's side. They had danced, talked, and flirted all night. She had him eating out of the palm of her hand, literally, as she plucked a lemon wedge from the center of the table and put it in his mouth so they could take shots of tequila.

"Mm-hmm." London nodded.

"Come home wit' me." He leaned toward her.

"You have to ask her." London tossed a shot back and pointed at me. "She's my girl. I want to, but the only guys I'm allowed to get with are the ones we get with together."

John's eyes widened, and he smiled at me. "Is dat true?"

"You're a big man, but do you really think you can handle both of us?" I said with a wink.

"Hell yeah!" Not wasting another second, he paid the tab, and within minutes, we were headed out.

"Are you sure you're down for this?" I asked London a while later as we followed John to his apartment.

"Why would you even ask that? I'm the one who initiated this shit," London replied.

I got serious. "Because shit is probably gonna get real once we get inside this fat fucker's place. I know you're married, so if you don't wanna—"

She stopped me before I could finish. "Look, I told you I was ready, and I am. If he knows where Vinnie Dash is, I'm gonna make sure he tells us." London nodded, staring straight ahead with a look of resolve. "Let's go." We had just pulled up and parked behind Jamaica John's car in front of a small house.

Jamaica John was waiting for us in front when we got out of the car. He unlocked the door, and we followed him inside.

"You going on a trip?" I asked, noticing two suitcases sitting near the doorway.

"Vacation," Jamaica John said, offering no more detail as he locked the door behind us.

"Where you going?"

"Somewhere warm," he snapped. It was obvious he didn't want to give up any details, so I left it alone. I didn't want to piss him off before we had barely gotten in the front door.

He led us into a small living area and turned on the lights. It was a typical bachelor pad, with a black faux leather sofa and chair, black lacquer coffee and end tables, and a large painting of a half-naked woman on the wall.

"This is nice," London lied as she looked around.

"Ya want some smoke?" He reached into a jar on his mantle and took out a plastic sack of weed.

"Sure." I shrugged. London didn't look like she wanted to be a willing participant. I said, "Do you still have to pee, Devin?"

"Huh?"

"You said you had to pee when we were in the car, remember?"

"Ohhhhh, yeah." She nodded.

"Bathroom is down de hall," John said, sitting on the sofa to roll a blunt.

Once it was lit, he took a long drag, then passed it to me. After taking a pull, I went and kneeled in front of him, blowing the smoke in his face. He closed his eyes and inhaled, smiling. Then, I took off my shirt. John stared at my perky breasts, looking like he wanted to devour me.

"You wanna go in your room and get started without her?" I suggested.

He reached out, and his pudgy fingers rubbed against my lace bra. "Ya fine as fuck, ya know dat?"

"I do." I nodded. "Come on."

He struggled to get off the sofa, and I contained my laughter. He took me by the hand and led me up the narrow staircase into his bedroom. There were clothes on his bed, which he quickly knocked onto the floor. Taking another hit off the blunt, he grabbed me into his arms and kissed me. My first instinct was to gag, but I calmed down and forced myself to kiss him back.

I pushed him onto the bed then straddled him, took the blunt from his hand, and put it into an ashtray on the nightstand, where another half-smoked blunt was resting. I reached into his sweatpants and was surprised by what I felt. Jamaica John's dick was just as large as his body. If it had been attached to someone better looking, I might have been able to enjoy myself; but what the hell. I wasn't there to have fun. I was there to do a job, so I got to work, stroking and pulling on it until he closed his eyes and started moaning.

"You like that?" I ran my finger gently back and forth against his swollen head.

"Suck it," he whispered. I frowned, because putting his dick in my mouth was not what I had planned on doing.

"I will," I lied, standing up and unzipping my skirt. It fell to the floor, and John became even more aroused as he stared at me, standing in front of him dressed in only a bra, thong, garter, stockings, and stiletto boots. I performed a mini strip tease as I eased out of my boots and unrolled the stockings one by one, then used them to tie him to the bedpost. It always amazed me how easy it was to get these horny motherfuckers tied up.

"Shit," he whispered as I ran my fingers down the side of his face and down his body.

"You ready?"

"Fuck yeah!" he said eagerly.

"Good. Devin, he's ready!" I called out. "What we are about to do is always better with three."

London walked in, gun in hand, and aimed it at him. She handed me another weapon.

John shook his head as if he had known all along that it was too good to be true. Bet he was feeling pretty stupid now. "What ya want? I got no money here. All I got is weed."

"We don't want no fuckin' money, John," London told him. "We want information."

"What? What ya askin' 'bout? Me don' know nothing!" he yelled.

"Shut the fuck up and listen, you fat fuck. You know a lot, and we know it. Now, tell us about Larry Duncan," I commanded him.

"Me don' know no Larry Duncan."

"Everyone knows about Larry Duncan," I spewed. "There's five hundred large on his head."

Whap! I slapped him across the face. For a second, it looked like he was more turned on than fearful of my assault. But when he tugged on the restraints and realized he was stuck, then his arousal turned into anger.

"You bitch!"

"Where the fuck is Larry Duncan?" I put the gun to his temple.

"I don't know. De number he gave me no work." He was sweating profusely.

"Where the fuck is Vinnie Dash?" London asked, taking a step closer to the bed.

Jamaican John tried to pull himself free, but I had tied him in such a way that he couldn't escape. "I don't know."

"Stop fucking lying to us, John. We already know that you were the one who orchestrated the drug deal between Larry and Vinnie." I aimed the gun at his head. That was enough to make him suddenly remember that he did, in fact, know something about Vinnie Dash.

"Vinnie is in de wind. He was in Jamaica, but he disappeared. Nobody knows where de fuck he is," John said as he continued to struggle. Sweat was dripping down his face and his neck. His shirt was now sticking to his body.

"Lying motherfucker. You know what? I'm tired of this shit." London left the room and returned with a large knife.

I looked at her. "What the fuck are you gonna do with that?"

"I'm about to neuter this bastard. Seems like the only thing these men understand is their dicks being cut off," she said angrily. "I ain't got time for games. I gotta get back to the hospital before Daddy finds out I'm gone, so I'm about to cut his dick off, inch by inch, until he tells us what we want to know."

She looked so serious that even I couldn't tell if she really intended to do it. "Dude, if I were you, I'd start talking, or that dick you were just begging me to suck is gonna be gone."

London moved closer, and for the first time, I saw actual fear in John's face.

"No!" he hollered and started violently thrashing his huge body to the point I thought he might break the bed; then, all the flaying ended abruptly. He screamed out in pain and then took a deep breath before going limp. His eyes were open, but they looked empty, staring at nothing.

"What the fuck happened?" I asked London.

"I don't know. I think he had a heart attack." She placed two fingers on his neck. "He's dead. Shit. What the fuck do we do now?" she said breathlessly.

"I don't know. Search his shit while I put my clothes on," I said, stepping into my skirt. I was leaning against the wall to put on my boots when I noticed London going through his dressers. "Did you find anything?"

"Nothing," she said as she rummaged through the clothes and tossed them on the floor.

"Check his pants pockets," I suggested.

London went into his pockets and pulled out his cell phone. She looked down at the screen and let out a little laugh. "You're not going to believe this, but his phone isn't even locked. Who doesn't lock their phone in this day and age?"

"Who cares? Check his text messages. See if he has anything from Vinnie or Larry."

"Bingo. He has a text message from VD that came in two days ago."

"What's it say?"

London scrolled through his phone and read: "Leaving Jamaica. Meet me at the marina in three days with my money."

"What marina?" I asked.

"I don't know. John just texted back OK. But three days is tomorrow."

"Well, we know one thing. He's going somewhere warm." I finished dressing and picked up my gun. "Give me his phone."

London did as I asked, and I went into his email. A smile spread across my face when I found what I had hoped would be there. "He's got a one-way ticket to Jacksonville, Florida for tomorrow afternoon."

Kenny

62

"Pull this fucking van over! Pull it over!" my dad screamed, repeatedly slamming his hand on the dashboard like a maniac.

He'd been screaming, yelling, and punching the dash nonstop for nearly twenty minutes. Curtis just ignored him, driving until we'd crossed well over the Queens/Long Island border. I was scared, because most of his tirade had something to do with me and how he wanted to rip my throat out and shit down my neck.

Curtis finally pulled into the driveway of the safe house, and my father, who looked like he was about to have a damn stroke, started coming over the seat of the van after me. At that point, all I wanted to do was get as far away from him as possible, because I couldn't be sure if he'd lost it enough to make me his next victim. The van had barely come to a stop when I jumped out headed toward the street. I had barely walked twenty feet from the van when he grabbed me from behind, spinning me around.

"So, what? You too good for us now, you fucking traitor?" my dad growled just before he punched me in the stomach. "You pussy-ass momma's boy."

I doubled over in pain and stumbled backward. Just as I gathered enough strength to stand back up, he charged at me. This time, I was ready and blocked him in time, which angered him even more. Not only was my dad a tall man, but he was also as strong as an ox for his age. It was natural strength that was more like a gift, because he almost never worked out to maintain it. What he didn't realize was that although I wasn't as cocky as he and Curtis, I had been blessed with his genetics and had that same natural strength. He underestimated me, mainly because I allowed him to smack me around. He glared at me, his eyes full of anger, and I retaliated with the same stare.

He came at me again, and we locked like two pit bulls ready to fight to the death. We wrestled one another to the ground, grunting as we exchanged blows.

"Kenny, Dad, stop it. Stop!" Curtis yelled as he tried to separate us. It took him a minute, but finally, he got enough space to push us apart.

I leaned against the car, my hands on my knees, trying to catch my breath.

"What the fuck is wrong with you? Why'd you let her go?" my dad spat at me.

"You said you weren't gonna kill her." I panted, positioning myself in a defensive posture in case he tried to attack me again.

"I didn't say I wasn't gonna kill her. I said I wasn't gonna kill her there at the fucking beauty shop." He began pacing like the madman he was. "Now you've gone and fucked everything up."

"Aunt Chippy did nothing wrong. She's always been nice to me and Curtis. This bullshit is between you and LC. She has nothing to do with it. How'd you like it if LC went after Mom?"

"You're a fucking disgrace. You've ruined it. I was going to take away the one thing LC loved more than anything, and you messed it up." He kept storming up and down the sidewalk, shaking his head while he talked. Then he stopped, turning toward the steps to the house. "I know, Momma. We're going to bring it inside." He turned back to me. "You heard your grandmother. Let's bring it inside. And don't think I ain't gonna kick your ass when we get in there."

"Will you stop fucking talking to her?" I yelled at him. I just couldn't take it anymore.

"What are you talking about?"

I pointed at the door he'd been looking at. "I'm talking about the fact that there is nobody over there. That Grandma Bettie's been dead twenty years."

"You little disrespectful bastard!" He charged at me again, but this time Curtis grabbed him.

"This entire time I've been quiet about it, and so has Curtis. We've been avoiding sitting in seats and making accommodations for a woman that's been fucking dead for over twenty years. Wake up, Dad! She's not here, so stop talking to her!"

"Leave it alone, Kenny," Curtis warned, struggling to hold him back.

"Sorry, but I can't do that, Curt. Not anymore. I can't turn a blind eye anymore. Our father is mentally ill, and he needs to be hospitalized. Uncle LC and them were right to have him locked away," I said, finally unburdening myself of the guilt that had been building inside of me. We'd been enabling my father to be as crazy and dangerous as everyone had tried to tell us he was.

My dad reached his arm behind Curtis, snatching the gun my brother always carried. He pointed it at me.

"Say it again and you're gonna be the one dead," he snapped. "You disrespectful motherfucker."

"Dad, it's okay." Curtis eased in front of him in an effort to get him to lower the gun. I could see the tears forming in my brother's eyes, and my heart raced. "Please, please, Dad, lower the gun."

"He's crazy, Curt," I whispered, now fighting my own tears.

My dad looked at Curtis and said, "Curtis, go take your grandma inside the house and y'all get ready, 'cause we gonna have to move out this house. The neighbors are watching us."

"Okay, Dad. But first, please give me the gun," Curtis pleaded.

My dad and I stood in the middle of the driveway, neither one of us moving. I steadied my breathing, finding solace in believing my brother loved me enough that he was standing in the way of a bullet. For a brief second, I wanted him to shoot me.

"Yeah, Grandma Bettie, we're coming right now," Curtis suddenly said, his voice sounding stiff. "Pop, Grandma Bettie said come on and get in the van with her."

"What?" My dad finally turned away from me.

Curtis gently took the gun from him and pointed to the truck. "She's waiting. We'd better hurry up before she starts cussing."

"Oh, yeah, you're right." My dad walked over and opened the back side door. "Come on, Momma. Curt, let's go!"

"Curt, he's crazy. He's gonna get you killed," I said as he followed him to the van.

Curt stopped and turned to me. "I gotta go with him, Kenny. I'm all he's got."

"What about me?" I asked.

"Go home, Kenny. You always got Ma." He got in the van, and I watched helplessly as he backed it up then drove away.

63

An array of emotions ran through me. As soon as I got the call that my wife had escaped an attempted abduction, I was both relieved and angry. Just a few minutes before, Vegas had received word that two of the men who were assigned to her detail were now dead, and Chippy was missing. I immediately knew that my brother had taken her, and fear seized my heart until I received the call a half hour ago that she was safe. She was now on her way home with Junior, who was closest to her location.

"How the hell did they get to her, Vegas?" I asked.

"I don't know, Pop. She had six guys on her detail, and one of them was your guy Willie."

Wasn't much I could say bad about Willie. He was a retired cop and Navy Seal.

The front door opened, and Chippy walked in. I rushed over and held my wife as Junior escorted her into our home. "Are you okay?"

"I'm all right, LC." Chippy sobbed into my chest.

"Did that bastard touch you?" I noticed the blood stains on the arm of her blouse.

"No, he didn't hurt me. I scraped my arm when I jumped out of the van." Her hair was standing all over her head, and her clothes were disheveled, but she had never looked more beautiful to me than at that moment. I kissed her forehead and hugged her again.

"Ma!" Paris ran down the stairs and over to her mother, her face full of tears.

"I'm okay, baby," Chippy assured her.

"I'm gonna kill him, Ma. I promise, if it's the last thing that I do," Paris snapped.

"We've gotta find him first," Rio commented, walking over and hugging his mother.

"Trust me, we're gonna find him," Vegas said.

"Ma, did he say anything?" Orlando asked.

"Not really. He just kept saying that he wanted his portion of the business that your father stole from him." Chippy looked at me. "I'll tell you one thing, LC. He's never gonna stop."

"Yeah, and he's knocking us off one by one," Rio said. He wasn't entirely wrong to be worried, either. Now that I knew Larry could get at us like this, the situation had risen to a whole new level of danger.

"I want this entire family on fucking lockdown. Everyone needs to be home now. Everyone! No one is to leave this compound without my permission. Am I understood?" I announced.

"Nevada. Where is he?" Chippy started to panic.

"I'm right here, Grandma." Nevada hugged Chippy, and she held onto him, but you could see he was angry.

"Junior, where's Sonya?" Chippy asked.

"She's upstairs with the kids. She's safe, Ma," Orlando said, putting his arm around her. "And so are you. We all are."

"I don't know about that," Vegas said, removing his phone from his ear.

"What the hell do you mean?" I asked, my concern matching the look on my wife's face.

"That was Bruce from London and Harris's security detail. London and Sasha never made it to the hospital. They aren't there," Vegas told me.

"What the hell do you mean, they never made it?" I demanded.

"That's impossible. I talked to London earlier, and she said she was already at the hospital and Sasha was with her. She said they were going to spend the night." Chippy turned and looked at me. Any relief I had felt when Chippy returned home was gone, replaced by fear for my first daughter and my niece.

"Where the fuck are they?" I snapped, and damn near everyone in the room jumped.

"We're trying to reach them now. Neither one of them are answering their phones," Vegas replied.

"Oh my God, LC. He has them. He has Sasha and London. How are we going to find them?" Chippy's eyes filled with tears. I put my arm around her and asked myself the same question.

"We don't know that, Chippy," I whispered into her still damp hair.

"Why don't you just ping their phones, Grandpa?" Nevada asked.

"Good thinking." I looked over at my grandson, and then to his father, and nodded.

"I'm already on it, Pop," Vegas said.

"Orlando, you take a team and check it out. Junior and Nevada will get you within a few blocks of the ping point. If you find something, don't try to be a hero. Wait for us before you go charging in. We may have to call the authorities in. There's been a lot of bloodshed associated with our name, so we want the cops on our payroll to handle it."

"I got it," Orlando said, heading for the door at the same time Nevada and Junior headed for the den.

My cell phone rang, and I took it out of my pocket. Seeing the name on the screen, I frowned. "Chippy, are you butt dialing me?"

"No, my phone is in my purse," she said, and then as she realized where her purse was, her eyes got wide. "Larry took it from me when we got in the van because he knew I had a gun in it."

I looked down at the phone again and inhaled deeply to steady myself before I hit the ANSWER button.

"Larry."

"How are you, LC? It's good to hear your voice. Not!" The sound of his voice caused my already brewing anger to build, but I forced myself to remain calm. I knew handling it with caution was critical. My initial instinct was to demand the whereabouts of London and Sasha, but my better judgment made me wait.

"Oh, by the way, did Chippy make it home okay? We spent a little time together," he said with a sick laugh.

"I'm trying to remain calm, Larry," I told him. "You're making it very difficult."

"LC, you don't wanna talk about how difficult you've made my life, do you?" Larry asked.

The good news was that he didn't make mention of London or Sasha, which made me think he might not have them. Otherwise, he would have been trying to use them from the start to throw me off balance. Still, I couldn't be sure, so I was determined to get my brother and his behavior under control some way. I had to gain the upper hand.

"This has gotta stop," I told him. "You have—"

"Don't fucking tell me what I've done. What about what you've done, LC? This is all your fucking fault! You were the one who had me locked away and stole my share of the company. You took everything from me: my life, my family, my money."

"Larry, you know none of that's true."

"Stop fucking lying to me, LC! This is why I shot your ass last time we were together—because you keep fucking lying!" Larry screamed like a madman.

"What the fuck do you want, Larry? Let's just handle this man to man, once and for all," I said, still speaking quietly so as not to set him off any worse than he already was.

Larry laughed. "Man to man? You don't really wanna do that, little brother. You were never that good and never will be."

"Try me and see," I suggested.

"You know what? You're right. Let's just handle this shit and finally get it over with," he said. "It's been going on long enough."

I felt a brief second of relief. At least now I would know where he was. "You name the place."

"I'm taking Momma back home for a few days, so why don't we meet back where it all started."

I ignored his reference to my mother. His insistence that she was still alive was more proof of how far gone he was, and pointing it out to him might just send him over the edge. "I'll be there tomorrow afternoon," I said.

"Take your time. It's going to take me at least a few days to get there. Unlike you, I don't have a Learjet. At least not yet." He hung up.

Larry

64

I stood smoking a cigarette as I watched Curtis prep the back of the van. It looked as if I was going to be able to kill two birds with one stone: having a face to face with my brother, and handling my business with Vinnie, who said he would lower his price to 20K a kilo if I met him down in Florida and took all his product today. So wasting no time, Curtis, Momma, and I loaded up the old van and headed down I-95. We had arrived in Jacksonville about an hour ago to meet Vinnie at a warehouse near the Julington Creek pier.

"What about Kenny?" Curtis asked.

"What about him?" I frowned. "It's clear that your brother don't give a shit about us; therefore, we ain't gonna give a shit about him. We got business to take care of. I don't have time to deal with his temperamental ass."

"But, Dad—"

"Curtis, shut the fuck up about your brother. Now, if you're that worried about his ass, you can get the fuck out and stay here. Is that what you wanna do?"

"No, sir." Curtis sighed then walked over and patted my back.

"I'm sorry, son. It's just . . . your brother, he broke my heart," I said sadly. "Go get those bags. Vinnie is here."

Vinnie was fifteen minutes late when he walked up wearing an all-white linen suit and a pair of leather flip flops, looking like a tourist.

"Larry Duncan." He extended his hand to greet me.

I looked at it and said, "You got my shit, Vinnie?"

Vinnie lowered his hand, and his smile weakened. "You got my money?"

Curtis walked over and tossed him a duffle bag full of cash. "Here."

He nodded and pointed to a box truck. "Dope is in the back."

I motioned for Curtis to check it out, and Vinnie tossed him the keys.

"You got that other thing for me?" I asked.

Vinnie shrugged and said, "Sure thing, Larry. Got it right here."

He handed me a brown leather briefcase. I took it out of his hand and gave him a knapsack of money. "Is that it?"

He handed me a telephone. "All you have to do is call me on this cell, and everything will be taken care of."

"Thanks, Vinnie." I put the briefcase on the floor in the back seat. Everything was falling into place.

"Where are you heading next?" I asked him.

"No particular destination. I heard Santorini is nice this time of year. I might head there." Vinnie shrugged. "Or I might hit up Italy, check out where the Dash family got their start."

"A'ight, Dad, we're loaded." Curtis tossed Vinnie the keys.

"Well, once again, Larry Duncan, it's been great doing business with ya." Vinnie grinned, extending his hand a second time. This time, I took it. "Good luck dealing with your brother."

I lifted the phone he'd given me and said, "I'll call you and let you know."

He laughed, picking up the duffle bag and starting to walk away.

"He's just gonna walk down the street with a million dollars in cash?" Curtis asked.

"Hey, like Momma always says: not my monkey, not my circus." I took a deep breath. "Come on. We have a lot of things to do if we're going to meet with the infamous LC Duncan."

Orlando

65

Pinging London and Sasha's phones hadn't given us an exact location, just a vicinity, which turned out to be LaGuardia Airport. We arrived at the terminal with five cars and ten men and began searching for my sister and cousin, but we came up empty until about an hour into the search, when Nevada gave me a call.

"What's up, nephew?"

"Well, Uncle O, I think we have a problem. I've been pinging Aunt London's and Sasha's phones, and all of a sudden nothing is coming back."

I didn't like the sound of that. "What's that mean, Nevada?"

"O, it's Junior." My brother cut in. "What it means is that either they turned their phones off or someone did it for them. You guys find anything at the terminals?"

"Nothing, but we still got a lot of ground to cover. I could use some help."

"Roger that. I'm gonna head over there with my guys right after I brief Pop and Vegas."

"There is one thing we haven't thought of," Nevada cut in. "They are at an airport. What if they're on a plane? We wouldn't get a signal if they're in the air," he told me. "Give me a sec. Let me check something really quick. Wait for my call." The boy genius hung up without waiting for my response. It took him nearly ten minutes to call me back.

"Damn, it took you long enough. What were you doing?" I asked.

"Hacking into Aunt London's American Express account to see if she's used her card today," he said meekly, because he'd been told about hacking into accounts. "Uncle Junior said it was okay."

"Then you're golden. You find anything?" I asked.

He hesitated, then said, "Looks like she was at the Lucky Dragon buffet in the Bronx, a municipal parking lot in Manhattan, she purchased tickets on Delta Airlines, and has a hotel room being held at the Marriott."

"Which Marriott?" I asked.

"Sawgrass Marriott Golf Resort and Spa in Jacksonville, Florida."

"Good job, nephew. I'm handing you my title. You're officially the smartest one in the family." I could hear Junior laughing in the background. "Junior, tell Pop I'm headed to Florida. I'll meet you guys down in Waycross once I find out what the hell these two are up to."

"Will do, O. Be safe, and smack both of them upside the head for me. We don't have time for this BS."

"Tell me about it."

Five hours later, I stepped off the elevator onto the eighth floor of the Sawgrass hotel and continued down the hallway until I arrived at room 878. Nevada had used his hacking skills to get me the room number of their suite. With a full detail of men behind me, I tried my best to calm down a bit and then tapped on the door, lightly at first. When there was no response, I knocked a little harder, then checked my watch. It was almost three in the morning, and they were probably asleep, but I didn't care. I knocked again, this time hard and loud. I finally heard muffled sounds and then, Sasha's voice.

"Who is it?" she asked gruffly. I took a step back so she could get a good view from the peephole I knew she was looking through. "Oh, shit! It's Orlando!"

"Orlando?" I heard London ask. To say I was pissed would be an understatement. Our family was in crisis, my crazy uncle was on the loose, and here were my sister and cousin, disappearing to a Florida resort like they didn't have a care in the world. "I told you we should have told someone we were coming here."

"Open the damn door," I yelled, banging on it again.

The door slowly opened, and Sasha stared at me, looking stupid as hell. I pushed past her and entered the room. There were two beds in the room. London was sitting in the center of one, and the other, which I assumed was Sasha's, sat empty.

"What the hell are you doing here?" London asked.

"The question is what the hell are you two doing here? Do you know how worried everyone is? Pop had everyone tearing apart the fucking hospital and the entire east side of New York City looking for you," I snapped. "What the fuck is wrong with y'all?"

"Calm down, O. I can explain," Sasha told me.

"No, I'm not gonna calm down, because our psycho uncle tried to kill my mother yesterday, and my sister, who was supposed to know better, along with my super responsible cousin, vanished into thin air without saying shit to anyone. There is no way I'm calming down," I lectured them.

"Wait, what?" London jumped out of bed with a sudden look of concern. "What did you just say about Mom?"

"Uncle Larry tried to kill Aunt Chippy? Oh my God. When? Where?" Sasha stood beside London. "Is she all right?"

"So now y'all interested. If you'd picked up the phone or answered a text you would know what happened to Ma," I shouted.

"Orlando, is Mommy all right?" London asked frantically.

"She's home safe now. Of all people, Kenny helped her escape, but Larry is still out there looking for God knows who to do God knows what to them. Which is why when we found out that you two weren't where you were supposed to be, all hell broke loose." I shook my head at their carelessness.

"I'm sorry, O. It's all my fault." Sasha's voice was barely above a whisper.

"It's nobody's fault. Look, we have a reason for being here. We're not just here for a getaway," London said with a sigh.

"I'm listening." I folded my arms and waited for her explanation.

"We know how to find Vinnie Dash," Sasha said after a few moments.

"Is he here in Florida?"

"He's supposed to be in Jacksonville today," Sasha said.

"So, if Vinnie Dash is here, why didn't you tell the rest of us?" I didn't know if I was more curious about their reasoning or angry at them for trying to go it alone. When it came to issues that affected the whole family, we never condoned this kind of lone-wolf shit. It was too risky.

"Because we don't know exactly where," Sasha explained. "Just that he's going to be at a marina in Jacksonville."

"Dammit, Sasha. Do you know how many marinas there are in Jacksonville?" I sat on the side of the bed, overwhelmed by everything, and began to rub my temples. "I need to call Vegas so he and Daryl can handle this."

"The hell you are! We were on this mission way before you got here. We were the ones who got the info from Jamaica John," London snapped at me.

"Well, technically we got it from his phone." Sasha shrugged. "And I'm sorry, but if you think for one second you're about to stop me from finding that bastard, you're crazy. He killed my mother—or did you forget about that?"

"And he tried to kill my mother and my husband," London added.

Now I understood why they had gone off half-cocked on this mission. They saw themselves as vigilantes for justice. People they loved had been hurt, and they wanted to be the ones to get revenge. The problem was that this was not a game or a movie; this was real life, with dangerous people, and they should have waited for help from the family.

"I'll tell you what. Why don't y'all tell it to Mom and Pop?" I pulled out my cell phone, pushed a button to dial, then set it on speaker so they could both hear it ring. Sasha didn't move, but London jumped, grabbing the phone and hanging it up.

We all looked at one another, at a silent impasse for a minute. Finally, Sasha said, "Orlando, sometimes it's easier to ask for forgiveness than permission. We knew what we were doing. We also knew that nobody would let us do it if we asked." She put two fingers together. "We are this close to finding Vinnie and, quite possibly, your son. We waste time trying to convince Uncle LC and Aunt Chippy, and Vinnie will be in the wind. Now, you got a whole team with you. Let's not waste time arguing. Let's go find that son of a bitch."

As crazy as it sounded, Sasha made a lot of sense. And if she was right that Vinnie was nearby, then that could mean my son was too. I didn't want to waste another second.

Ruby

66

I sat on the balcony of our new yacht, enjoying the view. The water was calming, the sky was magnificent, and the air was just as perfect as the boat we were on. Surprisingly, it had been a peaceful past couple of days. Despite being spontaneously uprooted from his home once again, my son was fascinated by the floating mini mansion that was our temporary home. The 63-foot Benetti yacht had three bedrooms, three bathrooms, and a crew cabin, as well as plenty of open space for him to play. It had taken Blake bribing him with a trip to Gator World to get him off the boat.

Seeing my son's enjoyment also helped me be a little more accepting of our living situation. My initial frustration with Vinnie putting us into this predicament once again was starting to slowly subside. There was also his promise that once he made this final transaction and sold the remaining dope, guaranteed to bring him another million dollars, he would be out of the drug game for good. The anticipation of our being able to live a somewhat normal life gave me a little hope. I was starting to relax and had even made love to my husband, something we hadn't done in over a week. After, as we lay in bed, we talked about our future and where we would live. Vinnie suggested Europe, far from the Duncans, the Asians, and anyone else who might have brought harm to our family. His excitement was infectious, and I allowed myself to feel some of the happiness that I could see he felt. I quelled the suspicions I had about Vinnie's involvement with my brother's death and told myself that I had to stop looking for answers that maybe I didn't need to know. I fell asleep in his arms, and for the first time in almost a year, I didn't dream of Orlando.

My cell phone rang, and Blake's name appeared. I quickly answered it, knowing he was probably calling because Vincent wanted to speak with me.

"Hello."

"Ruby . . . can . . . with . . . go." Blake was incoherent.

"Blake? What ya sayin'? I can't understand."

"Ruby . . ."

I looked at my phone and saw that my signal was weak. "Blake, I can't hear ya. Wait."

The call ended. I walked along the deck with my phone in the air, trying to get a stronger signal. As I made my way to the stern, the small bars in the corner of the screen slowly increased until they indicated a strong signal. I dialed Blake's number, and as it began to ring, I looked at the dock and spotted Vinnie heading toward the boat, carrying a large satchel. He waved at me, and I waved back.

"Ruby." Blake finally answered.

"Blake, can ya hear me?" I asked.

"Yes, I can. Me need fo' ya to listen to me." His voice was very serious, and I knew something was wrong.

"Blake, what's wrong? Is Vincent okay?" My thoughts went to my son.

"He's fine, Ruby, but I talked wit' de man I told ya 'bout. Ya got to git off dat boat. It's not safe. I got a car for us. We got to leave now while he's gone," Blake told me.

"Blake . . ." My eyes closed, and I struggled to catch my breath. I knew before he said it, and my heart sank. "Did he?"

"Yes, Ruby, he killed ya brudda. He paid de man to blow de house up! Ya got to leave. I'm on de way. Meet me at de marina parking lot in five minutes. I'll be in a green car."

The call ended, and I turned to leave. I had barely made it three feet when suddenly, I heard Vinnie's voice behind me.

"Well, my love, the deal is done, and we are one million dollars richer."

A chill went down my spine as I felt his arm on my shoulder. I turned and faced him; he stood smiling, holding the satchel like a newborn baby.

"Dat's good, Vinnie," I said nervously.

"Is that all you're gonna say? *That's good, Vinnie*? Ruby, this is what we've been working for. We finally got enough money to travel the world and be happy." He pulled me close and kissed me, but I couldn't bring myself to kiss him back. He placed his hand on my stomach and whispered, "We can have a baby. My baby. I can be a dad."

He wanted me to have his baby. The man who killed my brother wanted me to make him a father. My husband. The man I married. My brother's murderer. I needed to get away. I looked over Vinnie's shoulder in search of Blake and Vincent, who were going to be waiting for me.

"Ruby, what's wrong?"

I ignored him as I continued staring toward the parking lot, searching for the car Blake said he would be driving, but I didn't see them. I knew I had to leave now.

Vinnie turned to see what I was looking at.

"Fuck!" he said through clenched teeth. I took a step back from him, trying to figure out how I was going to get away. Vinnie grabbed my arm and said, "What the fuck are they doing here?"

"What? Who?" I was confused by what he was asking.

"Don't play stupid, Ruby! Shit! Fucking Larry must've told them where we were."

"Who ya talkin' 'bout?" I shook my head. My mind was a whirlwind. Vinnie was acting erratic, and I hadn't even tried to leave. I looked in the direction where he was pointing. There, in plain view, I saw a woman and two men in the distance.

Just when I thought things couldn't get any worse, they did. It was my son's father.

"The fucking Duncans, that's who! We gotta get outta here." Vinnie grabbed me and pulled me across the deck toward the stairs leading to the staterooms.

"Vinnie!" I yelled both from panic and the pain of his grip on my arm.

"Come on. I don't think they saw us," he said then yelled to the captain, "Start this motherfucker up. We're leaving now!"

Kenny

67

The bus ride home to Georgia was the longest ride of my life. I was paranoid at every stop we made, expecting my father or brother to be waiting for me. When we finally made it to Waycross, I was the last person to get off the bus. I stepped onto the platform and looked around, making sure it was safe. I didn't have any bags with me. All my belongings were still in New York, because there was no way I was going back inside the safe house to get them. I was never going back to that house again.

I caught a cab to the farm, and when I arrived, my mother was sitting in the living room, watching television.

"Hey, Ma," I said.

"Kenny! You startled me, boy." She jumped off the sofa and rushed over to hug me, then, glancing over my shoulder, she asked, "Where is your brother?"

"He's still with him, Momma."

My mother put her hands on my shoulders. "What happened?"

We went over to the couch, and I sat beside her. I didn't waste any time getting to the heart of my story. "He's always been crazy, but now he's dangerous. He's a maniac, Momma. He's killing people for no reason. He killed Aunt Donna, he caused Harris's accident, and then he tried to kill Aunt Chippy."

My mother gasped. "My God! Is she okay?"

"She's alive," I told her. "Momma, we had a fight, and he was about to kill me. Curtis had to stop him."

"Oh, baby, I'm so sorry." She pulled me in for another hug.

"I hate him. I swear to God, I hate him. I should've known when he first got home and started talking all this stuff about Uncle LC that something was wrong. And don't get me started about his constant conversations with Grandma Bettie." I stood up and looked out the window into the backyard. "I should've killed him myself."

My mother came and stood beside me. "Kenny, don't say that. You don't mean it."

"I do mean it. He's out of control, and now he's got Curtis with him out there somewhere."

"Come on, let's go." She took me by the arm.

"Momma, where are we going? I'm tired, and I need to take a shower. I've been on a bus for two days. I can't go anywhere like this." I motioned at the dingy clothes I was wearing.

"You're fine. Where we're going, it doesn't matter what you got on." She pulled me out the front door.

"Why are we here?" I asked five minutes later when we walked up to the small family plot.

"Because we need to talk, and I need to explain some things to you," she said, stepping carefully through the graves.

"We could have talked at the house, Momma," I said, but she kept moving. I followed her until we arrived at a gated area. She opened the rusted fence that enclosed a large mausoleum with the name *Duncan* on the outside. I paused before entering. In all the years I'd lived on the farm, we almost never visited my grandmother's grave. It was just too painful for my parents, even after Dad was sent away.

"Come on." She motioned, and I entered with her.

"Let me explain something about your father, Kenny."

"There's no explanation for him other than he's crazy. Isn't that what they've always called him, Crazy Larry?"

She shot me a sideways glance. As bad as he was, my mother had never wavered in her love for him. Then, she launched into a story that blew my mind.

"Listen, your father was an intriguing man who served his country in Vietnam, but when he came back, he was very damaged, like a lot of men. He's always been smart, like his father was before him and like his brothers. All Duncan men are, including you." Her hand covered mine. "But he's always had a fascination with guns. Over the years, his fascination grew. He was always buying and collecting them. They became his hobby, his passion, I guess.

"The only person who loved guns as much as he did was Grandma Bettie. They would sit around and talk about and compare guns all the time. That was their bond. Well, one day, the two of them were in the living room, and he was cleaning one of his guns. Curtis was in there with them. Then, the unthinkable happened. The gun went off, hitting Grandma Bettie in the chest and killing her instantly."

"What?" I turned and stared at her in disbelief. "Pops killed Grandma Bettie?"

"No, Kenny." She released a big sigh. "Curtis shot and killed Bettie. It was horrible. I was pregnant with you at the time. Your father took the blame for it because he didn't want anything to happen to your brother. It was natural for everyone to assume that he did it. After all, just like you said, he is Crazy Larry.

"But after that happened, his life took a very tragic turn. All of our lives did, actually. Your father became very paranoid and thought that everyone was out to get him, especially his brothers. I guess it was guilt, but Bettie's death triggered something. Then, hiding the fact that his son shot and killed his mother, along with the demons he carried from Vietnam, caused him to suffer a psychotic break. He became very violent: assaulting people, destroying property, and then he would say that Miss Bettie told him that people were plotting on him and that's why he had to do it. He got worse and killed a dozen innocent men.

"In order to keep him from going to jail, LC, Lou, and I decided it was better to have him locked up somewhere he could get treatment." Her eyes misted over with tears. "It was one of the hardest decisions we had to make. He was the love of my life, and he took care of his brothers after their father died and Miss Bettie went to prison. We all loved Larry, but we were forced to make a decision—prison or the mental hospital—and we chose what we thought was the lesser of two evils."

I sat and listened to my mother reveal things about my father and brother that I would have never thought possible. The bond between the two of them had always been strong for as far back as I could remember, and I never understood, because for most of our lives, my dad was locked away. Now it made sense. I felt some sympathy for both of them. I couldn't imagine the guilt of killing my grandmother, even if it was an accident. Then, all the horrible things that I'd been a part of over the past few weeks came rushing back, and I was angry all over again.

"You all made the wrong choice," I snapped, "because now he's out and back to his old ways. So, it's your fault that all of this is happening."

Tears fell from her eyes, and although I knew my statement was hurtful, I didn't care because it was the truth.

"What are we going to do?" she cried.

"The only thing we can do, Momma. We kill him."

She opened her mouth, but nothing came out as she nodded in agreement.

Orlando

68

We walked along the marina of the Julington Creek pier, where numerous yachts were docked. This was the sixth marina we'd been to this morning, and we had no idea what we were looking for. I was sure Vinnie Dash would be just as flashy with whatever boat he was in as that damn yellow Lamborghini he drove, but there were so many luxury yachts around here, there was no telling if one of them was his.

It was a gorgeous day, so there was a crowd of people on the pier, enjoying the weather. I scanned faces in the crowd, but none looked familiar.

"We don't even know if we're looking for a tug boat or a tanker. It's a lot of boats out here," Sasha said.

"Trust me, it's Vinnie Dash. He's gonna be in a nice boat," I told her.

"Hell, it's a lot of nice boats out here. It's Florida." She sighed. We continued walking a little farther, and then, she stopped. "Where the hell is London?"

I turned around and spotted London not too far behind us, looking back toward the street. We walked over to her.

"What's going on? You see Vinnie?" I asked.

"No, not Vinnie, but look over there." She motioned her head in the direction she was looking.

"Who?" Sasha stood on the other side of her.

"That guy over there with the long dreads."

I put my hand over my eyes to shield them from the sun, and I spotted the guy she was talking about. Sasha did too.

"The old guy with the kid?" Sasha asked.

"Yeah." London began walking toward them, and we followed. "Orlando, look at that little boy. Oh my God."

As we got closer, I focused on the little boy's face, and something inside of me leapt.

"Does he look like anyone to you?" London glanced at me.

"That big-ass head should look real familiar." Sasha laughed.

We stopped and waited, trying to look nonchalant as the man and the little boy came nearer. I couldn't stop staring at my son, who was happily eating an ice cream cone and talking to the man.

London smiled at them. "Hello, there," she said. "That ice cream looks good."

He smiled back at her and said, "It is good. Blake bought it for me."

Sasha stepped closer to the dread-headed man and opened her jacket slightly so he could see the handle of her gun and understand that now was not the time to make any stupid moves.

I kneeled down and looked at my son's face, almost choking up with emotion. "What's your name?"

He grinned at me and said, "Vincent."

"That's a cool name. Vincent. Where are you from?" I forced myself to stuff down any anger I felt at the fact that Ruby had named him after one of my family's enemies.

"I used to live in Jamaica, but now me, my mommy, daddy, and Blake live on a boat." He licked the ice cream. My cousin and sister were right; he did have my big head. He had his mother's eyes and dimpled smile, but he also had my complexion. He was beautiful, and it took everything within me not to grab him in my arms and hug him tightly.

"Oh, really? Which boat do you all live on?" London asked.

"Come on. I'll show you." He grabbed her by the hand and pulled her toward the pier.

Blake looked at the three of us. I could see him trying to decide on his next move.

"It's cool, man. We ain't gonna hurt you or Vincent," I whispered to him. "Just relax."

He chuckled. "Why would a man come all this way to hurt his son?"

I was a little surprised by how quickly he'd put the pieces together, but even more surprised that he almost sounded supportive. I nodded, and we followed Vincent and London.

"Which boat, Vincent?" London asked when he stopped.

"That one." Vincent pointed and then frowned. "But . . ."

"Wait, Vincent. Are you pointing at that boat down there?" I picked him up so I could be sure which one he meant. He nodded, and I put him back on the ground then turned and asked Blake, "Is he talking about the boat that's pulling off?"

Blake looked at me, almost apologetically, and said, "Yes, dat's de boat, Mr. Orlando."

69

The car ride from Brunswick Airport to Waycross was mostly quiet. Initially, I had told Chippy to stay home where she would be safe, especially in light of what had just happened with Larry, but my wife was headstrong. Despite the fact that an attempt was just made on her life, she insisted on traveling with us. After a nonstop flight to Atlanta, she and I, along with Junior, Paris, Vegas, and Daryl, headed with our security detail to the farm in search of my brother.

"Are you okay?" I looked over at her.

"I'm fine." She gave my hand a reassuring squeeze then turned to look out the window. "It's been so long since we've been here. I'm just trying to take it all in, I guess."

"Still looks the same to me," I said, staring at the familiar sights as we drove through my hometown. "Willie, turn down the next street."

"Yes, sir." Willie, our driver, nodded at me in the rearview mirror.

A little farther down the road, I instructed him to stop at a gas station. Willie pulled the SUV into the parking lot, and I rolled down the window and stared at the building. The same Pepsi sign still hung over the entrance. The feelings of nostalgia overwhelmed me as I recalled the day my brothers had given me this gas station, where I had worked for years while I attended college, as a graduation gift. The love and bond shared between the Duncan men had been unbreakable back then. I never would've dreamed our lives would be as they were now.

"This is where it all started," Chippy said with a sigh.

"That was a long time ago," I said, forcing my thoughts back to the present. I rolled the window back up, took one last look, and then directed Willie to our next destination. I sat back and closed my eyes in an effort to prepare myself for whatever was waiting for me when I got there.

I could feel the vibration of the truck increase, indicating that we were no longer on concrete, but the winding dirt road that led to the Duncan farm. I looked over at Chippy and saw that she was staring at me.

"Are you sure about this, LC?" she asked with a worried look.

I'm sure. Don't worry." I pulled her to me and kissed the top of her head. "I need you to stay in the car while we do this."

"What? You're kidding, right?" She sat up and looked at me like I was crazy.

"Chippy, I told you the only way you could come was if you promised to stay safe. That means in the car with Willie."

I caught Willie's eye in the rearview mirror and again, he nodded. Chippy opened her mouth to protest, but I shook my head.

"Do not get out of this car, Chippy. I mean it."

My phone rang, and I saw that it was Vegas, calling from the car behind us.

"What's the plan, Pop?" he asked when I answered.

"Have the men surround the house. I want someone at every door," I told him.

Vegas gave the orders, and when we parked, I watched as eight men climbed out of separate SUVs, guns drawn, and approached the farmhouse. The front door opened, and NeeNee walked onto the porch.

I kissed Chippy again, then opened the door and stepped out. My sons and daughter were by my side. I looked at them and instructed, "Hold tight."

"Are you sure, Daddy?" Paris asked, her eyes locked on her aunt.

"Yes."

"LC, what the hell is going on? What are you doing here?" NeeNee yelled.

"You know why I'm here. I'm looking for Larry."

"Larry ain't here," she said with a frown. "I ain't got nothing to do with this mess y'all got going on. You can take your goons and get off my property."

"What's wrong, Ma?" Kenny stepped onto the porch, and I saw the gun in his hand. I just hoped Vegas could keep Paris under control.

"I talked to him, Nee. He's around." I stepped onto the porch warily, keeping an eye on Kenny's weapon. For now, he was holding it loosely by his side. "How you doing, Kenny?"

"I'm all right, Uncle LC," Kenny said.

"I mean it, LC. You can go," NeeNee told me. "I don't want no trouble."

I could see that she was telling the truth, but I also knew she would side with her own family first, so I had to figure out where Kenny stood. From what I knew, he had helped Chippy escape, so there was a good chance I could keep things peaceful with him for now. As long as he didn't feel threatened, things didn't have to escalate between him and us.

I turned to Kenny and said, "You talk to your daddy? Do you know where he is?"

"No, sir. I don't. I haven't talked to him since . . ." His voice drifted off, then he looked at me sadly and offered some form of an apology. "I didn't know that's what he was gonna do. He's out of control."

"I know. That's why I'm here. Time to put an end to this." I placed my hand on his shoulder. "And I appreciate what you did for your aunt Chippy. You saved her life. But, I need to talk to your momma for a little while."

Kenny looked at his mother, and she told him, "Go on inside. I'm fine."

When he went in, she took a deep breath and shook her head. "Bettie Duncan is probably rolling over in her grave right now because of y'all. She ain't raised y'all to be like this."

"You're right. She probably is. Let's go see her," I suggested.

We walked down the steps of the house, passing one of the security guards who hadn't left his post. Of course, Chippy hopped out of the car and caught up to us. When I saw the way she and NeeNee hugged each other tight, I knew I couldn't send Chippy back to the car. These were two mothers who wanted nothing more than for their children to be safe.

"I am so sorry about what happened to you, Chippy," NeeNee said.

"I know, Nee. Now let's fix this," Chippy said, taking her hand as we walked down a long path to the cemetery.

The three of us were mostly silent until finally, we arrived at the place where my mother and father were laid to rest. We took a seat on a tiny bench in front of the plaques with their names.

"What happened to you boys, LC?" NeeNee asked. "Y'all were so close. You used to look out and take care of each other."

"I don't know what happened." I sighed.

"You wanna hear something crazy?" NeeNee said.

"What's that?" I reached in my pocket and pulled out a handkerchief to dust off my father's plaque.

"I always thought it was the money."

"The money?" I repeated.

"Yeah. I mean, you boys always worked hard and made a good living, but when that money started flowing like water, that's when things in the family began to change. Remember when you and Chippy first moved to Atlanta and then y'all moved all of us with you? Then we all moved to New York. We all got a taste of the good life and the power."

"That's true," Chippy said, "but I don't think that's what it was. The money had nothing to do with it. Things didn't really get bad until Levi—"

Just then, my cell began to ring with my wife's ring tone. Chippy and I exchanged a knowing look. Larry had her phone.

"Hold on a minute, Nee. I think this is your husband."

"Hello," I answered.

"I see you made it into town, LC," Larry said, throwing me off guard. I looked over my shoulder, half expecting to see him standing behind me.

"I did. Where are you, Larry?"

"Waiting to meet you. Let's sit down and have a drink."

"When and where?"

"Right now. And how about Big Shirley's, for old time's sake?" he said.

"I'm on my way." I hung up the phone.

"LC, you can't go meet with him. You know Larry as well as I do. It's probably a trap," NeeNee said nervously.

"I ain't worried. Truth is, it's probably more dangerous for him than me," I told her. This was one of the reasons I had brought a security detail with us.

"LC, are you sure you should—" Chippy started, but I cut her off.

"I love you, Chippy, but you know this has to be done. I told you that if you couldn't handle it, you should stay home, remember?" I stated firmly. She rolled her eyes at me but stayed silent.

We would probably fight about this later, but as head of the family, I had to take charge and take care of Larry once and for all. It was something I should have done as soon as I knew he was released from the mental hospital.

"You want me to go with you?" NeeNee offered.

"Naw, sister-in-law. If you wanna do something, why don't you take my wife and make her some tea?" I said. "I gotta be going."

NeeNee tried one last time. "LC, I don't know about you going to meet him. You know what's gonna happen, don't you?"

"I do. I'm wise enough to know that this is one meeting one of us ain't gonna survive." I gave her a hug and kissed my wife good-bye.

Ruby

70

As the boat pulled away from the dock, I could no longer breathe, because I'd spent every inch of air in my lungs to scream. My heart pounded in my chest as I fought to get away from Vinnie, who held me tight against him.

"Vinnie, we have to go back and get Vincent!" Tears streamed down my face.

I looked back at the view of the marina becoming smaller as our captain slowly maneuvered around the other boats in the harbor. We were still close enough to go back, but I had to act fast before we got much farther. Adrenaline kicked in, and my body went into fight or flight mode. I somehow became strong enough to finally push Vinnie away from me and escape his grasp. "You bastard! My son is back dere. We have to go back!"

"We ain't going back nowhere." Vinnie went to grab me again, but I moved just in time, putting a few feet between us.

I stared at him, breathing heavily. "We can't leave him, Vinnie. Please! Please, Vinnie."

"Ruby, I know you saw him. I know you saw Orlando. He's here to kill me. Do you want me dead? Is that what you want?" he bellowed as he took a step toward me.

"I want my son! Dat is what I want, Vinnie."

"You really want them to kill me?"

"Isn't dat what you did to my brudda?" Without thinking, I charged at him, clawing at his face and screaming through my tears. "I know you did it. You killed Randy!"

Vinnie grabbed my arms and tossed me to the ground, slapping me across the face. I struggled to get up, but he straddled me. "Yes, I killed him. Are you happy now? He's dead, and I'm sorry it had to be done, but I've been a good husband and father, haven't I? I've given you the best of everything, and this is the thanks I get. You're an ungrateful bitch, Ruby."

"Get off me!" I gasped for air. "I must get my son!"

"Fuck your son. He's with his real father now anyway, isn't he? Orlando Duncan, the man you dream about? I've heard you cry out his name in your sleep more than once. You're still in love with him." Vinnie's face was red, and his chest heaved as he raged on in a combination of anger and hurt. "You never loved me."

"Vinnie, let me go," I pleaded and then began struggling again.

Suddenly, he pulled out a gun and placed it against my temple. "You said you loved me, Ruby."

"Vinnie, please, no!"

"If I can't have you, neither will he. I wish your son's father was here to see this," he said with an evil laugh.

I closed my eyes and prepared to die.

"Her son's father is here, motherfucker!"

I looked over to see Orlando standing on the deck, soaking wet, a few feet away from us.

Vinnie turned to look at him, but before he could even react to the sight, two shots rang out. I screamed as Vinnie's body fell on top of me. A slight gurgle escaped his mouth as he took his final breath. I lay beneath Vinnie, terrified that Orlando was coming for me next.

I was trembling as Orlando shoved Vinnie's body off me. But then, instead of raising his weapon to me, he reached for my hand. I hesitated at first, then allowed him to help me to my feet.

"How?" I asked.

"It cost me five hundred dollars, but I rented a guy's Jet Ski and caught up with the boat," he explained. "If you got out of the harbor, I might not have gotten to you in time."

"Orlando, I am so sorry. I thought . . . when my brother Randy . . ."

He put up a hand to stop me. "Not now, Ruby. We have a lot to talk about when the time is right, but for now, we have one very confused son waiting for you at the marina." He put his arm around me, and we stepped over Vinnie's body as we headed up to the control station to tell the captain to turn the boat around.

LC

71

I sat in the back of Big Shirley's, nursing a beer and trying to be as inconspicuous as possible while I waited for Larry to arrive. Really, no one was paying me much attention. Most of the patrons were too busy focusing on the curvaceous stripper doing tricks with a beer bottle on a makeshift stage. The ones who weren't being entertained by her ability were haggling with other dancers over what services they could provide and at what price. One or two people had given me a second glance, suggesting my face might have looked slightly familiar to them, but I'd been away long enough that no one recognized me as a family member of the owners. Same for Vegas, who hadn't even been born when Chippy and I moved away from Waycross. He was sitting at a table near the front door, and Daryl was at the bar, both in positions where they could keep an eye on me in my seat. Junior stood behind me, and we had a few other security men in place, along with Paris and her team surrounding the building so no one could get in or out without our knowledge.

I had been glancing at the front door in anticipation of his arrival for more than twenty minutes, and still, Larry hadn't come in.

"Pop, I don't like this waiting game. Maybe we should get outta here," Junior said over my shoulder.

I shook my head. "Not yet. He's just trying to demonstrate that he has control. If we leave now, then he knows he's gotten under my skin. We need to stick around and finish this." I took another sip of the now warm beer and looked at the front door.

"Hello, LC. I hope I ain't keep you waiting long." Larry's voice came from my left. He must have come from another room. Maybe he'd been in the building the whole time.

Vegas and Daryl sat up a little straighter but stayed at their posts.

He sat in the chair across from me. I hadn't seen him since the day I was shot. My memory of that night was still hazy, but I didn't remember my brother ever looking so menacing. He was dressed as he normally was, in a suit, and carrying a briefcase, which I was sure had some type of weapon in it. It was bittersweet to realize that out of all of us—me, Lou, Larry, and Levi—he was the one who looked most like our mother. NeeNee was right; Momma would have hated to know that her sons had become enemies.

"Larry." I nodded.

He shot a glance at Junior. "So, we need a babysitter to talk now? I thought this was between you and me."

I turned to Junior and said, "Wait over at the bar."

"But, Pop—"

"Please, Junior. Let me talk to my brother alone."

He reluctantly walked over to the bar.

"Damn, LC, that's one big motherfucker you got there. Reminds me of a smart Levi," he said, chuckling. Then he leaned forward and asked, "So, how's Chippy?"

He was goading me, but I was not going to give him the satisfaction of reacting. "Look, Larry. This has got to stop. You said you wanted to talk, so talk. What the hell is it that you want?"

The smile had left his face. "You know what the fuck I want. I want what's mine. I want my fucking company back—no, what I want is my life back that you stole away from me, but I realized on the drive from New York that it's too late for that."

"I didn't steal anything from you, Larry. I have told you that over and over again. And I damn sure didn't take your life. Hell, I saved it."

"Fuck you, LC," he spat. "Is that what you've told yourself all these years to ease your fucking guilt? Yeah, you and Lou stole my money, my company, and had me locked away to save me? Is that what you're trying to tell me?" Suddenly, he laughed so hard that he started coughing.

I looked over to make sure Vegas, Daryl, Junior, and the other security men were on standby.

"Larry, this ain't got shit to do with money. I know you got plenty of cash, because you've been buying dope and giving it away like candy on Halloween. But if it's money you want, then how much?" I stared at him.

"I don't want money. I want Duncan Motors," he said.

"Duncan Motors?" I almost laughed my damn self. "I'm not giving you Duncan Motors. It belongs to my kids and grandchildren."

"What about my children? What about my boys?"

"When was the last time you looked in the trust?"

"The what?" he asked.

"Your family trust," I told him. "When you sold your share of the businesses, NeeNee had the money put into a trust for you, her, and the boys. There's probably fifteen million in it right now."

He frowned. "You are such a liar. And even if that was true, why would she be staying in that raggedy old house?"

"Because she loves that farm and she knows you love it too." I sighed. "NeeNee never needed all the glamour and glitz, Larry. All she ever needed was you."

He sat there quietly for a minute, and I thought he might be contemplating what I'd said. I hoped he was realizing the truth in my words. But then looked to his left and spoke: "I know he's lying, Momma. He could always spin a tale, couldn't he?"

Larry raised an eyebrow as he listened to whatever the imaginary person said back to him, and then he turned to me and threatened, "I want Duncan Motors, and if I don't get it, I'm gonna make your life, and the life of everyone associated with you, miserable by killing them off one by one."

"Look down, Larry," I said, pointing to his chest and shaking my head. Larry dropped his head a little and saw the small red dots that were now glowing, indicating where the bullets would enter his body if the triggers were pulled. "I've got at least ten guns on you right now."

He looked back up at me with a smirk on his face. "Now, LC, you really didn't think it was going to be this easy, did you?"

"It's as easy as you doing what I tell you to do, Larry," I told him, "or you die. Simple as that."

"Go ahead. Give them the signal to shoot me." He reached down nonchalantly and picked up the briefcase he'd brought, calmly placing it on the table. "The minute Curtis hears a shot, he's going to blow this fucking place to smithereens."

Curtis

72

I sat at a table in the back of the Chicken Shack and waited anxiously. Closing time for the restaurant was hours ago, so it was completely dark. The only sound in the place was the humming of the air conditioning, which wasn't loud enough to drown out the music from across the street. I stared at the linoleum floors, inhaling the scent of fried chicken, which caused my stomach to growl. I hadn't even realized I was hungry until then, but I was too nervous to eat anyway. I stared at the two-way radio in my hand, waiting and praying.

"Take this radio and wait across the street in your momma's place," my father had told me as we sat in the parking lot of Big Shirley's. "You listen while I'm talking to LC, and when you hear the code word, you hit the button. You understand?"

"I don't know about this, Pop."

He glared at me. "Ain't nothing confusing about what I just told you to do. What the fuck is the problem?"

"I just . . . " I tried to formulate the numerous thoughts in my head into coherent sentences, but I couldn't. I didn't know how to tell him that I didn't want to be a part of his suicide mission that would result in not only his death, but the deaths of my uncle, cousins, and plenty of other innocent people who didn't even know their lives were in danger.

"Look at me, Curtis," he said.

I turned and looked at him. "This ain't the time for you to punk out on me. Your brother done already did that. Now is the time to man the fuck up. You've always been the strong one in the family. Hell, even stronger than me. And besides, if LC cooperates and does what the hell I tell him to do, I won't even have to say the code word. Okay? I just need you to be ready, just in case."

"But, Pop, what if he doesn't cooperate? You know what you're asking me to do?" I tried to get him to see my point of view and the reason behind my hesitation.

"I know, but it can't be no worse than what they will do to me if you don't, son. You know what they say: death before dishonor. Now, come on. We both gotta get in position before LC and his boys get here." He held the small walkie-talkie out, and I took it. We got out of the Explorer, and he reached into the back and took out the brown leather briefcase.

"You remember the code word, right?" he asked.

"Yeah, I remember." I nodded.

He gave me one last look, and said, "I love you, Curtis."

I grabbed him and held him tight. "I love you too, Dad."

He headed inside Big Shirley's through the back, while I broke into the restaurant owned by my mother.

"Gimme a bourbon," my father's voice came blasting through the small speaker in my hand, and I jumped. I turned the volume down low, and then, unable to sit any longer, I stood up and began pacing around the small dining area. A part of me wanted to just walk away from everything the way Kenny had, but I couldn't. I didn't want to abandon my father. He had been let down by too many people once his mental illness got worse—which, if I had to honest with myself, started happening after Grandma Bettie died. And Grandma wouldn't have died if I hadn't picked up that gun. My father had taken the blame for me, and now I had to be strong for him, the way he expected me to be. The way he raised me. I owed everything to my dad.

Sweat began forming on my brow, and I picked up a napkin and wiped it.

"What are you doing here, Curtis?"

The voice startled me, and I spun around. Standing at the entrance to the kitchen were my mother and brother.

"Momma, what? How?"

"Boy, this is the twenty-first century. Don't you think I have cameras and a security system in place that lets me know when someone is in here?" She walked toward me. "What are you doing?"

"I . . . nothing."

The walkie-talkie crackled, and Pop's muffled voice came through the speaker.

"What the hell is that?" Kenny rushed over and tried to snatch the radio, but I moved away from him.

"Curtis, what is going on?" my mother asked.

"He's meeting with Uncle LC, and I'm listening, that's all," I told her.

"Why are you listening? What is he about to do?" Kenny sounded angry. "I know him. If you're here, he's about to do something real sneaky."

"Curtis, listen to me. Whatever your father has you doing, you have to stop." My mother put her hands on each side of my face and stared me in the eye. "You have to."

I looked at her and didn't fight the tears that formed. "I have to. I'm the only person he has. I'm all he has left."

"Baby, you're not. He still has family," she said.

"His family put him away all those years ago. They locked him away. And it's all my fault," I cried.

"It's not your fault, Curt. It was an accident." Kenny came and put his arm around my shoulder.

"You . . ." I shook my head and pushed his arm off me. "You don't know what I'm talking about."

Kenny didn't leave my side. "Mom told me everything. I know what happened. It was an accident. It wasn't your fault."

"Your father is sick, Curtis, and that has nothing to do with you. He's a sick man, and he needs help, but not the help that he's asking from you."

The speaker crackled again, and this time my father's voice was clearer, "Maybe not all of them, but I see two key figures, Vegas and Junior, in this room. Throw in your death, and Chippy can cancel Christmas!"

"I have to do it," I said to my mother and brother, reaching into my pocket and taking out the phone my father had given me.

"Baby, please don't do this. You can't!" my mother pleaded.

"You heard what the fuck I said, LC. You can cancel Christmas!" Pop repeated.

I looked down at the phone in my shaking hand.

Larry

73

"Now, LC, let me tell you how things are gonna go down, because if you don't, no one in this motherfucker will live to tell about it." I laughed, looking down at the red dots on my chest. With Vegas and Junior less than thirty feet away, and half the patrons being LC's men, I had him right where I wanted him. Yes, it was pretty much a suicide mission from this point on, but maybe, as the Klingons on *Star Trek* used to say, *Today is a good day to die.*

I'd never been afraid of dying. Hell, after Vietnam there wasn't much that could scare me. My only fear was not being able to leave my boys their proper legacy. But with LC and his brats gone, all Curtis would have to do was get his brother back on board. I was confident that the two of them could finish off whoever was left of LC's brood and start their own empire. I'd already given Curtis the locations of my last few stashes, and with the four hundred kilos we got from Vinnie, they'd be off and running.

"Larry, there are innocent people in here. This is between you and me. Let them out," LC said. Just like always, he was trying to tell me what to do, but fuck him. Those days were over.

"You're not worried about these people. You're worried about your boys, and maybe a few of your men." I glanced over at the front door and the bar.

He tried a different approach, since ordering me around wasn't working. "So, what do you want? What's going to resolve this?"

I shrugged. "Truth is, I think we're past resolution." I said as sincerely as possible, "You know, your wife made a statement the other day that really stuck with me. She said that our kids and grandkids were going to be fighting like the Hatfields and the McCoys. And that really bothered me."

"Bothers me too," he said.

"Yeah, but probably not for the same reasons." I sat back in my seat. "You see, you have six kids, plus Lou's daughter and a few grands. And me, well, I only have my two boys."

I could see the old wheels turning in his head as he tried to figure out where I was going with this.

"You know I never ran from a fight, and neither have my boys, but these odds just aren't in their favor, so I decided to even the odds."

"What are you saying, Larry, that you're going to kill my children? I'm never going to let you do that."

"Maybe not all of them, but I see two key figures, Vegas and Junior, in this room. Throw in your death, and Chippy can *cancel Christmas!*" I emphasized the last two words and then held my breath in anticipation.

Nothing happened.

"Didn't you tell that boy the code word was *Christmas*?" Momma yelled in my ear.

"Yes, Momma."

"Then why the hell are we still here?"

"I don't know," I replied as I felt my anxiety rising. Something wasn't right. This wasn't the way Curtis and I had planned it.

"What did you say?" LC asked.

"You heard what the fuck I said, LC. You can *cancel Christmas!*" this time I yelled it, and LC's brats and a few others stood from their seats.

"Hold off," LC said to his men. They stayed where they were but didn't sit back down. I could see Junior flexing his muscles like he wanted to jump across the table to strangle me, but he, too, followed LC's orders. His family revered him; I'd give them that.

A few of the regulars who weren't interested in sticking around for a fight started heading for the door. The dancer who'd been on stage grabbed her tips off the floor and headed to the back, and the bartender turned up the house lights. Between the sudden commotion around me, the bright lights, and the fact that my plan was backfiring, I was confused for a minute. LC sat and stared at me while I pulled my thoughts together to figure out my next move.

Finally, I pounded my fist on the table and shouted, "Dammit, Curtis, stop being a damn coward and make the call!" I took hold of the lapel of my shirt and yelled directly into the microphone attached there, "Cancel Christmas!" I stared at the briefcase, waiting.

"Larry."

I looked up, and there was my wife. My boys were standing on either side of her.

"Time to stop this, Larry."

"What the hell is she doing here?" Momma shouted.

"I don't know," I said, looking past NeeNee to Curtis. "Curtis, where is that phone I gave you?"

"You mean this?" NeeNee held up the phone that Vinnie had given me.

"Nee, I'm going to need you to give that to me, honey, and you and the boys need to get outta here." I stuck out my hand, but she took a step backward.

"LC, get everyone out of here, please," she said to my brother. He didn't hesitate, jumping up from his seat and rushing his people and any remaining bystanders out the front.

"Come on, everybody out! There's a bomb in here!" LC shouted, and folks started to scramble. That is, except for my wife, sons, and brother.

"Nee, please, honey. I need you to give me that phone. It's still not too late."

"You're right, Larry. It's not too late. Not too late for you to get some help." She turned to LC. "This is between me, my husband, and my boys. Stay out of it."

LC took a step back.

"What the fuck is that supposed to mean?" I yelled.

"You need help, Dad. And we're going to make sure you get it," Kenny said, and he and Curtis took a step toward me. "Now, put your hands out so we can tie you up."

I searched Curtis's face for some sign of loyalty to me. "Curtis, after all we've been through, are you going to be part of this?"

Curtis lifted his hand and showed me the rope they meant to tie me with. "Sorry, Dad, but Kenny and Mom are right."

"Right about what, you ungrateful bastard?" He came closer, and I took a swing at him. Within seconds, the two boys were on me, using the skills I had taught them to subdue me.

"Don't struggle, Dad! This is for your own good," Curtis said.

"Fuck you, you traitorous son of a bitch!" I screamed and fussed until NeeNee managed to stuff a sock in my mouth. They ended up hog-tying me and removing me from the building.

On my way out, I saw LC and his family staring at me, their faces full of pity. But they had no idea. I knew how to fool those people in the hospital, and one day, I'd be back to kill them all.

Chippy

Epilogue

I sat back and buckled my seat belt in preparation for takeoff. I was more than ready to go home and see my grandchildren, who I missed dearly, along with my pregnant daughter-in-law. With Vinnie dead and Larry in a new mental facility, I looked forward to our lives returning to a sense of normalcy.

I swiveled my seat around to make sure everyone was accounted for. Rio and Paris sat near the front, already sipping on mimosas and chattering. London was in the far corner of the plane, staring out the window. The tension between her and Daryl, who sat on the opposite side next to Vegas, was too thick not to notice. I was worried about my daughter, who was now in a constant state of frustration. Her leaving with Sasha and going after Vinnie had given her a convenient excuse to run away from her husband, his medical crisis, and their failing marriage, but now she would have to go back home and face reality. I didn't know if I should intervene or allow whatever happened to do so naturally. I loved my daughter, and the last thing I wanted to see was the pain she was in, whether it was caused by Harris or anyone else.

Across the aisle from her was Sasha, who sat beside Junior. I found it ironic that the two of them had suddenly become so close. Neither one realized that they were biological siblings. Since her mother's death, I had found comfort in knowing that he was there for her. I had to wonder if their strengthening bond was Donna manipulating things from the grave. It certainly didn't mean I was ready to reveal the truth to them, but I was happy that they had each other during this very difficult time for our family.

LC boarded the plane and took his seat beside me.

"Everything okay?" I asked.

"Yeah, we're ready to take off," he said. "You spoke with Orlando?"

"Yes. He and Ruby decided to stay in Florida. He didn't want to overwhelm Vincent by bringing him to a house full of Duncans. That poor baby is still petrified because Vinnie told him that the Duncans wanted to kill him and his mother."

"I can't believe he told that child that." LC sighed. "He needs to bring him home so we can show him otherwise."

"Baby steps, LC. They're gonna spend some time together so they can get to know one another. They're headed to Disney World, so I'm sure he'll like that." I smiled as I leaned back against the headrest. I looked forward to the day my newest grandson could be with us.

"That's good. But I want my family together under one roof." He gave me a knowing look.

"I know you do. LC, you know Larry is your family too, right?" I reminded him.

"I know that, Chippy."

"And so are NeeNee and Curtis and Kenny. Those boys are gonna need you, and so is he."

He didn't say anything.

"I'm sorry you had to deal with all of this. And NeeNee and the boys are committed to being there for your brother, so I need you to be there for him too," I said.

Larry was now living in Central State Hospital in Milledgeville, Georgia. Years ago, when it was agreed that Larry needed to be placed, Central State was the one institution that LC insisted his brother not be placed. He hated the thought of his brother being a patient in one of the country's largest asylums. Now, we all knew that it was the best place for Larry to receive the level of treatment he needed.

"I know." LC nodded, then added, "And I will."

I looked over at my husband and saw the pain and worry on his face. I knew that the recovery he had gone through after being shot was nothing compared to the healing he would need from the broken heart he now had. Getting back to normal was going to take longer than I thought, but we Duncans were strong. We'd made it through so many trials together, and we'd make it through this one too.